A
DARKNESS
STRANGE
and
LOVELY

ALSO BY SUSAN DENNARD

Something Strange and Deadly

A Dawn Most Wicked: A Something Strange and Deadly Novella
(available as an ebook only)

A DARKNESS STRANGE  LOVELY

SUSAN DENNARD

An Imprint of HarperCollins*Publishers*

HarperTeen is an imprint of HarperCollins Publishers.

A DARKNESS STRANGE AND LOVELY
Copyright © 2013 by Susan Dennard
www.epicreads.com

Library of Congress Cataloging-in-Publication Data
Dennard, Susan.
A darkness strange and lovely / Susan Dennard. — 1st ed.
    p.   cm.
Summary: "Eleanor Fitt flees to Europe to seek the help of the Spirit-
Hunters after a villain from her past resurfaces, only to find that, in Paris,
there's a new kind of evil lurking"— Provided by publisher.
ISBN 978-0-06-208329-6
[1. Brothers and sisters—Fiction.   2. Dead—Fiction.   3. Magic—
fiction.   4. Zombies—Fiction.   5. Paris (France)—History—19th
century—Fiction.   6. France—History—19th century—Fiction.
7. Horror stories.]   I. Title.
PZ7.D42492bDar   2013   2012038125
[Fic]—dc23   CIP
                                                                    AC

Typography by Lissi Erwin
13 14 15 16 17   LP/RRDH   10 9 8 7 6 5 4 3 2 1
❖
First Edition

For Sara Kendall and Joanna Volpe—you believed in me from the start, and I can never thank you enough.

CHAPTER ONE

When Jie's letter came in the mail, I was so elated I forgot I had no hand.

"Oh, thank heavens!" I cried, reaching for the battered envelope in the postman's grasp. "I've been waiting for this for over a . . ." I trailed off. My eyes locked on the postman's horrified face—and his eyes locked on my wrist.

Yet it was not the poor quality of my gray gown's lace sleeve that prompted his expression but rather the bandaged stump poking out from beneath.

I yanked back my wrist, and the postman's face erupted in red. "P-pardon me, Miss." He thrust the letter at me.

"Of course," I squeaked, snatching the letter with my left hand. Then I bolted from the post office into the Philadelphia morning.

Holding the hard-earned letter like a visor against the sun, I strode into the bustling Chestnut Avenue traffic. The road's cobbles were layered in a sticky, dried mud from yesterday's rain. It clung to my boot heels as I crossed into the rattling carriages, clopping horses, and distracted pedestrians.

As I passed by shop after shop with their giant signs overshadowing the offices wedged between, I cursed myself for my stupidity. Almost three months with no hand, and one would *think* I would remember. The empty wrist ached all the time—itching in the night as if my fingers were still attached, reminding me constantly of how much more than a hand I'd lost. If not for that wretched injury, maybe I could put all the summer's horrors behind me. Maybe I could push through each day instead of barely keeping my head above the darkness.

It always hovered there, threatening to drown me in memories of Elijah . . . and Clarence . . . and Mama. . . .

But it was not to be. Just as my hand would never return, this grief would never leave. Life—and death—did not work that way.

Though sometimes, if I squinted hard enough, I fancied I could see a blue sparkle of spiritual energy, as if the ghost of my hand wanted me back as much as I wanted it. What with all the flickers and flashes of spirits I'd started seeing in the past few months, it wouldn't have surprised me to learn that I *was* actually seeing the ghostly remnants of my hand.

As my brother, Elijah, had told me, if he had necromantic powers, then whether I wanted them or not, I did too.

I dabbed at my brow with my sleeve. Summer might have

been fading into fall, and the thunderstorms with it, yet the heat seemed determined to stay. The usual breeze carried from the Delaware River was missing, and I wished—not for the first time—that I hadn't left my parasol at home. The annoyance of holding it in my clumsy left hand was nothing compared to the sweat oozing down my back and beneath my bonnet.

I spared a glance at the envelope, and my breath caught. In Jie's meticulous print, it read *Paris*.

Paris! I hadn't heard from Jie in more than a month, and the Spirit-Hunters had been in Chicago then. I'd hounded the post office every day since, desperate for some message that would tell me where they were—in hopes that I could join them—but no word had come. Until today.

Heavens, if I only could go to Paris—leave Philadelphia so far behind the past could never, *ever* catch up to me.

I scampered out of a buggy's path and onto the opposite walkway, where I found the welcome shade of a storefront. It was Mrs. Binder's trimmings store, where Mama and I had once bought sewing supplies. With no concern for propriety, I clasped the envelope in my teeth and used my left hand to rip it open.

And for the first time in ages, my heart actually lifted—and, *blazes*, it felt good.

Eleanor,

Of all places the Dead would bring us, I never thought it would be Paris. This city is the strangest place I have ever seen. One minute people are screaming over the Dead (or les Morts, *as they call them) and then the next minute they're sipping their champagne and laughing at the latest scandal. Daniel calls them mercurial. I call them annoying.*

I snorted. I could just imagine Jie's scowl as she declared the Parisians all manner of undeserved foul things.

But it's not just the Parisians who are strange. The Dead are bizarre too. Not only are they walking corpses, but they're recently dead. Murdered. Joseph thinks it's some sort of sacrifice, but he can't tell what exactly. He spends all the moments he's not out fighting the Dead or speaking before the Sénat with his nose stuck in a book.

Our host, the Marquis du Bazillac, is generous enough, but he's demanding too. He seems to want Joseph and Daniel everywhere so he can show them off like prize cows. Daniel just saw me write that, and he's telling me to scratch it out. I told him I'd scratch out his eyes if he didn't go away.

I barked a laugh . . . but almost instantly, my stomach clenched. I missed Jie and Joseph and Daniel so badly it *hurt*. With a tight swallow, I kept reading.

You should see Daniel these days—you wouldn't recognize him. He's got this book on manners he carries with him everywhere; and not only does he always wear a suit now, but he's got a top hat to boot! Prize cow, indeed.

I hope you're well, Eleanor, and I wish you were here with us. I know your mother still needs you, though. Is she doing any better? Is she still at the asylum? And how is your hand feeling? Well, that's enough questions for one letter. Besides, Daniel wants to add something, and I'm almost out of space. Write me back and send it to the Hotel Le Meurice in Paris.

Regards,

Jie

Squeezed below Jie's letter, in Daniel's loping, slanted scrawl, it said:

Empress,

Stay out of trouble. I can't rescue you from across an ocean.

Daniel

My fingers tightened around the paper, and tears stung my eyes. Daniel might've broken my heart, but he was still one charming scalawag. A scalawag I missed . . . and *wished* could be—

I shook my head. "Stop. Don't think of him, Eleanor."

But it was too late. The regret trampled over me, aching in my throat. He had told me he didn't love me months ago; and yet at every note he added to Jie's letters, I inevitably turned into a pathetic ninny. Why was it that no matter how many times I scolded myself for caring, none of my stupid feelings would fade? Although . . .

I glanced at the letter again. Suits and a book on manners? What did *that* mean?

"Eleanor Fitt!" a girl's voice squealed. "Is that you?"

I stiffened. I knew that shrill voice—just as I knew the huskier one that followed.

"I daresay, it has been *ages* since we last saw you!"

Wincing, I stuffed the letter into my pocket and hid my bandaged wrist in the folds of my skirts. Then I turned to face Mercy and Patience Cook—or the Virtue Sisters, as I preferred to call them. Squat Mercy bustled over to me, beaming in her lavender gown, while lanky Patience, pucker-lipped and pink clad, ambled behind.

"How are you?" Mercy asked, grabbing my arm. "We have missed you at all the parties!"

I very much doubted this, but I merely bowed my head and said, "My mother is . . . unwell. As such, we have not been getting out much."

"Oh yes!" Patience said. "We had heard that." Her nostrils fluttered as if she smelled a particularly good piece of gossip, and I knew immediately what question would come next. "Is she still at Kirkbride's? Is she still . . . *unstable*?"

My chest tightened painfully, and a thousand nasty retorts flew through my mind. Yes, my mother was at Kirkbride's Pennsylvania Hospital for the Insane because *yes*, her mind had cracked. Mama's health was the only reason I hadn't chased after the Spirit-Hunters the minute my wrist had healed enough to travel. Kirkbride's was lovely, what with its progressive ideas on mental health and its beautifully flowered grounds; but it was also expensive.

Yet these weren't emotions I liked to dwell on, and *damn* Patience for forcing me to.

Fortunately, Mercy clapped her hands just as I opened my mouth to sputter something utterly inappropriate. "Oh, we were just in Mrs. Binder's, Eleanor, and we saw the most wonderful pistachio muslin! Didn't we, Patience?" She poked her sister.

"We did," Patience simpered, "and it will look lovely with Mercy's skin." She turned a smug smirk on me. "Mother has the latest *Harper's Bazaar*, you see, and it shows all the newest walking gowns for fall. We are going to have them made."

I grunted, unable to conjure any other response. As far as I could tell, there was absolutely nothing wrong with their current gowns. I was in the same gray walking gown I'd worn every day since June, and it was still perfectly functional.

My eyes raked over Patience's pink silk—*I could get fifty dollars for that dress at Mr. Rickard's.* And Mercy's lavender grenadine was easily worth seventy-five. After selling all of my own dresses to pay for Mama's hospital bills, I'd become quite adept at estimating what a dress would fetch at Mr. Rickard's Pawn Shop. I was also quite good at haggling for the best price.

However, I was not particularly adept at controlling my facial expressions.

"Eleanor," Mercy said, alarmed, "are you ill?"

I quickly schooled my face into a smile, but as my lips parted to reply, Patience cut in.

"Have you seen Allison Wilcox lately?" She lifted her eyebrows. "We have called and called, yet she is always away—that, or she is avoiding our company. Perhaps you have had better luck in your own calls upon the Wilcox home?"

Now I gaped at her and did not bother to hide my emotions. How *dare* she ask about Allison Wilcox when she knew perfectly well what had passed between our families.

Mercy seemed as horrified by her sister's question as I, for she reached for Patience's elbow. "Hush."

But Patience wouldn't be silenced. "Oh, but of course *you* wouldn't have seen Allison," she cooed. "Not after your . . . ah . . . how to phrase it delicately? *Scandals* with the Spirit-Hunters."

"Patience, stop that!" Mercy hissed.

"But it is true, is it not?" Patience batted her eyes innocently. "The Fitt family and the Wilcox family are no longer on friendly terms? I daresay, the fact that you were seeing both Clarence and the man who *murdered* Clarence would not reflect well—"

"Enough!" Mercy dug her fingers in Patience's arm and yanked her away. She flashed me an apologetic grimace. "I'm so sorry, Eleanor. I hope your mother gets better." Then, without another word, she hauled her sister into the busy street and disappeared from view.

I was rendered speechless. I couldn't even breathe. Tears I had fought every second of every day now rose in my eyes like a tidal wave.

I stumbled back until I hit Mrs. Binder's window. "You are better than she," I whispered to myself, blinking the tears away. "Stronger and better." If I could face an army of Dead, then the insults of Patience Cook should be nothing.

But they weren't nothing—not when they echoed with so much truth.

So I did as I always did: I forced my mind to dwell on other things. Normal, day-to-day things.

Spinning around, I stared into the shop's window. My eyes lit on a frilly parasol in the display's corner.

And the tears came boiling back with such a vengeance, I couldn't contain them. All I could do was keep my face hidden and let them drop.

Daniel had given me a parasol like that one. Back when I'd thought he might love me. Back when I'd thought Clarence was just a narrow-minded suitor . . . and my brother was just a victim. Back when I was naive and stupid and thought the world a good place. The world *wasn't* a good place. I knew that now, and no amount of distraction would let me forget.

As soon as I was in control of my emotions once more, I went to the bank to deposit my latest funds from Mr. Rickard. It was a small sum on which to manage living. I had stopped paying Mary, my mother's maid, long ago; and though I wasn't sure why she stayed with me—pity, friendship, or (most likely) guilt—I was grateful for the company all the same. My childhood home, emptied of furniture and devoid of life, would have been too much for me to bear on my own.

It was just as I strode between two columns and onto the marble steps leading down to the street that my right hand— no, the empty space where my hand had once been—began to tingle.

I froze midway. I knew this feeling, the feeling of electricity. Of soul.

I glanced down, certain I'd see a shimmer of starlight, like a little wrinkle in the world where my hand used to be. But nothing was there. Just the usual cloth bandages . . .

Which meant some *other* spirit was jangling at my senses.

Holding my breath, I whirled around to scan the crowded street. Simply because I knew I could sense the Dead didn't mean I was used to it. And it certainly didn't mean I enjoyed it.

My eyes raked over traffic and across building fronts, but

I saw no unusual shimmer or flash of blue. I gulped, my throat tight.

Why wasn't this throbbing going away? If nothing Dead was here, then . . .

Pain stabbed through my right arm, sharp and burning. A cry broke from my lips, and I yanked my arm to my chest.

Then light flared from my wrist, and for half a breath I could actually *see* my missing fingers. They shifted from static blue to solid pink and back again.

A screaming howl filled my ears. I whipped up my head, my heart lurching into my mouth. But when I scanned the area for some rabid hound, all I saw was the usual clattering carriages and purposeful walkers. The tobacco store across the street, the saloon next door—they all looked the same. Not a dog in sight. The cab drivers trotted by, their horses ambled on, and everyone continued as if they heard nothing.

Which meant I was the only person hearing this!

Then the pain shrieked louder, taking control of my mind and blurring my vision. Another howl came. I gasped. Two howls, then three, all roaring over one another like a pack of wolves on the hunt. Yet I still saw nothing.

I lurched around, certain I had to run. To warn others— and to *hide*. But I couldn't think straight—the dogs were so loud, they swallowed everything. I heaved up the steps and back toward the bank's door.

Then my gaze locked on a pair of eyes. Yellow eyes, gleaming from the shadows behind the bank columns.

I flinched and stumbled back as new fear erupted in my chest. The last time I'd seen yellow eyes had been on Marcus Duval. If he was here, then I was as good as dead. There was no way I could fight him—not by myself. He was a necromancer so powerful even Joseph had lost to his magic.

Oh God, oh God—what could I do?

The howling crescendoed. Louder and louder. A sudden wind blasted my face. Icy and damp, it clawed into my throat and froze my lungs, yet I couldn't move. I was rooted to the spot, held by those yellow eyes.

Then the bank door swung open. A customer walked out, and like a hypnotist's snap, my mind and body were suddenly freed. I burst into action, ripping my gaze away from the shadows and darting down the steps, toward the street.

Instantly the dogs stopped, replaced by the shouts and rattle of normal morning traffic.

A heartbeat later, the agony in my wrist ended with no trace of pain left behind.

But my panic didn't go. If I was right—if that had been Marcus in those shadows—then every second I stayed was a second closer to my death.

I kicked into a run, bounding into the street and aiming for home.

Not once did I check for the yellow eyes. I knew they would be as gone as the wind and the howls and the pain. Yet as I rushed down the street, my mind ran through scenario after scenario, trying to explain what had happened. It must have been black magic. Those yellow eyes—identical to the ones that haunted my dreams and my memories—*must* belong to Marcus.

And the only people who could help me were an ocean away in Paris.

But I was prepared for the day I would face Marcus again. He was a nightmare wearing my brother's skin, and I had vowed to destroy him. I wanted to fight Marcus—wanted to watch him *die*—but I would need the Spirit-Hunters to do that.

So I had to leave Philadelphia. I had to lead Marcus to the Spirit-Hunters. An ocean away or not, I could not let the distance or expense stop me. Not if I wanted to stay alive.

Eventually I managed to hail a streetcar on Market Street. By the time I reached my own tree-lined avenue, I was soaked through with sweat. I barreled down the road, finally reaching the low, wrought iron gate leading into my yard. The grass was tall and overgrown, the hedges wild. Only the white house I'd grown up in and the cherry tree out front looked the same.

I flew down my front path and up the steps, but before I could even fumble through my pocket for a key, the door burst open.

Mary, her chestnut hair falling from its bun, gaped at me. "Eleanor! Why're you running like the devil's after you?"

"Because," I panted, "he is. Marcus is here!" I shoved my way into the foyer and slammed the door behind. "Get my carpetbag. I've got to go."

Mary didn't move. She just stared, her eyes bulging. She was the only person in the world other than the Spirit-Hunters and Mama who knew the full story about my brother's necromancy and death. She knew how dangerous Marcus was—and she knew of my plan to find the Spirit-Hunters once Mama and my finances had been settled.

"Did you hear me?" I asked. "Marcus is *here*." Still she didn't budge. I stepped forward. "Mary, what is it?"

"You . . . you . . ."

"What?"

"You have a guest."

I stopped, my heart dropping to my stomach. "Who?"

"Me," said a new voice.

I jolted, my head whipping toward the parlor door. There stood a gaunt young woman in black, and though she looked nothing like the rosy-faced girl I'd once known, I instantly recognized her.

Allison Wilcox.

The last time we'd seen each other had been moments before I learned her brother, Clarence, had been murdered.

But the rumors behind his death were wrong: he had not been killed by the Spirit-Hunters. No, the truth behind Clarence's death was far, *far* worse.

For Clarence Wilcox had been murdered by *my* brother.

CHAPTER TWO

After Clarence had died and I had stopped my brother and his army of Dead, after the Spirit-Hunters had fled town—hated and blamed for crimes that were not theirs—I had called every day at the Wilcox home, trying to gain an audience with Allison. But I was denied each time, and after a month I had finally given up.

And now, weeks later, I found all my earlier desperation to speak with her—to set things straight—was gone. Now, of all times, was not the moment for my rehearsed explanations and apologies.

I gulped and met her dark-eyed gaze. Eyes like the ones her handsome brother, Clarence, had been blessed with.

"What are you doing here?" I asked.

Her jaw twitched. "No greeting? No refreshments?"

"I don't have anything like that to offer you."

She sniffed. "Nor do you have anywhere for your guests to sit." She waved to the parlor, where there was nothing left but flowered wallpaper and blank hardwood floors.

I tugged at my earlobe. Even though sofas and snacks were the last things I cared about, heat burned up my cheeks. "I'm sorry. I've had to sell everything."

"Even your hand, I see." She didn't smile. "How ever do you hold your parasol?"

"I very rarely do."

Her eyebrows rose, and annoyance rushed through me. I'd had quite enough verbal assault for one day, and if Allison was here only to hurt me, then so be it. I was not going to risk my life a moment longer.

I turned to Mary. "Get my bag. Now."

Mary nodded and curtsied to Allison before scampering upstairs.

"Nothing to offer," Allison said sharply, "*and* you ignore me."

I spun back to her. "I'm sorry, but I'm leaving town at this very moment."

"Leaving?" She blinked, and some of her frost melted. "Why? To where?"

"France, and I have no time to waste." I strode past her and into the empty parlor. A quick scan through the window showed no one on the streets. Yet.

Allison stomped into the room. I turned to find her cheeks bright with fury. "How dare you ignore me, Eleanor! I'm here to see *you*."

"Really?" I pursed my lips. "I've come to your house dozens of times, and you've always turned me away. So why are you *truly* here, Allison?"

For several moments we watched each other in silence. Mary's footsteps pounded overhead as she raced to add my final measly belongings to a carpetbag.

But at last Allison spoke. "My mother," she said slowly, "forbade me from seeing you. In fact, if she knew I was here right now, she'd kill me." Then, like a bursting dam, words poured from her mouth. "But I *need* answers, Eleanor. I can't wait anymore! Mother wants me to marry a rich man, you see, but I *can't*. Night and day, I'm forced into company with nasty old bachelors and nastier old widowers."

Gooseflesh pricked down my arms. Allison might have been telling my story from three months ago.

She stepped toward me. "I have to know what really happened with my brother. Mother might believe the newspapers, but I don't. *Tell* me how Clarence died."

I didn't move. Allison deserved an answer, yet I couldn't give it to her. Not when my life was threatened and every second counted. Mary clattered down the stairs. "Eleanor, I've got your bag!"

I didn't even spare Allison a glance before spurring myself back into the foyer. Mary held out an old black carpetbag. Her

17

hands trembled. "Now what?"

"Now," I said, turning cautiously to Allison, who hovered in the parlor's doorway. "Now I leave."

"No." Red flared onto Allison's face. "You can't just *go*. I asked you for answers."

"I'm sorry," I said, my voice flat though I actually meant the words. I had wanted to tell her the truth for so long. . . .

I shoved my left hand into my pocket, and withdrawing Jie's letter, I turned to Mary. "This is where I will be going. I'll telegraph once I'm in France."

"France!" Mary cried, taking the envelope. "What's there?"

"The Spirit-Hunters." I shot a glance at Allison, but other than a tightening in her jaw, she did not react to this name. I could not help but wonder: did she already know that the Spirit-Hunters had not killed Clarence?

I hefted the carpetbag from Mary's hands, forcing my mind to remain in the present. "Did you put the emergency money in the bag?"

"Aye. And your brother's letters too."

"Good. I'll be going straight to the wharf."

"I'll take you," Allison inserted. "To the wharf."

"What?" I spun toward her. "Absolutely not."

She glared. "Yes. If you are going to run off, I want answers first. You will ride with me."

I narrowed my eyes, and she matched it with her own stare. Two girls who'd once shared tea and gossip were now bound together by death.

But then it occurred to me that if I accepted a ride, I could move more quickly. I could even say good-bye to Mama, for her hospital was on the way.

Best of all, though, Marcus didn't know Allison. He wouldn't recognize her carriage, and I could travel to the wharf unknown. So although part of me felt bad for accepting Allison's offer under such selfish circumstances, most of me simply wanted to *go*.

"Fine," I finally said.

Allison nodded once, and her eyes grazed over Mary. "Where will your maid go?"

"I've family in California, Ma'am. Eleanor gave me money for a train weeks ago."

"You must remember to stay in touch with the solicitor," I reminded Mary. "Father trusted him, but still—I'd feel better if I knew you telegrammed him regularly. At least until the house sells."

Mary bowed her head. "Of course."

"You're selling the house?" Allison demanded. "Is that how you have enough money for a train ticket?" The look in her eyes—the implication that I'd gotten my money through some nefarious means—set my temper alight.

"The money," I spat, "came from that sofa you complained I don't have. And I'll buy my steamer ticket with the money I saved by not getting a prosthetic, by pinching coins for months, by selling off all my things. I have not yet sold the house, but we have interested buyers. It should sell soon—it *must* sell soon, for otherwise I cannot afford Mama's bills."

Allison's nostrils flared. "You could have married my brother, you know. He cared about you, and he would have treated you as well as he treated me. Then you would never have needed money and maybe . . ." Her eyes turned glassy, and her lips quivered. But she did not finish her thought. Instead, with nothing more than a slight sniffle, Allison turned and strode from the house.

Guilt exploded in my belly as I watched her go. I *would* have married her brother if it had come to that. Underneath his sharp exterior, he had been a loving man.

And like all the other ghosts I wanted to forget, his perfect face haunted me every day.

I towed my mind back to the present. After giving Mary a quick embrace and making her promise to leave the house immediately, I hurried outside and clambered into Allison's carriage. Her cool poise was back by the time I slid over the velvet bench seats. The last time I'd ridden in this carriage, Clarence had been alive and we'd been on our way to the opera. It was the night he had caught me working with the Spirit-Hunters.

It was also the night he was murdered.

"Now, Eleanor," Allison ordered as the horses clopped to a start, "tell me how Clarence died."

"First," I said, forcing an edge to my words—a strength I wasn't feeling—"take me to Kirkbride's. I want to say good-bye to my mother."

Allison's eyelids twitched down. "The gossip is true then. Your mother *is* sick."

I nodded.

"All right." She rapped her knuckles on the carriage wall and directed the driver to the hospital. Her gaze never left mine as she asked, "So your mother is sick with . . . what? Last I saw her, she was fine. What could possibly be the matter with her now?"

"Quite a lot, actually." I had to fight to keep from growling. "Mama was never right after my father died. When I told her about . . . well, when I told her everything I'm about to tell you, it was too much." I dropped my gaze to my bandaged wrist. "It's even worse than the papers say, Allison. Are you sure you want to know the whole story? Ignorance is easier."

"But not better!" she cried. "A few months ago, I never thought further than the end of the day. Now, I see my whole life before and my death at the end. Just tell me what happened, Eleanor. I deserve the truth."

"The truth," I repeated. The word tasted like ash. I took a deep breath. "The papers said it was the Spirit-Hunters who killed Clarence. But it wasn't."

Her spine deflated. "Who then?"

I twisted my face away and watched the neighborhood pass by. I'd always imagined looking into Allison's eyes when I told her this, but, in fact, I found the words wouldn't come if I met her stare.

"It all began with our fathers. They were once very good friends, you know. Then your father, Clay, decided to run for city council, and he . . . well, he was one of the Gas Trustees, who controlled most of the city's jobs—meaning he also controlled most of the city's voters." I inhaled deeply. "Clay offered my father a position in his ring of council members, but my father refused and opted to run for city council the honest way. He wanted to stop Clay from corrupting the city.

"Then—" My voice shook. I tried again. "*Then* your father decided to force mine out of the race by destroying his railroad supply company. He hired thugs to blow up my father's latest dynamite shipment, and he also told Clarence to make my brother's life a living hell."

Allison's breath hitched, but I didn't look her way. At this point in the story, Mama had already begun shrieking her denial. She would hear nothing against the Wilcoxes—the past was the past, she had said. All that mattered was the future and regaining the Wilcox family's favor.

She'd stopped screaming once the whole truth came out.

Shifting in my seat, I wet my lips and resumed my cold account. "The man . . . the man raising the Dead across the city," I said, "was my brother. Elijah killed Clarence out of revenge for our father."

Allison's body turned rigid, but she made no other indication that she'd heard. So I kept talking. "After Clarence died and I learned the truth, I went with the Spirit-Hunters to Laurel Hill Cemetery. Elijah was there, trying to raise our father's corpse. I—" My voice broke, and I had to grit my teeth to keep going. "I stopped Elijah, but then . . . he died." I glanced at Allison, finally meeting her eyes. They were hard—unnaturally so—and it took me a moment to recognize the emotion she wore.

Revulsion.

Yet before I could think how to react, we turned onto a new street and Allison spoke. "Why couldn't you simply tell me that all this was happening? *While* it was happening?"

"Would it have changed things?" I rubbed my wrist. "Clarence would still have died, and it would still be my brother's fault." *And Mama would still have cracked, and I would still be friendless, handless, and fleeing Philadelphia.*

Allison clenched her jaw and didn't answer for several long seconds. Then she said, "Why are you going to Paris all by yourself?"

I tensed. "How did you know Paris? I only mentioned France."

"Lucky guess." She frowned. "Now *explain.*"

"Do you . . ." I gulped. I had to keep talking—and I had to keep shoving my feelings aside as I did. "Do you remember the séance my mother held in June? The one where all the guests fainted?"

"Of course."

"Well, Mama *did* let in a spirit that night."

Allison's brows drew together. "So it wasn't all theatrics as you claimed?"

"I wish . . . but no. The spirit was a dead necromancer named Marcus. He'd been waiting for years to reenter the earthly realm. His time in death had made him strong, and once he was out of the spirit world, he found my brother. Marcus used Elijah's magic against him. When Elijah cast a spell to bring Father back to life, Marcus was able to use the spell instead to bring himself back to life . . . and he was able to possess the nearest corpse."

"Your father's body?"

"No. Elijah's." I cringed as an image of my father's skeleton, its jaws latched onto my brother's throat, formed in my mind. "My father's skeleton killed Elijah, thereby giving Marcus access to the freshly dead body. And the spell—a spell to bind a ghost to a corpse—was Marcus's ticket to a new life in the earthly realm."

A life I would end as soon as I had the chance.

Allison's eyes grew wide. "So you're saying your brother's body is walking around with this Marcus spirit inside?"

"Yes." Yellow eyes and howling dogs flared in my mind, sending a ghostly pain through my wrist. Distractedly, I massaged it.

"And your hand," Allison said, her nose curling up slightly, "what happened?"

"One of the Hungry Dead bit it." More memories, more flashes of blood and chaos, flooded through my mind. The Hungry who had bitten me—a long-dead Civil War soldier— had been so fast. So *rabid*. There'd been no chance for me to escape.

"By the time I broke free," I added softly, "it was too late. My hand was destroyed, and I had to have it amputated."

Her face paled, but other than that she was surprisingly calm. It was . . . *odd*. And so very, very different from Mama's reaction. "You are handling it all quite stoically," I told her.

Allison's eyes flicked to the window. "I would hardly call my reaction stoic. But I do not deal with my grief through *hysterics*." She spat the word.

"My mother does not have hysterics," I said sharply. "Mama has melancholia. For days I could not get her to eat, to leave her bed, or even to *speak* to me. Her mind—her will to live—simply vanished. And Kirkbride's," I tried to say in a gentler tone, "was the only solution I could conjure."

Allison gave no response, and I was grateful when, moments later, we rattled to the end of the street—to where Kirkbride's famous hospital for the insane stood. I scooted to the edge of my seat. "We're here." I pointed at the wrought iron fence, behind which were gold-tipped trees and an enormous white mansion. With its long, ever-growing wings and cupolas, and its beautiful grounds and gardens, the hospital was meant to be a soothing place for the mentally disturbed to regain their wits. A haven of peace and beauty right in the middle of Philadelphia's hustle.

I set my hand on the door as the carriage slowed to a halt before the entrance gate. "Thank you for the ride."

Allison's lips puckered. "I am not finished with you yet."

I hesitated. "I told you what you wanted to know."

"And I want to know more. Now shut pan and get out. I'll come with you into the hospital."

"No!" I lifted a pleading hand. "It's dangerous. Please, Allie—"

25

"Don't," she hissed. "Don't you *ever* call me that. That was *his* name for me."

Shame seared through my face, hot and heavy. I turned away. Of course I had to use Clarence's nickname right when Allison's heart was no doubt aching. But it was too late for apologies or for begging that she stay. I had lost the argument, and Allison was already pushing out the carriage door. I hurried after her.

We strode through the gate, where the guard bobbed his head at me in recognition. I spared a quick glance for the wide, grassy front lawn—sometimes Mama liked to sit there—but all I found were vacant benches and the bronze statue of William Penn standing guard.

"My mother is probably in the back," I murmured to Allison, waving to a gravel path that circled the huge hospital. Despite more than a hundred acres of gardens and forest to entertain the mental patients, Mama was always on that front lawn or beside the same azalea bush in the back. There was a low fountain there that kept the summer heat away.

We set off, our feet crunching on the gravel.

"So what," Allison said with carefully flat inflection, "does your mother *do* here? It seems like a holiday resort."

"It's meant to be that way." I glanced at her, but it wasn't until we reached the end of the white mansion that I added, "My mother needs calm, not violence and straitjackets."

Allison's eyebrows lifted. "And has it worked?"

No, I thought as we passed a wisteria bush. *But I do not think anything will work.* . . . I took in a breath to tell her this, to explain that I had tried *everything*, when a long, throat-rattling shriek rang out—a shriek I knew well.

Fright burst inside me, and I broke into a sprint. My heels kicked up gravel, and I could hear Allison running just behind.

We bounded past azalea bushes when another scream ripped out. With it came shouts.

I skidded around the last bush beside the fountain, only to find struggling figures on the other side of the low pool: my mother, screeching and wrestling with two nurses. I surged to the fountain's lip.

"Mrs. Fitt, settle down!" shouted one nurse, her uniform rumpled and her hat missing. She held Mama's hands clasped.

"Let go of me!" Mama shoved and tugged, trying to free her arms.

The second nurse spotted me. "Miss Fitt, thank heavens! Help us get her back to her room! We've dragged her across the entire grounds."

I stepped forward just as Mama whipped around. She yanked once, and her hands broke free of the nurse's grasp. My mother was a powerfully built woman—it was a wonder the two small nurses had managed to contain her this long.

"You!" Mama thrust a pointed finger at me. *"You!"* Her gray hair was falling from its usual bun, and her walking gown was covered in dust and twigs.

"Mama!" I moved to her. "What's wrong?"

"How dare you show your face here," she yelled.

"What?" I turned to the nurses. "What is she talking

about?" They only shrugged. I glanced back at Allison; she waited by the azaleas, her face pale.

"Do not look away," Mama hissed. "Do not pretend you do not *know*."

"Know what?" I stepped toward her. "I don't underst—"

"You told me Elijah was a necromancer," she cut in, her voice gaining in volume and speed. "You told me that he killed Clarence Wilcox and those other boys. You told me he was dead!"

My mouth went dry. "He *is* dead."

"Do not lie to me!" Her chest heaved, and her fingers curled into fists. "I do not know why I believed you when you had no evidence but a handful of Elijah's letters. There was no corpse!" Her eyes raked over me, more lucid than I'd seen in months.

"The newspapers were right," Mama went on. "You *were* working with the Spirit-Hunters to destroy the city. That criminal, *Daniel*"—she spat the name—"murdered Clarence."

A cry shot over the water. It was Allison, a gloved hand to her mouth. But did she believe my story or Mama's?

At that moment the nurses broke off and scampered toward the hospital. I forced my attention back to my mother, praying the nurses thought her words gibberish.

"Mama," I said, clenching my skirts with my left hand. "I told you the truth."

"The truth! The *truth*?" She shoved her face in mine. "I will tell you the truth, *Eleanor*. A truth I was too blind and heartbroken to see. You are a licentious, lying daughter. A harlot!"

28

My jaw dropped, and outrage coiled in my chest. "How can you say that to me? After all I've done to keep our family alive—"

"By consorting with criminals? By sneaking from the house?" Mama's eyes thinned. "You were seeing that criminal boy, were you not? You planned to run away with him, but then he and the Spirit-Hunters left *you*."

"Stop." My voice cracked out like a whip. "You have no idea of what you speak. I could have left the city—could have abandoned you—but I *stayed*. I sold all of my things to pay your hospital bills because you spent our entire savings."

"I will not listen to this!" She threw her hands over her ears.

"Then don't listen." I advanced on her. "But Elijah *is* dead, Mama. You have to accept that. I *saw* him die—"

"Lies! Elijah is not dead. He's not, he's not! I saw him today, and he was most assuredly *alive*."

I stared at her, speechless. It couldn't be. . . .

"He came to see me," she went on, clearly pleased by my horror, "dressed in the latest Parisian fashions and wealthier than you can even *imagine*. Yet most importantly, Eleanor, he was alive—*alive!*"

No! I clutched at my chest, suddenly unable to breathe, unable to think. Marcus had found my mother, and that meant it wasn't simply me or the Spirit-Hunters he was after.

"Oh God," I wheezed as the gravel blurred before my eyes. I staggered to the fountain rim and dropped to a seat. Allison was nowhere to be seen, but I was too stunned—too horrified—to care or even consider.

Mama stalked toward me, puffing out her chest. "It was only a matter of time before Elijah came to save me, and he will return for me again. He has promised to take me away as soon as I help him."

"Help him?" I gaped up at her. "Help him with what?"

She crossed her arms. "Help him find the things you stole."

"Stole?" I repeated, startled.

"Oh, do not pretend you do not know. You stole his book—and wherever you have hidden it, I intend to find it. Elijah has promised to take me away if I do." She stomped closer to me. "Tell me where you put it, Eleanor. Where did you hide his book and his notes?"

I backed away from her. If Marcus wanted a book, then there was only one it could be: the missing pages in a grimoire called *Le Dragon Noir*. The one thing Marcus hadn't been able to take from me before he'd fled Philadelphia three months ago.

"I will find them," Mama shrieked. "And I will return them to him, Eleanor! And then—*then*—you will wish you had treated me more kindly."

I stood as tall as I could and fixed my eyes on hers. "Mama, did you say 'notes'? You are certain he asked for a book and notes?"

She hesitated, her posture wilting slightly. "Yes. A book and notes."

I turned away, pressing my left hand to my lips. I knew Joseph had destroyed the pages from *Le Dragon Noir*—Jie told me in one of her letters that he had done so—but before the Spirit-Hunters had even left Philadelphia, they'd found an envelope of Elijah's unsent letters tucked in the grimoire's pages. But those messages, as all Elijah's letters were prone to be, were filled with nothing more than random ramblings and random names. . . .

But perhaps they weren't so random to a necromancer.

Cold gripped me. Thank goodness I had put the letters in my carpetbag. Marcus had come to Philadelphia for *Le Dragon Noir*, and he knew that I could lead him to it—or at least to the letters within.

Footsteps sounded nearby. I whirled around. But it was only a male orderly marching toward us with the nurses at his heels.

Mama saw them, and her chin lifted high. "You may try to lock me in this place, Eleanor, but Elijah will come for me." Her eyes locked on mine. "And if you know what is good for you, you will never show your face to me again. You are no longer worthy of the Fitt name."

Then she pivoted elegantly around and faced the Kirkbride attendant as if he were nothing more than a dance partner. "I will wait for my son in my room, thank you. My daughter is now dead to me."

CHAPTER THREE

"Don't let anyone meet her," I ordered the nurses. My blood pounded in my ears, but I clung to the moment's excitement—for if I did not . . . if I let Mama's words sink in . . .

"Lock her in her room. . . . I-I fear it's the only option we have for protecting her."

"We'll keep her safe, Miss," promised the hatless nurse before I turned to leave. After three months of a sluggish, dazed existence, my mother had suddenly returned to her old dragon self. *My daughter is now dead to me.* My only remaining family member saw me as licentious and deceitful. I would not think of it. I would push it aside with everything else, and I would keep walking with my chin high and my shoulders back.

There was truly nothing left for me in Philadelphia now. So

with my jaw set and my blood burning, I marched back to the street. Alone.

Yet once there, I found Allison's carriage waiting with its door swung wide. She leaned out, her eyes rimmed with red. "Are you coming?" Her voice was thick, as if she'd been crying.

"You . . . don't mind?"

Her lips curled back. "Oh, *get in.*"

I squinted, my heart picking up speed again. "Does this mean you believe me? Despite what my mother was raving about?" I wanted Allison to believe me. Needed someone else to know my story.

She sniffed. "Your mother is clearly unwell. And as ludicrous as it all may sound, your story is more believable than hers." She waved to the seat beside her. "Now get *in.*"

I obeyed, and moments later we were rolling down Market Street toward the Delaware River. I watched Allison for several moments before working up the courage to ask, "Have you been crying?"

"Of course I've been crying," she snapped. "This is a lot of new information, and . . . and seeing your mother act like that. It's just awful." She wiped at her nose. "I know how you care about her. And Elijah."

I didn't know what to say. Everything about her response was unexpected. So I gnawed my lip and waited for her to speak.

Except she didn't. She simply stared out the carriage window as storefronts and people blurred past. I was grateful for the silence as we rattled through Philadelphia's downtown, for despite my desire to leave all this behind, I had never expected to do so on such short notice.

I had been planning to leave Philadelphia eventually, but now it had become my duty—to protect my mother, I *had* to leave. Marcus wanted my letters, so it was my job to bring them to the Spirit-Hunters.

Lost in my musings, I didn't notice how quickly we reached the Delaware River until we were suddenly upon its panorama of puffing steamers and white ship sails. Allison still hadn't spoken to me, but she did manage to rouse herself from her grief long enough to order her driver to take us straight to the ledger office.

While much of Philadelphia was lined with clean streets and elegant buildings, the wharves along the river were dingy and crowded.

My nerves jumped back into action. Marcus could already be here, waiting. I scanned every face for Elijah's, for yellow eyes; but for each person who passed, I missed four. With the horses and cabs rushing about, searching the crowded wharf was nearly impossible.

Nonetheless, as we pulled to a stop in front of the brownstone ledger office, I couldn't keep my gaze from darting around. Or my ears from straining for howling hounds.

Allison cleared her throat, and I turned my attention to her. "Thank you," I said. "I . . . I appreciate everything you've done for me. Perhaps one day I can repay you."

She scoffed. "Don't worry. I intend to call in my debt one day."

"Of course." I blinked, again struck by her unpredictable moods. But not wanting to waste another moment on her fickleness, I nodded once and climbed out of the carriage.

As the driver handed me my bag, Allison slid to the carriage door. "Send me a telegram from Paris. Let me know you have made it alive."

Now I was truly startled. What did she want from me? Friendship or enmity?

With the hope that it was the former, I said, "Yes. I promise to write." I bowed my head. "Good-bye, Allison Wilcox."

She pulled back into the carriage. "Good-bye, Eleanor Fitt." Then, with the abruptness that marked all of her movements, she yanked shut the carriage door and left.

And so it was that I found myself standing at the harbor with nothing more than a carpetbag and a drumming heart. The area stank of fish and river—that muddy smell of turbid waters—while the wind I'd missed in the city's center swept over me with full force.

Before me was the brownstone ledger building; behind me was everything I knew. Sure, I had read of places all over the world and dreamed of one day seeing them, but I'd never actually left Philadelphia before. I had no *idea* what was out there.

But I did not look back.

As soon as I was firmly inside the ledger office, black and white tiles led me to a wall of ticket counters. However, planted directly in my path was a middle-aged woman in an olive dress that was at least five years out of style. She stood unfolding bills and counting—*aloud*—as I strode toward her.

Sympathy flashed through me as I circled around her. She wouldn't get far with only ten dollars. Worse, she was going to get robbed if she wasn't more careful. Why, she had her steamer ticket dangling halfway out of her pocket!

With a final cringe at how loudly she advertised her naiveté, I marched to the nearest counter, where a bearded clerk waited. I dropped my bag at my feet.

"I need to buy passage to Paris."

"Can't go to Paris direct," he said, his voice gravelly. "It's not on the coast."

"Obviously." I glared in my best Mama impression. "But I need to go to France."

"So to Le Havre, then."

"How far is that from Paris?"

"It'll be half a day's train ride." He consulted a booklet of timetables. "There's only one direct steamer to Le Havre, but it's full. Obviously." His eyes rose to mine. "What with the Exhibition, we got foreign travelers everywhere. You won't be able to get a cabin for two weeks."

I grimaced. I'd forgotten about the Centennial Exhibition. It had been running so long now—four months—it had blended into the background of Philadelphia for me. "Two weeks absolutely won't do," I declared. "I must leave *now*. What else is there?"

"Well, C.G.T.'s *Amérique* to Le Havre leaves in two hours." His eyelids lowered, as if I was wasting his time. "But that lady over there just bought the last second-class ticket." He motioned to the olive-clad woman, who *still* stood organizing her pitiful funds.

"Now," he went on, "there's only one cabin left, and it's the most expensive."

"How expensive?"

"Seein' as the *Amérique* is the first ship in the world t'have electric lights, that it don't take on steerage passengers, and that it includes every meal, the answer is *very*."

"I didn't ask for a history lesson," I growled. "I asked for the blasted price."

"Two hundred dollars."

"Ah," I breathed, rocking back. That *was* expensive—certainly more than my emergency money of a hundred and twelve dollars and forty-seven cents. But I kept my face blank because confound it if I would let *this* man know my financial woes.

"And how much does a train from Le Havre to Paris cost?" I asked.

He glanced at his booklet. "Average cost is . . . fifty francs." His gaze rose to mine. "Which is about ten dollars."

Ten dollars. An idea hit me—a reckless, desperate idea. An idea so low that if I thought about it too hard, my morals would come barreling in to interfere.

I glanced back at the middle-aged woman. She was finally putting away her money, and I could only assume she'd be leaving at any moment.

I spun back to the clerk. "And you're absolutely certain there's no other boat leaving today?"

"Nothin', Miss."

"And what is the cost of a second-class ticket?"

"Why d'you ask when there ain't one—"

"What. Is. The. Cost?"

"Seventy-five dollars."

"Thank you," I said through gnashing teeth. "And which steamer is the *Amérique*? I'd like to . . . observe it before I decide on that first-class ticket."

He jerked his thumb to the left. "The big one with the wheels. You can't miss it."

"The big one. Very clear," I muttered, and before my temper or conscience could get the best of me, I twisted on my heels to leave.

As I'd feared, the woman in olive was gone. So I hefted my carpetbag onto my shoulder, gathered my skirts in my fist, and darted for the street. By the time I stepped outside, it was to find her on the opposite sidewalk and almost to the municipal pier.

I surged after her, my mind racing as fast as my feet and with my scruples flaring to life. *You shouldn't do this,* they said. *This isn't like you.*

"But," I whispered in response, thinking how aptly Shakespeare had said it: "Diseases desperate grown. By desperate appliances are relieved." If I wanted to protect Mama—protect myself—then this was what I had to do. Marcus had come for

39

me because I had the letters. Now I was leaving Philadelphia, and I prayed that he would follow me to Paris. Follow me to the Spirit-Hunters.

I slowed only once in my pursuit, to yank out seventy-five dollars, and then I marched directly for the woman. Fortunately, she was as scattered in her walking as she had been in her money counting.

And even more fortunately, her steamer ticket still dangled dangerously from her pocket, flipping this way and that in the breeze.

"Pardon me," I called. "Ma'am?"

She hesitated beside a stack of crates around which dockers buzzed like bees.

Perfect, I thought, hurrying to her side. My heart was lodged far into my throat, pounding hard, but I still managed to don my most charming smile. "I believe you dropped this." I held up the seventy-five dollars and let the wind flutter it enticingly.

Her forehead bunched up. "No, I don't think I did, Miss." She spoke with a heavy Irish accent.

"Were you not just counting your money in the ledger office?"

A pair of burly dockers trudged past, and I took the opportunity to shimmy closer to the woman—and to her ticket.

"I am certain I saw this fall on the floor beside you." I pushed the cash toward her, and her eyes locked on the money.

Her lips moved as if adding up the bills. "I-I don't think this is mine, Miss."

"Well, it isn't mine either." I gave her a warm smile. "And it was on the floor where *you* stood. You must take it. I insist."

She lifted a quivering hand and slowly closed her fingers around the money.

My pulse quickened. Now was my moment. Keeping the rest of me perfectly still, I slipped my left hand over her ticket. Then all it took was a flick of my wrist, a reangling of my body, and that second-class ticket was mine.

I bit back a smile, my chest fluttery with triumph. "So you'll keep the money?" I asked, sliding the ticket into my own pocket and making a great show of readjusting my carpetbag. "It *must* be yours," I added.

"Y-yes . . ." She swallowed, her eyes darting to mine. "Thank you."

"My pleasure, Ma'am." I positively beamed at her as I bobbed a little curtsy, wished her a lovely day, and trotted as quickly as I could around the dockers and crates.

I did it! Jie would be proud! I'd been just as sneaky as she. I couldn't wait to tell her, and now, here I was, on my way to actually *seeing* her. . . .

But a tiny ball of guilt wound into my belly. I scowled, picking up my pace. It was done; I'd taken her ticket, and I was leaving. The end. Now all I had to do was shove the guilt aside and find the *Amérique*.

Surprisingly, once I passed all the local ferries, the "big one with the wheels" *was* rather hard to miss. Twice as tall and three times as long as any other boat at the pier, it blocked out all view

41

of the river. I had to crane my neck to see the white sails billowing at either end. Two red smokestacks stood proudly at the center, and most obvious of all were the gigantic paddle wheels, one on each side.

My bonnet ribbons swatted my face as I approached the ship and made my way around the swaggering sailors and ogling passengers. I checked for any olive-clad women, but my mark was nowhere in sight. No doubt she was still by the stacked crates, counting out her newest funds.

A quick scan ahead showed two gangplanks, one near the street and one all the way at the end of the dock. At the closer plank, stacked luggage outnumbered people, and the women's colorful gowns shimmered like butterflies. Clearly this was the *first-class* line.

The more distant line, however, showed men and women dressed like me: well-made but well-worn clothes. So after a final search for the woman in the olive dress and finding she was nowhere about, I trudged on.

But I only made it a few steps before my right hand—my missing hand—started tingling. Then the hair on my neck sprang up.

I froze midstride. *Marcus, Marcus, Marcus*—he was all I could think of. My eyes slid left and right, but I could find nothing unusual.

Yet the buzz in my hand did not dull, and now my breath was quickening.

Stay calm, Eleanor. Focus. With forced cool, I looked over my shoulder toward land and searched the area. But no light flickered or energy sparkled.

If Marcus or something Dead was nearby, it wasn't showing itself.

So I made myself turn back around and resume my steps. My movements were clunky and rushed, though, and my heart refused to settle.

Then from nowhere, a gust of wind knocked into me. *Hard*.

I swayed, and the air flipped around me, tugging at my skirts like a riptide. I spun around and frantically checked the dockers' and sailors' reactions. Except that none of them seemed affected by this gale.

Pain burst in my wrist. It was the scene from the bank all over again, and I knew I had to run. *Just get on the ship!* It was the only shelter around, and though I didn't believe walls could really stop Marcus, it was the closest thing to safety I could conjure.

So I thrust myself forward, leaning into the unnatural wind and gulping for air. But the throbbing where my hand once was—it shrieked so loudly, it dulled all my other senses. I shambled forward like one of the Dead.

Then came the first howl, and I froze all over again. It was an unmistakably long and plaintive baying, and with it came a smell. A pungent, dank smell that wasn't from the river. A smell I *knew*.

Grave dirt.

The stench of the Dead.

Marcus was here, even if I could not see him. He was here, and I was too late. But I would *not* go down without a fight.

The wind battered against me as if trying to push me back to shore. I had to fight to stand tall while I scanned every shadow for yellow eyes.

And as each of my heartbeats skittered past, the howling dogs grew louder. Closer. I could not see them, but I could certainly imagine them: rabid, fanged monsters larger than any real dog.

That was when I saw him—not Marcus, but a young man in line for the second-class gangplank. His slender frame listed like a tree in a tornado, and his head spun about as if he too was searching for these raging hounds. He looked a few years older than me, with wildly flying chestnut curls and a charcoal suit.

He was beautiful—the features and garb of some fairy-tale prince.

And whoever he was, he was as affected by these hounds and this unnatural wind as I was. Perhaps more so.

I stumbled back, too stunned to be scared. Who *was* this young man? He couldn't be Marcus, could he?

In the space of two ragged breaths, the wind died down. The howling grew distant and then stopped altogether.

But I barely noticed. My gaze was locked on this young man as I slowly walked toward him—and the more I stared at him, the more familiar he seemed. Yet I couldn't pinpoint why.

My toe hit something, and I tumbled forward. My arms windmilled, yet just before my face hit the pier, a docker threw out his hands and righted me.

"Th-thank you," I whispered, painting a grateful smile on my lips. He merely looked at me as if I'd had too much drink and resumed his work. I used my distracted moment to regain my wits. To gather up my skirts and dash onward to the second-class gangplank.

But by the time I got there, the young man was gone— presumably on board the ship. It wasn't until after I had waited in the long queue and finally handed the porter my ticket that I realized something.

Both times my right wrist had ignited with pain and I had heard the hounds howling. And both times it had all ended when I turned my concentration elsewhere.

But what the devil that meant, I didn't know.

CHAPTER FOUR

At the top of the gangplank, a middle-aged man took my bag and guided me inside. I promptly scoured every nook and shadow for yellow eyes, but the world-famous electric lamps (molded into fish, I might add) clearly illuminated everything—and I quickly realized there was nowhere a person could hide. The bloodred carpet, the wood-paneled walls, and the velvet-padded handrails were constantly trod on or grasped at by servants in black uniforms scurrying past.

By the time we reached a wide staircase at the ship's center, where a large mermaid balustrade stood guard, my pulse had slowed to its normal speed.

I'd had to steal a ticket to get on this boat, so unless Marcus had bought that final, expensive ticket, he couldn't get on board.

Except rules like that don't apply to Marcus. I ignored that thought. If he got on the steamer, if that raging wind and those baying hounds followed me here, then I would deal with them.

We finally reached my stateroom, and after I tipped the porter, he left me with a key and scooted off into the flow of server traffic. Just as I was about to unlock the door, it swung back on its own.

My heart leaped into my throat, but it was only a pretty young woman in black. *"C'est votre chambre?"*

"Uh . . ." I was too busy trying to calm my pulse to follow her French. "What?"

"This is your room?" She dipped her head and peered at me from the tops of her eyes.

I nodded. "Yes."

"Then we are roommates."

"Roommates?" I repeated stupidly. I hadn't even considered the possibility, but *of course* second class would mean sharing a cabin.

"Mais oui." She stepped aside so I could trudge in, and with a wave to a set of bunks in one corner, she said, "I took the top bed."

"Oh . . . all right." I crossed to the bunk and heaved my carpetbag on it. Then I shifted around to inspect the stateroom.

My eyes instantly lit on two more bunks and two elegant black trunks stacked beside them. So, not roommate but *roommates.*

I turned my attention to the rest of the room. White enamel walls with walnut fittings surrounded portholes and large electric lights. The beds were made up with crisp, white linens, and a navy curtain hung elegantly over them. Squeezed into the center of the room were two navy satin armchairs.

At that moment, the young woman stepped in front of me. "I am Mademoiselle Laure Primeau," she drawled, holding out a dainty hand. "And you are?"

"I'm Eleanor Fitt." I gulped, suddenly hot with embarrassment. "I-I'd shake your hand, but . . ." I lifted my bandaged wrist.

Her eyes widened. "*Mon Dieu.*" She hastily withdrew her hand. "I am sorry. That looks . . . painful."

"Yes, it was." I twisted around to my carpetbag, not wishing to dwell on my injury. "Where can I put my things?"

She sighed. "I fear the other ladies 'ave already claimed most of the space." Skirts rustled behind me, and when I glanced back, she was draped over one of the chairs. "If you do not 'ave much, then you should use the drawer beneath the bed."

I nodded and set to placing my few items—extra underclothes, a hatbox, a nightgown—in the drawer. At the bottom of the bag, I found the stack of Elijah's letters.

Gnawing the inside of my mouth, I eyed them warily. Then, as quickly as possible, I withdrew them and stuffed them beneath my spare petticoat before finally crawling onto my bed.

Laure eyed me from her chair, and I eyed her right back. She looked to be a bit older than Jie—twenty-five years at the most.

"You are traveling alone?" she asked.

"Yes. And you?"

"*Oui.* But I am an old maid—you are so young. How can you travel alone? You 'ave no family?"

My stomach twisted. *My daughter is now dead to me.* I dropped my gaze. "No . . . I have no family."

"Ah. But that is sad, *non*? I 'ave a family, but—"

The cabin door flew open, cutting her off. I shot to my feet, ready to fight . . . but it was only an angular, gray-haired woman shuffling in. An auburn-haired girl of eight or nine skipped happily behind her.

Laure's expression soured, and with clear displeasure, she stood. "*Bonjour*, Madame Brown. We 'ave our final roommate." She motioned to me. "This is Mademoiselle Fitt."

The older woman curtsied primly, all the while openly examining me. "You are traveling alone?"

"Yes, Ma'am," I said, not bothering to hide my own return-examination. She was long faced and unfortunately hairy around the chin.

"This is my granddaughter, Lizzie." Mrs. Brown motioned to the girl, who gave me a bright grin—revealing her own unfortunate feature: exceptionally large front teeth. "Lizzie, get your parasol. We are going to the promenade deck to watch the ship depart. Would you care to join us?"

Nothing about her expression suggested she wanted me, so I forced a polite smile. "No thank you, Ma'am."

Her gaze shifted to Laure. "*Mademoiselle?*"

50

"*Non merci.*" Laure bared her teeth in a terrifying grin.

"Found it!" Lizzie trilled, whipping up a lacy parasol. She skipped back to Mrs. Brown's side and, after giving Laure and me a little curtsy, trotted from the room. Mrs. Brown followed.

Once the door was firmly shut, Laure's lips twitched up mischievously, and she rubbed her hands together. "*Mademoiselle,* you 'ave scandalized her."

"You mean by traveling alone?"

"*Oui. C'est magnifique.*" She snickered. "Now, if you will excuse me, I believe I will go to the promenade deck and watch us depart—*without* the Browns for company." Then, with a wink, she left.

I fell back onto my bed and draped a hand over my eyes. As much as I also wanted to see our departure, it was safer to stay locked away until the Philadelphia wharf—and I hoped Marcus too—were long gone. Once we had sailed the hundred miles of Delaware River to reach the ocean, *then* I would allow myself to roam the ship.

An image of the chestnut-haired young man flashed in my mind. If he could hear those dogs and feel that wind, then perhaps he would know what was happening. Perhaps he could explain. Or—if he was as lost as I—we could try to muddle through it together.

And since he was somewhere on this ship and we were stuck here for well over a week, I had every intention of finding him—and finding out what he knew.

* * *

51

Hours later, I found myself curled into a ball on my bed. After an evening of rocking, I was so queasy, I couldn't even stand— much less try to explore the ship. When I heard the Brown ladies come in to change into dinner attire, I could only screw my eyes tighter and pray that this nausea would vanish.

"*Oh la,*" Laure said, hovering over me. She had just finished donning her evening wear. "You are ill?"

I cracked open an eyelid. "The boat . . . it won't stop moving."

She laughed. "*Oui.* That is 'ow it usually works." She flicked her hand toward the portholes. "It helps to be outside, you know. Watching the 'orizon keeps your digestion calm."

She dragged me into a sitting position. "And it is best on the first-class promenade deck."

"But we aren't first class."

"*Pas de problème.* One must simply sneak onto the first-class deck when all its passengers are at dinner."

She helped me stand. Her eyes briefly settled on my missing hand but then passed on to my undoubtedly green face. "I can take you there and then we can go to dinner."

"But . . ." I waved helplessly at my gown as we made our way to the door. "This is all I have to wear." Heat crept up my neck, and at the sympathetic swoop in Laure's eyebrows, I dropped my gaze.

She sighed. "Then you can stay on the deck, where it is no matter what you wear, and *I* will go to supper." She towed me toward the main stairwell I had circled around earlier, and we climbed it three floors up before finally stepping into the first-class saloon.

"This is where all of the first-class passengers will spend most of their day-to-day time," Laure explained as we walked through. "It is not so different from the second-class saloon."

I nodded, my eyes flicking around. The room reminded me of my family's parlor—or as the parlor *used* to look before I had sold everything. There was a grand piano in one corner, oak and ebony bookcases along the walls, and red velvet armchairs and sofas strategically placed throughout. Skylights overhead showed an orange sky, and plate glass mirrors shone with reflected light.

We reached a door at the end of the room, and Laure planted her shoulder against it and shoved. "The wind outside is strong. Nice but strong."

The instant she got the door open, air blasted into me. My heart flipped, and my ears strained, expecting to hear hounds at any moment.

But no—this was a different wind. A real wind.

Tugging at my sleeves, I followed Laure onto the giant, empty deck. Smokestacks and masts spanned before me with awnings placed strategically between. Chairs and benches were also around, and Laure guided me to one at the ship's aft.

"Sit 'ere!" She had to shout to be heard over the wind. "It is the best view, and you can watch the sunset. I will 'ave a server bring you something to eat." She deposited me on a bench facing the western sky. "And if you think you will lose your stomach"—she patted her bodice—"do not do it in our room, *oui?*"

"Yes." I gave her a tight smile. "Thank you."

She swatted my words aside. "See you in the cabin later." Then she whirled around and strode off. With a sigh, I slumped back on the bench. I *did* feel better now.

We were still within sight of the coast, but it was too distant for me to discern much beyond marshland.

A squat waiter soon arrived with sea biscuits and an orange. He declared them the "best foods for a sea-ailed stomach" and then left me to munch on my meal.

I rather liked the biscuits. They were crisp and salty and did much to put my stomach right. I stayed there on the promenade deck until long after the sun had faded. Until swaying electric lights blocked out any starlight, and when I eventually found myself shivering, I decided it was time for bed.

But of course, just as my luck would have it, I heaved back the saloon door to find the room completely full. Worse, at least fifty pairs of eyes immediately turned to me.

With a gulp, I slipped my stump into the folds of my skirt and walked inside with as much poise as I could muster.

But the wind grabbed hold of the door and slammed it shut with a loud *bang!*, shooting me forward like a drunken rocket.

All at once, *hundreds* of pairs of eyes shot to me. All the women in their beautiful pastel gowns—gowns such as those I'd once worn and loved myself—and the men in their black suits, so crisp and handsome, watched me. To think this life had almost been mine . . . to think I'd been reduced to picking pockets to get on board . . .

Someone nearby giggled. Then came a chortle, a whisper. In less time than it took for me to gather up my breath and resume my steps, the room erupted with twittering.

My face ignited. Sweat popped out on my brow. With my gaze cast to the floor, I strode through as fast as I could. It wasn't until my stateroom was in sight that I slowed to a normal pace and sucked in air. I paused at my door and chided myself for being so daunted by a bunch of silly people. After facing an army of Dead, one would think a saloon full of rich folk would be as easy as pie.

Jie would have found it all hilarious—nothing scared her.

Joseph would have given me a knowing smile, his back straight and his demeanor a thousand times more elegant than any of *those* people.

And Daniel . . .

I leaned against the door, my legs suddenly too wobbly to stand.

I always tried so hard to *not* think of Daniel. To avoid remembering how his lips twisted up mischievously when he laughed. How he glowered when I got too close to his inventions. How he doffed his gray flat cap or flicked my chin with his thumb.

Or how he'd tasted when we'd kissed . . .

I huffed a breath and fumbled for my room key. *You are strong and independent,* I told myself as I unlocked the door.

Capable and clever. No males needed.

I turned my cabin door handle and pushed in. *You are powerful and—*

My thoughts broke off. I screamed. Crouched beside my bunk was a slight young man with chestnut hair and a charcoal suit. He turned his head toward me. "Eleanor—you're here! It's about time."

My breath froze in my lungs, but not because he knew my name. I couldn't breathe because staring out from his handsome, round face was a pair of gleaming yellow eyes.

CHAPTER FIVE

I screamed again, but this time I scrambled back to run. Marcus—it had to be he!

But Mama saw him in Elijah's body. The thought flashed but was instantly swallowed up by another. *Yellow eyes! Run!*

"Eleanor, wait!" the young man shouted.

I sprinted down the hall toward the middle of the ship, but then the boat swayed, throwing off my balance. I tangled in my petticoats and slammed into the wall.

Footsteps pounded behind, so with a shove I lurched on, charging my legs to go faster. The main stairwell was just ahead. Those steps would lead me to the first-class saloon—to people and safety. But stairs would be too hard to climb.

"Wait!" the young man shouted again.

I reached the mermaid balustrade, and, without thinking, I grabbed her tail and slung myself around, behind the stairs. I flew into the next hall. Far ahead was a bright doorway. The dining room? Somewhere that had people, at least.

I surged on, and the hammering feet rounded the stairwell behind me.

"Please, El!" he shouted. "Wait!"

El? That was my brother's name for me.

I faltered. My skirts flew around my legs. Then the boat listed sharply right. I toppled forward. Instinctively, I threw my hands out to catch myself, but I had only one hand to stop my fall.

Agony ripped through my stump as a shriek boiled up my throat and out my mouth.

Tears sprang to my eyes, but I made myself draw in my legs—I had to keep *going*. I was too slow, though. Too winded and hurt. The footsteps were upon me.

"El, are you all right?" The young man's cheeks were flushed scarlet.

"Stay away!" I scuttled against the wall.

His hands flew up. "I won't hurt you. I swear, El." He lifted a foot as if to approach.

"Get back!" I screeched.

He froze, his gaze snapping toward the door ahead and then back to me. Clearly he thought as I did: surely all this noise would draw *someone* into the hall.

I tried to blink back the tears blurring my vision. Pain

screamed in my wrist, but it was from the fall—not from spiritual energy. There were no dogs howling or winds roaring.

Still, the young man had yellow eyes. That told me I was in danger.

I drew in a shaky breath, ready to scream.

"No, please!" he blurted. "Just talk to me."

"Get away from me," I growled. "I vowed to kill you—or did you forget that?"

He recoiled. "Kill me?" He shook his head. "I don't mean you any harm."

"Go to hell, Marcus." I spat the name.

"Marcus?" The young man's forehead wrinkled. "My name isn't Marcus. I'm Oliver."

"Whoever you are, I will kill you." I slid my legs slowly sideways, hoping to stand and make a run for it. "Now get out of my way."

"I swear!" he cried. "Didn't you read about me in Elijah's letters?"

I tensed and sucked in a breath, my fear and fury skipping a beat. There *was* an Oliver in those letters.

"You recognize me," he said. "Oliver. My name must be in them. Your brother and I were together all the time—"

"You mean when you stole his body and started living in it?" I shook my head and bounded to my feet, my blood boiling back into a rage. "I promised I would send you to the hottest flames of hell for that."

He skittered to the other side of the hall. "Look. I'll stay right here. Just talk to me. *Please*."

"I have nothing to say to you." I slunk right. The agony in my wrist had pulled back to a distant throb, and the unbidden tears had dropped away. "Don't you dare come near me, Marcus."

"Why do you keep calling me that?" the young man cried. "I'm *Oliver*."

"And you just happen to have the same yellow eyes?"

He frowned. "Yellow eyes? Is Marcus a . . . a demon? As in a creature of spirit bound to this world by a necromancer?" His hand lifted to his collar, and he slipped out a long golden chain.

My heart stopped when I saw it. So did my careful trek. I knew that round locket hanging from the chain's end. "Where did you get that?"

His golden eyes never leaving my face, the young man dangled the chain toward me. "You know it, don't you?"

I didn't answer. I couldn't. Any words I wanted to say were trapped in my throat. I had bought that necklace for Elijah just before he went abroad. Inside was a picture of the thirteen-year-old me.

The young man let the chain and locket drop. "My name is Oliver, and I'm Elijah's demon."

"Demon," I whispered, the word filling every space in my mind. "Elijah's *demon*." For several long seconds, I simply stared. Then my heart and body jolted into action. I staggered back into a run.

Oliver did not follow me.

I reached the doorway at the end of the hall, and it *did* lead to the dining room. Only a handful of guests remained, sitting at a table that spanned the middle of the room. Judging by their sloppy posture, they were thoroughly drunk.

Demon, demon, demon. The word pounded in my mind with each step.

A black-uniformed waiter glided to a stop in front of me. "May I help you?"

Demon, demon, demon . . .

"*Mademoiselle*, may I help you?"

I gaped at him, tongue-tied. I couldn't say "Help! A necromancer who claims he's a demon is following me." Especially because Oliver—or Marcus, if his yellow eyes meant what I *thought* they might mean—was nowhere to be seen.

I finally stammered, "F-food?" and the waiter nodded, guiding me to a table against the wall. I dropped onto a red-upholstered chair and ordered a plate of buttered toast.

Then, trying to slow my breathing, I massaged my wrist and watched the door.

"A demon," I whispered. Would that make sense in the context of Elijah's letters? I couldn't remember. The only thing I knew about demons was that they were supposedly bad, and it was probably in my best interest to avoid them.

Laughter erupted from the group of drinkers, and while I watched with mild interest and disgust, they all lifted their glasses in a wild French cheer.

I glanced back at the entrance and started.

Oliver had ambled in, his jaw set and his hands in his pockets.

I sat, rod straight, as he sauntered almost casually to the table of drinkers and bellowed, *"Vive la France!"*

As they all roared their approval, he swiped a bottle off their table and then strolled toward me.

"Stop," I ordered once he was ten paces away. "Not an inch closer."

He nodded. "All right. I'm stopping. I am not coming a single inch closer." He strode to a table nearby and dragged a chair to the precise spot I'd told him to stop. Then he plunked down, yanked his stolen bottle to his chest, and turned his yellow eyes on me. "I intend to drink all of this gin."

My eyes narrowed. "All right."

He frowned. "Well, you could at least protest a little. I thought you didn't like it when Elijah drank. He said you got all worked up when he sipped your father's whiskey."

Somehow my spine straightened even more. I *had* done that, but the only person who would know was Elijah. "For one," I said carefully, "I was more worried about Elijah getting caught than getting drunk. For two, I don't care in the slightest about *you*." I dipped my head toward the bottle. "Drink up."

His lips twitched down. "You're just as bossy as he is."

"As he *was*," I snapped. "Elijah's dead."

His face paled. "Dead?" He clapped a hand over his mouth and turned away.

"Yes," I said. "He's *dead*, and Marcus stole his body."

"Blessed Eternity." The young man grabbed at his hair. "No wonder I can't find him. If he's dead and his body has been possessed . . ." He popped off the bottle's top and gulped back a long swig. Then he dropped his head in his hands and began to weep.

I blinked, completely stunned. Either he was trying to catch me off guard or he was genuinely crushed to learn of Elijah's death. But I was saved from deciding which by the arrival of my toast.

The waiter looked as horrified as I was by Oliver's tears— especially when Oliver suddenly roused himself enough to latch on to the waiter's sleeve. "Another bottle of gin, please."

"Your cabin and name?"

"I'm with them." He motioned to the inebriated Frenchmen.

The waiter's eyebrows arched with disbelief.

Oliver, his eyes now bloodshot and nose puffy, shouted, *"Vive la France!"* And again the table burst into cheers.

"See?" Oliver demanded.

The waiter glowered but didn't argue.

And all the while, I watched in sick fascination. "You're not Marcus," I said at last.

"No." Oliver rubbed at his eyes with his sleeve. "Is this Marcus the one who . . ." His voice cracked. "Who took Elijah's body?"

"Yes."

"I should've been there." His jaw clenched. "Oh God, if *only* I had been there."

My eyes narrowed, and in a wary tone, I said, "I thought that demons could not say the Lord's name."

He gave me a look halfway between a repulsed sneer and an amused smile. "Then you clearly know very little about demons. The myth is actually that I cannot say 'Jesus' and yet the name just crossed my lips, did it not?"

"Yes, it most assuredly did." My words came out harsh. "So, pray tell, why should I believe you're a demon then?"

"*Why?* Did you not see this?" He yanked out the locket, wrenching it full force against his neck. Over and over, each movement more frantic than the last, he tried to snap the chain. Soon an angry red line was scored into his flesh.

Yet still he ripped at the necklace.

"Stop!" I cried.

"Only if you believe me. Do you see this, El?" Another yank. "I am *bound*." He flung out his hand, releasing the locket. "Simply because the rumors fail to accurately portray my kind does not make me any less *real*."

"Though nor does a chain that won't break," I retorted. "If you really want to convince me, you'll have to give a better reason than that locket."

Oliver rubbed the bridge of his nose, and an ache flared in my chest. It was such an Elijah-like gesture—the old Elijah, the skinny, child Elijah—that I could have been sitting next to my brother at that very moment.

No wonder he seemed so familiar on the pier.

Yet of course, this similarity was not enough to make me trust him. "I'm listening," I said. "For *now*, so you had best tell your story quickly."

He sucked back another swig of gin, and I noticed with a start that the bottle was almost empty. Then, smacking his lips, he said, "I was . . . well, *born* isn't the right word . . . more like *created* two hundred years ago. You see, demons are a lot like humans, only we live in the spirit realm. We grow and age and eventually go where all spirits go."

I picked at the edge of my toast. "I thought spirits went to the spirit realm."

"Oh no. There's a final afterlife. First, though, your spirit has to travel through my home."

"And your home is the spirit realm."

"Yep. And demons"—he splayed his fingers gracefully across his chest—"start there before eventually passing into the great unknown."

"So you're dead."

"No!" He snorted. "I'm very much alive. I merely come from a different realm is all. I'm made entirely of spiritual energy. Plus, I live—*exist*—a great deal longer than humans."

Behind him, the Frenchmen burst into an animated debate. I had to lift my voice to be heard. "So if all you do is *exist*, then why are demons painted as creatures of evil?"

His eyes flashed. "Because people are scared of us. We're creatures of pure spiritual energy—we have a lot of magic at our command. But the truth is, demons are exactly like humans: good, bad, or"—he gave me a withering smile—"neutrally disinterested."

At that moment, the Frenchmen's debate ended with a

rousing chorus of unintelligible, off-key singing. Oliver glanced back, his body perking up. Then, with very deliberate movements, he rose and stumbled over to their table, his now-empty bottle in hand and voice chanting along.

While he swayed and sang, the waiter returned. He set the new bottle of gin on my table, shot a disapproving look at the happily drunk carolers, and then glided away.

I nibbled at my toast and waited with growing impatience. There was only so long I could maintain my veneer of calm and strength—especially when memories of Elijah hovered so close to my heart's surface. Several moments later, though, Oliver returned with a new bottle tucked under his arm. He dropped into his seat and inspected the label. "Rum. Delightful. A personal favorite."

"Three bottles of liquor?" I sniffed disgustedly. "And all of them stolen."

Oliver shrugged. "They have the money. I do not."

"No? Then how did you buy a ticket onto this ship?"

"I did not *buy* a ticket per se. I found one . . . no, *borrowed*." He nodded as if *this* was the proper term.

"In other words," I said, "you stole the ticket. Just like you stole the alcohol." Even though I too had stolen my ticket, I'd at least had enough conscience to compensate the poor woman— and to feel like utter scum for taking it in the first place. Oliver obviously had no such morals.

"You're welcome to *buy* me more alcohol," Oliver said, smiling sadly. "I intend to get so rip-roaring drunk that I don't remember a thing tomorrow."

"All because Elijah died?"

He winced. "How can you say it so . . . so callously? Yes, because I just learned my best *friend* died. My master. My only—"

"Enough," I snapped, sitting taller. He was *definitely* getting too close to topics best left alone. "I don't care one whit about your grief or your supposed demon feelings. I want to hear how you knew Elijah. Now talk."

The muscles in his jaw twitched, but he didn't argue. "As I was saying, I was simply existing. Then one day, a few years ago, I was summoned. It's like . . . like a tugging in your gut. One minute I was watching the universe unfold, and the next I was being yanked into a dingy hotel room in London. Suddenly I had a body *and* a skinny young man standing in front of me."

"And from where did the body come? Is it yours?"

His nose wrinkled up. "Of course it's mine! I didn't take some poor person's corpse, if that's what you're thinking."

"Well, how else does one get a body?"

"It's . . . it's like water and ice," Oliver said. "Phase changes. On the spirit side I was water. Then as I stepped through the curtain into the earthly side, I became ice."

I broke off more toast, considering this. "So was it *you* hiding in the shadows downtown?"

He stared blankly—clearly clueless as to what I referred, which could only mean I *had* seen Marcus in Philadelphia.

But then a new question occurred to me. "Why are your eyes yellow?"

He ogled them at me. "That's pretty standard for anyone whose natural form is raw energy."

Meaning Marcus's true form was pure soul—which it *was*, since his body had died years ago. "Does this phase change happen to everyone? Because Marcus—the spirit who stole Elijah's body—crossed from the spirit realm, yet he stayed in his spirit form. A ghost."

"As for that, I'd guess it's because he was dead." Oliver guzzled back more rum and then wiped his lips. "Basically, this fellow's body and soul were separate. When he crossed the curtain, he stayed in his spirit form because that was all he could be. However, if a man still possesses both a body *and* a spirit, then he would change phases. For example, if *you*"—he tipped his head toward me—"went to the spirit world, you'd change into a watery soul form."

I grunted. It made sense. "So you had a body and then Elijah bound you? Why did he need to use the locket?"

"The guardians," Oliver drawled, as if that was the most obvious answer in the world. "The ones who keep unwanted humans out of the spirit world—they also do a rather good job of keeping demons and spirits *in* it. When a necromancer calls something over, he has to hide it from these guardians right away. Hiding is done by *binding*; and to bind a demon, you have to use an object of significance. Elijah chose this. It binds me to your world, hides me from the guardians, *and* keeps me completely powerless."

"Powerless?"

"Yep." Oliver ran a finger along his chin. "I can't do any magic. Only Elijah can use my power—at least until our agreement ends."

I leaned forward. "But Elijah's dead."

He twisted his face away and took another pull of rum.

"So," I said, forcing Oliver to look at me again. "Does a spirit or demon *have* to be called by a necromancer? Because Marcus crossed over without a necromancer's help."

Oliver's eyebrows jumped. "The guardians didn't sense him? He must be very strong then. Of course, yellow eyes would suggest that too."

I fidgeted in my seat. My emotions were stewing in a way I knew best to avoid. Anger seemed the best approach, and if there was one feeling I could summon easily, it was *rage*. "First Elijah hid you from the guardians, then he made you his slave, and now you can't use your magic. Plus, your master died." My lips curled back. "Why, I'd say you're not a very good demon, are you?"

Oliver cringed.

"And," I continued, "I have to wonder why you weren't in Philadelphia with my brother. Why didn't you protect Elijah?"

Oliver screwed his eyes shut. "It was his necromancy that killed him, wasn't it? He must've done something stupid and . . ." His words faded, fresh tears welling in his eyes.

For some reason, this only infuriated me more. "So you *could* have saved him? Why didn't you, then? Why weren't you there?

If you really are—no, *were*—his demon, then why weren't you with him when he died?"

Oliver flinched as if I'd slapped him, but his eyes stayed close. "E-Elijah sent me away. He knew he had to give me some impossible task so I'd be out of his way and couldn't interfere."

"That is quite a convenient excuse," I said sharply, my voice rising. "Why, exactly, would he send his demon away?"

Oliver's eyes snapped open. "He knew I'd try to stop him. I didn't like what he wanted to do—the killing, the black magic. We argued. A lot." He dabbed at his eyes and then guzzled back more rum, swishing it around in his mouth.

"You know what I think?" I watched him from the tops of my eyes. "I think you were careless. You didn't *want* to save him or be with him—"

"No," Oliver breathed. "El, he gave me a direct command. I couldn't disobey him—not while we were bound. I told him— so many times—that there was nothing good in *Le Dragon Noir*. I told him any ghost in the spirit realm should stay there, but Elijah . . . he was determined to resurrect your father."

"Determined?" I gritted my teeth. "More like insane. Where did he send you?"

"We were in Luxor. He sent me to Giza to find the Old Man in the Pyramids."

"The who?" I snapped.

"The only person in the universe who knows how to raise a . . . a terrible creature. The Black Pullet."

The Black Pullet. That sounded familiar. Then I remembered some of Elijah's final words: *I'll go back to Egypt. I'll resurrect the Black Pullet, and we'll live in wealth for the rest of our days, and everything will be all right.*

"And did you find the Old Man?" My voice was a low snarl. "Was this mission that kept you from saving Elijah at least a successful one?"

Oliver's head shook once. "I couldn't find a bloody thing, and by the time I got to New York to meet Elijah, he had already left for Philadelphia. He was probably already dead."

I hugged my arms to my chest. It was a lot to take in, and the hot rage in my chest was spreading to my throat.

Here was some person—some *monster*—who not only knew my brother, but had spent the last three years with him. Three years that should have been mine. Three years during which Elijah had transformed from my loving brother into a vengeful murderer.

My eyes stung, and I bit my lip to keep the tears away.

"You know," Oliver said, popping open the locket and glancing inside. "You've changed a lot since this photograph was made." He tilted his head and squinted at me, his eyes over-bright. "No wonder I didn't recognize you sooner."

My whole body stiffened. "Were you trying to find me?"

"No. I was *trying* to find Elijah's letters, and, well . . . they led me to you."

My heart beat faster. The letters—it was always about those *damned* letters. I glanced at the table of Frenchmen. As long as they were still here, I could keep talking to Oliver with some semblance of safety.

I looked back to the demon. To his unnatural beauty . . . and increasingly drunken comportment. "What," I said, my voice dangerously soft, "do you want with the letters, Oliver?"

"They're all the ones I wouldn't let Elijah send. I thought if I found them, I'd find *him*."

"You mean you *kept* him from sending me letters?"

"Egads, yes!" Oliver blinked quickly, as if it took a lot of concentration to focus. "They're filled with explanations of necromancy—of spells and translated grimoire passages. It's dangerous stuff. Plus, he wrote to you almost every day. Like you were his diary."

"Oh?" I wound my fingers in my skirts. "I don't have three years' worth of letters."

"The ones you have are the ones he considered most valuable. He must've destroyed the others. But I know he cast a spell on the important ones. A finding spell, so that one day—in case things went wrong—they would reach you and you would understand."

"But I *don't* understand." My teeth were grinding so hard, my jaw had started to ache. "I have read the letters, Oliver, yet I *still* can't fathom what Elijah was doing."

Oliver jabbed a thumb to his chest—or he tried to. His movement was sloppy, and he swayed back in his seat. "I can try to explain them to you. I was there for everything."

"No," I snapped. "You are not allowed near my letters." *Especially not if they have secrets of necromancy in them.* "And," I added, "I still do not see why you were trying to find them in the first place."

"No? I thought I was being *very*"—spit flew with the word—"clear. It was *my* magic that made the finding spell, so that means I can track the letters. I sensed the letters were boarding the ship, so I *might* have picked a pocket to get on board."

"I don't believe you." I slid my uneaten toast away and pushed back from the table. "You were in my room just now, and you were searching through my things—not for Elijah or for me. You were searching for my letters."

His eyes darted sideways, and he swallowed several times. But before he could weave some clever excuse, I stood and puffed out my chest. "I've heard enough from you, Oliver. I'm going to my cabin now, and if you follow me, I will scream."

"B-but . . ." His lip quavered. "I thought we could . . ."

"Could what?"

He tapped his rum. "Grieve together."

I rolled my eyes. "I dealt with my grief months ago. I'm not doing it again."

I strode past him, giving his chair a wide berth, but I wasn't far before Oliver called after me—his voice barely audible over the rowdy Frenchmen. "I'm sorry for going into your room. I won't do it again."

I paused, my left fist curling, and strode back toward him— but only far enough so he could hear me speak.

"No, you won't go into my room again, Oliver. You won't come *near* me ever again. I want nothing to do with you, do you understand? Elijah wasn't the only necromancer in the family." I thrust out a pointed finger, wishing with all my heart that my charade could be real. If only I *were* a necromancer. If only I *were* powerful enough to destroy those in my way.

But Oliver did not know I was bluffing, so I said with all the authority I could muster, "If you dare come close to me without my permission, I will use everything I know to destroy you."

CHAPTER SIX

I thought I would start bawling the moment I reached my cabin, but, in fact, being away from the depressed demon and his drink and walking with long, purposeful strides was enough to lift my mood—or at least to clear away some of the pulsing anger.

But not enough to calm my thoughts.

A demon? Bound to my brother by a necklace? An old man in Egypt?

I was more confused than ever . . . but I felt I could be certain of one thing: the drunk young man in the dining room was *not* Marcus.

I found Mrs. Brown in her dressing gown, lounging in one of the armchairs and reading. "Miss Fitt," she said with a nod.

I winced. "Please, just call me Eleanor." Ever since I'd realized Miss Fitt sounded identical to "misfit," I had vowed I would never use my surname again.

She sniffed. "As you wish."

"Where's Lizzie?" I asked, crossing toward my bed.

"The bathroom, preparing her evening toilet."

"Oh." I peeked at what Mrs. Brown was reading as I passed: a book on manners. My lips twitched, and I wondered if it was the same book Daniel toted.

At that thought, an image of Daniel in a black evening suit materialized in my mind . . . and my mouth went dry. If anyone could fill out a dress suit well, I was certain it was he.

Clarence filled out his suit well too—

My lungs clenched shut, pushing out my air. I did *not* want to think of Clarence. Dwelling on his memory would stir up emotions I did not need.

I sucked in a shaky breath and dropped to the floor before my drawer. As I yanked out my nightgown, I checked quickly for Elijah's letters—still nestled beneath my spare petticoat.

Right then the door swung open. Laure strutted in. "Ah, Mademoiselle Fitt! You were not in the saloon—you missed the most wonderful card game." She stopped beside me and leaned onto her bunk, adding in a lower voice that smelled of wine, "Please tell me you did not spend the evening with the old goat."

"The who?"

"Madame Brown." She motioned to her chin and mouthed, "Beard. Like a goat."

Despite my rattled nerves, I couldn't help but laugh. "No, I spent most of the evening on the promenade deck."

"Ah, do you feel better now?"

"Much." I smiled.

"*Magnifique.*" She bent down to her own drawer and withdrew a white shift. "Come, let us prepare for the night's slumber. I wish to 'ave great dreams of true love and adventure."

A little snort came from the armchair. Laure whirled around and wagged her finger in Mrs. Brown's face. "Oh, what do you know of *l'amour*, you old—"

"That's enough." I grabbed her arm and towed her to the door.

Laure hooted a laugh. Once we were in the hall and headed toward the bathroom, she whispered, "But she *is* an old goat, *non*?" She raised her voice in song. "Old goat! *Vieille chèvre*! Old . . ." She trailed off as a wide-eyed Lizzie Brown walked by, her head swiveling to watch us pass.

I had to press my fingers to my lips to keep from laughing.

After we had used the bathroom, a stewardess came to our cabin to help us remove our dresses and—in Laure's case—corset. I hadn't worn one in months, and I rather liked the snide glares people gave me for it. One day the suffragists and I wouldn't be the only ones foregoing the whalebone prisons.

By the time we were in our nightgowns, Laure's wine giddiness had faded into wine exhaustion; and once the stewardess left, I practically had to carry her to her bunk. The Browns were already tucked in, and I waited until I could hear Laure's heavy breathing before I switched on an electric lamp beside my bunk, pulled Elijah's letters from my drawer, and spread them over my bed.

There were only eight in total, and if Oliver spoke the truth, then these were the most important. I started with the first, dated from the summer of 1873, when Elijah had first left.

As they had seemed when I'd originally read them, the letters were a confusing, rambling mess. Mentions of his work were dropped in with names. A hotel steward, a cab driver, a librarian—they were all sprinkled around his day-to-day activities.

And then there were the lines addressed to me. The descriptions of places he thought I'd like, stories he knew I'd laugh at, and promises to come home soon.

In the second letter, Oliver's name appeared twice, but it was only in reference to a joke. There was no mention of Oliver in the third letter, nor did anything crop up in the fourth or fifth.

Until my eyes lit on the name "Ollie" in the final line of the fifth.

Once, in Marseille, Ollie told me a hilarious riddle about Jack and the beanstalk, but since we were in the crypt of Notre-Dame de la Garde, our laughter echoed around all those soldiers' tombs until the priest finally made us leave.

"Very useful story, Elijah," I muttered under my breath. "You don't even share the riddle's answer." All the same, now I knew that he must have called Oliver "Ollie," and that nickname did appear rather frequently.

A yawn took over my mouth, and my eyes stung with exhaustion. I sank back on my bed. It was late, and I had eight more days of sailing to sort out things with this demon. I hadn't felt a single twinge in my hand since leaving Philadelphia, and I had three roommates to awaken if anyone entered our cabin. For now I felt safe.

It wasn't long before the rocking ship lulled me to sleep.

It was a dream. I *knew* it was a dream—I'd had it so many times before—and as always, I was terrified it would end.

Daniel, Daniel, Daniel. Smelling of machines and forest, tasting of salt. His lips pressed to my neck, his hand on my waist.

My hand—my *right* hand—pushed against his stomach, and my left scratched his back. My eyelids fluttered open, and I pulled back slightly. A yellow streetlamp shone on his sandy hair and sun-roughened skin.

"Empress," he whispered. His lips locked back on mine, and I sank into the embrace.

Then, as always happened no matter how hard I clung to the kiss, the dream shifted.

Daniel sat at the edge of my hospital bed, his face cast in shadow. My wrist ached—my hand having recently been amputated—and was wrapped tightly in a bandage. My heart was cracking right down the middle, yet as long as I focused on my hand, on the laudanum pumping through me, I could keep going.

"You're not in love with me, are you." I spoke it as a statement and tried to ignore my pounding heart.

He twisted his head away. "It's not that simple."

"It's a yes or no."

"Then . . ." He set his cap on his head. "Then no. No, I'm not."

A howl burst through the night.

Daniel's head shot up. For a single breath, all was silent and still.

Then the howl came again. This was *not* part of the dream, I knew.

Daniel lunged at me. "Run!"

At that instant a wind broke through the open hospital window, as loud as a locomotive and filled with angry baying.

Daniel yanked me up. My bare feet landed on cold tile. "Run!" he roared, but when I glanced at him, I found someone else entirely.

Clarence Wilcox, dressed in an evening suit just as I'd seen him last. "You have to go!" He grabbed my elbow and pulled me into a sprint. We bolted for the hospital's hallway.

No, now it was the ship's hall. We were racing toward the main stairwell, red carpet underfoot. And the boat rocked, fighting me.

"Faster, Eleanor! Faster!"

Another hand grabbed me from the other side. I choked at the sight of Elijah, filthy and huge—just as he had been before he died.

"Go!" he screamed, and suddenly we were racing twice as fast. My legs spun like wheels, but still I could barely keep up with the two young men.

"Don't stop," Clarence shouted. "They're almost here!"

The hallway blurred, shifting like paint into a murky, gray landscape. Barren, endless, this world was only broken by pinpricks of light across the sky.

Our feet pounded on wooden slats, and I realized with horror that we were on a rickety dock. Splinters sliced into my bare soles, and a wind beat at us from behind. My nightgown whipped up into my face.

The howling of the dogs was deafening.

"We're too late," Clarence cried.

"Just keep going," Elijah urged. Then he and Clarence released me, and they both fell back.

Somehow I pushed on. Ahead, a golden glow beckoned to me, growing closer and closer. I ran and ran and—

The wind shoved me. I flew forward onto my chest. My face slammed into the gray dock, and the roaring hounds swallowed everything. I tried to scrabble to my feet, but the moment I lifted my face, the howling stopped.

And I froze.

The dogs were there. Four of them, lips drawn back and fangs bared.

They were huge—bigger than me, bigger than a horse. Hulking, black, and with eyes of sun-bright yellow.

Eyes that were locked on me.

"Eleanor! Wake up!" I heard the voice, distant and dim.

I was shaking. Someone was shaking me.

"Wake up, El—wake up!"

And I knew that voice. This dock was a dream.

The moment the realization hit, the world winked out of existence. My eyelids popped open. I was staring at polished tan wood. The air was frigid.

"Eleanor, please wake *up*!"

I lifted my head, dazed, and found Oliver crouched over me.

"Where am I?" I tried to sit up, and he helped me rise.

"You're on the bloody promenade deck—you almost walked off the *edge*."

My eyes widened, and the contents of my stomach rose into my throat—because Oliver was right. Three feet from my face was the railing.

And beyond that was the roiling, gray sea.

Somehow, I had sleepwalked onto the deck.

Oliver gasped. "Oh no."

I wrenched my face toward him. "What?" In the swaying electric lights, his eyes were shining and his face was pink.

"Your . . . your face," he said. "And your dress."

"What do you mean?" I lowered my gaze. My nightgown was ripped to shreds. "Oh God." I wrapped my arms around myself.

Then I realized who knelt beside me, and my eyes jerked back to his face. "Get away from me—I warned you!" I tried to scuttle back.

His jaw fell. "But I just saved your life!"

"What are you talking about?"

"The Hell Hounds, El. Didn't you see them?"

My throat clenched shut. I stopped crawling. The Hell Hounds. The dogs from my dream. "H-how do you know about them?"

"Because my entire existence depends on it." A gust of wind thrashed over us, sending his chestnut curls into his eyes. He had to shout to be heard. "My life hangs on making sure the Hell Hounds never find me!"

And in a flash it all made sense. "The Hell Hounds"—my vocal cords strained over the ocean wind—"they're the guardians of the spirit world?"

"Obviously!" He swiped his hair from his eyes. "But why are they after you?"

"After me? What do you mean? It was just a dream." I struggled to my feet, my head spinning and the wind fighting me. Oliver reached out to help, but I bared my teeth. "*Stay back.*"

He retreated, his hands up. "I'm back! I'm back! But, El, that was *not* just a dream." He pointed to my face. "Just look at yourself."

I reached up and touched my cheek. "Ow!" I whipped back my hand. It was covered in blood.

For half a breath I stared blankly. Then I darted away from him, fear churning in my gut, and tottered to the nearest wall. My bare feet slapped on the smooth wood, and the wind whipped my gown in all directions.

I found a porthole, and in the yellow lamplight, I could clearly make out my reflection.

Lacerations lined my chin and nose. I leaned into the glass, and a new terror jolted through me, for there, embedded in my flesh at jagged angles, were giant splinters of dark, gray wood.

I glanced down at the deck and stomped my foot to be sure.

But no—there was no way this damage had been done by the deck.

And that could only mean one thing: my dream had not been a dream at all. It had been real.

CHAPTER SEVEN

As if my narrow escape from death was not enough agony for one night, things soon became even more complicated. After ogling myself in the porthole for a solid minute, the relative calm of the windy promenade deck was shattered by a childlike squeal.

My heart stumbled, and I spun around to find a terrified-looking Lizzie chasing toward me—her grandmother and a groggy Laure in tow.

"What happened?" Lizzie shrieked. "You're hurt!"

Mrs. Brown gasped. "Oh, Miss Fitt, we must call a doctor!"

"*Qui êtes-vous?*" Laure's eyes were locked on Oliver. "Who are you?"

"The poor man who found me," I blurted before he could say anything stupid.

"But what *happened*?" Lizzie demanded. "I saw you get up and walk outta the room, but when I called, you didn't answer."

"Sleepwalking," I said, my eyes darting from face to face. "I . . . I have a sleepwalking problem."

"And now you're injured!" Mrs. Brown cried. She hurried to my side and inspected my face. "Dear, your face is *destroyed*."

"It's not that bad," I mumbled, dabbing at my face. But I instantly grimaced. The bleeding might have lessened, yet the cuts still stung.

"Oh, it is *that* bad," Laure insisted. With a groggy yawn, she stepped to my other side. "But Mrs. Brown is right—you must see the ship's doctor."

"I can take you," Lizzie offered. She held up her finger, around which was a small bandage. "I already visited him today. He's on the bottom level."

"Thank you," I said, attempting a smile, "but this gentleman here can guide me." I waved to Oliver, who looked anything but willing to escort me to a doctor. "You're in your nightgown, Lizzie, and should go back to the cabin."

"*C'est vrai*," Laure chimed. "I vote we let the *jeune homme* take her."

"But how inappropriate," Mrs. Brown proclaimed. "Her nightgown is in tatters, for heaven's sake."

"But he's already seen me this way." I tried—with little success—to keep impatience off my words. "Please, I appreciate you coming to my rescue, but I can get to the doctor just fine now."

Laure gave a jaw-cracking yawn. "That is good enough for me, though perhaps you should lock the cabin door when you return."

"Yes, I certainly will." I waved good-bye to her—and Lizzie and Mrs. Brown—before turning to Oliver. "I'm going to find the doctor." He stepped toward me, but I flicked up my hand. "You are *not* coming with me."

"But they said I must escort you."

"And *I* don't want to be anywhere near you."

"The Hell Hounds are after you, El! You almost died. Don't you realize what just happened? You *crossed into* the spirit realm. You can't keep walking around by yourself—it might happen again!"

I didn't answer, but simply pivoted and strode for the saloon door. As I knew he would, Oliver followed. And for some unfathomable reason, I let him . . . and I was even a bit glad to have him.

Was I so lonely that even the company of a demon was welcome? *No, you merely want answers, and he's the only creature alive who can give them to you.* Yet even as these thoughts slid through my mind, part of me knew they weren't true. Oliver was just so much like Elijah. . . .

I glanced back at him. "Why," I shouted over the gusting wind and my smacking feet, "would these Hell Hounds be after me?"

"I haven't the faintest idea," he yelled back. He lengthened his stride yet was smart enough to hang behind a few feet. "I thought the Hell Hounds were after me, actually. When they showed up at the wharf in Philadelphia, I thought it meant my binding spell was failing. That Elijah was dead, and the Hell Hounds were out to get me."

"Should the binding spell end with Elijah's death?" We reached the saloon door. I motioned for him to open the heavy thing, and he hopped in front and heaved it wide.

"I thought it would," Oliver said, "but . . . I don't think it did. I certainly can't do any magic, and I'm . . ." He paused, and I had the distinct impression he was debating how much to tell me. At last he finished, "I think I must still be bound."

And I knew in an instant he had opted to *hide* something from me. My distrust for him ramped up a notch.

As I strode past him and through the open doorway, he said, "You were in the spirit realm, you know. Right on the edge."

"So it wasn't a dream?" The door slammed behind us with a bang.

"No. It was real," Oliver said, speaking at a normal volume.

I wiped at my face, trying to ignore how *that* made me feel. "Let's say . . . well, let's say I believe you. How did I get there? And why?"

"I don't know, El."

"Can you at least tell me what the dock was, then? Or the golden light at the end?"

"That whole area is the border between worlds. The dock is like a no-man's-land, and that golden light was the curtain to the earthly realm."

"That's all very complicated." I resumed walking. The saloon carpets were soft and welcome beneath my feet.

"It's not complicated," he retorted, following after me. "Ghosts that won't settle collect at the border. They wait for their chance, for the Hell Hounds to look away, and then they run for that golden curtain."

"But I saw Elijah there." I glanced back at Oliver. "Does that mean he wants to come here?"

Oliver scratched his head. "You're certain it was him?"

"Yes. And I saw an old friend of mine—one of Elijah's victims, actually."

He grimaced. "It sounds like their spirits were there to help you—on *purpose*—which makes me think that somehow they knew you were in danger. Like maybe they were watching out for you."

"So that was *really* Elijah?"

Oliver nodded. "His spirit, yes."

My throat closed tight. Elijah *and* Clarence—two people I'd have given anything to speak to again.

It would seem Oliver was thinking the same thing, for he said, "Did Elijah, um . . . well, did he say anything?"

"Like what?" I stepped onto the main stairs, paused, and gripped the left handrail until my knuckles were white.

"Like maybe a message," Oliver explained. "For me."

"No." I resumed my descent, adding gruffly, "There wasn't exactly time."

"Right." He shambled after me. "Of course not. Silly of me

to have hoped." He stared at the steps, his pace steady. Then his head snapped up. "Never mind. We have more important things to dwell on. Like seeing the doctor. And figuring out why the Hell Hounds are after you—oh, and figuring out how they keep *finding* you."

"We?" I paused on the next landing. "I don't trust you."

"No." He tapped his chin, and his lips curved up in an almost arrogant smile. "But even if you don't, I'm the only person who can help you right now. You told me you knew about necromancy, but obviously that was a lie. The first lesson in necromancy has to do with the Hell Hounds: Don't mess with them. They'll blast your soul straight into the final afterlife. No second chances. No questions asked. There's a reason I never let down my guard, and those dogs are it. If they manage to sense me here—to recognize I'm in the wrong realm—I'll be gone in an instant."

"So . . ." I bit my lip, my grip still tight on the handrail. "If you hadn't woken me just now . . ."

"No more Eleanor Fitt."

I sucked in. There *was* a lot I didn't know—and now I owed my life to a demon because of it. Fantastic.

Oliver cleared his throat. "It was total luck, actually. Like I said, I never drop my guard. When I sensed the Hounds were here and *not* after me, I thought . . . well, I assumed the worst. I saw you on the dock in Philadelphia, you know—saw how you reacted when the Hounds came. And so I ran to see if you could sense them this time. To make sure you were all right. Luckily I was able to distract you—by waking you up—and that sent the Hounds away."

"Distract me," I repeated slowly. "It seems that every time my thoughts are elsewhere, the Hounds disappear." I lifted my wrist. "And so does the pain in my hand."

His eyes grew wide. "Your hand? It hurts when the Hounds come?"

"Yes, and it even starts flickering—like the ghost of my hand is somehow here."

"Because it is!" He sprang onto the next landing and spun to face me. "Oh hell, it's clever—don't you see?"

"No, I don't see at all."

"Your hand—or the spirit of your hand—is trying to cross the curtain. The Hell Hounds are doing what they do best: stopping it."

"But why would my hand try to cross?" I clutched my wrist to my chest and strode past him onto the next flight of stairs. "Does it have its own spirit?"

Oliver joined me. "Sort of. Remember what I said about phase changes? Well, the spirit form—the, ah, *water* form—of your hand still exists. Only your ice form—your earthly body—is missing a hand. You must have cast a spell that's calling your soul hand here. Then, because it's not hidden from the Hounds, they attack every time it tries to cross."

"Except that I haven't cast a spell."

"So someone else is calling your hand then. Someone who wants you dead, I'd say. But your hand isn't magically *bound* to you, so it's not hidden from the guardians."

My eyes widened. "Marcus! He must be the one calling my hand!"

"You mean the necromancer wearing Elijah's . . ." Oliver's face tightened. "Him?"

"Yes. He's the only person I can think of who could cast a spell like that. He wants something from me——" I broke off. I didn't want Oliver to know Marcus wanted the letters as well. Not before I knew what exactly was in those letters that made them so valuable.

Beside me, Oliver shivered. "This Marcus must know quite a few tricks to cast such an advanced spell. If he is really the one behind this, he must know a lot about you as well—if he knows your hand is missing, I mean."

I gulped. Mama must have told him.

"There's no way you'll be able to escape him," Oliver went on. "Not without learning some necromancy."

"No," I spat. "I'm not doing that." We rounded another landing and moved onto the final flight.

"You have no choice, El. Not with the Hell Hounds on your trail. You have to learn how to hide your hand—just as I am hidden from their senses."

"I am not learning necromancy." My voice came out a growl. "It's too *awful*. Look at what Marcus has done. And Elijah!"

Oliver winced. "You're right." He slid his hands into his pockets. "But then that leaves you with only one other option."

"What?"

"Bind yourself to me."

I stopped midstride. "What did you just say?"

"Bind yourself to me." He paused and glanced at me. "Then you have access to all my power—"

"No."

"And then you can set me free."

"No!" I shrieked, pushing past him onto the lowest level. "Set you free? Bind to you? Absolutely *not*." I scanned the hall—it split in two directions.

"I was afraid you might say that," Oliver called after me. Yet nothing about his tone sounded afraid. If anything he seemed smug—as if my refusal was precisely what he wanted to hear.

"But bound to me or not," he continued, now following me once more, "you've got to protect yourself, El."

"Why do you think I'm going to Paris, Oliver?" I whirled around to face him. "There are people there who can help me."

He shook his head. "You don't have enough time. It's only a matter of days—hours, even—before Marcus's spell is too strong for you and distraction won't be enough. Then you'll be dead, and I'll be trapped in the earthly world for all eternity."

"Trapped?"

His eyes met mine. "My master may be dead, but as you can see, I'm still bound to his blood. Only someone with that same blood—*you*—can set me free. But"—he shrugged casually—"I can't *make* you do it. I'm just a man as long as this locket stays chained to my neck." With a huffed sigh, he pointed left. "I'm pretty sure the doctor is that way. Now, can you at least *consider* my offer? Then maybe, if you're still alive in the morning, you'll have come to your senses." He nodded his head to the stairs. "I'm two levels up, right by the stairwell. Room three-oh-four—*if* you decide you need me." He gave me one last melodramatic sigh before ambling off.

I didn't sleep the rest of that night. How could I? For one, the doctor—a nice old sailor with muttonchops and an easy smile— had rubbed a stinky white salve all over my face, thereby forcing me to stay locked in one position in my bed lest I disrupt said salve.

For two, Lizzie came every hour to poke me and make sure I was all right. And though I appreciated this gesture, I also wanted her to *stop*.

And three, terror of the Hell Hounds blazed through me. I'd been so close to death. To complete and final oblivion . . . Would it happen again if I fell asleep?

So I lay in bed, and I ran through my dream over and over again. Though the fact that Clarence and Elijah were watching out for me was partly comforting, it was mostly disconcerting. If only I had known they were real at the time, maybe I could have found a way, a spare second, to ask Elijah about his letters. About Oliver. For no matter what the demon said, I didn't trust him. Why would he want to bind to me? Was it true that *I* was the only person who could free him? And what would a "free demon" even mean?

I stared up at the bottom of Laure's bunk, and an idea formed in my mind. What if I could go back to the spirit realm—knowingly and intentionally go there? What if I *could* talk to Elijah? The thought of seeing him again . . . of seeing Clarence—my heart squeezed so hard, I couldn't see straight.

I would have to ask Oliver how, though. He was the only one who might be able to tell me how to cross the curtain intentionally.

Of course, waiting until the morning turned out to be especially difficult. By the time the sun rose, a gray pink at our porthole, I was barely able to keep my eyelids up. I felt gritty and heavy with exhaustion, but I forced myself to wait for the sun to crest before dressing and marching down to Oliver's floor.

It didn't take many knocks before a blustery man threw the cabin door wide. He wore a long nightshirt and only seemed capable of keeping one eye open. "Who're you?"

"Um . . . I'm looking for—"

"Me." Oliver bounced in front of the man. He wore the same gray suit as before, but it was wrinkled and untucked—as if he'd slept in it. "What is it, El?"

"I want to talk. Somewhere very public but where we can't be overheard."

He ran a tongue over his teeth. "How about the saloon?"

I nodded. "Lead the way."

Two flights of stairs later, he led me into the second-class saloon, which was—as Laure had declared—much like the first-class saloon. There was rich upholstery and an elegant grand piano, yet the ornamentation was calmer. Less nauseating, and more importantly, no one gave me or my gown a second glance.

"There." I pointed to a nook in the back corner with two green chairs, and we strode over. With a grateful sigh, I swept my petticoats aside and eased to a seat. Rolling back my head, I let my eyes flutter shut. Though I hardly liked sitting with Oliver, I was too tired to maintain any of the fury I'd carried the night before.

But Oliver seemed to misunderstand my relaxation. "Does the rocking bother you?"

"Why do you ask?" I opened my eyes.

"Elijah didn't like it either." He dropped onto the seat across from me and gazed out a porthole. "He got his sea legs eventually."

"When did you travel on a boat?"

"From England to France and then again when we went to Egypt." He sighed through his teeth. "I offered him relief, but he was funny about using my magic. He never used it unless he had to. I was more a companion to him than a tool. We were . . . friends." He turned to me, his brow knit. "Though for a friend, you'd think he'd have let me win at chess every now and then. I swear, the man was ruthless."

I couldn't help it. I laughed. "He was, wasn't he? We used to play every day, and not *once* did he go easy on me—even when I didn't know the rules yet!"

"That sounds like him. He was the same with riddles. He'd always pose those tricky little mind games—"

"Like the eight-queens riddle?"

"Exactly!" Oliver slapped his knee. "How do I fit eight queens on a chess board? I haven't the bloody faintest."

I grinned. "I never figured it out either."

"Well, perhaps if we both set our minds to it"—he tapped his forehead—"we could finally solve it." He bent toward me, a smile spreading over his lips. "Now, I assume you've brought me up here to make some deal?"

"Yes, though *not* the one you're imagining, so wipe that look off your face." I tugged at my earlobe. "I saw Elijah last night. I crossed into the spirit world, and he was *there*."

"I know."

"So, I want to know if I can go to the spirit dock on purpose. Can I cross over and talk to him and—" I stopped speaking. Oliver was shaking his head emphatically.

"No. For one, the Hell Hounds would be on you in a second. For two, that's *very* advanced necromancy. You'd need years and years of training."

"Oh." I gulped. "Even . . . even with your magic? Could you send me over?"

He blanched, and his pupils swallowed up the gold of his eyes. "No. *No*."

"What is it?"

"Your brother . . . he wanted the same thing, but I can't. I wish I could—maybe none of this would have happened if it were possible. But if I try to cross, the Hell Hounds will destroy me."

I deflated back into the seat. "What about voodoo? Can other magics cross into the spirit realm?"

He wrinkled his forehead. "I don't know, El. I've only learned what Elijah learned."

"So only necromancy."

"Yes——" He broke off as two little boys came barreling past in a rousing game of tag. Once they were out of earshot, Oliver continued, "I believe you could call Elijah if you had his body, since a soul and its body have a special connection, but . . ."

"There is no body." Disappointment swooped through me. "Damn Marcus." I looked away.

"I'm sorry," Oliver said softly. "If there was a way I could talk to your brother, I swear to you, I would."

I sniffed. He sounded just like Elijah, and I didn't like how it made me feel.

At that moment a yawn cracked through my jaw.

"You *know*," Oliver drawled, "one of the easiest spells to learn in necromancy is a dream ward. Because necromancers are so vulnerable in their sleep, blocking dreams is one of the first spells they ever learn." He shot a pointed finger up and recited: "A spell can't hit its target if the target's concentration is else-where." He curled his finger back down and dropped his hand. "Spirit world, earthly world—it doesn't matter. If you're dis-tracted, the spell can't hit."

"But if all it takes is distraction to deflect magic, it sounds like necromancy would backfire constantly."

"Sure, but you've seen how hard it is to distract yourself with monstrous dogs salivating for your soul. A non-necromancer wouldn't know he had to concentrate elsewhere, and the average person wouldn't even be *able* to." He shrugged. "Plus, distracting yourself when you're asleep is almost impossible. However, if you cast a *dream ward*"—he dragged out the two words—"you'll be safe and sound until the morning."

"The spell is . . . easy?"

"Very." He scooted toward me, his face animated. "And if you're even half as powerful as Elijah, you'll be able to cast it with almost no effort at all."

I pinched my lips together, considering his words. He wanted me to do necromancy. *Necromancy.* The black magic that had destroyed my brother and created monsters like Marcus.

But I couldn't stay awake indefinitely, and the more tired I became, the less I would be able to defend myself with this distraction technique.

And . . . there was just the tiniest corner of my heart that wanted to know what Elijah had done. Wanted to know what this magic was that had made him—and made Marcus too—devote his life to studying it.

Then another part of me—that roiling part in my gut that would do anything to kill Marcus and take my brother's body *back*—wanted to see just what kind of power I had living inside me.

"This simple little spell," I said warily, "you're certain it will protect me?"

"It's not a permanent solution to the Hounds, but it'll keep them away a bit longer."

I wet my lips, and before I could reconsider said, "All

right. Tell me what to do."

His lips curved into a grin. "Focus your power and repeat after me."

"Focus my power?"

"It's quite easy—or I think it is, based on Elijah. Close your eyes."

"How do I know you won't kill me or make me cast some horrible, world-destroying curse?"

"Because that wouldn't help me, now would it? I need you— alive—to set me free."

"That's a *very* comforting response, Oliver. Of course I can trust you implicitly when all you care about is using me for your own designs."

"Well, if it makes you feel any better, I've been thoroughly lonely and bored until you came along. So . . . I don't *want* to lose you."

I grunted, and his face sobered. "You really are just like him, aren't you?" He blinked quickly. "Never mind. Just close your eyes and feel for your power—your soul."

I squeezed my eyes shut and imagined sending my senses out to the very edge of my limbs.

"It's like taking a deep breath," Oliver said, his voice low. "With each breath, draw power into your chest. The magic is part of you—it's your very soul—and all you have to do is gather it into one place. You're making a *well*. That's what Elijah called it."

I sat up tall, inhaling until my lungs were full. I tried to pull every drop of spiritual energy into my body.

It happened immediately—a tingle that started in my toes and fingers and buzzed up to my chest. It was warm. Soothing.

"Wow," Oliver breathed.

"What?" I mumbled, keeping my eyes shut. This was nothing like the burning pain in my hand or the electric crack of Joseph's methods.

"You're glowing."

My eyes sprang open. "I'm *what?*"

"Just concentrate!"

I looked down. My entire body was emanating a soft blue light. I stared in horror at Oliver. "M-my skin!"

"It's fine." He threw his hands up. "No one's looking at us. Trust me, El. Don't worry. It just means you're strong. *Bloody* strong."

I gulped. "Wh-what do I do now?"

"You've got plenty of power here for the spell, so just repeat after me: *Hac nocte non somniabo.*"

"What does that mean?"

"I will not dream tonight."

"Oh." I drew in a steeling breath. I could do this—I could cast a spell.

"*Hac nocte non somniabo,*" I whispered. Warmth rushed through me like a wave, and the magic twirled around my heart—once, twice—before coursing back through my limbs and out. A heartbeat later, all the magic was gone.

I collapsed back onto the seat.

"You did it!" Oliver clapped. "And on your first try. Do you feel all right?"

A tired smile tugged at my lips. "Actually, I feel *amazing*." It was as if balmy bathwater lapped at my skin, and all my worries had fallen away.

"A complete sense of well-being?" Oliver's eyes crinkled knowingly. "That usually happens with necromancy. You ought to go to bed now—while you're relaxed. Your body needs to sleep anyway, to replenish the soul you just used. I'll be here—at the bar—if you need me."

I nodded, too exhausted and happy to do much else. Necromancy hadn't been what I expected at all, and I suddenly understood exactly why Elijah might have turned to it.

For not only was it a dark magic—it was a strange and lovely magic too.

I slept like a stone for the rest of that day. It was far more sleep than a single waking night warranted, yet I wrote off the exhaustion as part of the necromancy.

And I also blamed the necromancy for the abysmal pit of hunger in my stomach. Laure kindly ordered sea biscuits and oranges to the room, but no matter how many I stuffed into my face, the hunger never seemed to fade.

Nonetheless, I managed to ignore it long enough to conk back out and sleep straight through the night. I spent the next morning gluttonously eating—this time with something more substantial than seasickness fare—and writing letters to Mary,

Mama, and even Allison.

I reveled in the fact that I felt safe. That, for the first time in months, not a single cloud of grief blackened my sky.

Eventually Laure convinced me to dress, and she looked on as the stewardess's fingers flew deftly up the final buttons on my gown.

"Mademoiselle Fitt," Laure drawled, lounging against our bunk, "you must be the easiest woman to dress on this boat."

"Why do you say that?" I asked, giving the stewardess a thankful nod as she left our room.

Laure arched an eyebrow. "You 'ave no stays to pull or laces to tie."

"It's much more comfortable." I smiled and patted my corset-free belly. "Perhaps one day all women will forgo the wretched—" I broke off as an itch began in my missing hand.

Holding my breath, I glanced down—and found the air over my wrist shimmered. *Distract yourself, Eleanor. Focus elsewhere. Distract!*

"The wretched . . . ?" Laure prompted.

"Um." I wet my lips, attempting to recall what we'd been discussing. "Uh, one day we'll forgo the wretched things and start wearing trousers instead—"

Pain rammed into me—so hard and so fast, a moan broke through my lips.

"What is it?" Laure stepped toward me.

"It's my hand." I grasped my wrist to my chest, hoping she couldn't see the glow.

Then a single, long howl burst through the room.

It was happening again. The guardians had found me.

Without thinking, I bolted for the door. I needed Oliver—now! He would know what to do.

Laure shouted after me, but I shoved into the hall without a backward glance.

Snatching my skirts in one hand, I barreled down the corridor and toward the stairs. My absent hand throbbed with each step, and I didn't have to look to know that it glowed. The bluish light shone in my eyes like a lantern.

I reached the stairwell and headed toward the bar. Moments later, I burst into the second-class saloon. Shocked faces turned toward me, and I ran my eyes over each one. But none of them had the familiar rosy cheeks and rounded jaw I needed.

"Eleanor!" a voice yelled behind me. It was Laure, but I didn't turn. At that instant a howl burst through the saloon, carrying with it the dark stench of grave dirt.

Every lamp flickered and winked out.

Screams erupted—high-pitched and terrified—and I realized that, for the first time, it wasn't only I who could hear them. But what did that mean? Did it mean the Hound was here—actually in the earthly realm?

No, not hound. *Hounds.* There were several now, growling and barking over one another.

I spun around until I spotted the exit onto the second-class deck. Then I surged back into a run, my good hand out to shove people aside and my right hand a beacon to see by. If people noticed my glowing hand, they didn't react—they were too busy scrambling and screaming in the dark.

"Move!" I shrieked, shoving people harder.

But I only made it halfway across the room before an icy wind blasted into me. I toppled forward and hit the ground. Pain burst in my chin, and the recent scratches ripped open. All around, the passengers' shouts grew louder.

I dragged myself to my feet and trudged onward to the door. The wind was so strong, it felt like slogging through mud. Then came the sound like a full-speed train. The Hell Hounds were here—right behind me, with roars so intense they consumed every piece of my mind and being.

My legs pumped harder, my knees kicking high, and the bright square of daylight grew closer and closer. Just as I reached the door, a new voice shouted my name. "Eleanor!" Oliver's figure formed in the doorway, arms outstretched. *"Faster!"*

It was exactly like the dream. Faster, I had to run *faster*.

I reached the door, and Oliver grabbed my sleeves and yanked me aside just as the Hounds galloped past—screeching like tornados and fully visible now.

We ran as clouds crowded in overhead, blocking out the sun.

We reached the smokestacks at the center of the boat. Oliver shoved me between them. "You've got to hide!"

"How?" My breath came in short gasps. "They know I'm here!"

He shook his head. "You've only got seconds." He grabbed my stump and lifted it. My hand was there in its entirety, pulsing from blue starlight to pink flesh and back. "You've got to hide this!"

"*How?*" I strained to keep breathing. I wasn't ready to die—to have my soul obliterated! But the howls were racing closer, back on my trail. The smokestacks wouldn't protect me from the Hounds' supernatural jaws.

Oliver glanced desperately toward the sea. As my heart battered my lungs, I grabbed Oliver's sleeve and yanked him to me. "If I bind to you, can you save me?"

His yellow eyes locked on mine. "Yes."

"Then do it!"

He pulled me close. "Promise to set me free."

The Hounds were so near, I could hear each snarl and the gnashing of their phantom teeth. "I can't set you—"

"Promise to set me free," he shouted, "and then I'll save you!"

"Fine! Yes!" I shrieked over their raging howls. "I promise!"

Triumph flashed over his face. Gripping my left hand, he started whispering words I didn't recognize and could barely hear. Then he leaned in until our foreheads touched. "Say *Sum dominus et veritas.*"

I hesitated.

"Say it, Eleanor—now!" The boat tipped dangerously, and the Hell Hounds' growls shattered through my skull.

"*Sum dominus et veritas!*" I screamed.

Blue light flashed in Oliver's eyes, and he tugged my glowing right hand up. The air around it sparked, cracking with electricity. Oliver's eyes flashed the same color as my hand.

Abruptly, the wind stopped, and with it the howls.

But not the smell of grave dirt.

I turned to face them. The guardians of the spirit realm. They looked exactly as they had on the spirit dock, but now they stood still, confused. Four dogs towering over us, their noses sniffing and yellow eyes staring.

"Wh-what do we do?" I croaked.

"Give them a minute," Oliver whispered. "Their target— your hand—just vanished. They should leave soon . . . I *think*."

After what felt like hours of holding my breath, the dogs finally did twirl around and leave. I darted forward to watch them go.

Over the ship they bounded, their feet barely skimming the wood, before they leaped up off the edge and winked out of existence completely.

I spun to Oliver. "They're gone?"

"Yes. Gone."

My breath whooshed out. I almost doubled over. Oliver slipped his hand around my waist and guided me to the nearest bench, where we both plopped down and swallowed in air.

"That . . . that was close." I was coated in sweat, and my scratches were scabbing over anew.

"Too close." Oliver leaned onto his knees and held his head. "But that was smart of you, El. To bind to me, I mean."

I winced. Maybe it had saved my life, but at what price?

"Don't look so miserable," Oliver grumbled. "You got to keep your life, *and* you got your hand back." He reached for my right wrist and held it up.

My jaw sagged. All I could manage was a shocked sputter.

For there, wiggling at me as good as new, was a very flesh-colored, very *real* hand.

CHAPTER EIGHT

The first thing I did with my new hand was pinch Oliver.

"Hey!" He scooted away from me on the bench.

"Is it real?" I leaned toward him to pinch again, but he wriggled away.

"Of course it's real! Well, mostly."

"What do you mean 'mostly'?" I held it to the light, flexing and straightening the fingers. My body blazed with a warmth ten times more powerful than after the dream ward was cast. The closest I'd ever come to a feeling like this was when the doctors had fed me laudanum after amputating my hand. But this was a much, *much* better feeling. Instead of a happy lethargy, I felt ablaze with energy. I could do *anything*.

Oliver returned to his seat, eying me cautiously. "It's a phantom limb—it's only here because of my magic."

"A phantom limb," I repeated, shaking my head. "And will it stay forever?"

"About that . . ." He fixed his eyes on his feet. "It's bound to *me*."

"Meaning?"

"Meaning the hand only exists as long as I exist."

"So if I set you free, I lose the hand."

"If?" Oliver wagged his finger at me. "*When*, you mean. You just made a binding agreement."

"What happens if I don't follow through?"

He bit his lip. "There is, um . . . a time limit. If you don't set me free within the next two months, then your new hand will vanish. *And*, if Marcus's spell is still in effect, then the Hell Hounds will come after you just like they did five minutes ago."

"So I'm really no better off than before!" I cried. "All I did was sign over my life to you!"

"And I signed over mine!" He threw his hands up. "You ought to be thanking me, El! You've got absolute control over my magic now—anything you want done, I have to do."

I deflated slightly. "Why two months?"

"The longer the time frame, the longer the incantation. We were in a bit of a *rush*, you know."

"And now . . ." I stared at my fingers, torn between staggering relief and pulsing terror. "Now you're my demon? Like a djinn?"

"Precisely. And you're *my* master."

"Will you call me Master Eleanor?"

"No." He looked horrified. "I never called your brother Master Elijah."

"What if I command you to?"

"Then I *have* to." He groaned. "But is that really the sort of command you want to give?"

I shrugged. "Well, I have nothing else to ask for . . ."

"Then it's a damned good thing I haven't taught you the words of command yet."

I fixed my eyes on him, and he shifted uncomfortably. "Of course, I *will* tell you." He crossed his legs and lowered his voice, leaning close. "*Sum veritas*. You said it when you bound to me. It means 'I am the truth.'"

I drummed my new fingers on my thigh, savoring the feeling. "So all I do is give you a command and add those words at the end?"

He nodded.

"All right. Go to the edge of the boat"—I pointed at the railing around the deck—"and wait for me. *Sum veritas*."

A warm wave rolled over my body, and for a split second Oliver's eyes shone blue.

He blinked, and then a scowl cut into his forehead. "Truly, El? That's your command?" He slid off the seat, muttering, "Abuse of power."

I shoved up and hurried after him. "Can you not resist?"

He slowed and clenched his teeth. "It . . . hurts. Don't you feel it?"

I frowned and focused on my body. Sure enough, there was

a strange sense growing in my belly—as if my breakfast wasn't sitting quite right.

"All right," I said, "I cancel the command. You can go wherever you want. *Sum veritas.*" Again the pleasant tingle coursed through me, and Oliver exhaled sharply. We padded back to the bench and sat.

"No more abusing power," he ordered. "*Please.* You might turn me into a Rakshasi, if you're not careful."

"Turn you into a what?"

"A who. Rakshasa are demons. Very angry, very *awful* demons. For one, they have a fondness for making their fingernails venomous."

"Venomous?"

"Nasty, isn't it?" He shuddered. "I had the same reaction when Elijah told me about them."

"So you haven't met any?"

"No. Demons don't exactly cavort in the spirit world, and most Rakshasa who cross into the earthly realm head straight for the Orient. For some reason, they seem to thrive there—perhaps they like the taste of rotting Asian flesh more than European? Who can say? But, oh dear"—his lips twitched up—"you're looking a bit green, El."

I grimaced. "I daresay rotting flesh isn't the ideal topic for . . ." I trailed off. A figure had just appeared on the deck, her usual dark hair falling over her shoulders and her sleeve ripped jaggedly. Laure's eyes met mine, and relief washed over her face.

"Invisibility," I blurted. My happy warmth receded fast in

the face of fear. "My hand—make it invisible."

"What?" Oliver reared back. "I can't do that—"

"Well, hide the blasted thing somehow."

"Why?"

"My roommates have seen me *without* it."

His face paled. "I can't do a spell like that, El—it's impossible."

"But it's magic," I hissed. "You can do anything!"

"It's *spiritual energy*," he hissed back, "and there are limits." He grabbed my sleeve and tugged. "Just pull it down. You'll have to pretend."

So I did precisely that, and just in time, for Laure had reached us. "*Mon Dieu!*" she cried. "You are all right! How did you know that was coming?"

"How did I know what was coming?" I asked carefully. Had she seen the Hell Hounds? My eyes flicked to Oliver's, but he merely lifted one shoulder.

"That thing—that *cyclone*!" Laure wrung her hands. "Every lady is lost in a faint."

"Cyclone?" I pressed.

"*Oui.* Made of water."

Ah—a waterspout. Interesting explanation.

"Was there any damage?" Oliver inserted.

She turned to him, and recognition flashed in her eyes. "You are the young man from the other night, *non?*"

"Yes, he is," I rushed to say. "He was on deck too when . . . when this *waterspout* hit." I shifted my new hand beneath my skirts. "But was there any damage to the ship?"

"*Non*. It is the strangest thing. Other than some items knocked over and the icy water on everything, it is all fine." She dropped to a whisper. "But I did hear that the captain wants to turn around. People are in a panic. For some reason, many think they saw *dogs* and not a waterspout. So the captain now believes we should return to shore."

I sat up, alarmed. "Aren't we too far? Surely we're halfway to France by now."

"*Non*—not quite, and there are so many Americans. They want their own soil." She rolled her eyes. "You should see Mrs. Brown—'er poor granddaughter must wave smelling salts beneath her nose. And the little girl is one of those swearing that the waterspout was really a pack of wild dogs." Laure giggled, as if it were the most absurd idea in the world.

Oliver snickered too, so I forced my own laugh. "Listen, Laure," I said, "surely there are enough French people to keep the captain from turning around."

"*C'est possible*." She pursed her lips. "I can speak to any passengers who are still conscious. Perhaps we can make the majority."

"*Je peux vous aider*," Oliver said, his voice unusually silky.

Interest flared in Laure's eyes. "*Parlez-vous français?*"

"*Bien sûr*. Of course." He gave her a smile—a disarmingly handsome one.

A pleased flush burned on her cheeks. "I would welcome your help." Her eyes flicked briefly to me. "Eleanor?"

"I don't speak French," I muttered. "Or at least not enough to help."

She shrugged. "*Très bien.* You"—she flourished her fingers at Oliver—"will be enough."

"I will join you momentarily." He bowed smoothly, and as Laure sauntered off, I couldn't help but notice the extra sway in her hips.

The instant she was out of sight, I slid close to the demon. "Listen: you have to keep the captain from taking us back to New York."

"How?"

"Magic."

He recoiled. "A compulsion spell? Absolutely not! You have to sacrifice a living person to do that."

My insides flipped sickeningly.

"Exactly," he said, seeing my grimace. "You have to cut out all the body parts you want to control. So to compel the captain's tongue, I'd have to—"

"Cut out someone else's tongue," I said quickly. "I get it . . . but is there not some other way? What can you do with your magic?"

"Basic things. Mostly I just give you my power so you can cast spells. But . . ." He tapped his chin for a moment. "I suppose I could interfere with their navigation."

My eyebrows rose. "Do I have to cast a spell for that?"

"No." He jumped to his feet, his lips twisting up. "You see, I'm an incredibly persuasive demon. All it takes is a little conversation, charm . . . *alcohol* with the captain, and this boat will not be turning around." He winked. "I'll find you later, *Master* Eleanor."

Then, arms swinging, he strode off to the saloon.

Oliver found me hours later in the dining room, shoving whatever I could find into my mouth. I felt wretched. Tired, hungry, and drowning in shame. Why had I bound myself to Oliver? What had I done? And what would the Spirit-Hunters say?

Oliver slumped into the seat beside me, his nose wrinkled. "Elijah said you enjoyed food, but this is disgusting."

I gulped down some coffee and cleared my throat. "I'm sorry, Ollie. Demons may not eat, but *humans* do."

"Demons have to eat too," he retorted. "My body might not die as easily as yours, but it still needs food—and sleep." He set his forearms on the table. "But you, Eleanor, are not eating. You're gorging."

I scowled. "I can't help it. No matter how much I eat, I find I'm still hungry at the end."

"I wonder . . ." His eyes thinned. "Finish your coffee so we can start studying necromancy."

My heart bounced. Before I even knew what I was doing, I said, "All right." But then I stopped, horror rushing through me. No—I didn't want to learn more. Necromancy could only bring evil, and I would *not* do that.

"Actually," I began, but then my stomach gurgled with such agony, I couldn't speak. Maybe I *had* overindulged. "Actually," I tried again, "I don't need to learn it, do I? You told me the other day I could learn spells *or* bind to you."

Oliver bit his lip. "Well . . . you're forgetting the agreement."

Another rumble churned in my belly. I gulped. "What agreement?"

"The one in which you promised to set me free within two months."

Again the excitement shivered through me, but it was rapidly quelled by my conscience. I did not want this. *No.* "Set you free, set you free," I muttered, hugging my hands over my stomach. "Is that all you care about?"

"Blessed Eternity!" he swore. "I just saved your life—"

"Only so I would save yours!"

"Well, you're bound to this promise whether you like it or not." He pounded the table. "Set me free or be Hell Hound lunch."

"O-or," I said, watching his face, "I can just take you to the Spirit-Hunters in Paris. Joseph can set you free."

"Who can set me free?"

I winced as a hot wave of nausea hit me. No more eating three lunches in a row. "The Spirit-Hunters—they're the ones who will help me with Marcus. Did Elijah not tell you about them? They were in Philadelphia when he . . ."

Oliver scowled, his eyebrows dropping so low they shaded his eyes. "When, pray tell, would Elijah have told me? He wouldn't let me come to Philadelphia, remember?"

"He didn't write?"

"No," Oliver spat. "He didn't bloody write." He turned away, his jaw muscles twitching.

"Oh," I murmured. Then, with a deep breath, I explained who the Spirit-Hunters were and how Joseph's specialty was blasting spirits back to their realm.

"The important word there is 'blast,'" Oliver said, shifting back toward me. "He'll probably destroy my soul like a Hell Hound."

"You're just being dramatic." Sweat beaded on my brow, and I dabbed at it. I craved water to cool me, but I knew there wasn't any space in my stomach for it.

"I am *not* being dramatic." Oliver glared, offended and . . . and something else. Something dark. Something *angry*. But I couldn't tell if it was directed at me, the Spirit-Hunters, or someone else entirely.

The lines on his face relaxed, and he said almost flippantly, "How about this: you learn necromancy. Then you can set me free the old-fashioned . . ." He stopped speaking, and his eyebrows drew together. "Are you ill? You look a little green."

I swallowed. "I . . . I think I ate too much."

"Of course you did!"

"Can you help me walk to my cabin?" I made to stand up, but he flicked up his hand and stopped me.

"Not that you deserve this after intentionally stuffing your face, but I can ease your gluttonous pains if you wish." He fingered the chain around his neck. "All you have to do is say the words."

"*Sum veritas?* How will that make my stomachache go—"
I broke off and dropped my gaze to my belly. The trickle of warmth was sliding through me, glowing faintly blue.

I gasped because, oh, I loved it. It was two long heartbeats of perfection, and then when the haze cleared, I realized my nausea had vanished.

And fear grabbed hold of my chest. I jerked my head toward Oliver. "Wh-why'd you do that?"

His eyes were wide, scared. "I'm sorry."

"I didn't ask for it!" I was terrified because my body wanted more—*needed* more—of that magic.

"Actually, you did." He lunged to his feet. "Don't be mad—but you said it. You said the command."

I stood. "That's all it takes? I just say those words and the magic comes?"

"Not normally." He backed up several steps. "It's just that you were thinking about relief and I was *also* thinking about relief, and then you said the words, so . . ." He snapped his fingers.

I advanced on him, my mind a jumble of terror and desire. "If it's so easy to use your magic, Oliver, then am I always at risk?"

"Not all spells are a risk. This one was good, right? Your face is healed too."

"What?" I roared. Other passengers turned to stare, but I didn't care. I frantically patted my face—it was smooth. Perfect. *Unnatural.*

My breath came in gasps. I had to get out of here!

I tried to march by Oliver, but he grabbed my elbow. "Where're you going?"

"Away!" I wrenched my arm free. "This . . . it's all too easy, Oliver!"

"But not normally. This was just circumstance."

"Then let's not put 'circumstance' to the test anymore today." I massaged my forehead, willing my heart to settle. "I'll be in my room if you need me—though I'd prefer you *not* need me." Then I dropped my hands and stalked away from him.

"I really am sorry," he called after me. But nothing in his voice sounded sorry to me. I was shaking with nervous energy— with fear.

I couldn't deny that magic felt *good*.

Worse—and what truly scared me—was that for all my proclamations of not casting more spells, I desperately wanted more.

We reached Le Havre five days later on a bright Tuesday morning. I still refused to learn necromancy, and Oliver still refused to meet the Spirit-Hunters—though, it was not so hard to understand why. They *had* been Elijah's enemies, and they *did* hunt creatures such as him.

The closer we got to France, the more a strange panic seemed to boil in my chest.

One would think that the safety of the Spirit-Hunters would *soothe* my anxiety. Certainly Joseph's solid reliability was welcome—as was Jie's friendship.

But Daniel? Our awkward final moments had been bad enough. Add in my constant waffling from indignant hate to pathetic longing, and I was a veritable typhoon of contradictory emotion. Half of me was desperate to see him; half of me hoped never to lay eyes on him again.

"Shakespeare had no blasted idea what he was talking about," I growled, leaning against the promenade deck's rail. I had given up my pride and let Laure convince me to sneak up with the first-class passengers so we could watch our arrival in Le Havre.

"*Pardon?*" she asked. "What about Shakespeare?" She pronounced the name "Shock-eh-spear."

"I said, he had no idea about love or anything."

"You're in a fine mood," Oliver said, coming to the rail beside me. "Something the matter?"

"No," I growled, swatting a bonnet ribbon from my face. Laure and Oliver exchanged mocking glances, and with a groan, I marched away from them. They'd become the best of friends ever since discovering their mutual interest in flirting. And, while I'd been grateful to have the demon occupied elsewhere, I had begun to find their tendency to gang up on me thoroughly insufferable.

I moved to another empty spot on the handrail and focused on the approaching city. The climate was perfect, thanks to the sea—sunny, yet cool—and the view was absolutely picturesque. Le Havre was a city of white buildings that hugged the shore while great, black ships paced the harbor in front. Sunny quays with shady streets gave it the look of an old watercolor Mama had once hung in our parlor.

Less than an hour later, I found myself handing over as much as I could spare in tip to the stewardess and disembarking onto French soil—into a world unlike anything I had ever seen. Truly, no amount of reading or daydreaming could have prepared me for the city.

For one, Le Havre was *old*. I'd always fancied Philadelphia a historical city, but in comparison to Le Havre—and the rest of Europe, I supposed—Philadelphia was just a newborn babe.

Every building looked as if it had defied the test of time for centuries. Every steep-roofed house seemed to have a story, with the colorful gables and shutters and the flowerpots draping from each window.

As Laure, Oliver, and I stood at the end of the pier, local women in their white caps and fishermen with nets draped over their shoulders streamed around us. On the cobblestone street before us, travelers and coaches clattered by.

And it was all so lovely, I felt compelled to wander the city slack-jawed. Fortunately, Oliver and Laure were completely unimpressed. The demon took my carpetbag on his arm, and Laure motioned to a road leading straight into the city.

"The train station is that way," she told us, "but the Paris train will not leave for many hours. You must join me for lunch— I know the perfect place, and I will even go so far as to pay."

At the word "lunch," my stomach gave a stormy bellow.

"Food *would* be nice," I said. *Free food even more so.*

"*Très bien*. Then it is decided."

"Are we going to walk?" Oliver asked, looking longingly at a passing cab.

"*Bien sûr*. Of course." She poked him playfully with her parasol. "You 'ave been in America too long. Over here, everyone walks. It is said to be a way of life. Now"—she popped open her parasol and hooked her arm in Oliver's—"follow me."

The pair set off down the wide street, and I followed. I let them continue in front of me the entire time, thereby allowing me to keep my right hand out in the open. I even drew off my glove so I could enjoy the sheer pleasure of sunshine and breeze on my fingers.

By the time we reached our destination, sweat trickled down my spine, and I had decided the French had drastically different ideas of time and distance than Americans.

"Only two steps away!" Laure had insisted over and over, yet it still took us at least twenty minutes to get to a tiny inn, called Le Cupidon Belle, that was set apart from the main bustle and blessedly well shaded.

The restaurant was actually situated inside an open-air courtyard around which the inn stood. Bubbling happily amid rickety wooden tables was a fat, stucco fountain shaped liked Cupid. A little white-capped boy seated us directly under Cupid's gaze, and then a round-faced, wide-hipped landlady took charge of serving us the day's meal, beginning with a platter of fruit.

When the first grape exploded in my mouth, I almost wept,

enraptured by the tart sweetness of the fruit.

Then came the bread—a simple baguette—and my eyes really did fill with tears. Such a flaky, crisp crust around the fluffiest, saltiest bread I had ever tasted. I closed my eyes and simply breathed in the scent of it.

"Eleanor," Oliver said, sounding alarmed, "are you all right?"

I nodded, almost frantically. "It's just so amazing."

Laure laughed happily, and when I opened my eyes, I found her cheeks pink with pleasure. "France 'as the best food in the world, *non*?"

"I believe you're right." I moaned, ripping off another bite of baguette.

She gave Oliver and me a pretty pout. "I will be so lonely traveling to Marseille by myself." She then told us about an inn her family ran outside the city and a fishing boat her uncle had. As we worked our way through six courses of food—mussels and fish and apples and more bread—she forced us to promise multiple times that we would come visit.

The remainder of our meal—cheese and wine—passed amiably, though I was sad when the last plate was cleared away and Laure wrote out her address. It was all so final.

The walk to the train station was shorter than our journey to the inn. Before I knew it, we had reached the Le Havre depot, a long, modern building that was disappointingly identical to the stations back home. Enormous, multipaned windows stretched from floor to roof, and running beside the station were the tracks. Oliver and I quickly navigated the crowds, exchanged the rest of my money for francs, and purchased two second-class tickets to Paris. The train didn't leave for another hour, so I used the time to mail my letters to Mama, Mary, and Allison and to telegram Jie my intended arrival time in Paris. I didn't expect her to meet me at the station, but I also didn't want to arrive at the Spirit-Hunters' hotel with no warning.

When Oliver vanished for a time, I took the opportunity to relax and digest on a shady depot bench. Oddly enough, hunger still writhed in my stomach. I *knew* I was full, yet somehow I wasn't.

So I decided to distract myself. I closed my eyes and focused on my heartbeat. Its rhythmic thump was pleasant, like the gentle rock of the ship. I inhaled, filling my lungs until they pressed against my ribs. My chest buzzed with air—

No! I snapped my eyelids open. That wasn't only air. I had drawn in spiritual energy! I dropped my head, and sure enough, I could see a dull glow in my chest where I'd accidentally gathered my magic into a well. For several moments it just sat there, pulsing.

I jumped up. I had to find some private place to chant the only spell I knew: the dream ward.

I darted toward the nearest porter, folding my arms over my shining chest. "Excuse me," I squeaked, "wh-where is a water closet?"

But he shook his head. "*Je ne parle pas l'anglais.*"

"Toilet?" I squeaked, grasping for some other word. "*Les toilettes?*"

He grimaced and pointed across the room to a white door. I scurried over and pushed inside, grateful to find the beige-tile room empty. After locking the door behind me, I looked down at my chest and flinched. It was very, *very* bright, but worse, it was starting to burn like a breath held too long.

When I tried to inhale more, the pain only grew—as if someone had my heart clamped between two bricks.

I squeezed my skirts in my fingers and rasped, "*Hac nocte non somniabo.*" A tiny, familiar trickle buzzed through me, but it wasn't enough—not even close.

I tried inhaling again, but my chest was so full, I could barely wedge in more air. The well of power in my chest hadn't shrunk enough.

"*Hac nocte non somniabo,*" I repeated. Nothing happened. I tried again, panic rising in my throat. But still nothing happened.

I frantically scanned the room for something—anything—to inspire me, but my vision was turning spotty. I couldn't breathe!

I slumped onto the ground as the room spun around me. *Oliver, help! Someone, please, help! Elijah . . .*

And with that thought, power burst from my hands. Blue light was everywhere. It seared into my eyes and into my brain. I squinted, watching as the dingy bathroom transformed into . . .

It can't be.

I gulped in a ragged breath and dug the heels of my hands to my eyes. I couldn't be seeing right—except when I lowered my hands, the velvet sparkle was still there.

I was staring at the curtain between realms, and I could just make out the dock on the other side. Someone was on it—someone walking toward me.

"Elijah?" I threw out my hands, reaching for the starry world. "Elijah, is that you?" But I knew it was. I had just called him, hadn't I? Now all I had to do was cross, and then we could talk.

"Eleanor! Are you in there?" Oliver banged at the bathroom door. I blinked rapidly as the world around me dissolved back into the water closet.

"Please let me in!" His voice sounded panicked. "I can feel something isn't right."

I lurched to the door, but my body was like pudding. I fumbled over and over with the lock. Finally, I managed to get the door open, only to find Oliver with his arms up, ready to pummel it.

He froze. "Blessed Eternity," he swore. "What have you done?" He slid an arm behind me. "Come on—everyone's staring."

I glanced into his young face. He was wearing a new brown top hat. "That is a *lovely* hat. Wherever did you get it?"

His forehead wrinkled. "You're drunk."

"No, I'm not." I rolled my eyes skyward . . . though I *was* feeling oddly fuzzy. And good—very good. "I can't be drunk. I haven't been drinking."

"Off magic, I mean." He glared at me accusingly. "What did you do?"

"I'm not entirely sure, but I found the curtain, Ollie! And the dock."

His eyes grew huge. "Oh no. Oh *no*. Come on." He tugged me toward the nearest window and patch of sunlight.

"Stand here," he muttered, "and maybe no one will notice how much you're *shining*. Foolish girl!"

"I'm shining?" I asked, glancing at my body. My sleeves seemed to twinkle, and my skin was as luminous as starlight. "Why?"

"It's an effect from whatever spell you just cast. What spell *was* that, by the way?"

"None. It was all an accident. I was simply breathing, and somehow I made a well of power. Then . . ." I waved vaguely in the air.

"*Then*," he said, "you realized you can't collect your body's power like that without expelling it. Foolish, foolish girl!"

"Stop saying that. You should have warned me." I sighed and rubbed at my eyes. "Can we sit?"

"No—not until this spell wears off. And I would have warned you had I known you'd be stupid enough to try necromancy by yourself. Next time you decide to do it without me, *don't*."

"And I told you, I wasn't trying. It simply happened."

"Meaning you're a lit fuse, El. Don't you see? You're too bloody powerful. Now that you've started learning necromancy, your body is using its magic on its own." He gave a low moan. "You're *sure* you saw the curtain?"

"And the dock—and Elijah was standing on it. I called for help from you *and* Elijah." I grinned, utterly pleased with myself. "You both came."

"Or else Marcus has some other finding spell on you. He could've been trying to lure you over. You were this close"—he held his thumb and pointer finger to his eye—"to walking over and right into the Hell Hounds' maws."

"Oh." I frowned.

"You need training or that lit fuse is going to go too far. An explosion of foolish girl."

I sniffed. "Or foolish man. Don't leave me to go buy new top hats." I set a hand on my hip. "If you have enough money to buy that, then why did *I* buy our train tickets?"

He turned away, his cheeks reddening. "Because I don't have the money."

"You stole it! Just like your boat ticket and all that alcohol."

"Shhh!" He leaned close, his eyes scanning everyone around. "Yes, I might have *borrowed* it, but I was attracting too much attention without something covering my head. We're in France now. If you think the rules of society mattered in Philadelphia, they are *nothing* compared to what awaits us in Paris."

"Oh, pshaw. The Spirit-Hunters aren't concerned with society, so I don't see why we should be."

Oliver rolled his eyes as if I was the most naive creature in the universe. "All thoughts on the morality of stealing hats aside, we have to work extra hard at keeping ourselves anonymous. You have a team of Hell Hounds and a powerful necromancer after you. The last thing we need are stories about us in the *Galignani's Messenger*."

"The what?"

"It's a newspaper for English-speaking visitors in France. It details what everyone is doing, thereby fulfilling the gossip needs of society—and you can be certain that a glowing girl with a handsome lad such as myself is the sort of story people talk about."

"You're changing the subject." I puffed out my lips. "If I really am a lit fuse, then I suppose you'll have to teach me necromancy."

"Are you joking?" He folded his arms over his chest. "What do you think I've been trying to do for the last week?"

"Well, I was scared. I am scared. It *is* scary, don't you think?"

He grimaced. "Remind me never to drink with you. You babble like an idiot."

"Humbug." I snorted. "But I do want to learn it now. It feels so good! And I don't want to cast any more accidental spells. Plus . . . *oh*! Just imagine what I could do to Marcus with necromancy. *Boom!*" I wiggled my fingers like an explosion. "Fight fire with fire, you know."

"Or you could simply talk him to death. I feel on the verge of suicide myself—"

"I'm *serious*, Ollie. Teach me necromancy. I order you to."

"Fantastic." His mouth quirked up, the faintest sheen of

triumph in his eyes. "But in about ten minutes when this stupor wears off, do not forget what you said. Now come on." He held out his hand. "The train is here, and you have a team of Spirit-Hunters to find."

CHAPTER NINE

The view outside the train was exactly as Henry James described it in *Madame de Mauves*: trees of cool green, meadows rolling onto the horizon, and a gray light that made the sky look silver.

I pressed my face against the window while Oliver maintained his usual slouch in the seat across from me. I groaned inwardly. Why had I ordered Oliver to teach me necromancy? And why, now that the magic had worn off, was I not regretting that decision more?

What was *wrong* with me?

Despite my frustration with my scruples (or lack of them) and despite the fact that my legs were going numb sitting on the hard seat, before I knew it I had dozed off against the polished wood wall. I was soon traipsing through *As You Like It*'s Forest of Arden with Orlando shouting his love to me and posting love poems on all the aspens.

Although, when I awoke five hours later, it occurred to me that the grassy green of Orlando's eyes and the wool of his gray flat cap were entirely too similar to a certain Spirit-Hunter's I wanted to forget.

"Did you have a nightmare?" Oliver asked. "You look awfully pale."

I gulped and sat up straighter. "I just . . . dreamed of someone. Someone I'd rather not think of."

"That inventor fellow?"

I gaped at him. "H-how did you . . ."

He chortled. "Let's merely say that when you told me about the Spirit-Hunters, your careful avoidance of discussing him, combined with the lovesick look on your face—"

"I am not lovesick!"

"Of course not," he said flatly. "Does *he* know how you feel?"

"I refuse to discuss this with you."

"Fine. Suit yourself." He shrugged. "It's good you could nap. You wore yourself out with that spell."

"And blazes, am I hungry now." I folded my arms over my stomach. "I cannot *wait* to feast on croissants."

He grinned. "They are the best pastry in the world, aren't they? Did you know they were brought to France by Marie Antoinette? They're actually an Austrian creation."

"Really?"

He lifted a flat-palmed hand. "I swear. I met her ghost. She was *not* pleased with death. She kept moaning, '*Pas chance pour l'amour.*' No chance for love."

"Is that true? Is there no love on that side?"

"Of course it's not true. You saw Elijah. His love for you hasn't faded or else he wouldn't have come into your dream and saved you from the Hell Hounds."

I frowned and turned my gaze out the window. Russet and gold-tipped trees were sprinkled over foliage still clinging to summer-green. As we roared by, it all blurred together like some Impressionist painting.

If Elijah had come to my rescue out of love, then what did that mean about Clarence Wilcox? Why had *he* saved me?

"However," Oliver continued, "there is a much higher chance for broken hearts in the spirit realm. More often than not, lovers get separated." He spoke as if he'd experienced that separation firsthand.

I swallowed, my mouth suddenly dry. "Ollie, have you ever loved?"

He nodded slowly. "I loved your brother, and . . ." A shy smile spread over his lips. "I find I am starting to love you."

I shifted in my seat, surprised by his honesty. "You do not mean . . . that is to say, you do not love me romantically."

He barked a laugh. "Egads, no! Not for you—no, no." Then his face sagged, and he turned away to stare out the window.

I desperately wanted to ask "For whom then?" but the way his lips compressed . . . he looked so utterly sad that I could not bring myself to do it.

Plus, at that moment, he withdrew a silver flask from his coat pocket and drank back something that smelled like whiskey.

"Where did you get that?" I demanded.

He smacked his lips. "I saw it in your roommate's luggage and decided it was the perfect size for my hand."

"You stole from *Laure*? But she's your friend!"

He frowned. "Not Laure. That old goat-faced lady—"

"Mrs. Brown?" I squealed. "No! *No!* She carries a flask?"

"Carried," he corrected.

I sniffed. "You're awful. And you really must stop stealing."

He opened his hands in a noncommittal way, and then after taking another long swig, he slumped down in his seat. "You know," he drawled, "I actually know quite a lot about love from my *many* years of watching the universe—"

I groaned. "Oh, the wise demon doth speak. Hark so that we all may learn!"

He laughed, straightening slightly. "I'm serious. I've seen a lot of souls pass through my home, and I've seen a lot of loves still hanging on. Those long-lasting ones"—he tapped his heart—"are the ones filled with tenderness and smiles."

"Oliver, the demon poet," I said drily.

He rolled his eyes. "One last piece of advice, El: if this Spirit-Hunter does not love you back, then good riddance. Real love isn't about drama or heartbreak. Real love just is."

I ran my tongue over my teeth and stared silently outside. Oliver was right—I knew he was right. With a sigh, I turned back toward him. "You remind me of Elijah, you know. The way you talk to me. The things you say. You're just like he was before . . . before . . ." I shook my head, unable to say the words.

A heartbroken smile dragged at Oliver's lips and eyes. "I'm not surprised. When a necromancer calls for a demon, the one that answers is the one most similar to the necromancer." His fingers went to the locket. "Elijah was a good man before revenge took over his mind."

I tried to swallow, but my throat was pinched too tight. "He sacrificed himself at the end—jumped in front of one of the Hungry to save me."

"That doesn't surprise me." He bent forward, propping his elbows on his knees. "He cared about you more than anyone else in this universe. Even more than *me*—hard to imagine, I know." The edges of his mouth twisted up.

"Tell me about him," I urged. "Tell me what you used to do together."

"Other than chess and riddles?" Oliver's face shifted into a frown. "There was a great deal of eating . . . and sleeping. Oh, and studying. Can't forget all the bloody libraries he used to drag me to."

"What about . . . what about necromancy? I know you said you were more his friend than his tool, but surely he used your magic *some*. What spells did he have you do?"

Oliver's frown deepened. "I'd rather not talk of it."

"Please?"

"No." He sat up. "Please, El. It's too . . . too fresh."

"Oh." I hugged my arms over my stomach. "Then perhaps later?"

"Or perhaps never."

"But why?"

He clutched at his heart and turned away. "Because it's personal, that's why. Can't you be satisfied with knowing that he cared about you?"

"No." I slid to the edge of my seat. "I *can't* be satisfied with that. I need to know more—"

"Well, you won't learn more from me." He gestured almost tiredly to the window. "We're coming into Paris, if you care to see."

That ended my protests immediately, and I pressed myself as close to the window as I could get. In the distance, cast in pink, was a crowded city with layers that rose up like a cake and crawled with movement. It was like watching the dancers in a ballet, and I felt a sudden, deep urge to write bad poetry.

But the closer we got, the more the charm started to vanish. And the more complex the labyrinth of streets and buildings around us became, the more the filth and soot stood out.

"It's so . . . so dirty," I said at last.

"Ha!" Oliver barked. "Isn't every city?"

"Philadelphia certainly is, but . . . I had this idea of Paris being . . . well . . . perfect." I gnawed my lip. "Where are all the electric streetlamps? Or the bridges and gardens? The ones you see in the prints?"

"Oh, you'll see them—just wait until we reach the center of

the city. It's always dirtiest on the edges."

Soon enough we were zooming through the Paris of which I'd dreamed. All around were the quintessential beige buildings with their iron-fenced windows and dark, shingled rooftops. Chimneys poked up in organized rows, silhouetted by the evening sun.

But what impressed me most was the number of electric lamps that rose up, elegant and iron, to illuminate the streets. City of Light, indeed! It was like a fairy world twinkling at sunset, and I could honestly say I had never seen or imagined anything like it.

"Tell me what everything is," I ordered, my face smashed against the window.

Oliver scooted beside me and pointed. "There's a house, there's a house . . . *that* looks like a *boulangerie*, and over there's another house."

I glared at him. "I mean the famous places. The Arc de Triomphe or the Louvre or Notre Dame or—"

"All the places that aren't beside the train tracks." He snorted. "Patience, El. You will see them in good time. But look." He pointed to the hill with its jagged rooftops and crooked, ever-rising angles. "That hill is Montmartre, the home of the bohemians: the artists and Gypsies who don't want to live in the city." He grinned as if remembering fond times. Then he pointed again, this time to where the train was aimed. "And that, up ahead, is our train depot." He turned toward me, opening his hands wide. "*Et voilà Paris, Mademoiselle.*"

* * *

The interior of Gare Saint Lazare was disappointingly foul—especially after the glamour of the city's streets. We pulled into the triangular-roofed station built of exposed metal and wood and were soon filing off the train—only to be greeted by row after row of locomotives. With so much smoke billowing from each, it was a wonder the high skylights of the depot weren't any blacker.

Oliver, my carpetbag in his hand, strode toward red archways marked SORTIE. I scurried after, and in moments we reached a set of steps heading down to tall-windowed exits.

"Where do you want to go?" Oliver yelled to be heard over the noise of the trains and people. An old couple swerved around us, glaring at our sudden stop, and a gust of perfume ran up my nose.

I coughed into gloved hands. "So many people!"

"Welcome to Paris, El." Oliver smiled. "Do you want to find the Spirit-Hunters' hotel now?"

"Only if you agree to meet them."

"Absolutely *not*."

"You must see them at some point," I insisted, though secretly I was relieved. I wasn't sure *I* was ready to face the Spirit-Hunters with my new necromancy, much less with a demon in tow. Joseph had made it plain enough how he felt about necromancy, so until I could find a way to prove I *wasn't* doing anything wicked, it seemed best to simply pretend it had never happened. Why darken my easy friendship with the Spirit-Hunters with something over which I had no control?

Oliver closed his eyes, his head cocking to one side. When he opened them again, they flashed blue.

I started. "Wh-what was that? I thought you couldn't do magic without my command."

"I can't." He shook his head. "I was merely testing our bond. In case . . . well, in case we get separated. You can find our bond too. You simply . . . *feel* for it."

I mimicked the movement he had made, closing my eyes and angling my head. Sure enough, now that I searched, I could sense the slightest thread winding its way around my heart.

I opened my eyes. "I feel it, but what do you mean by 'get separated'?"

He flashed his eyebrows. "Your friend is here."

"Eleanor!" shrieked a high voice.

My heart swelled, and I spun toward the sound. There was Jie, bounding over a bench, skidding around a pile of luggage, and then throwing her arms around me. "You're here!"

"I am!" My voice came out as a squeal; and after squeezing me so hard I choked, Jie pushed me back for inspection.

"You look tired—it doesn't suit you." She poked me in the belly. "Though you're lace-free, yeah? I'm proud."

I scanned her right back, from bald forehead to booted toes. "Well, *you* haven't changed a bit—though I daresay, these are fine clothes." I fingered the tan wool of her suit jacket.

"You think this is nice? Wait'll you see Joseph and Daniel. You won't even recognize 'em. They are"—she twirled one hand in the air—"*à la mode*. Our host buys them so many hats and gloves and ties." She rolled her eyes. "It's ridiculous. He tried to get me to start dressing like the Parisian ladies, but then I threatened to punch his face in. We finally compromised on a few new suits instead." She tugged at her lapels, teeth bared in a smile.

I scrunched up my forehead. "The boys sound foppish."

"Don't tell them that, yeah? Daniel will bite your head off, and Joseph will just frown until you feel like a rotten lowlife for speaking your mind."

I laughed tightly. "And here I thought joining you all meant I needn't worry about clothes or society anymore!"

"You don't with me, Eleanor." She pointed to my carpetbag. "This all you brought?"

"Uh . . ." I twirled around. Where was Oliver? *Get separated—ha.*

I turned back to Jie and beamed. "Yes, that's mine. Now tell me everything!"

"You first!" She swooped my bag up over her shoulder, and we joined in the flow of people leaving the station.

"I'd rather wait," I said, choosing my words carefully. It was all going so well, and I wanted to cling to that a bit longer. Later—I could always talk about Oliver, Marcus, and the Hell Hounds later.

"I'm tired," I continued. "It's been a long day. You tell me about Paris first."

"Fair enough." She smiled. "But let's get a cab, yeah?"

Several seconds later, I took my first steps into Paris, and my heart grew so big, I had to shuffle to a stop and simply soak it all in.

In some ways Paris was as familiar to me as Philadelphia—the carriages rattling on the cobblestones, the people hurrying home, the smell of horses and mud and *city*—and yet in most ways it was so, so different.

The same beige-faced buildings and gray roofs I'd seen when entering the city now peered down at me from every direction, and I couldn't help but imagine all the people behind each tall window and down each winding street.

And with the sun setting beyond the rooftops, the streetlights seemed to glow even more brightly, casting all those lives and smiles and heartbreaks in an unearthly warmth.

I grinned until my cheeks ached. I had done it! I'd left Philadelphia far behind, and my troubles were long lost in the dust. Or . . . they were at least somewhat behind me.

Oh, don't think of all that, I ordered myself. I was in Paris and with my dearest friend. I ought to give myself at least a few hours to revel in it.

Jie let me gape for several minutes, but then her usual impatience kicked in, and she hauled me down to the busy street. After waving over a hansom cab, she rattled off the hotel name and a few French words. The driver helped us inside the coach.

"Learning the language?" I asked, impressed, as we settled onto the bench seat beside each other.

Jie twirled the end of her braid. "I don't like relying on Joseph to talk to everyone, and I *hate* not knowing what people say about me." She sighed and stared out the window as we clattered to a start. "But we've only been here a month. I haven't learned much."

Some of my excitement melted, and for a moment I pressed my hands to my lips and watched her. She was the same girl from the summer—fierce, quick to smile, and unafraid—but there was a new dullness in her eye.

"You don't like it here," I stated.

"Is it that obvious?" Her eyes slid to mine. "It's not the city's fault, or even the Parisians'. Truth is, I've just been lonely."

"Me too." I sighed and hooked her arm in mine. "But now we're together."

She chuckled. "And I'm glad for it, yeah?" Suddenly her breath caught, and she wrenched free. "Eleanor, you have two hands! How?"

"Uh, w-well," I stammered. It was all fine to avoid mentioning Oliver, but *this* would certainly need an explanation. Stupid Eleanor! Why hadn't I prepared an answer for this?

"I used . . . magic," I finally said.

"How?"

I shrugged one shoulder. "I simply figured it out, I suppose."

Her eyebrows shot up. "Simply . . . figured it out?"

I nodded, relieved when she didn't question me further and only said, "Joseph did say you had power."

Taking my new hand in her own, she slipped off the glove. She spread out my fingers and held them to the light. "It's just like your old hand!"

"It *is* my old hand." I pulled it back, embarrassed. "I . . . I managed to call it through the curtain and bind it here." That was mostly the truth.

She whistled. "That sounds like dangerous stuff. You should've waited for Joseph."

I only grunted in response, and Jie seemed to notice my discomfort. She dropped my hand. "You don't wanna talk now—sorry. You should look at the city, yeah?"

"Right. I'm in Paris." I forced a smile, sliding to the window. But the streetlamps glared off the glass, making it hard to see much beyond the cobblestone streets.

"Or," Jie said with a laugh, "maybe you should look at the city tomorrow. In the daylight."

I turned back toward her. "So where is your hotel? And, um . . ." I scratched at my ear. "Do you think I could stay with you?"

"Of *course* you can stay with me." Her eyes lit up. "Besides, I'm sure the instant Monsieur LeJeunes knows you're here, he'll offer you a suite."

I exhaled heavily. "Thanks, Jie. Is this *monsieur* the host you mentioned in your letter?"

"*Oui.*" She batted her lashes. "He's the Marquis du Bazillac, and he's in the Senat—though he's running for the presidency. He was the one to write to us in Chicago. Of course, he thought we were three men. Imagine his surprise when he realized I was a woman." She grinned wickedly.

"And he doesn't care about the Centennial Exhibition? About the fact that you're wanted *fugitives*?"

"Naw. He knows it's not true, and he's trying to win the people's hearts by saving them from *les Morts*. Though he has had to work extra hard to keep the gossip . . ." She trailed off, searching for the right word. "To keep it *clean*. I think that's why he makes us do so many events. Parties, balls, Senat meetings. But I can't complain." She opened her arms. "We live like royalty, yeah? Our hotel is fit for Empress Tz'u-Hsi herself. And we're right across the street from these amazing gardens called the Tuileries. You'll definitely want to see those tomorrow." A bright-toothed smile suddenly split her face. "Oh boy, I bet the Marquis will buy you new gowns and jewelry. Why, look at what his friend gave me." She whipped the end of her braid up to my face. It was held by a jade lotus hair clasp. "It's Chinese, yeah?"

"Oh my." I took it gently in my hands and stroked the delicate petals. "It's beautiful, Jie."

She grinned happily and flipped her braid behind her head. "Just wait—you'll probably get something beautiful too. And I *know* the Marquis will want to take you to all the teas and dinners he makes Joseph and Daniel attend." Her smile fell. "In fact, Joseph is off at some *salon* tonight, so you won't see him until tomorrow. The man is so exhausted from all the visits he has to make, but he'd much rather have the city's love at the price of sleep than go through what we did in Philadelphia."

My brows drew together. "So when do you get any work done?"

"It's . . . slow." She flicked a piece of dust off her pants. "Everything about our job is a mystery. But listen, I want to hear more about you. What sights do you want to see tomorrow?"

As if on cue, my stomach grumbled angrily. I grinned.

"First, I would really like to *eat*."

She laughed and rubbed her hands together. "Then let's get you a baguette!"

The Hotel Le Meurice was so grand, I was terrified to step inside. Like a moth in the butterfly garden, I absolutely did not belong. But if Jie could swagger into the gleaming marble foyer with its white columns and gold chandeliers and not mind the stares, then so could I.

Jie gave a nod to the navy-uniformed man behind the front desk; and before I had a chance even to see what was beyond the main entrance, she whisked me left, beneath an enormous crystal chandelier and on to a grand stone stairwell.

"This marquis," I said, ogling the pink marble walls, "he's rich, I presume?"

Jie laughed. "Very. He probably sleeps on a mound of gold."

Two flights up, we stepped into a hall that ran off in either direction. Teal rugs muffled our footsteps, and lamps every few feet gave a steady stream of electric light.

"I am in awe," I declared. "All of Paris is so elegant, and this is downright opulent!"

"You haven't even seen the best part yet." Jie pointed directly across from us to a white door built into a wall of glass-paneled windows. White curtains blocked whatever was on the other side. "That's the lab. Now you'll *really* be impressed." She slipped out a key, and moments later, the door swung back.

I gasped, rooted to my spot in the doorway. "Impressed"

was an understatement. The same teal carpet as the hall's was underfoot, while mauve armchairs lined the room's edge. Simple mahogany bookshelves covered the walls, and in the middle of the room were three wide worktables—all lit by dangling chandeliers.

"Wow," I breathed.

"It's supposed to be a parlor for the three suites in the corner." She motioned to the back, where a tiny hall connected to three doors. "But the Marquis paid for us to make a lab."

"Do *you* all sleep on mounds of gold?"

She snickered. "Just satin, I'm afraid." She slid her hands into her pockets and ambled in.

I stepped carefully after her. "And you think the Marquis will pay for me as well?"

"Yeah. I'm sure of it." She guided me around the paper-strewn tables and toward the corner hall. "The Marquis has more money than he knows what to do with. He's paying for Daniel to visit Germany."

My heart skittered. "Daniel . . . isn't here?"

"No. He's studying with the German army to learn about weapons and flying machines—pretty much anything that might be useful to us."

"Oh." Disappointment slashed through me, so sharp, it actually *hurt*. I bit the inside of my mouth. "And for how long," I asked, trying to keep my face passive, "is Daniel away?"

Jie shrugged. "The Marquis offered to send him for a whole month, and Daniel jumped at the chance . . . but I think he decided to stay only two weeks in the end." She shuffled into the hall, which was really nothing more than a narrow room with a door on each wall. "So that means he should return in a few days."

My heart stumbled again, but I stoutly avoided thinking about my feelings. The last thing I needed to worry about was a young man—even if he had left me somewhat heartbroken.

I cleared my throat. "So which room is yours, Jie?"

She motioned to the door on the right, and then with a flick of her wrist, she spun the knob and pushed inside.

I moved to follow but instantly stopped again. My jaw went slack. The hardwood floor was covered in an elaborate violet carpet that matched the chaise longue and two armchairs. A huge, plush bed in sky blue stood beneath a draping blue curtain that contrasted perfectly with the maroon-and-gold window curtains. A writing desk, two bedside stands, and even a full-length mirror stood guard against cream walls.

"Wow," I said. "Your situation has really changed. To think you were living *and* working in a closet only a few months ago—to think that Philadelphia *still* believes you're to blame for all those deaths and walking corpses."

She opened her palms. "Like I said, I think that's why the Marquis makes Joseph go out so much—to counteract the bad gossip. And to help his own presidential campaign. Either way, we're the only people who can help Paris, and unlike the stupid Centennial Exhibition, no one here expects us to pretend the problem isn't exactly what is. These sacrificed Dead are walking, yeah? And it's our job to find who's behind it all."

I frowned. "Tell me more about the Dead. What's happening exactly?"

"We call them *les Morts*, remember?" She crossed to the bed and flung herself on her stomach. "The basics are that these Dead show up randomly . . . but they're the Hungry Dead. Rabid and *fast*."

"Is it a necromancer?"

She propped herself on her elbows. "We don't know. See, all *les Morts* have one thing in common: they were murdered first . . . and their ears and eyes were cut off."

I shrank back, my stomach coiling. "That's what you meant by 'sacrificed'?"

"Yeah, and it's not nice. They keep showing up reanimated. Or they *were*. We haven't seen any in almost three weeks. But listen, Joseph can explain it better. He has some theories, and he can tell you about 'em once he's back from"—she twirled one hand in the air—"living the tiring but very glamorous life."

"You sound as if you don't like the glamorous life." I pointed at the nearest window. "But a view of Paris? Free clothes and trips to Germany? What is there to dislike?"

"A lot." She rolled her eyes. "You should see how the women fall over Joseph and Daniel; it's . . ." She clamped her mouth shut.

"It's what?"

"Nothin'." She rolled onto her back and watched me through half-lowered lids.

"What is *that* look for?" I demanded.

"This is my I-know-how-you-feel-about-Daniel face."

"Excuse me?" I hitched up my skirts and stalked to the bed. "How do I feel about him?"

She tipped her head to the side. "You two are like . . . I dunno, like something that's completely in love but won't admit it."

"*What?* That's utterly absurd." I dropped onto the chaise at the foot of the bed.

She crossed her arms. "You seem awful defensive."

"Honestly." I moaned. "Why does everyone seem to think this about me? I am *not* in love with Daniel Sheridan."

"Who else thinks it?"

"Oh, um—" I paused, not wanting to mention Oliver. "My maid." I glanced to the right. "But I'm not. In love, I mean."

She swung her legs around and leaned back onto the pillows. "Isn't there some line about protesting the truth too much?"

"The lady doth protest too much, methinks." I sighed dejectedly. "It's from *Hamlet*, and you're probably right. But listen, I thought . . . well, I thought there was something between us. But when I asked him how he felt, he told me very plainly that he was *not* in love with me."

Jie winced.

"Surprise." I wiggled my fingers halfheartedly in the air. "Now can you please drop these silly notions."

"But have you considered that maybe it's a complicated situation because of—"

"Enough," I cut in. "*Please.* I do not want to discuss Daniel a moment longer. Please finish what you were saying before. About all the women."

She nodded slowly and clasped her hands behind her head.

"Well . . . the ladies are in love with Joseph and Daniel, and it's sickening." She watched me, clearly waiting for my reaction.

"Don't worry, Jie." I gave a tight laugh. "The women can have them both. I have other things to worry about. *Les Morts*. Marcus."

"Marcus?" She sat up. "You mentioned him in your telegram, but I didn't understand."

"Um . . ." I gulped, searching my brain for any topic that *wasn't* Marcus. I only needed a few minutes to get a solid story in order. A story that carefully avoided any mention of Oliver. I cleared my throat. "Can we possibly order dinner first?"

"Right!" She scooted off the bed. "I promised you a baguette. I'll get you some food, and then you can tell me what's going on. And *then*"—she waved to my enormous yawn—"I'd say it's time for bed."

I patted my mouth until the yawn passed. "That sounds absolutely perfect."

She grinned, her eyes crinkling. "I'm glad you're here, Eleanor."

I grinned back. "And I'm glad to be here."

CHAPTER TEN

The next morning, Jie woke me with her usual finesse.

"Up!" She jabbed my ribs. "The sun has been high for hours, yeah?"

I cracked open an eyelid. "How do you have so much energy?"

"'Cos it's the middle of the day!" She pushed her face in mine. "Joseph and I have already fought one Dead—"

I bolted upright, almost hitting her chin. "The Dead? *Les Morts* have returned?" I glanced out the window; the sun was *not* high. "What time is it?"

"Eight." Jie snickered at my stricken face. "Early for you, but *les Morts* wait for no one."

Jie assisted me with dressing, and as she buttoned my gown,

I couldn't help but wonder where Oliver might be—though I supposed he had managed this long by himself. One night alone in Paris wouldn't kill him.

Once Jie and I had pinned up my hair, we marched into the lab. A tall man with skin the color of hazelnuts stood over the middle worktable. He looked as handsome as always—no hair out of place, no wrinkle in sight.

"Joseph!" I leaped toward him.

He spun around, his face splitting with the biggest grin I'd ever seen the Creole wear. "Miss Fitt." He swooped into a bow.

"Now, now," I scolded, "call me Eleanor."

He lifted, his eyes twinkling. "It is so wonderful to see you, *Eleanor*. The last time I saw you, you saved my life." His hand moved to his left cheek, where jagged white scars puckered—scars that could only be the remnants of Marcus's attack. "I must say you look as lovely as ever."

Heat flooded my face. "Joseph, I had no idea you could be so charming."

He spread his hands, laughing. "It is this Paris air. *La joie de vivre*." He hooked his foot around a stool and slid it out. "Sit. Talk!"

My stomach twisted hollowly. "As long as I can still eat after . . ."

Jie snorted. "Breakfast'll still be there."

I gave her a playful glower, but as I moved to sit, the view outside caught my eye. "Paris!" I darted to the window, my mouth falling open. "Look, it's Paris! In the *sunlight*! And oh, it does look exactly like the prints."

Joseph chuckled and joined me at the window. "We have a lovely view, *non*? Here"—he unlatched the window and pushed it wide—"lean out and take a look."

I bent halfway out and gawked at all that lay before me. Directly below was a cobblestone street *packed* with carriages and carts and people—so many people. Smells of horse and sweat wafted up; and for a moment, like last night, I was briefly struck by how similar it was to a Philadelphia street except . . .

I strained to push myself farther out, to hear the rolling rhythm of the language. It floated over the clopping horses and rattling wheels, and *that* wasn't like Philadelphia.

Nor was that breeze whipping over the city and tugging me out. *Come,* it seemed to say. *Come see the city.*

Jie stepped beside me. "Those are the gardens I told you about." She pointed to an iron fence across the street. Beyond its bars were red-tipped maples and chestnuts swaying in that playful wind. "If you look that way," she went on, directing me to look left, "you can see all the flowers and hedges, yeah?"

I followed her finger until my eyes met manicured bushes and perfectly organized rows of flowers. "Yes," I breathed. "And what is that beyond it?"

At the far end of the garden was an enormous, hollowed-out structure. Its roof was missing and its walls charred.

"That," Joseph said, "is the Tuileries Palace. It was destroyed in a fire several years ago."

"And that?" I pointed right, to the other end of the gardens, where a giant, needle-like column poked up toward the sky.

"That is the Place de la Concorde," Joseph answered. "It is an Egyptian obelisk . . ." His words faded off, so I glanced back at him—and found his eyes locked on my right hand.

I slowly drew back through the window. "You can ask about it."

Rose patches appeared on Joseph's cheeks. "May I see it?"

"Of course." As I slid off my glove and extended my hand toward him, I prayed he didn't have many questions. My reluctance to share the truth was somehow even greater this morning than it had been last night. Why muddy the clear waters? Things were going so well.

And heavens, how I had missed Joseph and Jie. Missed having friends who liked me exactly as I was . . . *Besides,* I told myself, *you are making it easier for them too.* No need to worry the Spirit-Hunters when they had an entire city of people to protect.

"*Kaptivan,*" Joseph breathed. He inspected my palm like a fortune-teller at the fair. "How did you make this, Eleanor?"

I licked my lips. "I-I'm not sure how. It was bothering me . . . hurting when spirits were near, so I just, um . . . called to it. And it came."

He squinted almost imperceptibly. "Surely it was not so simple."

"Perhaps not, but I . . . I can't really remember the details."

A flicker of something passed over his face. Anger, perhaps, except that I'd never seen Joseph angry—at least not with me. "I urge you to remember the details, Eleanor. It is very important."

"I-I'll think about it." I glanced off to the right and withdrew my hand. "Maybe I can remember something."

"Hey," Jie said, fidgeting with her hair clasp. "I'm gonna go down and order breakfast, yeah?"

Joseph nodded, and I took the opportunity to bolt to the table and waiting stool. "Jie told me you battled a corpse today."

"*Wi.*" Joseph closed the window and followed me to the worktable. Sharp lines puckered his brow, and I noticed new creases around his eyes. He looked so very tired.

"This corpse was our first in quite some time," he continued. "It was one of the Hungry, as they always seem to be. She was a baker's wife, and the poor man . . . his son died a few weeks ago, and now he must deal with this too. Needless to say, he is devastated."

"Jie only told me the basics about *les Morts.*" I pretended to focus very hard on adjusting my skirts around my stool. "What exactly is happening?"

He eased onto the stool beside me. "Before we came, there had been forty-eight walking corpses. This was why we were called in, and within the first week of our arrival, we encountered twenty-two more. Seventy Dead in all. Then . . . nothing for the past three weeks—until this morning, that is."

"And they've all been *murdered?*"

"Yes." He sighed, and his shoulders sank a few inches. "We are at a loss for who might be responsible, though. Not a single corpse has appeared in the same place. From the rich to the poor, no class has been untouched—and there is no way of predicting when or where the next person will vanish. Nor when or where that person will reappear as one of the Dead—or the Hungry, rather, for they are not attached to a necromancer. Recall that a corpse *not* controlled by a necromancer is free and desperate only for its next meal of soul."

My gut twisted and I fidgeted with my gloves. "Well, what if you kept track of all missing persons? Would that help you predict the next victim?"

"The police do provide us with a new list each week, but there are over two million people in Paris. Most missing people are completely unrelated to our murders. . . ." His voice trailed off, and I realized his attention was focused back on my phantom hand. And the wrinkles in his brow were even deeper.

So before he could direct the conversation to my magic, I blurted, "Oh, Joseph, I almost forgot about Marcus!"

His eyes leaped to my face. "What about him?"

"He came to Philadelphia. That's why I left—why I'm here. Marcus wants the pages from *Le Dragon Noir* and the letters Elijah left inside." I went on to explain how I'd seen yellow eyes, how Mama had thought she'd seen Elijah, and how I'd been forced to flee on the next steamer bound for France.

I however did *not* mention Oliver. "Then I came here," I finished at last. "To you, for I didn't know what else to do."

"It was right for you to come." Joseph massaged the scars on his cheek, his back stiff and straight. "Do you believe that Marcus will follow you? Will he come to Paris?"

"I . . . I think so. He must know I have the letters, and . . ." I bit my lip. By omitting Oliver, I'd had to omit the Hell Hounds, and *that* meant I was going to have to tell a lie now. But only a little one—one I could take back later. "I believe . . . that is to say, I'm rather certain Marcus saw me board the steamer. He knows I have left Philadelphia."

"Good." Joseph dropped his hand. His scars were tinged with pink from rubbing. "I *hope* Marcus comes. Is it possible he might have boarded with you?"

"No." I shook my head. "If Marcus had been on the steamer, I would have known. He would have sought me out."

"True." His gaze shifted to the window. "Do you perhaps know when the next steamer departs?"

I frowned, trying to remember what the ticket clerk in Philadelphia had said. "The next direct boat won't leave for another few days. As for an *indirect* boat, I haven't any idea."

"Nonetheless, he will be at least a week behind you. At best." His lips twisted up in a slight, private smile. "But when he comes, I will destroy him. This time, Eleanor, I will be prepared."

Chills slid down my body, and a fresh wave of desire—of hunger to face Marcus once and for all—clawed at my insides. And with it came the faintest flicker of magic, warm in my chest. I almost smiled.

But then a thought occurred to me, something I hadn't considered yet *was* possible. "What if Marcus does not follow? What if he stays in Philadelphia, Joseph?" *And uses more magic and spells to reach me from afar.*

"If Marcus does not follow," Joseph answered, his voice barely audible, "then there is only one solution, Eleanor."

"What?"

"We will go to him."

The moment Joseph and I reached the bottom of the hotel's main stairwell on our way to breakfast, a high-pitched squeal broke out.

I jolted, yet before I could calm my heart, we were set upon by a flock of brightly clad girls in all manner of flounce and lace.

"Monsieur Boyer! Monsieur Boyer!"

Pastels and curls swarmed around us, and with no warning, Joseph was yanked away from me. Two breaths later and I was left standing alone, mouth agape.

"Aha!" exclaimed a male voice. "Finally we have found you!"

I jerked my gaze to the foyer. The speaker was an expensively dressed gentleman. He moved down the stairs with the aid of a cane and the stooped posture of an old man—though he couldn't have been any older than my mother. His dark mustache shone so brightly in the electric lamps that I was certain oil would drip off the long hairs and splatter on his white collar.

On his arm walked a petite, middle-aged woman. She was a full foot shorter than the man, yet if you took into account her enormous coiffure of onyx-black hair, she almost reached his crooked height.

The couple entered into the foyer, and the man bowed gingerly before me.

"I am Monsieur Frédéric LeJeunes, Marquis du Bazillac. And you, *Mademoiselle*, must be Eleanor Fitt." He took my hand and dropped a kiss on the air above it. "*Enchanté*."

"It i-is a pleasure," I stammered, thrown off by the realization that *this* was the Spirit-Hunters' generous benefactor. The exact man I had to woo if I wanted a place to stay.

"Zis is Madame Renée Marineaux," the Marquis added, nodding to the woman.

She beamed at me, making her angular face almost pretty and her hazel eyes almost golden. It was quite a stunning effect on a woman who seemed unimposing—perhaps even plain—at first glance. "How do you do?" she murmured.

I bobbed a polite curtsy.

"I was told," the Marquis began, "by Mademoiselle Chen that you are taking breakfast now, *non*?"

"Yes sir."

"Then you must—how do you say?—*join* us. It is right zis way." He motioned happily to a set of open doors beyond the foyer, and I couldn't help but notice how odd his cane was. And beautiful. The handle was made of ivory and carved into the shape of an open hand.

Dragging my eyes from it, I bared a polite smile. "Thank you, sir. Breakfast would be perfect—I cannot wait to try all the French delicacies."

He barked delightedly and set off toward the restaurant. I glanced back at Joseph, but all I could see was a top hat floating above a sea of feathery bonnets. So I moved after the Marquis. *I suppose those are the girls Jie mentioned. . . .*

"Where are you residing?" the Marquis asked, cutting into my thoughts.

"To be honest, sir, I stayed with Miss Chen last night." I fluttered my lashes in what I hoped was a sweet and helpless way. "I came here quite suddenly and have nowhere else to stay."

"Then you must take a room here," said Madame Marineaux, moving to my side. She spoke with a faint accent—though it did not sound French. "The Marquis is friends with the owner, you see, and he is taking care of these *amazing* Spirit-Hunters. You must allow him the privilege of hosting you as well." She shot the Marquis a raised eyebrow. "Surely that can be arranged, *Monsieur?*"

"*Mais oui!*" The Marquis stomped his cane against the floor. "I will take care of everyzing."

"Thank you very much." I gave them both a grateful grin. "*Merci beaucoup.*"

Moments later, we entered the restaurant. Pistachio-colored curtains lay over ceiling-high windows, and crystal chandeliers hung like icicles. A navy-uniformed waiter with a rigid posture and even stiffer mustache helped me sit as the Marquis assisted Madame Marineaux. Then, after taking a flurry of orders from the Marquis, the waiter glided off.

The Marquis set his strange cane against the table, allowing me full view of the gnarled ivory fingers, and I could not help but stare. The detail that met my eyes was amazing: the fingers were tipped with long, sharp fingernails, and the lines carved into the palm were astonishingly lifelike. But it was the fingernails that held my attention. They seemed dangerous, yet alluring. *Exotic*, I thought.

"Ah, you are admiring my cane?" LeJeunes tugged at his mustache, grinning. "It is *magnifique*, *non*?"

"Yes," I said warmly. "I have never seen anything like it. Where did you get it?"

"From me," Madame Marineaux answered, a pleased flush spotting her cheeks. "I am glad you like it. I found it on my travels. When I was in India, I visited a small village for which this symbol"—she dipped her head to the cane—"is considered good luck. And it has certainly brought the Marquis luck." Her gaze landed on LeJeunes with fondness.

"*Oui, oui*. It has." He clapped his hands. "Such success in zee Senat elections, and I hope"—he winked in my direction—"I will have the same success in zee presidential elections. All thanks to my *Madame* and my . . . what is zee word? Good luck charm." He placed a gloved hand tenderly over Madame Marineaux's.

I shifted in my seat, intrigued by the Madame. "You have done much traveling?"

"Oh yes." She smiled, her hazel eyes crinkling. "All over the world." She angled her head to one side. "But surely that is of no interest to a young girl such as yourself." She gave a tinkling laugh. "Usually all the girls I meet wish to speak of parties and fashion!"

"Oh no!" I cried, shaking my head. "Your travels sound fascinating. My dream is to do just that, actually—to see the world."

"You have made a good start!" The Marquis tapped the

table, his smile spreading beyond the edges of his mustache. "You are in the City of Light. The best conversation and the finest parties are to be found here. *La joie de vivre, Mademoiselle*! Society and museums and lovely sights. You must see all of it while you are visiting your friends."

At that moment our waiter strutted back into the room, pushing a trolley laden with breads, pastries, and richly scented coffee. As he laid out plate after plate, the Marquis motioned for me to serve myself. So I did, grabbing two croissants, a tart drizzled in chocolate, and a generous helping of butter.

After the Marquis had filled his own plate—it would seem he had a fondness for anything with cherries—he turned his eyes to me. "I have an idea, *Mademoiselle*! We are hosting a ball to celebrate all zee success our Spirit-Hunters have had."

I froze in the middle of slathering butter on my first croissant. A ball? It seemed a dreadful time for a ball if *les Morts* roamed the streets.

"You must attend," the Marquis urged. "Everyone who is anyone will go."

Somehow, I grew even stiffer. It was bad enough that the Spirit-Hunters would have to take time off to go to the ball, but me as well? I couldn't possibly attend such a gala when I had only *one* dress in my possession. Yet before I could protest, Madame Marineaux clapped excitedly. "That is a grand idea, *Monsieur*!" She turned to me. "You absolutely *must* come, Mademoiselle Fitt! It is in two nights."

I set down my croissant and wiped my hands on my napkin.

"I-I would love to, but I fear I have brought nothing suitable to wear to such an affair."

Madame Marineaux clucked her tongue. "Do not be silly. Such a minor inconvenience. Why, I know a dressmaker with premade creations. She can tailor something for your, eh . . ." Her eyes dropped to my ample waist and then to my crammed plate. "For your *needs*."

Heat flooded my face, and I realized that the Madame had nothing more than half—only *half*—a pastry on her own plate.

I snatched up my buttered croissant. "I-I'm sorry, *Madame*, but I'm afraid the expense of a new dress would be too much for me." I chomped almost frantically into the flaky bread.

"Expense?" LeJeunes repeated. He gulped down coffee and then wiped his mouth. "*Pas de problème. I* will cover zee costs, and zis weekend you will attend zee grandest gala Paris has ever seen!"

I gulped back my bread, trying not to choke. "Sir, I could not possibly impose—"

"Nonsense!" Madame Marineaux wagged her finger at me. "I will send the dressmaker over this very afternoon. You cannot say no to new dresses."

Dresses? Plural? Yet as I sat there, flustered and outvoted, the Marquis laughed happily. "*Parfait!*"

A moment later, a harried Joseph rushed into the dining room. He glanced over his shoulder repeatedly, as if expecting girls to appear behind every table and chair. He looked even more exhausted than before.

The Marquis waved. "Monsieur Boyer, come! Sit. Eat."

Joseph nodded quickly, and as he darted for the table, I felt an odd twisting in my stomach. I frowned—it was a familiar feeling, yet it took me a moment to realize why.

Then it clicked. I had felt this when Oliver tested our bond at the train station. The demon had to be nearby. I whipped my gaze to the door, and sure enough, a slight, gray-suited figure lounged in the hallway beyond.

I shot to my feet. "I-I must use the necessary. Pardon me." I wobbled a curtsy, embarrassed by the three pairs of surprised eyes yet also certain I did not want Oliver seen. Moments later, I dashed into the hall and veered sharply left. I strode away from Oliver and away from the restaurant's view.

As I knew they would, Oliver's footsteps clicked after me. It wasn't until we had passed through two doorways and the hallway twisted sharply left that I slowed to a stop.

"You fool!" I turned and, grabbing his coat, yanked him to me. "They might have seen you."

"That Joseph fellow did see me."

My breath caught. "What? Did he recognize you?"

"No." Oliver smirked, obviously entertained by my panic. "Why would he? We've never met."

"But you're a . . ." I dropped my voice to a whisper. "You're a demon. Can he not tell?"

"Not unless I'm doing magic. *I* couldn't even sense another demon if the demon wasn't actively tossing around spiritual energy. Like the rest of the world, all your Spirit-Hunters see is

166

an incredibly dashing young man." He flashed his eyebrows at me. "Besides, I was under the impression that you wanted me to meet Joseph Boyer."

"I do want you to meet him. Just . . . just not yet."

He scratched his chin. "So you aren't mad at me for leaving you at the train station?"

"Well, uh . . . no," I said at last, "though I am wondering where you have been all this time."

He spread his arms wide. "It's Paris, El! I've been everywhere. Enjoying my old haunts and finding new ones. Why, I discovered a charming bar in Montmarte, and while I was there"—he dipped toward me—"I heard about *les Morts*. Bloody disgusting. And bloody ambiguous."

"What do you mean?"

"I mean that those missing eyes and ears could be any number of sacrificial rituals." He tapped his chest. "And I am glad it's not me tasked with finding the person behind it."

"But we *are* tasked with that."

"Er, why 'we' exactly?"

I frowned at him. "Well, the Spirit-Hunters are after *les Morts*, so I suppose I am too."

"But what of Marcus—"

"He's not here, so I will deal with him when he comes."

"—and Elijah's letters, your necromancy, and . . . am I forgetting anything? Oh yes." He glowered. "Setting me free."

I ground my teeth. "And I will get to all that when I am good and ready. For now, Marcus *isn't* here and *les Morts* are. If I want

Joseph to help me, then I must first help him."

"But *I* am good and ready now, El. I thought we were friends."

"We . . . are." My face scrunched up, and I realized that he *was* my friend. He knew more about me than even the Spirit-Hunters, and I didn't want to lose that. And yet for all that Oliver knew of me, I knew almost nothing about him. "For a friend," I said slowly, "you keep an awful lot of secrets. About my brother."

He gave me a cool, sidelong glance. "And I have told you, that's my personal business."

"But maybe your *personal business* would help me understand Elijah's letters."

"Well, you could make it easier for the both of us if you simply gave me those letters." He bowed toward me. "I *could* take them, you know. But I haven't."

Now it was my turn to gaze at him sidelong. "Why not, if it's so easy?"

For a moment he did not reply, and I could see in the shifting of his pupils that he was rummaging through various replies. At last his eyes narrowed and he declared, "I haven't stolen the letters because I want you to trust me. I *need* you to trust me. We can't make this partnership work if you don't. I want to see the letters for personal reasons, so I am . . . *content* to wait. At least for now."

I swallowed, unsure how to respond. I so desperately wanted to trust him too—wanted the easy reliance I'd shared with Elijah. "What if . . . what if we make a deal?"

"Ah." His yellow eyes flashed bright gold. "I *do* love deals.

What do you propose?"

"You help me with *les Morts*, and then I'll let you see Elijah's letters."

His lips curled up. "What a lovely idea, El. I daresay, with me on this case, *les Morts* will be solved in a matter of days— nay, *hours*. And then those letters will be mine."

My eyebrows twitched down. I had the distinct impression I had fallen into some unseen trap—that I'd offered Oliver precisely what he wanted all along. Yet, as far as I could see, whatever it was he wanted matched up with my own desires, so I merely answered with "Thank you."

His smile widened. "See if you can't get me one of the bodies—that would help immensely."

"Get you a body?"

"Yes. Missing eyes and ears could be a variety of things— all of them *bad*. But if you get me one, I *might* be able to—"

"Eleanor?" Joseph's voice rang out from the hall. "Are you here?"

My heart skittered into my throat. "Go," I hissed at Oliver. "I'll find you later."

He grinned, almost rakishly. Yes, he definitely enjoyed my panic. I shot him a glare before darting back into the main hallway.

After intercepting me in the hall, Joseph informed me— tiredly—that he had to attend a meeting with the Marquis and Madame Marineaux.

"But I would like very much for you to come to the lab once I am back. There are . . . *things* we must discuss." His gaze flickered to my phantom limb. "I will let you know when I have returned, *non?*"

Dread cinched around my neck like a noose, yet as we walked into the foyer, I forced myself to give him a chipper "Of course!"

He nodded. "Until later, then."

He was gone only moments when a porter came to my side and informed me that he would guide me to my room. Excitedly, I followed him up four flights and into a smaller version of Jie's room—though mine was blessed with a balcony that overlooked the gardens and the hollowed-out palace.

I had barely finished exploring the luxury of my new home when a dressmaker arrived, sent by Madame Marineaux. Before long, the sun was in the middle of the sky and Jie was dragging me to lunch in the dining room.

Joseph still had not returned, and Jie explained over our meal—her words laced with annoyance—that his daily absences were more the norm than the exception.

I hastily swallowed my mouthful of roast duck. "But where does he go?"

"Parties, *salons*, more parties." Jie stabbed her fork into a potato.

I swallowed and wiped my lips with a napkin. "But shouldn't he be working?"

She shrugged. "He wants to, but *les Morts* haven't been here in three weeks, yeah? The demand for our services hasn't been very high."

"Oh. Right." My forehead creased, and I chewed absently on a piece of a baguette. *Well, I suppose this gives me more time to come up with a good story about my hand.*

Except that my afternoon of planning excuses was not particularly successful. I had become too adept at ignoring my problems . . . or perhaps it was simply the magic of Paris. Either way, as Jie took me walking through the Tuileries Gardens and down to the river Seine, I found myself far more focused on this new, grand city than on the ever-present darkness lurking in my mind.

At first I fidgeted with my new gown, smoothing at the bodice and tugging at the skirts. Though the dress was of shockingly good quality for something premade, the muddy brown color left much to be desired, and I was painfully—and surprisingly—self-conscious in front of all the Parisians. They looked so effortlessly stylish, and they carried themselves with a grace I knew I could never match.

But no amount of fidgeting could improve my dress, so once more I mimicked Jie's carefree stride until, soon enough, I was so lost in the gardens around me, I was able to forget about myself—and my problems.

Why, it was the most *wonderful* thing to see, for there were whole families in these gardens doing the things we Philadelphians usually reserved for more private areas. Children played while men read and women embroidered—and they did it all beneath the warm Parisian sun, the changing leaves, and the never-ceasing wind off the river Seine.

And the river—the first thing that struck me was: *We do not have rivers like this in America.* Our rivers might have been used for transport and industry, but they were still owned by Nature herself. The Seine belonged to Paris. It was the very heart of the city, and the buildings grew up straight from its banks into the crisp blue skies overhead. I could stand in the very middle of the Pont Solférino, look left and then right, and know—deep down *know*—that with a single glance I was seeing everything Paris had to offer. And what Paris had to offer, first and foremost, was beauty. Just as the Parisians carried themselves in a way no American ever could, with a sense of poise rooted directly in their bones, the river Seine carried itself with the same grace.

If I could have left the world behind right then and set up camp in a tiny attic overlooking the city—if none of my troubles existed—then I would have. Gladly.

But alas, the church bells tolling three and Jie's thumb gesturing back to the hotel reminded me that I could not escape. Not today . . . and perhaps not ever.

By the time we'd walked back to the Spirit-Hunters' lab, the sun just starting to set, dread began to resume its coil around my neck. I had willingly let dreams of Paris squeeze out everything else, and all because I didn't want to face the reality of my life. Of *death*.

But I had to confront it now. When I finally skulked into the lab, I found Joseph bowed over books. His hat and gloves were off, yet he looked as crisp as always. Examining his reading fare, I headed for a stool beside him.

But I instantly pulled up short, my mind filled with a single thought: *No!* The titles stacked before me were all focused on one topic. *A History of Demonology in Eastern Religions*; *The Rise and Fall of Famous Necromancers and their Demons*; *Amulets, Spells, and Black Magic.*

"Wh-why the interest in demons?" I squeaked.

Joseph didn't glance up. "I believe we may be dealing with such a creature for *les Morts.*"

A second surge of panic flooded my brain. A demon behind the sacrifices? A demon such as *Oliver?* I sputtered a cough. "Wh-why would you think a demon is behind *les Morts?*"

Joseph closed his book and glanced at me. "The sheer number of sacrificed victims suggests more than a single necromancer at work."

"Could . . . could it be several necromancers then? And not a demon?" My words sounded pleading.

"It is doubtful. According to *Summoning Demons for Power*"—Joseph rapped the page—"most magical partnerships are made with demons. As such, I believe we are dealing with either a necromancer-demon pair or a free demon."

"A free demon?" My forehead wrinkled up. "Does a demon not have to be bound to a person in order to stay in our realm?"

Joseph's eyes slid to me. "You know a great deal about demons, Eleanor."

"Not really." I squeezed my fingers around my skirt and

forced my face to stay neutral. "Only stories from books. And church."

"Ah, but of course." He looked away, and I could not tell if he believed me or not. "A free demon," he went on, "can exist in this world as long as it is hidden. Masked, you could say." Joseph ran a hand in front of his face. "The mask is created by the necromancer to hide the demon from the spirit world's guardians. Thus, a free demon is not *bound* to a necromancer but in an *agreement* with one. The demon can still use its magic at will—it does not require a necromancer's command. Does this make sense?"

"I think so." I nodded. "The necromancer *agrees* to hide the demon with a mask, and the demon is free to use its magic."

"*Precisely.*" Joseph rubbed at his scars for several moments, watching me. Then he lowered his hand. "But listen to me, Eleanor. Only someone very foolish would ever go into an agreement with a demon. The allure of necromancy is nothing compared to that of a demon's magic. So whomever we are up against—demon, necromancer, or both—is likely very desperate and very corrupt. Do you understand?"

I didn't answer. I couldn't. I knew the minute I tried to speak, my words would fail. I had been desperate, hadn't I? But corrupt? No. *No.* I had had no choice but to bind to Oliver—the Hell Hounds would have destroyed me. . . . I would have died and Marcus would have gotten the letters and . . .

Joseph shifted in his seat. He was waiting for my answer.

"I still do not see," I said as flatly as I could, "why it cannot be several necromancers together."

Joseph frowned. Sharply. I had not answered his question; he had noticed. "Eleanor, consider that most necromancers seek control and power. They do not like to share. And"—he tapped the book again—"according to this book, there have only been a handful of paired necromancers since this type of magic first evolved.

"Marcus's parents," he continued, "are a perfect example of how rare such pairs can be. His father was trained in voodoo and his mother in necromancy. They wanted to control New Orleans."

"And they worked together?"

"*Non*, quite the opposite." He huffed out a weary breath. "From what I gathered from Marcus, I would say they worked *against* each other more than anything—and this is what usually happens with such pairs. Both mother and father were always trying to recruit their son, yet neither ever realized he had his own dark plans to take New Orleans for himself. But listen, this is not why I have called you here."

"No?" I fidgeted with my skirt.

"No." Planting a hand on the closed book, he angled toward me. "I need to know how much magic you have used, Eleanor. How many spells you have learned."

And I knew right away that Joseph considered "spells" bad. Suddenly the conversation about demons seemed more appealing.

"Spells?" I asked in a tight voice. "I-I don't know what you mean. What is a spell?"

"When magic is built on self-power," he said, his gaze never leaving my face, "when it uses the spiritual energy inside you, we call that a spell. Because I use electricity and it comes from outside my body, I do not cast spells."

I bit my lip. "Have you *ever* cast one?"

"Absolutely not." His jaw tightened. "I do *only* white magic, Eleanor. Black magic—spells, necromancy—is too dangerous. It corrupts and festers the soul. All while feeling wonderful. An opium of magic."

I held my breath. Was this true? Was I *rotting* away each time I cast a dream ward? *No,* I told myself. *You feel stronger than you have in months.* Besides, how could Joseph even know if he'd never cast a spell?

"What about voodoo?" I asked. "Its practitioners don't cast spells?"

"No. They connect to the spiritual energy of the world, of each other. It is a religion—not a means of *power.*" He spat out the word as if he wanted nothing to do with it.

And it hit me: his hatred of spells and necromancy extended far more deeply than mere disapproval of power.

"Marcus," I breathed. "This is because of Marcus, isn't it?"

Joseph drew back. For several seconds he didn't answer. Then he turned away. "Yes. Yes, it is to do with Marcus. To learn that my best friend was . . . was not what he seemed. To learn that he had spent years fooling, not only me, but our teacher—the Voodoo Queen herself. And then, despite every-thing I did . . ." His voice cracked. "Despite everything I did," he repeated, his fingers curling into fists, "Marcus still died . . . and then he *returned*—"

"But it isn't your fault," I interrupted. "You take all of Marcus's deeds onto your own conscience, Joseph, but what he did—all his horrors are separate from you."

He twisted back toward me, the bags beneath his eyes pronounced. "And do you do any differently, Eleanor? Have you forgiven yourself for what Elijah did?"

My lungs seized. *Do. Not. Go there.*

Joseph's posture deflated. "Forgive me. If anyone can relate to my story, it is you. I . . . I should not bring up such things. I merely worry about you." His eyes locked on mine, unblinking. "About this power of yours."

"I told you. I am not casting spells." My words were snipped. "My power comes *naturally*. I did not ask for it. It's simply there."

He held my gaze. "You are certain?"

"*Yes.*"

He blinked once, slowly. "Then you will not, I hope, disagree with my request."

I lifted an eyebrow.

"Would you consent to study with me?" he asked. "I can teach you to control your natural power. To use it properly."

No. The word flamed through my mind and burned in my stomach. *You already use it properly. He will teach you to not use it at all.*

But, I argued with myself, *he knows more than I. I should learn from him. He's my friend.*

Finally, I managed to make my head nod, a tiny, jerky movement.

"Good." Joseph pulled back his shoulders. "Then let us begin with your first lesson: ignoring your powers."

"Ignoring?" I screeched. Ignoring my magic seemed like ignoring a growling stomach or a jaw-cracking yawn. Unnatural. Unhealthy.

That was when I noticed a large, gleaming bell hanging over the window. I pointed, so obviously trying to change the subject, and asked, "What's that?"

I was shocked when Joseph actually followed my finger and answered. "That is our newest version of the Dead alarm."

I licked my lips, trying to focus on what he'd said. "No telegraph system?" In Philadelphia, Daniel had rigged a system much like the fire department's alarms. When the somber Dead alarm had sounded, a telegraph machine in the Spirit-Hunters' lab had jumped to life, alerting them to the when and where of the latest Dead attack.

"A telegraph would be impractical here," Joseph said. "The city is simply too big." He dipped his head toward the bell. "When a new corpse is found, someone usually comes here seeking help. However, we quickly learned that Le Meurice has certain . . . *restrictions* about the types of people it allows through the door. At first, some of the lower-class victims were not admitted, so Daniel built this. Now all a person must do is tug a rope outside the hotel, and we know instantly that we are needed."

"It is a wonder," I said, hoping to ease my tension with

sarcasm, "that the Hotel Le Meurice even let me in their door with such tight restrictions. But I am not surprised to hear that Daniel found a solution. He would."

"A primitive solution, but one that works." Joseph glanced at me, his head cocked. "You are sad that Daniel is not here?"

"*What?* I'm—" Fortunately I didn't have to continue, for just as I drew in a deep breath to protest, the Dead alarm burst into life.

Clang, clang, clang!

As one, Joseph and I lunged for the window. He threw open the lowest pane.

Down on the street, dressed in a black uniform and apron, was a gray-haired woman yanking the rope.

"*Les Morts*!" she shrieked. "*À l'aide*!"

CHAPTER ELEVEN

Joseph reacted instantly to the bell. "*Nous venons!*" he shouted to the woman. "We come!" Then he darted to a cloth-covered mound beneath the worktable. I recognized the bulky shape: the influence machine.

It was a device that looked like a spinning wheel, but rather than wooden wheels for making thread, it had two glass wheels for making electricity. Joseph used the electricity to blast the Dead back to the spirit realm, and it was, I realized, the reason Joseph never needed self-power.

But it was also bulky and inefficient.

"Help me carry it," Joseph ordered, crouching beside the device and dragging it out.

The machine was as high as my knees and twice as long.

At the sight of it, annoyance blazed through me. As corrupt as Joseph might have insisted spells were, at least they did not need an enormous, heavy machine to produce.

I knelt and gripped the machine's wooden base. With a grunt, we stood. Then, with Joseph moving backward and me following, we trudged as quickly as we could to the stairs and down.

By the first landing I was already gulping in air. "You really ought to keep this in the carriage. It's too heavy to transport every time."

"I proposed this," Joseph panted, his gaze intent on the steps, "but Daniel threatened to quit if I put his precious machine in danger like that."

"Danger?"

"He's certain someone will steal it. Or break it."

I scoffed—or tried to, but my breathing was too labored. "You would think it was his child."

Joseph smiled weakly. "He invests all his heart in his creations, so in some ways I suppose it *is* his child." His foot rocked onto the final step, and we picked up our pace, scooting through the foyer.

Jie met us on the street. "I heard the bell ring from the restaurant and got a carriage ready. The woman is already inside."

"*Mèrsi*, Jie. You are fast and effective—as always."

A red flush ignited on her cheeks. "Come on." She guided us to the waiting black cab, and after shoving the influence machine on the floor, we all clambered in. The carriage rattled to a start, and as we traveled down the street and past the Place de la Concorde with its enormous gold-capped obelisk and fountains, Joseph tried to speak to the distraught maid. This proved especially difficult, though. The woman babbled incoherently.

"Oh *non*," Joseph breathed, motioning to the maid. "Her employer, the lady of the house where this Dead runs loose—it is Madame Marineaux."

Jie and I gasped.

"It is worse, though." Joseph gripped his hat brim with a gloved hand. "The Madame is trapped in the same room as the corpse, so we will have to work fast. As capable a woman as Madame Marineaux is, no one lives long with one of the Hungry nearby." Then, with a grimace, he added, "Let us pray she is still alive at all."

Moments later, the carriage came to an abrupt halt, and at the maid's terrified shriek, I realized we had reached our destination. While Joseph and Jie hauled the influence machine from the carriage, I climbed out to gawk at the beige stone house. It was typically Parisian, yet it was at least three times as large as any other home on the street. *No wonder she and the Marquis can afford to buy me dresses.*

Joseph and Jie moved past me, scuttling sideways for the front door.

"And how," I asked, scurrying after, "did the Madame get trapped in the room *with* the Hungry corpse?"

"It was an accident," Joseph said. "The servants managed to shut the butler's corpse in the lady's dressing room, but they did

183

not realize the lady had locked herself in her water closet."

"*Plus vite*!" The maid cried. "Faster!" She barreled through the black front door, and we chased behind.

The instant I crossed the threshold into the elegant front hall, a wild pounding hit my ears from the floor above.

My eyes rested on the steep, winding staircase at the end of the room. "We're going up there?"

"That's where the butler is," Joseph said.

I pursed my lips and stared at the stairs. They were fine for a graceful human, but they would be treacherous for a clumsy corpse. At that realization, an idea unwound in my mind.

"What if we don't go up," I started, "but instead lure the butler downstairs?"

Joseph and Jie ground to a halt, glancing at me. Their chests heaved, and the influence machine rocked between them like a ship on high seas.

"Continue," Joseph breathed. "What would we do next?"

I hurried to them. "Leave the machine here. We'll draw the butler down, where we'll be waiting with our attack."

Joseph squinted slightly. "That *would* give us more time to prepare." He nodded at Jie. "Set it down." They eased the device to the floor.

"Joseph," I continued, "I will let the corpse out while you and Jie get the machine spinning."

"No." His voice was sharp. "*You* and Jie prepare the machine. I will let the Hungry loose."

I opened my mouth to protest, but he cut me off. "It is an

order, Eleanor. Now start spinning." And with that, he tossed his top hat to the floor and bounded for the stairs.

Jie turned to me. "You wouldn't get far in that dress anyway." She dusted off her hands and dropped to her knees to spin the wheel. "Plus, you can stop a corpse like Joseph can, yeah?"

I didn't answer but simply exhaled slowly through my nose. Only once had I laid bodies to rest, and it had been a tedious, *slow* process. Not to mention, it had been three months ago, and I'd had no idea what I was doing.

Yet, if Jie saw my hesitation, she did not comment. She simply placed her hands on the machine's knob and began to turn.

Surely I can do it again. I certainly wanted to.

At that realization, the hunger flared to life—but this time it wasn't confined to my belly. My chest ached, my fingers itched, and my mouth watered. All I could think about was magic. Using my magic to stop this corpse.

I forced myself to inhale, to push this need aside, to focus.

It was then that the noises from upstairs ceased.

One breath passed. Then two, and the only sound was the whir of the glass.

Then the calm was broken.

"It comes!" Joseph roared. "Be ready!" Heavy, sure footsteps banged through the hallway.

Then a new pounding came in an awkward counterbeat to Joseph's. A split second later, Joseph hit the stairs and came flying into view. "Hurry!"

Jie spun the wheel faster. But the momentum was too

much—the handle flew from her hands. "No!" She caught the handle and started over.

Joseph hit the main floor, his eyes white and bulging, and dove into a crouch beside Jie. Behind him came the hollow punch of limbs against tight walls, the snap of bones on steep, crooked stairs, and the chomping of jaws in search of prey.

All of our eyes stayed glued to the stairs—each step was slowing the butler, but was it enough?

A black-shoed foot toppled into view. Then the other, and I knew with a sickening certainty that the Dead would reach us before the machine could make sparks.

Now I could see the man's face: empty, bloody holes where his eyes had once been and crusted, brown blood all over his wrinkled skin.

Without thinking, I acted. I threw my hands up, latching onto my spiritual energy, and drawing in a warm, buzzing well of power. Then, like cracking a whip, I flung it at the body.

The instant my magic touched the Dead, a leash formed between us—but not a leash I could control. This corpse wasn't bound to a necromancer. It was one of the Hungry: animated by a spark and searching frantically for any soul to consume.

I had no idea how to blast its magic back to the spirit realm. That was Joseph's trick, and it needed electricity. Yet I found I *could* affect the corpse. I *could* pump my will into it.

"Stay!" My voice ripped out, high and desperate. "Stay back!"

The Hungry hesitated, then it slogged forward as if in waist-deep mud.

"Stay!" I yelled again.

Sweat dripped down my face. Despite the pleasant heat licking through me, holding this corpse was exhausting me. Why wasn't the influence machine making sparks?

"Stay, stay, stay!" I shouted. The Hungry's teeth clacked in spurts now, but with less time between each bite. And no matter how hard I strained, the corpse was gaining ground. Faster with each passing breath . . . until it was almost to the bottom step. Until it was only feet from reaching us. From reaching *me*.

"Stay!" I shrieked. "Stay, *stay*!" I couldn't maintain this much longer.

At that moment, a *pop!* filled the hall. Joseph made his attack. As the machine sparked again, he thrust his left hand into the electricity. It flew into his skin, and as he tossed up his right hand, lightning blasted from his fingertips.

Blinding blue webs of light seared my vision, and my focus scattered. Instantly, the corpse lurched into a full sprint. Off the final stair and right for me.

I flung up my hands.

Crack! Electricity sizzled past me, hitting the corpse like a bullet to the chest. Then again and again.

For half a ragged heartbeat, the Hungry hovered upright, his jaw wide. Then he collapsed in a heap on the floor.

And we all stared at it for several long, shaking breaths. The air was heavy with thunder and humming with static. And when no twitch came, Jie let out a great whoop.

"That was amazing, Eleanor! I've never seen anything like

it!" She threw her arms around my neck. "I'd say you're now *officially* a Spirit-Hunter."

But the instant Jie released me from her embrace, Joseph cast me a deep frown that emphasized his scars, stark and white. He was furious. Yet he did not say anything; he merely snatched his top hat off the floor, hopped over the corpse, and went upstairs.

I felt too good—too mind numbed and *incredible*—to give his reaction much thought.

Instead, I studied the butler's corpse. In addition to the bloody gashes around his empty eye sockets, beneath his white hair were gaping holes where his ears had once been. Yet what really struck me as odd was the fine dusting of white powder that seemed to coat his entire body. Before I could consider what it might mean, though, the front door swung wide and a squeal erupted. The old maid scurried to my side, wailing, "*Pauvre Claude, pauvre Claude!*" Over and over, she cried.

Until Jie's temper finally cracked. "Enough," she snapped. "How're we supposed to clean him up if you won't shut pan?"

"But 'is wife!" the maid howled. "She died two weeks ago and now 'e die too—*oh, pauvre Claude!*"

"You said he has no family?" I asked.

"*Nooooon!*" she howled.

"So would it be possible for us to keep the body?"

"What?" Jie asked, staring at me. "We don't take the bodies."

"Why not? If we keep it, we can inspect it. For other

mutilations or *something* to help us investigate." *And then Oliver can look at it.*

Jie's face bunched up. "It won't be long before it starts to rot, yeah?"

I raised my shoulders. "I know, but is it not possible we're missing something? A clue?"

"Taaaaake 'im!" the maid sobbed.

I gripped the woman's upper arms and tried to get her to look at me. "Calm down. We need your help. We need you to hail us an extra-large cab. And get us something to wrap the body in."

The woman shook her head. "I must ask Madame Marineaux about a wrap—"

"Use a bedsheet," a woman commanded from above. I snapped my head up just as Madame Marineaux rounded the staircase's corner. Other than a slight flush to her angular face, there was no sign of her harrowing experience with *les Morts*.

This impressed me enormously. What kind of woman could travel the world, face off the Dead, and command Parisian high society with ease? The sort of woman I wished to be.

Madame Marineaux paused by the corpse to inspect him, her brows drawing together. "This is . . . well, sad does not seem sufficient." Her gaze lifted to Jie and me. "Thank you, *Mesdemoiselles*. You have saved my household . . . and my life. The water closet door was almost broken." She shivered and clasped her hands to her heart. "Did I hear properly that you wish to take this corpse?"

She looked so disgusted by the prospect that an embarrassed

flush ignited on my face. "Er, yes. We can study it for clues."

"Oh. I had not thought of this." She stepped around the corpse, her gaze firmly placed elsewhere. "I suppose that is a very clever idea then."

My mortification instantly shifted into pride.

Joseph trotted down the stairs and came to Madame Marineaux's side. "I see no other signs of *les Morts*. This poor man is the only Dead in your household."

"Thank heavens," she murmured. "And thank you, *Monsieur*."

"You are most welcome, *Madame*. Now I fear we must depart." His eyes met mine, and it was clear what he was trying to tell me: *you and I need to talk*.

"Oh, do not go," Madame Marineaux begged. "I owe you a million thank-yous. Please, stay for dinner. We can discuss plans for the ball this Friday."

"*Je suis désolé*," Joseph replied, "but I cannot. Now that *les Morts* have returned, I must not be away from the lab for too long."

"We have to wait for the Dead." Jie nodded to the body. "*Eleanor* wants to bring it back to the lab."

"Oh?" Joseph popped on his hat. "All right. I presume there is an excellent reason for this, so let us get it into a carriage. Hurry—"

"Or," I blurted, "I could stay. You two go on to the hotel, and I will make sure the butler gets to the lab."

"A grand idea!" Madame Marineaux exclaimed. "And then

you can stay for dinner. I would so like to have company after my terrifying afternoon."

Again Joseph's nostrils flared, but I could see in the straightening of his back that he would not argue with Madame Marineaux.

Instead, he spun to me. "I expect you to find me the instant you return."

Jie's forehead wrinkled. "Is something the matter?"

Joseph did not answer. He simply bowed to Madame Marineaux and strode from the hall. Jie flashed me a worried look, but I gave her a smile in return. Whatever Joseph's problem was, I found I did not much care. My blood still bubbled with the thrum of magic, and all I wanted to do was make this happy moment last as long as I could.

So I turned to Madame Marineaux and said, "I would love to stay for dinner. *Merci beaucoup.*"

Madame Marineaux's house turned out to be as elegant and entertaining as its owner. She led me through her hallway and into a private sitting room.

"I never let people come here," she said with a wink, "but I believe you will find it enjoyable."

She was right—the room was fascinating. It was like being in a museum: on this shelf was a collection of tribal masks, on that table was an assortment of enormous seashells, and on the windowsill was a row of exotic orchids. The floors were covered in Oriental rugs and the windows draped with thick, scarlet drapes. A fireplace burned with a small, cozy fire, and every-thing felt so tasteful. So lovingly tended.

It was precisely what Mama had tried to create in our own home, but our knickknacks had been fake and cheap by compari-son. And, of course, all those knickknacks were now long gone.

While Madame Marineaux went to check that her servants were recovered enough to make a small dinner, I wandered the room with a slack jaw. After examining everything I laid eyes on, I ended up before a shelf on which lay two hair clasps like Jie's.

"Admiring my souvenirs?" Madame Marineaux asked. I hadn't even heard her enter the room.

Smiling, I turned toward her. "Oh yes. Did you give Jie one of these?"

"I did." Madame Marineaux moved to my side, her skirts swishing. "I thought she might like something from her home-land."

"She does." I nodded warmly. "She likes it very much."

"I am glad." She motioned me to a pair of rose-colored arm-chairs beside the fireplace. "Let us sit. We will have an *apéritif* before our meal."

As we crossed to the seats, I noticed a collection of portraits over the fireplace. One was of her, one was of the Marquis, and one was of an auburn-haired woman whom I did not recog-nize . . . though something about her reminded me of Madame Marineaux.

"Who is that woman?" I asked, dropping into a chair as she

eased into the other. "Your sister, perhaps?"

For a moment the Madame's shoulders drooped, and she did not reply. But finally she said, "No. The Marquis's sister, actually. Her name was Claire." She gave me a sad smile. "And she was like a sister to me—my closest friend in all the world. But . . . she died almost seven years ago."

"Oh, I am so sorry."

"Do not be. We must lose everyone we love at some point or another. *C'est la vie*." She clasped her hands in her lap. "Now tell me, what do you think of Paris? What have you seen so far?"

"Not much, but what I *have* visited is truly beautiful."

"You shall have to see more then! I will steal you away as soon as you are free and show you my favorite places."

"Oh, *Madame*, I would love that! But you've already done so much for me. Why, I haven't even thanked you for this dress yet. It is so nice to have something new to wear."

Her lips quirked up happily. "I fear the brown is not the prettiest of colors, but I promise"—she tilted almost conspiratorially toward me—"you will have something far more magnificent for the ball."

"Th-thank you." I fidgeted with my gloves. "I don't know how I can ever repay you."

"By telling me stories." She clapped her hands. "I love hearing about other parts of the world. Tell me about Philadelphia—oh, or, I know, tell me how you met the Spirit-Hunters."

"Oh, um . . ." My forehead puckered. I didn't want to tell her how I had met the Spirit-Hunters, for that would mean telling her about their criminal status back in Philadelphia—about my own unsavory status. Instead, I opted to change the subject. "It amazes me how popular they are here."

She nodded. "They are the city's favorites—though how much longer that will last, I do not know."

I blinked. "What do you mean?"

"Only that it is . . . *difficult* to keep the city entertained. As odd as it may sound, the less they work and the more parties they attend, the higher their favor."

"That is odd." I tugged at my ear. "Would the people not *want* them to stop *les Morts*?"

"Of course! But they also want to *see* the Spirit-Hunters out and about, living a glamorous life. And you cannot forget that everyone loves the macabre. The newspapers benefit by having stories to tell, the Marquis benefits by protecting the city, and the Spirit-Hunters benefit by being showered with love." She laid her hands in her lap, grinning slightly. "Do not frown like that, *Mademoiselle*. It is merely something to consider."

Right then, a maid—not the hysterical woman from earlier—bustled into the parlor with a tray of champagne. The crystal flutes rattled, and the woman's face was pinched, clearly indicating that she was not fully recovered from the afternoon's drama.

Just as she finished pouring the sweet drink and handed one to me, Madame Marineaux exclaimed, "*Non, non*! Look what you have done!" She glowered at the maid. "You have dirtied her glass with your finger! Please, take *my* drink, *Mademoiselle*."

She extended her flute toward me, her face lined with annoyance. "And accept my apology for this foolish maid."

"That's all right." I smiled reassuringly at the maid. "I do not mind."

"No," the Madame insisted. "I cannot have you drinking out of a tarnished glass. Think what people will say of me!" She pushed her glass at me once more, so I accepted it—and was instantly rewarded with one of her beautiful smiles. Then, after donning another, quick scowl, Madame Marineaux sent her maid away and waited for me to drink.

I sipped it—the added syrup was far too sweet for my taste—but since the Madame was clearly waiting for a reaction of approval, I forced myself to tip back the whole thing.

When I was done, she picked up our earlier conversation. "So you see, *Mademoiselle*, as long as *les Morts* continue, the Spirit-Hunters will remain popular. It is quite the . . . conundrum."

I nodded, although I suddenly found it quite difficult to focus—and I was too warm and relaxed even to mind. It would seem the alcohol had gone straight to my head.

And, hours later, when I returned to the Hotel Le Meurice, I found that not only could I not recall a single word from the evening, but I had completely forgotten to bring the butler's corpse with me.

Or to find Joseph.

But most worrying of all, I realized *none* of this until the next day.

* * *

I awoke exhausted, throbbing with hunger and so befuddled, I questioned my own sanity. How can one forget an entire evening *and* night?

Unless it's the necromancy.

I heaved the absurd thought aside and replaced it with visions of a hot bath and copious amounts of fresh bread. In all likelihood, I had imbibed too much champagne. I could deal with my necromancy later. Deal with the Dead and Oliver and everything else in the world *later*.

But of course, none of my plans came to fruition. Just as I heaved up my foot for the final step through the restaurant doorway, someone shouted my name.

"Mademoiselle Fitt! Eleanor!"

With a monumental amount of effort, I turned myself back around. And instantly beamed, for it was none other than Laure Primeau.

She bustled toward me, her face split with a grin and her dark sapphire dress cinched tightly around her waist. How she got her corset so small, I couldn't imagine, but she certainly made it look effortless. And she certainly wore that magnificent color effortlessly as well.

"What are you doing here?" I strode toward her, my hands outstretched to clasp hers. "I thought you were bound for Marseille."

"And I decided to take a detour. I 'ave friends in Paris whom I 'ave been meaning to see. I thought I would come visit you on the way." Her lips quirked up. "Especially when I heard you are companions with the famous Spirit-Hunters. *C'est vrai?* "

"Yes. It's true."

Her eyes crinkled—partly with pleasure, but mostly with mischief. "I suppose that explains how you got a new hand, *non?* "

I yanked my hand back, heat bursting on my face. "Yes. That's . . . that's it."

"Oh, I did not intend to make you uncomfortable." She hooked her arm in mine and gave me a wide—and very genuine—smile. "I 'ave hunger and would very much like a treat in the 'otel's famous restaurant."

I laughed. "You had me at the word 'hunger.' Come—it is my treat this time."

We were halfway through our second round of pastries (though how the devil she fit three chocolate croissants *and* all that coffee inside her corset, I haven't the faintest idea), when a flurry of noise began outside. People trickled past, one by one . . . until there were suddenly *many* people—all of them rushing and all of them headed for the street. A quick glance out the window showed people pushing onto the Rue de Rivoli. Traffic was almost at a halt.

But most curious of all was that every person's face was lifted up.

Laure dabbed at her mouth with a napkin. "What do you suppose it is?" She did not wait for an answer before waving over the nearest server. After a quick conversation in French, her eyebrows jumped high, and she twisted back to me. "He says it is a giant balloon over the city."

Now *my* eyebrows jumped high. Then, without another word, we both bounded to our feet and scrambled for the door. "A giant balloon?" I repeated as we hurried through the crowded front hall. "Are you sure you understood right?"

"*Oui!*" She began with a glare, but she didn't finish speaking, for now we had left the hotel and had a full view of the sky.

And both our jaws were sagging.

Floating over the city, exactly as the server had described, was an enormous white balloon. It was like the war balloons from the Civil War but much, *much* larger. And shaped like an egg.

No wonder the whole city was outside! The balloon floated closer and closer, faster than any bird or carriage, and as I ogled with the rest of Paris, all my earlier concerns dropped away. I wanted to see this balloon up close, wanted to see what sort of machine could navigate the skies.

"Come," Laure urged. "Everyone is going into the gardens." I let her drag me along and we wound our way around stopped carriages, huffing horses, and wide-eyed spectators until we reached the fence surrounding the Tuileries.

"*Mon Dieu!*" she cried. "Look! It is *landing*!" She tugged me toward the gardens' entrance. We darted and wove and twisted until we were both coated in sweat, yet no one seemed to mind our unladylike comportment—not even when Laure started stabbing people with her parasol to get inside the gardens. Everyone else was poking as much as she.

At last we managed to find a small gap between bodies at the bottom of the stairs. By that point almost everyone had stopped moving, their faces upturned at the now rapidly sinking balloon. So, with our hands as visors, Laure and I turned our own faces upward with the rest of Paris.

The closer the balloon came, the more detail I could see. It was at least three times the size of a war balloon yet shaped like an ellipse. With a long gondola dangling beneath, it had the look of a boat with enormous white sails.

And never—not ever—had I seen anything like it. Not even at the Centennial Exhibition back in Philadelphia, which supposedly contained all the world's wonders. Clearly they had missed this one.

I couldn't keep the grin off my lips. The words *magnifique* and *incroyable* flew around me, and not once did Laure stop her own exclamations.

Soon the balloon was low enough that the crowds were forced back, and a space was cleared at the center of the gardens. Blue-uniformed men rushed forward. I squinted and then blinked. One of those servants was the rigidly mustached waiter from the hotel.

But before I could consider what it might mean, one of the portholes in the gondola popped open. A rope flew out. Then, one by one, each porthole burst wide and ropes came tumbling through. The servants from Le Meurice—for those were who they all were—rushed forward to snatch up the ropes.

I strained on my tiptoes, trying to glimpse how this

monstrosity would be tied down, but then my attention was diverted—the gondola's door was opening wide.

A folding ladder dropped down, and onto the first rung stepped a gleaming, black boot.

Applause rippled throughout the crowd and then finally burst forth in a thunder of clapping hands. And it was as if someone took the clock and locked it in place.

I felt every brush of wind, every drop of sweat. I heard every whisper and shout around me. Heard Laure's elated laughter bubbling beneath. My heart grew and grew until I thought it might break free from my chest.

Perhaps it was the dregs of necromancy or perhaps it was the way the perfect breeze kissed my face, but in that moment, I did not think I had ever seen anything more beautiful in my life. Or inspiring. What kind of person did you have to be to tame the skies?

I held my breath, waiting for the rest of this unknown pilot to appear.

A gray-trousered leg came next, followed by a gray coattail, a sandy-blond head . . .

And then the pilot turned to face the crowd. To face me.

It was Daniel.

CHAPTER TWELVE

My knees buckled.

Daniel. *Daniel Sheridan!* Here. Now.

I swayed into Laure. She looked over, alarmed, and tried to steady me. She shouted something. I didn't answer—I couldn't. All I could do was stare stupidly at the balloon, my breath frozen in my lungs.

Daniel leaned into the gondola, and when he came back out, he popped a top hat on his head. Then he spun around to wave at the crowd. A confident grin split his face.

And all of Paris cheered—except for me.

How many times had I tried to forget that blasted smile? The way his forehead relaxed and his green eyes crinkled?

A growl escaped my throat, and I squeezed my skirts in my

fists. When Jie had said he was due back soon, I had not envisioned that his arrival would be quite so grand.

Laure gazed over at me, worry creasing her forehead. "Are you ill?" she shouted. I nodded and, taking her arm, swiveled about. I *had* to get away.

With far more violence than before, I shoved my way toward the garden gates and towed Laure with me. Perhaps if I ate croissants until I was sick, locked myself in my room, and pretended my pillow was Daniel's face, then this enormous lump closing off my throat would go away.

Surprisingly, people stepped aside and let us pass. It was as if my misery were a storm cloud to be avoided at all costs.

And for some reason, this only made me angrier. I stomped on, Laure plying me with concerned questions the entire way.

We were almost up the stairs when I realized that the crowds really *were* clearing a path—but it wasn't Laure and me they were avoiding.

I halted on the top step, pulling Laure to a stop with me, while ahead the Parisians continued to draw back.

Laure turned around. "Ah," she breathed.

"Ah what?" I asked. But she didn't have to answer, for footsteps pattered behind and a voice I knew entirely too well called, "*Excusez-moi, Mesdemoiselles. Est-ce que je peux vous aider?*"

Laure's lips puffed into a coy smile, her lashes batting prettily. But she said nothing, and so providing a response fell to me.

I drew in a ragged breath and forced myself around. Then I looked him square in the eyes and said, "Hello, Daniel. A fine

202

afternoon for an overly dramatic balloon landing, don't you think?"

His eyes doubled in size, and his mouth bobbed open like a fish. If the situation wasn't so awful, I would have laughed at his shock.

He tried to speak, his usually tan face devoid of all color, but nothing came out.

Then, as if matters weren't already uncomfortable enough, they somehow worsened. The entire crowd fell silent. Every single person stopped speaking and waited to see what Daniel would do.

Life ticked by in painfully slow seconds. My heart pounded in my ears, and I fought to keep my face still.

Someone coughed. Laure flinched. Then Daniel flinched and stumbled toward me.

"Miss Fitt," he said.

"Do not call me that." My voice came out surprisingly composed—though I desperately wished the crowds would cease their silence and ignore us. "I'm Eleanor to you, Daniel. You know that."

His eyebrows twitched down, and with that, his own composure seemed to return. He swooped off his top hat and bowed. "Eleanor, what a . . . pleasant surprise." He lifted and motioned to Laure. "Who is your companion?"

"This is Mademoiselle Laure Primeau," I said. "Laure, this is Mr. Daniel Sheridan."

"How do you do, *Mademoiselle*?" He gave another elegant

bow, and I almost laughed as my discomfort melted away. Jie was right. I didn't recognize this young man at all. This Daniel Sheridan was not the escaped convict I had fallen in love with three months ago. Whatever that book on manners was that Jie had mentioned in her letter, it had turned Daniel into a perfect copy of every other polite and *dull* gentleman in the world.

"You know each other?" Laure asked, her lips twisting up wickedly. "What a magnificent . . . coincidence, *non*?"

"He is one of the Spirit-Hunters," I muttered, grabbing her arm. "Let's go back to the hotel now, *please*."

Daniel leaned toward me. "The Hotel Le Meurice?"

I nodded grudgingly, avoiding his eyes. "We were just headed back, were we not, Laure?"

But she didn't answer. Her smirk merely deepened. "You are going to the same 'otel, *Monsieur*?"

He tugged at his collar. "Yes."

"*Parfait*," she murmured under her breath. Then, with an arch smile at me, she said, "Then he must escort us, *non*? It is his responsibility as a gentleman."

I opened my mouth, a hissing retort on my tongue, but Daniel was already leaping up the remaining steps to us. "Allow me," he said, swooping another graceful bow.

And it was as if all of France released its breath. That single movement sent a wave of sighs through the entire audience (for crowd they were no longer). Instantly, conversations resumed; the world returned to its natural course.

Laure's lips stayed in a smug pucker as she took Daniel's left arm and I took his right. Then we began an awkward promenade toward the hotel. He was as tall and lanky as ever, and I had to roll back my head to meet his eyes.

"That was quite an entrance," I said, lifting my voice over the now-roaring crowds. "You would do well in the circus."

"*C'est vrai,*" Laure chimed. "What was the purpose?"

He chuckled tightly. "The Marquis asked me to do it. When I returned to Paris, he told me to make it grand. So I did." He spoke slowly, putting a great deal of emphasis on each word. "What brings you to Paris, Miss Fitt?"

"And why . . . are you . . . speaking so slowly? Also, do not call me Miss Fitt."

"I ain't—I mean, I'm not talking slow . . . slow*ly.*" His teeth gritted, and I could see Laure bite her lip to keep from laughing. "I'm merely surprised to find you here," he continued. "And with a . . . lady at your side."

I wrinkled up my face. "Merely" was not a word in Daniel's vocabulary.

"Eleanor was my roommate," Laure explained as we walked down the sidewalk beside the busy street. "We were on the same ship to France."

Daniel only gave her a cursory grunt, his focus still on me. Laure looked daggers at him—it would seem she wasn't fond of being ignored.

But inwardly I grinned. Even in my mud-colored gown and unlaced waist, Daniel wanted to speak to *me.*

"You have not answered my question," Daniel said, his

205

eyebrows drawing together.

"What question?" I asked.

"Why are you here, Miss . . . er, Empr . . . uh, Eleanor."

My breath skipped. He had almost said Empress, and strange behavior or not, *that* was too intimate for me.

I swallowed. "If you must know, *Daniel*, I was chased out of Philadelphia by Marcus, and now"—I flourished my left hand in the air—"here I am. And what about you? I thought you were due in later."

He grunted again and lengthened his stride. Since we were attached, Laure and I had no choice but to pump our legs faster. I didn't mind. The hotel was close now, and the columns of Le Meurice beckoned to me.

"What will 'appen to your balloon?" Laure asked

Daniel peered at her, giving an absentminded smile. "Actually, I prefer to call it an airship. Once I unload my things, I'll move it outside the city, to a big warehouse that holds bal— er, *airships*."

"And what will you unload?" she pressed, still trying to draw his attention.

But he didn't answer right away. We strode through the street's traffic, somehow walking even faster than before. It wasn't until we were almost to the other side that he lifted his voice.

"I'm an inventor, *Mademoiselle*, and I have new inventions for my employer." His face shifted back to me. "Things for Joseph."

"Fascinating," I inserted before Daniel could go into any detail. I was *desperate* for some space. Plus, we had reached the sidewalk on the other side, and I could just make out the hotel's white marble foyer. Freedom was so close! "We left our breakfast half eaten, Laure."

Laure snorted. "*Très horrible*," she said flatly. "To think of a breakfast unfinished—the world might stop spinning." She pulled free of Daniel and sauntered toward the door.

"Must you be so sarcastic?" I demanded, trying to free my own arm from Daniel's and scurry after her.

"Oh, I am only beginning," she called, already disappearing into the hotel.

I pulled harder, throwing a glare at Daniel. "Let go."

"No. Wait . . . Please."

I frowned as he tugged me, and against my better judgment, I let him guide me between two columns. He bent toward me, his gaze roving over my face—some of his old slouch back. "Did he hurt you?"

"Who?"

"Marcus."

I reared back slightly. "Oh no. I managed to get away before he could do anything."

"Is he here?" Daniel leaned in more closely. "Are you in danger now?"

"No—not yet. At least, I don't think so. I cannot be entirely sure." I was rambling—Daniel's proximity was making my head spin. "I do think he will follow, though—"

I didn't get to finish, for at that moment, Daniel's eyes landed on my right hand. "What is that?"

"My hand." I curled my fingers into a fist.

He grabbed my wrist and pulled at the glove, but the instant he saw flesh, he let go, repulsed. "How? How's this possible?"

"It's a long story." I tugged my glove back in place. "One I would rather not share."

"Tell me!" His voice lashed out like a pistol shot. "I have a right to know!"

"A right?" I hissed. "What, pray tell, gives you *any* right to know about me?" I backed up two steps. "Have you forgotten how *you* left things between us in Philadelphia? You cannot simply show up in a fancy balloon, Daniel, and expect me to fall at your feet. I am not some girl to be trifled—"

"I ain't expecting that!" he snapped. "I just wanna know where *that* came from."

A female squeal burst out behind me. "Monsieur Sheridan!"

I whirled around, and my stomach flew into my throat. Rushing toward us, all smiles and perfect couture, was beautiful girl after beautiful girl. Their lashes batted so wildly I thought they might be having conniptions.

Daniel stood, clearly bewildered as the array of silly girls came nearer and nearer. And though this was easily the worst nightmare I could ever conjure, it was also an opportunity to escape Daniel's temper.

So as fast as humanly possible, I fled for the restaurant. Yet I was almost immediately intercepted—by Joseph and Jie.

"Eleanor," Joseph said, beckoning for me to follow him out of the lobby and into the relative quiet of the main stairwell. He and Jie paused at the bottom step, and then he turned a hard eye on me. "You did not come to the lab last night."

"I'm sorry," I said tiredly. "I did not get in until quite late."

"Did you have a nice time?" Jie asked, sliding her hands into her pockets. "Was the Madame's house really—"

"You could have come this morning," Joseph cut in. "It is imperative that we fix your magic as soon as possible."

"Fix it?" I repeated. "It's not as if it is broken."

He dipped his chin, watching me from the tops of his eyes. "That is precisely the problem, Eleanor. It *is* broken, and yet you act as if what you did yesterday was of no consequence."

"What are you talking about?" I glanced at Jie, but she merely shrugged—and looked incredibly uncomfortable with the turn of the conversation. "What did I do yesterday?"

"You used your necromancy." Joseph's voice was curt. "You used your own power to stop that corpse."

"But I *stopped* the corpse, didn't I?"

"Not properly, *non*."

"Properly?" My voice came out shrill with annoyance. "What should I have done, pray tell?"

"Not relied on self-power."

"Joseph," Jie said, pleading, "you're being a little rough on her, don't you think?"

"She knows the dangers of self-power," Joseph replied, not taking his eyes off mine. "We had discussed it only moments before the Dead alarm rang." He leaned toward me, his voice low. "Eleanor, your body is so accustomed to using its own magic, you are automatically reacting with spells. Your body wants to use its power, and this is very dangerous. If this is how you respond when a single corpse is present, I shudder to imagine what will happen when we finally face Marcus. You *must* resist your magic. Do you understand?"

"Yes," I snapped, my temper flaring to life. "Though it might help if you would teach me how to actually *do* that, wouldn't it?"

"And I will—as soon as I return from this assembly."

I bit back a groan. "Fine. Let me know when you have returned from your assembly. Now, if you will excuse me, I have breakfast to finish." Then, with nothing more than an apologetic smile for Jie, I stomped off to the restaurant—and found Laure ordering a fresh pot of coffee.

"Where 'ave you been?" she demanded.

I ignored the question, shifting from foot to foot as I asked, "Would you care to see my room?" I wanted something—anything—to distract me from the last twenty minutes. "We can have the rest of our meal sent up. I have a lovely balcony."

Laure hesitated. "Is this to escape that young man—"

"No." I moaned.

Her lips pursed with disbelief.

"All right, perhaps it *is*. Now come with me. Please?"

With a smug grin, she complied, and soon enough, we had escaped the first floor.

Yet of course, as my luck would have it, taking breakfast on the balcony proved to be a colossal mistake. For an inhumanly *long* hour I was not only cursed with a perfect view of Joseph as he left the hotel, but with all the Parisians who came to see the enormous balloon.

And worse—far worse—all the Parisian ladies who came to see its pilot.

At the first tap against my bedroom door that afternoon—hours after Laure had left—I swung the door wide, already saying "Land sakes, I thought the world had forgotten about . . ." I let the words die, for it was only the dressmaker with a frazzled assistant and a wealth of fabric in tow. My shoulders dropped. Had I alienated Jie by snapping at Joseph? I had searched for her after Laure left, but according to the man at the hotel's front desk, she was away "on business."

The dressmaker and her assistant bustled inside, and without even asking, they dragged me to the center of the room and began to undress me down to my petticoats. Once my gown was off, they set me atop a stool and then subjected me to a tirade of pins, needles, and lace. Madame Marineaux—true to her word—wanted me to have a magnificent ball gown in an eye-catching scarlet. The Marquis had already paid for everything: the silk, the gown, and the hard work.

I couldn't help but love it. It was neither a color nor a cut I would have selected for myself, yet the low neckline accentuated my feminine figure, and the scarlet made my skin positively glow.

"That dress suits you," a man drawled.

Oliver.

I spun on my stool, startling the assistant, and found the spry demon dressed in his usual charcoal suit, his stolen top hat clasped in his hands and his yellow eyes shining with mischief.

"How did you get in?"

"The door wasn't locked, and"——he bared his teeth in a grin——"I'm *quite* stealthy."

"Well, you cannot be here," I said over the annoyed clucking of the dressmaker. "I'm half dressed——"

"Yet fully covered."

"——and you're a man——"

"Some might argue otherwise."

"——in a lady's bedroom."

"Though obviously these women don't care." He motioned to the dressmaker and assistant, who were far more concerned with the effects of my unexpected twirl than with the pretty-faced young man lounging in my doorway.

"You should have knocked," I added with a glare. "And where have you been for the last two days?"

"It's barely been more than a day, El. Stop being dramatic."

I growled as the dressmaker tapped my ribs. I flung up my arms so she could mercilessly stab me with more pins.

"I've been working, as agreed." Oliver draped his hands behind his head. "Gathering clues, keeping an eye out for Marcus . . ."

"Marcus?" Fear——and hope——awoke inside me. "Is he here?"

"I haven't seen him if he is. I am merely on the lookout for him since clearly *you* are too busy to worry about your safety." He motioned to the dress, a single eyebrow quirked.

"I *need* this gown. Madame Marineaux wants me to have a stunning gown for the ball tomorrow night—"

"Who?"

The dressmaker spun me around, so I had to look over my shoulder to keep talking.

"Madame Marineaux. She's the most fascinating woman I have ever met, Oliver. She's been to all sorts of places and . . ." I trailed off. His eyes were cold. "Wh-what?"

"You have enough time to gallivant with Parisian ladies yet stopping *les Morts* or dealing with Marcus is entirely too much to ask."

I pulled free of the dressmaker and whirled around to face him. "Are you angry at me?" I asked incredulously.

"Egads, yes! If you're going to gallivant, El, I would like you to bloody well gallivant with me." He scratched the bridge of his nose, his face set in a scowl . . . and looking so much like Elijah.

I sighed through my nose, glad I hadn't mentioned Laure's surprise visit to Paris—or my time spent with her. It would only serve to make him more jealous. "What do you propose we do together then?"

"Search for *les Morts*, read through your letters so we can figure out what Marcus is after, train your powers . . ." His words faded and he fixed his yellow eyes on me. "Any preference?"

I swallowed, suddenly breathing fast. Train my powers—I

wanted that. My whole body wanted that. But I made myself ignore it and heed Joseph's warnings. "We should deal with *les Morts*. If I want the Spirit-Hunters to help me with Marcus, I first need to stop *les Morts*."

"Or," Oliver said, inspecting his fingernails, "you could simply build up your power and then stop *les Morts* and Marcus with magic. You could learn to fight."

The hairs on my arms pricked up. *Learn to fight.* Oh, how I needed it. Needed to use this energy inside me. To use it to fight. To use it to *hurt* . . .

"No!" I snapped. The dressmaker flinched, and Oliver's brows drew together. I waved for the dressmaker to continue, and then, with a deep breath, I fixed my eyes on Oliver. "No. I will not train."

Oliver didn't react, though I could have sworn his yellow eyes almost glowed. "And may I inquire why not?" he asked calmly.

"Because I promised Joseph—"

"Oh, did you now?" He clasped his hands behind his back and ambled two steps toward me. "Because I distinctly recall a promise you made to me. A *binding* one. So unless this promise you gave to Joseph is on the same . . ." He glanced off, as if searching for the word. Then his eyes shot to mine—and the irises were definitely a brighter gold than usual. "On the same *scale* as our promise, then I urge you to forget the one you made to him."

I swallowed. "You mean my death."

"That's exactly what I mean." He sighed, and all of his poise vanished. "Bloody hell, Eleanor, you have only two months to free me, and it's not some simple spell. It requires a great deal of training to master."

My stomach knotted, and I gazed down at my right hand. *I'm sorry, Joseph*, I thought.

But the truth was, I wasn't sorry. I *wanted* this—and judging by Oliver's growing smile, he knew precisely how much my body craved more magic.

"All right, Oliver." I squeezed my fingers into a fist. "You win."

CHAPTER THIRTEEN

A half an hour later, with the dressmaker and her assistant gone, I made my way to the front of the burned Tuileries Palace, where Oliver had told me to meet him. The day had turned dreary—overcast and damp—and now that the balloon was gone, there was little to draw visitors to the gardens.

"We have to be careful," he said as I approached the palace's crumbling grand front doorway. His head swiveled as he checked for any observers. "The police don't like people in here—though they really only patrol at night, when the bummers crawl in. I don't see anyone now." He motioned for me to follow, and together we crept inside.

The charred floors were laden with weed carpets, and shimmers flickered in the shadows. Gooseflesh rippled down my body.

"There are a lot of ghosts here," I murmured as we picked our way over a toppled wall.

"It was a big fire," Oliver answered, guiding me down a hallway. Our feet crunched over the rubble.

"Can we talk to them?" I waved to the shadows. "To the spirits?"

"No. I told you that."

"You said I couldn't talk to spirits on the other side of the curtain. You never said I couldn't reach ghosts on *this* side."

He grunted and tugged me through a shattered window into an open courtyard. "These aren't spirits. They're merely pieces of souls. Stuck here. They have no voice, no memories. The Hell Hounds don't even bother them."

"Oh. That's rather sad."

"Death is always sad business to the living." He exhaled loudly. "Why else would people want the Black Pullet?"

"What do you mean?"

His mouth bobbed open with disbelief—but it quickly transformed into a smirk. "You don't know what the Black Pullet is, do you?" He stopped walking, and the breeze swept through his curls. "All this with Elijah and yet you have no idea what he sought."

Bristling, I stomped my foot. A cloud of charred dust swirled up. "You're right. I know nothing about it. I haven't *wanted* to know."

Oliver's expression turned grim. "Refusing to understand what Elijah became—refusing to learn about what he wanted and why . . . that won't help you. You have to let him go, El—let go of whatever memories you have. When he died, Elijah wasn't the boy you grew up with . . . or the man I f—" He broke off. "The man I knew. The person he became wanted the Black Pullet. Wanted immortality and endless wealth. You *have* to accept that."

No, I don't. My memories of Elijah were all I had left of my old life. My life with a father, a brother, and . . . and a mother who still cared. I bit my lip and bowed over to wipe the dust off my skirts. "So is that what the Black Pullet does then? Give one immortality and wealth?"

"Yep."

I lifted back up. "Well, no wonder Marcus would want it."

Oliver stiffened. "Marcus wants it?"

"Yes. He told me after he took Elijah's body—"

"Blessed Eternity, El! No wonder he's after your letters! *Le Dragon Noir* was the only text in the world that explained how to find the Old Man in the Pyramids. That was one of the reasons Elijah was trying to get his hands on the missing pages."

I winced. "Which means when Elijah sent you to Cairo, he *did* know that . . ."

"That I would fail to find the Old Man? Yes." Oliver sat back, his jaw tightening with anger. "Elijah *wanted* me out of his way. That's something *I* have to accept." He snorted, a humorless sound. "Of course, as you told me on the boat, all those key pages from *Le Dragon Noir* are now gone—destroyed by your wonderful Joseph. And that leaves me with an unfulfilled command and only one place in the *entire* universe with a clue to finding the Old Man."

"My letters," I whispered.

"Think about it, El. If you want to stop Marcus, then there's only one solution that I can see: you have to figure out what secrets are locked in Elijah's letters."

"But they're all gibberish."

"Not if you know what you're seeking." He splayed his hands on his chest. "Remember, I was Elijah's demon. *I* would know what to look for. Give me the letters, El. I can help."

"Can you? Is *this* why you've wanted the letters all this time? To . . . to chase the Black Pullet?"

"What?" Oliver's voice was barely above a whisper. "How can you say that? If all I wanted was to find the Black Pullet, I would have *stolen* those letters a long time ago. Yet I haven't, El. I have kept your trust. I won't deny those letters mean something to me, but it has nothing to do with the Pullet."

"So what *does* it have to do with?" Then it clicked—something else he had said clicked firmly into place. "Your command," I breathed. "Your final command from Elijah is unfulfilled, so it still drives you. You *have* to find the Old Man in the Pyramid."

He twisted his face away.

"Does it hurt you to resist it?"

"Yes," he whispered, emotion thick in his voice, "but I keep hoping that if you learn necromancy and free me, then the command will end. Or if I could just find this Old Man— before Marcus does—I can fulfill Elijah's final order. Then this

220

constant ache will stop. And *then*," his voice turned into a snarl, "I can destroy the bastard who stole Elijah's body."

But to free Oliver—or destroy Marcus—I would need to train my necromancy. I wet my lips, almost relieved that I *had* to train if I wanted to help my demon.

No! I screamed at myself. *You can't practice necromancy! You promised Joseph.*

A frustrated groan slid from my throat. What was happening inside me? Why were my heart and my head in such disagreement?

Oliver's forehead knit with concern.

"Go on," I said shakily. "Let's find a place to . . . to train." I gestured for him to lead the way, and he pulled me through a crumbling doorway and into a grand hallway. In one corner a wide staircase curled up . . . only to stop halfway, with a pile of smashed marble beneath. Overhead, the gray clouds floated somberly by.

I found a broken column and eased down. Oliver insisted on first dusting off his own broken column—"Do you know how hard it is to get limestone off a suit?"—before finally settling across from me.

My stomach grumbled. "What a shock," I said drily. "I am hungry. *Again*."

"It's part of the necromancy, you know."

"Yes, I guessed that. Whenever I do a spell, I find I'm famished afterward."

"No." He shook his head. "You're only famished when

the spell wears off—and you will stay famished until you cast another."

I tensed. "What are you saying?"

"I'm saying you cannot make that hunger go away unless you train."

"So, this"—I patted my stomach—"is a craving for more magic? Why didn't you tell me sooner?"

Oliver didn't reply, but the wariness in his eyes told me all I needed to know.

"So I *am* like an opium addict?" My voice grew high-pitched and sharp. "I need more spells to feel good? To feel normal?"

"You're too bloody strong. I didn't expect this to happen so quickly. You have a lot of magic to control, but it means there's a lot of magic to control *you*."

"You knew this would happen. You should have told me! I don't want to be *addicted* to necromancy, Oliver." I jumped to my feet and staggered to the foot of the broken stairs. I wanted . . . no, I *hungered* to destroy Marcus—that was all—but what was the price?

I pressed my hands to my face. *Stupid Eleanor.*

Footsteps thudded behind me.

"What if I do magic the way Joseph does?" I demanded, my hands muffling my words. "Will the hunger stop?"

Oliver strode in front of me and pulled down my hands. Everything about his expression—from the slant of his brow to the sag of his lips—was apologetic. "I don't know if that will stop the hunger, El."

"But I would be using electricity—external power instead

of my own." I searched his face for an answer. "Would that end this . . . this addiction?"

"Perhaps," Oliver said, his nostrils flaring. "But then you'll be using electricity. A magnificent idea in theory but ultimately absurd."

I gulped. I remembered thinking something similar at Madame Marineaux's—about how inefficient the influence machine was.

"There are limits to what you can do with electricity," Oliver continued, releasing my hands. "You cannot make a phantom limb, you cannot cast a dream ward, and you certainly cannot defeat Marcus."

"Why not?"

"Because it is *weak*, Eleanor." He lifted his chin imperiously. "Electricity isn't *natural*. It's . . . it is a fake power."

"How do you know?" I asked. "Have you ever used it?"

"No," he spat. "And I never will. Setting fire to my veins? It will *change* me. Kill me. And for what? A single blast of power that I can't even control. I use real magic, El. I am *made* of soul, and using my power is as safe and natural as breathing. Just as your magic is."

"But my natural magic is addictive." My voice came out quick. "And in the end I'm limited. I only have so much spiritual energy inside of me."

"But you can enhance your power, El." He drew back his shoulders. "And you *can* control the cravings. Without Joseph's method."

"How?" I breathed. *"How?"*

"Supplement your magic." He took a step toward me, staring straight into my eyes. Not once did he blink.

He looked dangerous. *Demonic.*

"Blood," he whispered. "Sacrifice."

For half a second I considered the words. But then the weight of those words careened into me. I staggered back. "No, no, *no.*" I lifted my hands. "You told me you didn't approve of sacrifices."

"I don't mean human." He sniffed. "Spiritual energy is in the blood of any living thing, El. Simply drinking the blood of an animal will—"

"Stop!" cried a high voice from another room. "Stop!"

Gravel skittered, and Oliver and I whirled around just as Jie hopped through a burned-out window and into our room.

"Did I hear him right?" She stared at me, her eyes huge. "Are you talking about sacrifices? And necromancy?" She punched a finger toward Oliver. "And did he call himself a *demon*?"

"J-Jie," I stammered. Where had she come from? "I can explain."

"Yeah?"

"Yes." But when I tried to say something, I found that my mouth would only spring open and closed. I turned a desperate face to Oliver, but he looked as stunned as I felt.

"Well?" She planted her hands on her hips. "Say something, Eleanor. Is he really a demon?"

I nodded slowly. All the blood left her face. "Oh God," she whispered, shaking her head and backing up. "I have to tell Joseph." She spun on her heels, spraying pebbles, and hurried toward the nearest doorway.

"Wait!" I darted after her. "Please—I'll tell you everything. Just don't tell Joseph."

She paused. "Why not? He's already worried about you—and you know he is. He told you to stay away from black magic."

"But I have no choice!"

"You *always* have a choice," she snarled.

"No. I *don't*. I would have died had I not used my magic, had I not bound myself to Oliver."

She retreated two steps and gasped. "You *bound* to it?"

"Him," Oliver snapped. "I am a—"

"Shut pan." Jie bared her teeth at him. Then she turned to me. "I'm telling Joseph about this."

"No!" I lunged for her. "Please! Let me . . . let me at least explain."

"I don't want to hear any explanations from you." Her eyes roved over me, repulsed. Betrayed. "You know a demon is causing *les Morts*. What if it's him?"

"What?" Oliver straightened. "How ridiculous—"

"Really?" She thrust her chin at him and then at me. "For all I know, you're *both* raising the Dead."

"Jie!" I reared back. "How can you say that?"

"Easy. We think a demon is murdering these people, and what do you show up with? A demon. And on top of that, you're learning necromancy. It's not a hard conclusion to make—especially when the moment you came to Paris was

225

the moment *les Morts* started rising again."

"No." I grabbed the sides of my face. "Jie, you know me! I'm not a murderer!"

"I *knew* you," she spat. "And that Eleanor wouldn't do necromancy. But fine." She threw her hands up in defeat. "You wanna keep secrets from me, then keep 'em. But Joseph has to know about this."

"And I'll tell him!" I blurted.

"Why should I trust you?" she sneered. "You've lied to us—lied to *me*."

"No!" I shouted, anger rising over my fear. "It's *not* Oliver. It can't be Oliver. He was in America. With me."

She shook her head, her lips clamped tight. "You're a necromancer now, Eleanor, and that makes us enemies."

Then, with a final jaw clench, she pivoted around and burst into a run. I immediately shoved after her. Oliver shouted for me, but I didn't hear. I had to stop Jie. Had to make her see things *my* way.

I pushed my legs faster. By the time I reached the open courtyard, I had broken into a full sprint. My ankles twisted on loose stones and white dust puffed onto my skirts, yet Jie stayed far ahead.

So I ran harder. My lungs seared and my vision turned hazy, yet still I ran—out of the ruins and into the gardens after Jie's shrinking figure. Flowers blurred in the corners of my eyes as I barreled onward, aiming for the street. For the hotel. For the almost-vanished Jie.

By the time I reached the hotel, my body shaking, I had given up.

Joseph was going to find out sooner or later anyway. What was the difference in defending myself to Jie than in doing it to the both of them? Let Jie tell him. For now I wanted to be alone to process everything that had happened—that was happening. I didn't know what I was doing anymore.

So I hauled myself up to my bedroom, sat on the edge of my bed, and stared at the carpet. Thoughts flashed through my mind one after the other—from the letters to animal sacrifices to the Black Pullet. Now I knew with almost complete certainty *why* Marcus was seeking my letters—and why Oliver wanted them as well. Yet this knowledge did me little good. I was no closer to stopping Marcus than I had been before, for I had now lost the only people who could help me.

After a few minutes of these agonizing thoughts, I realized that simply *waiting* for the inevitable—for Joseph to find me— was more than my nerves could stand. So I decided to put my brain to work.

I had new information; I should at least try to use it. It was time to dig through my sheaf of confusing letters. I could focus on those without thinking about myself. I would push all my other problems to the back of my mind, and I would go to the library to see what I could learn about the Black Pullet.

Of course, it wasn't as easy to leave the hotel as I had anticipated. As soon as I found Elijah's letters in my carpetbag and hurried back down the main stairs, a tugging began to tickle in my gut.

At the final step, the hair on my neck stood straight on end. Oliver was near.

Yet I didn't see him anywhere, so I resumed my trek—carefully, slowly—toward the foyer. It was as I passed the gentlemen's smoking room, gray smoke billowing through its doorways, that I realized where he was hiding. So I crept to the heavy red curtains that draped the entrance and risked a glance inside. Through the haze, I could make out bulky scarlet sofas and beyond that a gold-and-black bar.

A bar over which hunched a gray-suited young man, no doubt nursing a gin between his long, demon fingers. For several seconds I watched him, yet not once did he turn.

I can sense him, yet he's not sensing me. What I couldn't tell was whether his obliviousness was from the gin or from a lack of desire to find me. But either way, this was my chance to sneak out unnoticed and conduct my research alone. So with my letters in one hand, I gathered up my skirts in the other and twisted around to walk away.

But I instantly stumbled back. A tall figure stood squarely in my path.

"*Excusez-moi,*" he said in stilted French, "*mais je ne—*" The young man broke off, his eyes widening in recognition. "Empress?"

That was when my own recognition kicked in. I choked.

Of *course* I had to run into Daniel Sheridan at that precise moment. He was dressed to the nines in a wheat suit, white tie, and even whiter pair of gloves. As if that wasn't out of character enough, there was a gleaming gold monocle lodged in his left eye and a book—*the* book on manners, I realized—in his hand.

Despite looking unusually foppish, he also looked rather spectacular—ridiculous monocle and all. The wheat of his suit blended into the sandy blond of his hair so that, in the brightly lit hall, he positively glowed.

I cowered. Had Jie talked to him? And what if Oliver decided to come over *right now?*

"What are you . . . doing here?" Daniel spoke with the same strange pauses he'd used earlier in the day.

I forced my knees into a curtsy. "Mr. Sheridan. I was just, um, taking a peek at the room." I flourished my letters toward the smoking room. "I thought perhaps . . . Jie . . . was in there?"

"Um, no. It is for men . . . *gentlemen* only."

"Oh! So you haven't seen Jie in there? Or . . . at all?"

"Not since this morning."

My breath shot out. Daniel didn't know. "Well," I said, beginning my retreat, "if you see her, please tell her I was look-ing for her—"

"Wait!"

I paused, my heel midair. "Yes?"

"Um, how are you?"

"What?" My foot dropped with a thud. "I am fine. And . . . you?"

He tugged at his tie. "Fine, fine. Thank you."

"All right, then." I let my gaze flit over his shoulder. Oliver was still focused on his drink—thank the merciful heavens. Now if I could somehow slide my conversation a few feet to the right . . .

Daniel swiveled his head into my line of sight. "Are you looking for someone?"

"No!" I squeaked. "I mean, that is to say, of course not—I don't know anyone in Paris, do I?" I laughed shrilly. "No, I am merely soaking in every detail of this fine room. Lovely example of Parisian decor."

Oh dear, what was I blathering on about? "Well," I rushed to add, "good day to you, Mr. Sheridan!" I whirled around to hurry for the street.

But Daniel slung out a long leg and stepped in front of me. "Are you going to the post office?"

"What?" I frowned.

"You're carrying a stack of letters."

My gaze dropped to my hand. Sure enough, Elijah's letters were still grasped tightly in my left fingers. "Ah, right. These *do* look like documents worth mailing, but no . . . no, I'm not going to the post office today." I made to scoot around him.

He sidestepped, blocking me once more. "Then where are you going?"

I hesitated and wracked my brains for a good response, but all I could conjure was the truth. "Well, I-I'm going to the library. These letters are from Elijah, and I thought there might be a clue in them."

"A clue?"

I lifted one shoulder. "Something to explain why Marcus wants them. He came all the way to Philadelphia—even approached my mother for them."

"Oh?" Daniel slid his hands into his pockets, waiting for me to go on.

"I believe Marcus wants the Black Pullet, yet no one knows how to raise it—whatever *it* might actually be. All I know is that it's some creature from the spirit realm that can grant its master immortality and endless wealth, but there's some critical step in this whole summoning process that remains unknown. It's possible Elijah figured out what that step is, and maybe"—I held up the letters—"there's an answer in here."

Daniel nodded once. "Would you . . . would you like some company?"

"No!" The word shot out before I could stop it.

Bright pink exploded on Daniel's face. "Oh, uh . . . of course. I just thought you might, um, want a companion. And by companion, I meant you might want *me* to join you . . . to keep you safe, of course. You did say Marcus might show up at any time, and . . ." He trailed off, dabbing at his hairline.

One would think that seeing Daniel—the young man who'd had his fair share of pleasure in discomfiting *me*—at a loss for words would be wholly entertaining for me. Instead, it made my insides squirm.

"I-I know where the library is," he continued, still stammering. "I could keep a lookout while I guide you there. And I have research to do myself, so . . ." His eyes dropped to his shoes. "Never mind. It was rude of me to . . . to intrude. Forgive me."

He turned to go.

Maybe it was the way his cheeks burned scarlet or the way his shoulders dropped a few inches. Or maybe it was the way he said "forgive me"—the way he actually seemed to *mean* those two words. Or maybe I was simply desperate to get him away from the hotel before Jie told him the truth. But whatever the reason, the outcome was the same. "Daniel!"

He stopped and looked back.

"I . . . I don't actually know the way." I took a step toward him. "So an escort—and bodyguard—would be welcome."

And with those words, Daniel's lips cracked wide in a breathtaking smile.

My heart jolted, and a thousand emotions—emotions I didn't understand, didn't *want* to understand—exploded in my chest. But biggest of all was a hollow ache that seemed to start in my heart and radiate outward.

I jerked around before he could see the horror no doubt lining my face, and as I scurried for the entrance, all I could think was, *Why did I just agree to let him join me?*

And why, why, why did he have to go and smile?

CHAPTER FOURTEEN

Much to my chagrin, Daniel insisted on being a proper escort. Not only did we walk at a painfully slow, lady-like pace, but I was forced to rest my left forearm as lightly as possible in the crook of his elbow.

It was an excruciating walk across the street to the Tuileries, and if he had still been toting that dratted book on etiquette, I'd have commanded that he burn the thing. Thank *goodness* he had dropped it off with a footman on his way from the hotel. As we trailed the sidewalk beside the gardens, I inhaled deeply. The air tasted crisp—like new beginnings—in the way only an autumn afternoon can.

"Nice day," Daniel mumbled, guiding me east toward the burned-out palace.

I nodded. It was more than just a nice day. It was a stunning one. I wanted to skip and shout and kick at pebbles and pretend that this moment was nothing more than a September afternoon ripe with opportunity. Pretend there weren't monsters hiding in the shadows. That there weren't demons, or binding agreements, or hateful mothers, or best friends I had betrayed . . .

Or Daniel Sheridan holding my arm.

Gritting my teeth, I rammed it all from my mind. I refused to let my roiling emotions for him confuse me right then. *Focus on Paris,* I ordered myself, turning my face toward the gardens. The river's breeze caressed my cheeks, cooling the sun's heat, and though the chestnut trees beyond the fence whispered at me, their rusted-red leaves were too distant to offer any relief from the sun.

"Should I . . . buy you a parasol?" Daniel's voice shattered my calm.

I huffed out a breath. "Well, seeing as you have already given me one parasol I do not carry, a second would be a total waste, don't you . . ." I trailed off. His lips were crammed so tightly together, they had turned white. I had hurt him.

I gave a second, even heavier exhale. As much as Daniel had upset me, *he* wasn't the one I was angry with. Nor was he the one who was angry with me. So as we ambled past the charred palace, I said as cheerfully as possible, "I like your monocle."

Daniel blinked, and the monocle popped from his eye. Then, flushing as purple as a turnip, he shoved it back in place. "Thanks." His voice was gruff. "It was a gift. From Madame Marineaux."

"Oh!" I perked up. "She has wonderful taste, no?"

"Er . . . I suppose," he murmured, and we descended back into silence. Soon we were beyond the charred palace and to the Musée du Louvre. It was as the ruined Tuileries Palace would look if it were intact: all elaborate carvings, elegant archways, and lifelike statues beside each window.

I turned to Daniel. "Have you been inside the museum? To see the art?"

"No." Regret dragged at the word. "We . . . we haven't had much time for sightseeing. *But*"—he nodded emphatically, as if promising himself—"I will go in one day. See the art and the architecture that makes Paris, well . . . *Paris*."

I gawked at him. There was such passion in his voice—even with his affected manner of speech. His cheeks flushed, and he glanced down at me. "Sorry. I ain't . . . I *haven't* gotten to see much of the city. Yet."

"Right. Because you were in Germany?"

He nodded, his eyes brightening. As we crossed into the clamorous Rue de Rivoli and left the Louvre behind, he said— shouting to be heard over the traffic—"I worked with a general there. Von Zeppelin. He's the one who invented that airship." We reached the opposite sidewalk, and Daniel added in a normal volume, "Von Zeppelin's a genius, and it was a brilliant idea of the Marquis's to send me east."

His brows knit suddenly, and he looked at me. "But here I am talkin' . . . *talking* about myself. I should be asking about you. About your mother and Philadelphia."

With that simple subject change, it felt as if all the white-faced buildings on the street suddenly closed in on me. Their gray roofs blocked out the sun. The rattle and clop of traffic filled every space of my hearing—a drone of meaningless noise to play beneath the single thought running through my brain.

My daughter is now dead to me.

Somehow a response formed in my mouth. "Mama is not well."

Daniel stopped before an enormous, buzzing intersection and tugged me in front of him. The noise was almost deafening, and it was only the movement of his lips that told me what he said: "Still?"

I looked down and did not answer.

He hunched forward until his mouth was close to my ear. "Do you wish to speak of it?"

I started, suddenly realizing how close he stood. I had managed to avoid all thought of Mama for this long, to avoid all those black memories.

I *refused* to fall into that pit now.

I grabbed Daniel's arm, saying loudly, "Let's resume our walk."

Daniel frowned but did not argue. He guided me around the carriages and pedestrians until we finally squeezed through the other side of the intersection and into a narrow street. More beige buildings and gray roofs peered down at us. A baker here, a butcher there, and many small hotels. Eventually we reached a grassy square surrounded by great, old chestnuts.

A giant fountain of four bronze women pouring water rippled and churned with fallen red leaves.

"Library's just there," Daniel said, pointing to a white stone building across the street. Other than the ornate details around the windows and the letters over the door declaring Bibliotèque Nationale, it looked like the rest of Paris.

"Why are *all* the buildings this same beige stone?" I grumbled. "How does anyone know what building is what?"

"You sound annoyed." Daniel grinned. "They're all that same beige limestone because that's what's most available. Directly under the city." He stomped his foot. "There are quarries beneath all of Paris. And it's all built in the same style because it was all conjured up at the same time and led by one man. Georges Haussmann. He wanted to make Paris cleaner and more manageable."

I held my breath. The passion was back in his voice. He had been talking like the old Daniel. The *real* Daniel, and oh, how I wanted him to stay . . .

"So if we wanna get in the library," he continued, "we have to go 'round the other—" His words broke off, and he cleared his throat. "That is to say, the entrance is on the other side."

My stomach sank.

"There . . . is a large reading area that is separated from all the books," he added. "A capital place for studying."

Capital. I winced. Where had he even picked up that word? Well, I refused to give up hope yet. Perhaps if I could get him to talk more about architecture or his inventions, he would go back to himself. "What sort of research are you doing, Mr. Sheridan?"

"I have something that is almost finished. A surprise." He pulled me back into a walk, and we left the fountain behind. "What about you? What do you intend to research?"

Failure. I couldn't contain my sigh. "I guess I will look for any books on the Black Pullet. I think Elijah was in Paris when he first learned of the creature, so there must be something."

"Can you read French?"

My footsteps faltered. "No. I hadn't even thought of that!"

His eyes bunched up and his lips pressed tight, as if he was trying to fight off a laugh, but at last he gave up. He slapped his thigh. "Well, I can't read it either, Empress, so it looks like we won't be gettin' a whole lot done."

My lungs swelled, yet I found I couldn't breathe—was afraid to breathe. He had called me Empress, and he had spoken completely like himself. At last I beamed up at him. "I-in that case, we will just have to find what we can and have someone translate later."

"I reckon so." Daniel gave me a rakish wink, and I almost melted right there on the cobblestones.

"Maybe we can figure out a few words," I continued, trying—and failing—to hide the quaver in my voice. My heart was banging like a timpani. "For example, we know Elijah learned something in *Le Dragon Noir*. We can search indexes for it."

"Good idea." He nodded approvingly. "We can also cross-reference all mentions of *Le Dragon Noir* with the letters. Look for connections."

"Yes!" I squeezed his arm. "That's perfect. Now if we only can make the librarians understand us."

He doffed his hat playfully. "You just leave that to me, Empress."

Moments later, we reached the library's entrance on the other side. "This library is old," Daniel said as we passed through an archway into a flower-filled courtyard. People milled about, lost in their books, their feet crackling on the gravel. "And as it ages, it keeps getting bigger and bigger. More space and more books." He grinned and held open an enormous oak door for me. Beyond was a simple marble-floored hall with a winding staircase.

The moment I stepped inside, I eased out a breath I hadn't even known was trapped. Being in a library was like a gentle balm. No matter the city, no matter the time, you always know what you'll find. My home was halfway around the globe, yet here was something as familiar to me as myself.

The last time I had been in a library, Marcus had tried to kill me—but not even that could upset me now. I could forget about everything here. Let it fade into a meaningless whir in the back of my brain . . .

Daniel nodded to a dark wood door at my right. "This way, Empress." He set his heel against the door and turned to face me. "Prepare to be amazed." Then he rocked back, and the door creaked open.

My heart hitched. I gasped.

Spanning before me was row after row of desks. There was nothing to distract the devoted reader.

Gaping, I scuffed into the room and stared at the ceiling's domes and circular skylights. Then I caught sight of the walls, and somehow my mouth fell open even farther. From floor to ceiling were shelves—three *floors* of shelves, to be precise.

"That's not even the beginning," Daniel whispered. "*Le magasin central* is where most of the books are actually kept." He pointed straight ahead, to where the floor sank down into a recessed area of endless shelves.

"Sakes alive," I breathed. "Where do we even begin?"

He flashed his eyebrows and tugged me over to the nearest desk. "You can start by organizin' all your brother's letters. I'll find the reading material." He pulled out a gold-upholstered chair, helped me sit, and then swept me an easy bow.

This time I *did* melt. The instant he twirled around, I sank back into my seat like butter on a hot skillet. Whatever oddness had been between us, it was gone now. The air was easy. Daniel was simply Daniel, and I was simply Eleanor.

I laid out all my letters, and soon enough, Daniel came marching back with a stack of books teetering in his arms. He eased them onto the desk. "We'll start with these. The librarian's going to bring us anything else he finds."

Snagging the top book—*Étude des Grimoires*—I flipped to the index. Instantly, a giggle broke through my lips. "It's here!" I tapped the page. "*Le Dragon Noir.*"

"And here's *La poule noire.*" Daniel leaned over my shoulder and planted a finger on the opposite page. "The Black Pullet. Not a bad start, Empress."

All I could manage was a nod. He was so close—so close that I could see the stubble he had missed shaving. Could see each muscle in his jaw.

But it was the smell of him that almost undid me. Metal and salt and everything he had always smelled of came rushing into my nose, and with it came the memories. Swirling. Intense.

My back to the lamppost. His hands cradling my face. His lips pressed fiercely to mine.

A low moan escaped my mouth.

Daniel flinched, his face jerking toward me.

I clamped a hand over my mouth. *Oh God. Please say I did not make that noise aloud.*

His brow knit with concern. "Are you all right?"

I nodded frantically, my eyes nearly popping from my skull. "Hungry," I said behind my hand. "Sorry."

"Well, we can eat after we finish this." Grinning, he hooked his heel around the chair next to mine, drew it out, and plopped down.

I bowed over my book and avoided meeting his gaze. For several moments I could feel him watching me. It made me hot—miserably, boiling *hot*—and just when I thought I would explode with sweat and flushed cheeks, he turned away.

I drew in a long, shaky breath, and when I finally had the courage to glance at Daniel, it was to find him fully focused on my letters.

"Your brother," he drawled, "makes about as much sense to me as French politics."

"It makes no sense to me either."

"Who's this Ollie fellow, d'you suppose?"

"Uh . . ." I bit the inside of my mouth. What could I say?

"Or Monsieur Girard in the last one?" Daniel went on, oblivious to my sudden panic. "Or this random hackney driver?"

I sank back in my chair. "I-I don't know. Perhaps we should focus on the books first." I grabbed up the letters and shoved them aside with far more force than necessary. But again, Daniel didn't seem to notice. He simply shrugged, and in a matter of minutes we had sunk into a rhythm. Daniel scanned indexes, I marked pages, and the librarian—a soft-spoken Frenchman— continued to bring us book after book.

Minutes slid into hours, and after examining forty-seven different books and determining that only thirteen were useful, we came to the final text in our stack: *Napoléon et la campagne d'Égypte*.

Daniel flipped to the index. "I don't know what Napoleon would have to do with grimoires, but we might as well . . ." He trailed off.

"What?" I asked.

"It *is* here. One page about *Le Dragon Noir*. Page fifty-seven." He thumbed through until he found the right page, and then we both read the passage.

"Here." I tapped the middle paragraph and haltingly tried to translate. "'Many Egyptians . . . thought Napoleon had a necro-mancer . . .'"

"'But,'" Daniel said, following along, "'there was never'—I don't know what that word is."

"Me neither, but look here." My eye caught on a paragraph further down on the page—on a French phrase I knew well. "'The soldier,'" I continued translating, "'who was famous for . . . for discovering *Le Dragon Noir* was a known necromancer.'" I straightened. "Does that mean the grimoire was found in Egypt?"

"Sure sounds like it. And look: the soldier's name is Jacques Girard."

"Monsieur Girard!" I snatched the letters off the table and found the last one, sent from Egypt. But my shoulders drooped as I read aloud, "'Monsieur Girard was not home today. I fear I wrote the wrong address. If I cannot find him, then I will have no choice but to find the pages.'"

"Huh," Daniel said. "It *could* mean something or it could just be someone with the same last name."

I groaned.

Daniel shot me a concerned look. "Don't get frustrated, Empress. Why don't we head back to the hotel now? I'll have the librarian send the books to the lab."

I nodded, too tired to worry about Jie—or Joseph—waiting for me at Le Meurice. While Daniel dealt with the books, I wearily gathered up my letters and considered this latest information. Elijah wrote that he needed pages. Those had to be the missing pages from *Le Dragon Noir*. The ones that had been displayed at the Centennial Exhibition—and the whole reason Elijah had even come back to Philadelphia all those months ago.

There was some other connection here, though. Something I was missing.

But at least I could be certain of one thing: whatever was hiding in these letters, I was going to find it. Even if it meant consulting Oliver on it. Yes, it was time to share the messages with my demon.

Daniel and I left the library, moving as slowly as when we had come, but now it was different—now I *wanted* the moments to drag by. Soon enough we would reach the hotel. Reach Jie and Joseph . . . and reach the truth.

But not yet. For now I could still wrap myself in this. In *Daniel.*

As we ambled past the chestnut-lined square, I suddenly realized something. "Daniel!" I yanked him to a stop. "We did none of *your* research! I'm so sorry—I took over all of your time."

He smiled shyly. "I didn't actually have any research to do, Empress. I just wanted to . . . Here, come with me." He pulled me into the square and over the grass to the fountain's edge. As the water poured out from the bronze women's vases, he slowed to a stop and angled himself toward me. "Will you be at the ball tomorrow night?"

"Yes," I said slowly. "Why do you ask?"

He shrugged one shoulder, gulping furiously. When he didn't say anything for several moments, I said, "Is that all you wan—"

"I need to apologize," he blurted.

My eyebrows shot up. "Oh?"

"I shouldn't have been so rude this morning. In front of the hotel." His eyes flicked down. "Although you *were* the one to lose your temper."

"Lose my temper? I only lost it after *you* . . ." I let my words fade. His lips were twitching up. "Oh, I see. You're *teasing* me."

He reached out and popped my chin with his thumb.

I gave a mock gasp. "How dare you, sir! Touch me again, and I shall call the foxes."

"Foxes? As in the police?" He fought off a laugh—and failed. "I never pegged you for such criminal language, Empress."

I rolled my eyes. "And I'm not as highfalutin as you might think."

"Listen to you! 'Highfalutin.'" He whistled through his teeth. "Next thing I know, you'll be swearing and spitting."

"Only because I learned it from you." I gave him a superior smile. "And if *anyone* here is highfalutin, it's you, Daniel Sheridan." I grabbed hold of his monocle and tugged it to my eye—but of course it was laced around his neck, and I wound up tugging *him* to me too.

My heart stopped. His face was only inches from mine. I could feel his breath, gently brushing my cheeks. I could see every line in his jaw and every shade in his lips—and oh, his lips. They were so close.

"Eleanor." His voice was faint and rough. "There's something I need to tell you."

"Yes?" I dragged my eyes from his lips and met his gaze.

It almost undid me. I could see the longing in them—see the desire in the way his pupils widened and shrank in time to his breathing.

"That night in the hospital, when you asked me if I—"

"Eleanor!" a voice roared.

245

As one, our heads whipped toward the sound. Stalking toward Daniel and me, his cheeks bright and his eyes glossy, was none other than Oliver. "Eleanor!"

Acid churned into my throat. Daniel jerked away from me.

"What the devil are you doing here?" Oliver shouted, almost upon us. His features were masked with fury.

Daniel pushed in front of me. "Who the hell are you?"

Oliver ignored him, staring at me over Daniel's shoulder. "I've been waiting around for you for hours, El! Then I come here, and what do I find?"

Daniel whirled around to me. "Do you know this man?"

"I-I . . ."

"Of course she *knows* me," Oliver spat. "I'm her—"

"Hush," I hissed. Panic beat wildly in my chest. "You're drunk!"

Daniel recoiled. "So you *do* know him. Is he your beau?"

Oliver opened his mouth, but I shot him a fierce glare. "Don't, Ollie."

"Ollie?" Daniel repeated, somehow standing up even taller. "From the letters?"

"Yes," Oliver said at the same instant I cried, "No!"

"You were her brother's friend," Daniel said, his eyes on Oliver. "And I . . . I've seen you somewhere before. . . . At the hotel—that's it, isn't it? You've been in the hotel." He turned to me, his eyes creased with pain. "He *is* your beau. How else can you explain this?"

"Please," I begged. "It isn't like that at all."

"God, I've been an *idiot*." He retreated two steps, his head shaking. "A new hand, a new man. I don't know who you are anymore."

"Yes, you do!"

"No, *Miss Fitt*." He wrenched his top hat low over his face. "You're not . . . you're not who I thought you were."

There was so much venom in his voice—venom I didn't deserve—that all I could do was stare. *He* was the one who had changed. Not me. Why couldn't he—or Jie—see that?

But I never had a chance to tell him. Before I could speak, he pivoted sharply and strode off—away from the square, away from Oliver, and away from me.

I immediately rounded on the demon. "How could you do this to me? You stupid drunk!"

"El, I—"

"Don't," I shouted. "Do not speak to me. Do not come near me. Don't even *look* at me." I stomped away, but I only made it several steps before looking back. "Is this what you wanted all along? For me to have no one but you?"

"No. Of course not." His eye shone, but with emotion or gin, I couldn't say. "I was waiting for you, El. Waiting for you to . . . to come . . . and I followed our bond here, so—"

"I do not care," I said softly. "Two of my friends are gone, and it's all because of you."

And with fury and shame pounding in my ears, I twisted around and left.

CHAPTER FIFTEEN

On my way back to the Hotel Le Meurice, I stopped by a post office. A telegram from Allison, a note from Mary—anything from home would have been welcome. I just wanted to know I wasn't alone.

But I *was* alone. There were no messages for me.

So I trudged to the hotel and was soon clambering up the main steps. On the second floor, I slowed and glanced into the lab. The door was ajar, the white curtains drawn back, and Joseph was within, focused on a stack of papers.

As if he sensed me, his gaze flicked up. A furrow dug into his brow. He beckoned to me.

And I realized with crushing relief that Jie had not yet told him about Oliver. *You should tell him,* my conscience whispered. But I knew I would not. He was the only Spirit-Hunter left who did not hate me . . . and I wanted to cling to that for as long as I could. Who knew how much time I had before I was on my own—left to face Marcus by myself?

So, with a fortifying breath, I stepped to the doorway and poked my head in. "I thought you were away."

"My business ended early. Perhaps *now* would be a good time to train." He rubbed the back of his neck. "It is very important that you learn to fight your magic."

"Right." I slunk in—but almost instantly stopped again. Four waist-high, pine crates stood in a row beneath the windows.

"Daniel's latest inventions," Joseph explained. "Yet you have not seen our other . . . *decoration*." He flourished a hand to the far-right table. Atop it lay a man-shaped mound beneath a white sheet.

"The butler?" I asked.

"*Wi.*"

Despite being an incredibly morbid reaction, the corpse's presence made me smile. Madame Marineaux must have remembered, even if I had not.

Joseph hurried to the body, waving for me to follow. I gathered up my skirts and warily approached, the faint stench of carrion drifting into my nose. He waved to the corpse's head. "So far, the ears and eyes are the only regions I have found that are desecrated."

"You inspected the whole body?"

"Not yet. I cleaned one of the ear wounds. I thought perhaps I would uncover a ritualistic way in which the organ had been removed—some special incision I could find referenced in my books." He ran a gloved hand along his jaw. "But I found nothing."

"May I?"

At Joseph's nod, I gulped in clean air and yanked back the sheet. Up close and a day older, the butler managed to look even worse than he had before. Though his mouth was clamped shut, the waxy skin around his lips had stretched to the point of ripping—presumably from chomping so desperately.

And I was most assuredly *not* standing on the cleaned side. Crusted blood was all over the butler's face, a layer of brown streaks, and his ear . . .

Placing a gloved hand over my mouth, I moved in close. Through the jagged flesh—it had not been a clean cut—was the beige gleam of the man's skull.

It was sickening . . . and yet *fascinating*. To think that a person's blood could have so much power—

I straightened, horrified by my thoughts. This man had been murdered. I ought to be repulsed. Disturbed.

But you aren't, my conscience nagged.

Yes, I am, I insisted. *I* am.

I swallowed tightly. "Do you think he was dead when he was cut up?"

Joseph winced. "Judging by the amount of blood around the wounds, he was alive during this procedure."

My stomach flipped—that *was* truly horrifying. "The poor, poor man," I murmured, and my eyes settled on the white powder on his shoulders. I had noticed it at Madame Marineaux's, except now there seemed to be much less of it. I motioned to it. "Do you know what this is from?"

"*Non*. We have seen something like it on several bodies, but it could be anything. Dust from an old building, crumbling paint—there is no way to tell. These Hungry cover so much ground and are so violent." He exhaled loudly and replaced the sheet over the man's destroyed face. "I wish we had more facts with which to work instead of only half clues and ignorant musings. The only thing of which I am certain is that these sacrifices *must* be the work of a demon."

A demon. Sacrifices.

My stomach curdled. What if it *was* Oliver? I had no proof he had been in America—and a three-week lull in *les Morts*? That was enough time to leave Paris and return. . . .

I towed my mind back to the lab—I would deal with that darkness later—and, glancing at Joseph, I tried to don a happy face. "So . . . shall we begin this first lesson?"

"Yes." He scratched absently at his cheek. "To begin, you must first understand why using self-power is so dangerous. It is no different from opium—each time you draw on your spiritual energy, your soul rots."

"Rots?" I repeated doubtfully. He had said something similar the day before, and even knowing that the magic was addictive, I still found the idea of a festering soul to be rather . . . dramatic. I told Joseph as much.

"But nonetheless, it is true." He scrubbed roughly at his scars, motioning with his other hand that we should return to the main table. "It is addictive, Eleanor, and as with any addiction, one's morals degrade."

"So what you're really saying," I declared as we moved to

the stools, "is that my scruples will rot—not my soul."

Joseph's jaw clenched. We reached the table, but neither of us sat. "Eleanor, look at what became of Marcus. Of Elijah. They lost all sense of what was right and wrong—"

"But I am *not* Marcus, and I am *not* Elijah." The ferocity of my words surprised me, but I couldn't seem to stop them. "Self-power is fast—natural—and it doesn't keep me tethered to a machine. Spells have so many uses, Joseph."

"You are right that I cannot raise a body or make a phantom limb, yet I can blast away the Dead. That is all that I need to do."

"But that is limiting."

"Listen to yourself," he hissed. "Do you not hear how the magic controls you, even now?"

"That isn't true," I said, teeth gritting. "I have fought and *fought* my magic today—just as you ordered. I have not used it once."

He relaxed slightly. "Good. I am glad you say that. You must keep fighting. All you need is electricity."

No, I thought. *Electricity cannot stop Marcus when he comes.* But I did not say this. Instead, I scanned the room for some other evidence of electricity's limitations. My eyes landed on the butler's corpse, and an idea hit—something I *did* want to do yet could not achieve, even with necromancy.

I swept my skirts to the side and took a seat. "Can I talk to a spirit with electricity?"

His eyes thinned. "Why do you ask?"

"If we could talk to *les Morts*, we could know who killed them. No more running aimlessly around the city. Or," I continued, another idea forming, "there's a soldier from Napoleon's army that might know something useful." I quickly explained what Daniel and I had found at the library. "So you see, Joseph? We could solve everything if we could only talk to these people. Is that possible with your method?"

"Talk to these *Dead*," Joseph corrected. "You must remember that they are no longer people. Their desires and dreams are not what they were in life. Nonetheless, you do make a good point." He bent over the table and grabbed a thick, gray book called *A Treatise on Spectres and All Other Manifestations of Spiritual Energy*. "I, myself, have never heard of a way to do this—even with spells—yet that does not mean one does not exist. Perhaps we can find something in this book." He glanced up at me, waiting.

He was offering me a truce, and though I didn't agree with Joseph, I *did* know when to stop fighting.

I nodded, and with a hesitant smile Joseph pushed his stool close to mine, sat down, and flipped back the book's cover. But we barely made it through three pages before we were interrupted.

"Monsieur Boyer," said the Marquis. "I have a meeting you must attend." He limped into the lab with neither a knock nor an apology.

"Meeting?" Joseph repeated, sliding off his stool.

"*Oui*. I realize you have only just returned, but it is . . . how do you say? Critical. Several senators are discussing zee new measures you suggested."

Joseph straightened. "My suggestions for working with the police?"

"*Oui.*" The Marquis leaned on his cane, his chest heaving as if the climb to the second-floor lab had left him entirely spent. He bobbed his head at me. "*Mademoiselle*, I hope you do not mind. I can call Madame Marineaux to attend you, if you wish."

"Oh yes!" I cried, instantly excited. My last time spent with the Madame had been so happy . . . even if I couldn't remember what exactly had passed. "I would love to see her again—that is, if she is not too busy, of course."

"*Je ne pense pas.* I do not zink she will mind—not for you." He stroked his mustache and tilted almost conspiratorially toward me. "She told me you remind her of my sister."

Pleasure fluttered through my chest. "That is quite a compliment."

"*C'est vrai.*" He nodded. "My sister was a wonderful woman. Actually"—he turned to Joseph—"she lived in New Orleans for a bit. Did you ever know a LeJeunes?"

A line moved down Joseph's forehead. "No, I do not recall anyone by that name."

"Too bad," the Marquis said heavily. "You would have liked her." He spread his arms, holding out his cane. "Everyone liked Claire. She had—what is the word? *Présence.*"

The Marquis continued speaking, but I did not hear. My gaze was locked on his cane. It looked different than the last time I had seen it. Three of the fingers had furled in, as if the hand were about to make a fist.

"Does my cane bother you?"

I blinked, suddenly noticing that the Marquis had stopped talking. I gave him an embarrassed grin. "Oh no . . . not at all. I

255

merely thought it looked different."

His mustache wiggled. "Different?"

"Were its fingers not more like this the other day?" I mimicked an open hand.

He snorted a laugh. "I do not zink so, *Mademoiselle*. It is ivory." He flicked a carved fingernail. "It does not bend."

"That's why I was surprised. I could have sworn it had changed shape."

"I zink you are, eh . . . *imagining* zings." He gave me an indulgent smile. "Perhaps you ought to sleep."

"Yes," I mumbled, confused. "Perhaps I ought."

"In zat case, I will tell Madame Marineaux not to keep you up *too* late." LeJeunes shoved to his feet, his eyes shifting to Joseph. "Come, Monsieur Boyer."

I hopped off my stool and curtsied good-bye. As the Marquis shuffled from the room, Joseph turned to me. "I am sorry, Eleanor, but I must attend this. If we could get a unit of patrolmen to help us—it might be precisely what we need to corner the demon behind *les Morts*."

"I understand."

"Perhaps you can study this book until Madame Marineaux arrives, and then we will talk about it in the morning."

"Yes, I will." I gave him a tight smile.

"And remember: you must keep fighting these magical urges. Please—I beseech you."

"All right," I said, nodding, but as he gathered his hat and coat, I couldn't help but bite my lip. Joseph had never cast a spell, so what did he *really* know?

And while I did not agree with Oliver either—sacrifices were absolutely not an option—at least with my self-power I could do more than simply banish the Dead. I was caught between doing what might be morally right (at least according to Joseph) and what might actually *work*.

For the problem before us was larger than *les Morts* or a renegade demon. The ultimate problem was a necromancer whose power had been crafted in life and honed in death. The ultimate problem was Marcus, and would Joseph's methods stand against him?

No. They would not.

With a determined set in my jaw, I turned to the book on specters and read it—right there in the lab with a butler's corpse to keep me company. It was filled with dull language but was at least written recently (an 1874 publication, according to the title page) and was also incredibly thorough. Necromancy, voodoo, shamanism—any and every form of magic pertaining to spirits was mentioned within its gray covers.

I scanned the chapter headings for something about speaking to ghosts, and with surprising ease, I found information written in as dry a manner as the rest of the book.

Summoning spirits is ill-advised under any circumstances. For one, ghosts are rarely amenable to leaving the earthly realm once there. For two, the amount of magical training and power needed is extensive. Necromancers, for example, must rely on blood sacrifices to rip a temporary hole in the curtain. Voodoo requires group sessions of up to a hundred

*priests to open a hole. Ultimately, all methods are likely
to incite the attention of the Hell Hounds (also known as
barghest, black shuck, or Cŵn Annwn, see page forty-seven
for more detail).*

*However, mediums of the mid-1800s discovered a
method that allows the curtain to remain closed and the
ghost to be "called" via a séance. One must know the
spirit's name and time of death (the latter information used
to adjust the strength of the "call." A longer-dead ghost
will require more power and therefore more people).*

I gnawed my lip. That was it? A séance? It certainly sounded
harmless enough. My own mama had hosted séances for years
(with no success) in an attempt to speak to my dead father.
Admittedly, she had also allowed Marcus to enter the earthly
realm during one of these sessions, but *I* wouldn't be so foolish.

And I had magic on my side. *So let Marcus or any other spirit
come.* I smiled, but almost instantly my lips twisted down.

Why hadn't Joseph and Oliver known about this method? It
was so easy. . . .

A gentle buzz suddenly twirled in my gut, and I knew without looking that Oliver was near.

Two breaths later, the lab door cracked open.

"What do you want?" I snapped. My eyes never left the
page.

"To talk. To . . . apologize."

"Well, I don't accept."

"I messed up, El."

"Yes, yes you did." My teeth gnashed together, and against my will, I glanced up. Oliver stood, head hanging, in the doorway. "Why did you do that?"

"I . . . I was drunk."

"Really? Because you seem quite sober now."

"Drunk and jealous," he whispered. His yellow eyes crawled up to mine. "You're my only friend. My family."

"And?" I slammed the book shut and stood. "I have no family either, Oliver. Did you forget that? Did you forget that my father is dead, my brother is dead, and my mother has renounced me? I have no money, no home, and no chance at a real life. And now—*now*—the only three people who are able to look beyond all that . . ." My fingers clenched into fists. "I am about to lose them too."

Oliver hunched even further into himself. "You still have me."

"That's not *enough*!"

"It was enough for Elijah. He and I used to do *everything* together."

"And I am *not* Elijah."

"I know," he murmured. "Trust me: I *know*."

"What does that mean?"

"It means," he retorted, his spine unfurling, "you don't want to learn how to free me. It means you run off with Madame Something-or-other and silly inventors when I'm right here waiting to teach you. Elijah never missed a chance to learn more. Now, do you accept my apology or not?"

"I do not accept." I glared at him. "One minute you behave like my oldest chum—the spitting image of Elijah. Then the next minute you're manipulating me. I don't trust you, Oliver."

He sniffed. "I never asked you to."

"No, you're right. You did not." I got to my feet. "Yet for some reason you still seem to *expect* a great deal from me. Elijah might have made you his companion, Oliver, but for me you are nothing but a tool."

Pain flashed across his face, but it was quickly replaced by a smug arch to his eyebrow. "I see what you're trying to do. This has nothing to do with that Daniel fellow at all. You're afraid of something, and you're taking it out on me. So what is it, El?" He left the doorway and strode to me, only stopping once he was inches away. "What is it you're afraid of?"

His eyes held mine—daring me to look away. I did not. "Are you the demon raising *les Morts*?" My voice was barely a whisper. "Tell me."

"And if I do not?" He sneered. "Will you *command* me? Command your tool?"

"Yes, I will."

"So do it then." He rolled his eyes. "You're being ridiculous, though. You know I can't do any magic without your command."

"How do I know that?"

"Well, I suppose you do *not* know for certain." He opened his arms. "But go ahead. Ask me for the truth. Just be prepared for the consequences."

My heart lurched. "What consequences?"

"In a few hours, once Joseph knows about my existence, I really *will* be all you have left. So even if I am the demon behind *les Morts*, do you truly want to know?"

I thinned my eyes. "Now I see exactly what *you're* trying to do. If I command you, you will hold it against me—hang it over my head as leverage. Elijah used to play the same childish game." I flipped my hand out and in a mocking voice said, "'Oh, El, you *owe* me. Remember that time you blamed me for stealing the cherries?'" I backed away from Oliver, turning dismissively toward the butler's corpse. "Well, I do *not* truly think you're behind *les Morts*. And I won't fall for your tricks. Now come here. I want you to take a look at this corpse."

At that word, Oliver's footsteps sounded behind me, and together we went to the white sheet.

"This is one of *les Morts*?" Oliver grabbed the edge of the sheet and yanked back. "I bet I can—oh, blessed Eternity." His hand flew to his mouth, and his face turned a putrid green.

"Does it bother you?" I set my mouth in a stern line. "*You*, the boy who wanted me to sacrifice an animal?"

"When I said sacrifice," he said, his voice muffled by his fingers, "I did not mean this atrocity."

"How am I supposed to know that? Now, inspect this corpse and tell me if you recognize the spell."

Oliver gulped and slowly lowered his hands. "I cannot tell much by simply looking. There are thousands of spells it could be. . . ."

"But?"

"But if you command me to, I can sense for the magic."

"Will you be *angry* if I command you?"

He shook his head once.

And at that movement the hunger flared in my belly, so sharp and so fierce I could not breathe.

You promised Joseph you would resist. Except this was vital information, wasn't it? If we could learn the spell, we would be one step closer to stopping *les Morts*. I *had* to use Oliver's magic.

I wet my lips, and before guilt could stop me, I said, "Sense for the spell on this corpse. *Sum veritas.*" The magic curled over me, pleasant and warm, before sliding off me like smoke.

Oliver's eyes flashed blue. Then he snapped them shut, and his brows drew together.

"Well?" I asked. "Can you feel it?"

"Give me a minute," he growled. But it only took him a few seconds to begin nodding. "There's something there . . . a faint trace of power around the ears and eyes . . . and the tongue." His eyelids lifted, and, using the edge of the sheet, he eased open the corpse's jaw.

We both leaned forward and peered inside. "The tongue is still there," I said.

"Yes, but look at how slashed and swollen it is."

"Is that not from all the chomping?"

Oliver's head flicked once to the side. "No. It was cut. Drained of blood."

I recoiled. "What does that mean, then? Can you recognize the spell?"

"I think I can, yes." He straightened, and when his eyes met mine, they were winced with revulsion. "But it's bad, El. Very bad. I . . . I think it's a compulsion spell."

That sounded familiar. I kneaded my wrist, trying to figure out *why*. Then I remembered. "You mentioned that on the boat, didn't you? You said to control a person's actions, you had to sacrifice body parts." I looked down at the butler. "So this spell is meant to control someone's ears and eyes and tongue?"

"Yes, what they see, hear, and say . . . but not just one person, El."

"What do you mean?"

"I mean there have been over seventy victims."

The full weight of his words slammed into me, and I stumbled back. "Someone has cast seventy-two compulsion spells."

"Except . . ."—he waved toward the corpse's head—"there are still traces of the magic on this body, which means the spiritual energy from this corpse has not yet been used. It's still with the body—hoarded, almost."

I scrunched up my face. "I don't understand. How is that possible?" I took the sheet from his hands and replaced it over the butler's face.

"It's possible with an amulet—an object that holds a spell. The necromancer will build the spell over time, adding more and more spiritual energy to the object. Then one day when he's ready, he leaves the amulet where he wants it to cast, he goes far away from the danger area, and then . . ." Oliver's hands spread wide. "He lets the spell release."

"Blazes." I swayed back on my heels. "So it's an undetonated bomb."

"Exactly."

"Does this mean we are up against seventy-two amulets?"

"More likely we're up against *one* amulet with seventy-two spells inside."

"So if Joseph . . . or I wanted to stop it, could we?"

"Not easily. Possibly not at all." He circled his hands on his temples. "Whenever this necromancer—or demon—finally decides to cast the spell, he'll gain compulsion over seventy-two people."

I hugged my arms to my stomach, feeling ill. "Seventy-two people?"

"That or a single person for—well, I would estimate at *least* seventy-two days."

"I don't understand."

"It's simple, really. A compulsion spell is only in effect temporarily. The stronger the necromancer, the longer the spell. If he wanted to control a person for an extended period of time, he'd need multiple spells." Oliver swung his head side to side, his face grim. "But that's not even the worst of it, El. A compelled victim won't be able to tell when they're possessed . . . and nor will *we*."

It was only moments after Oliver explained the horrors of an amulet to me that a steward came to fetch me. Madame Marineaux had arrived and so I dismissed Oliver and met the Madame in my room.

Her visit was as wonderful as I had hoped. The perfect

distraction to the thoughts—and fears—roiling through me.

I had to tell Joseph about the amulet and the compulsion spells. I also had to figure out what I would do—what Oliver and I would do—as soon as Joseph learned about the demon.

But all those worrisome thoughts faded into the background the moment Madame Marineaux arrived. We drank delicious French wine on my balcony and talked about the ball the next evening, the places I wanted to see, and . . . well, I could not remember precisely what else. The wine must have clouded my head at that point. Either way, I awoke the next morning feeling alive, alert, and ready to take on the day.

I could face Joseph. I *had* to face Joseph, and in the end, wouldn't I rather the truth come from me than from Jie?

However, as I descended the main stairwell, my jaw set and my stride determined, I was accosted by outraged bellows from the floor below. My resolve instantly shattered.

"I can't believe it!" Daniel roared. "You didn't consult me in this at all."

I paused on the middle landing and craned my neck around. Through the lab's open door and curtains, I could see Daniel standing beside his crates, waving a crowbar wildly. Jie was nowhere to be seen.

Joseph sat on his stool, his back rod straight. He lifted his hands. "I do not need to consult you, Daniel. I am in charge, and there was never any question of her joining us or not. Her skills are an asset to the team."

"Skills?" Daniel shoved the crowbar into a crate top. "What

skills? Necromancy? Lying?"

I gulped. They were discussing me . . . but did they know of Oliver?

Joseph began ticking off on his fingers. "She fought an entire cemetery in Philadelphia. She helped us at Madame Marineaux's. Yes, she has a great deal of self-control to learn, but she is undeniably powerful."

They don't know what Oliver is yet.

"I have never seen anyone with so much natural magic," Joseph continued. "Once she learns my methods, she will be incredible."

"More like disgusting," Daniel spat. "You're letting a necromancer into the group. Just think about that."

Fury cramped my gut. Daniel had no right to say such things, for he had no idea what I had been through. *No idea.*

"She has stopped," Joseph declared. "She fights the call of black magic—and ultimately, Daniel, it is none of your concern what magic she uses. I am in charge, and I say she is in the group. I expect Marcus to arrive any day—any *moment*—and we need her power, no matter what form it is in. As such, when she arrives, I expect you to control your temper."

A strangled cry came next, but other than that Daniel made no more sounds.

I dug my palms in my eyes and waited until the normal murmur of conversation picked up. Then, my hands shaking, I strode as steadily as I could down the remaining steps and into the lab.

"Ah, Eleanor," Joseph said with a tired smile. He waved to

a stool. "Have a seat." The butler's corpse still lay on the farthest table. And though the windows were all opened, it wasn't enough to kill the body's stench.

"Where's Jie?" I asked.

Joseph glanced at me sidelong. "We assumed she must be with you. She left a note"—he gestured to a slip of paper on the windowsill—"that said she was going out."

"But that was yesterday afternoon," Daniel said gruffly.

"And she has not come back yet?" I gaped at them. "Aren't you worried? We should look for her!"

"It's Jie," Daniel said. "She can take care of herself."

"One does not simply 'go out' for an entire day," I snapped. "Not Jie, at least."

Joseph scratched his neck. "I will send out one of our new patrolmen to check for her."

"Please," I begged.

"Yes. I will do it the minute I leave the lab."

My shoulders sank. I had not even realized I had held them tensed. Perhaps I was overreacting—Jie *could* take care of herself, after all.

"So," I said to Joseph, "I suppose you received the patrol force you wanted?"

Joseph bowed his head in acknowledgment. "We did. And did you learn anything about contacting spirits?"

"Actually, yes." I swallowed. "I read about séances."

"Séances," Joseph murmured. "They are very hard to successfully employ, and there are certainly dangers involved.

However, it *is* an avenue worth researching. But first . . ." He set his hands on the table. "Daniel, I would very much like to see your newest inventions."

I, however, had no desire to see them. I stood. "Perhaps I should go—"

"*Non*!" Joseph's hand shot up. "This equipment is as much yours as mine, and I believe it will help you control your powers." He gave an encouraging nod. "Look at these items as your tools."

"Um, all right." I reclaimed my seat, and Joseph motioned for Daniel to continue.

"Well, this box"—Daniel nudged his boot against the middle crate—"has two new influence machines. Nothing exciting." His voice was coated with the odd, stiff affectation once more. "This other box contains the pulse pistols." He shoved his crowbar into the crate he'd been prying at before I entered the room. As the nails squeaked, he said, "Do you remember the pulse bombs in Philadelphia? The dynamite propels a magnetic rod, thereby creating an electromagnetic pulse. That pulse laid the Dead to rest."

"Quite useful and ingenious." Joseph's words were overenthusiastic, as if he was trying very hard to keep Daniel pleased.

"Useful," Daniel agreed, "but slow." He yanked the final nail from the crate. "You had to have matches, and you had to wait for the fuse to burn. Well, no more of that." He hefted off the lid and swept aside straw, revealing a device shaped like a revolver. Copper wire coiled around the barrels. "These are the pulse pistols. No more wasting time. You merely pull the trigger, and the Dead go down. There are two limitations, though. First, the range isn't as wide as the bombs." He tapped a munitions box beside the gun. "Second, the guns only hold one shot at a time, so either you carry a few loaded pistols all the time or you hope you can reload faster than the Dead can reach you."

That's quite a limitation, I thought. And beneath that, another thought flashed: *I don't need that.*

Daniel tossed a pistol to Joseph, who caught it deftly and held it to the light.

"Incredible. This would have made things at Madame Marineaux's easier, I daresay." He glanced at me, a hopeful smile on his lips.

And that smile rankled me. A great deal. Why was he pretending to be pleased with me when the truth was he considered me and my magic an abomination?

Daniel strode to the last crate, his spine straightening. "This last invention is something I'm real . . . I mean . . . something of *which* I'm very proud." He spent a few minutes working the nails out. Once the lid was off, he pushed aside the straw and dug out an ornately designed, cream-colored box. It was much like a lady's hatbox, all soft designs and curves. Instantly, pain swept over his face. He dropped the box roughly on the floor. It hit with a heavy thud.

"What is in there?" Joseph asked.

"Nothing." Daniel's voice was barely above a whisper. "It's . . . it's empty."

Joseph gave me a glance, and I tugged at my earlobe. That box was most assuredly *not* empty, but before I could ponder what might be inside, Daniel fished out a second, smaller box. He placed it tenderly on the table and slid off the top.

My eyes widened.

Inside, nestled on a velvet cushion, was a crystal the size of my fist. Though it was rough and uncut, it still glittered like sunlight on water.

Daniel slid his hand beneath the velvet pillow and withdrew what looked like a crooked, copper wrench. On one end was a clamp and on the other was a spring-loaded handle.

"I call this a crystal clamp," he said. "It latches onto the crystal like so. . . ." He spread the clamps wide and set the crystal within. Then he clasped the handle. "Now, you squeeze this. That in turn squeezes the crystal and creates an electric current. As long as you're squeezing, you have electricity."

I gasped as comprehension hit me. "It's like my amethyst earrings. Piezoelectricity, right?"

Daniel's eyes flicked uncertainly to mine. "You . . . you remember that?"

Of *course* I remembered it. The day he had taught me that word was the day he'd carried me home in an unconscious heap. The day he had given me a new parasol. The day I had finally started to hope for more than just friendship . . .

"I am not sure I remember." Joseph drummed his fingers on the table. "Though I do recall something about squeezing quartz and getting an electric current, *non?*"

270

"Exactly." Daniel nodded. "When you squeeze quartz, the mechanical stress creates an electric charge. That charge moves through the copper clamp and into your arm. The copper also magnifies the charge, and of course, the bigger the crystal, the bigger the initial current. It's not as powerful as a spark from the influence machine, but it should be enough to stop a corpse or two."

"*Kaptivan*," Joseph said, gently taking the contraption into his gloved hands. "A portable source of electricity."

"You should try it out," Daniel suggested.

"I cannot." He laid the device back in its box. "If I take in the electricity, I must shoot it back out again. I learned *that* the hard way." He shot me a smile, as if I might understand.

I *did* understand—all too well. Yet I had assumed it would be different with external power. Instead, it would seem that no matter the source, no magic could be held indefinitely. You had to use it.

And that was simply one more limitation to electricity.

"Why don't *you* try it," Daniel said, his eyes settling on me. "I bet . . ."

He gritted his teeth as if he didn't want to finish.

"Bet what?" I pressed. "Tell me what you were going to say, Daniel."

"I was gonna say," he snarled, "that *you* should try it out because I bet that new hand of yours can squeeze this clamp like a real professional."

I stiffened. "Joseph said it's dangerous."

"Right." He folded his arms over his chest. "Silly of me to forget."

"You *want* me to hurt myself, is that it?"

"I didn't say that, did I? Thing is, I'm just startin' to wonder, *Miss Fitt*"—his words came out faster and louder—"what's so great about that phantom hand of yours."

"Stop." Heat blazed up my body.

"What amazing tricks can it do? Can it stop the Dead? Or—I know—can it *raise* the Dead?"

I knew Daniel wanted to hurt me like I had hurt him, but this time he'd gone too far. I pushed onto my feet and marched around the table toward him.

"Show us some tricks," he said, wiggling his fingers at me. "Show us your amazing necromancy with that shiny, new *hand*."

"You jealous, spiteful *ass*," I hissed. "Do you want to know what my phantom hand is good for, Daniel?"

"Please," he said with a sneer.

"This." I slapped him straight across the cheek, so hard that even with my glove, the blow flamed up my arm.

Then, before he or Joseph could react, I turned on my heels and stormed from the lab.

CHAPTER SIXTEEN

I had just reached my room, ready to pound my pillow into a pulp, when the Dead alarm rang. I rushed to my window. A scruffy boy was yanking the bell rope and hollering, "*Les Morts! Les Morts!*"

"Number seventy-three," I murmured, but I didn't go down to the lab.

Nor did anyone come up for me.

Minutes later, just as I moved away from the window, two top hats hurried into a carriage, and I couldn't help but note that they did *not* carry an influence machine. I supposed Joseph trusted Daniel's newer, more portable inventions.

I also couldn't help but notice Jie's absence. They might not have been worried about her, but I was.

Yes, I knew Jie could take care of herself. I had seen her barrel through a line of corpses with nothing more than a casual flying kick. Yet why would she leave? And do it all of a sudden with nothing more than a vague note? It was not like her.

So I went to the hotel's front desk and asked if anyone had seen her. They had not. I asked in the restaurant, the men's smoking lounge, and even in the shops nearby. But no one had seen a bald Chinese girl dressed like a boy. Not since yesterday.

As I strode back into Le Meurice's marble foyer, wishing I had read the note she'd left for Joseph, a voice trilled, "Eleanor!"

I whirled around to find a violet-clad Laure hurrying toward me, her lips at their usual mischievous slant.

"*C'est vrai?*" She whipped a newspaper from her purse. "Is it true? The *Galignani's Messenger* says you and that balloon pilot 'ad a fight." She glanced down at the tiny print. "Ah, *mais oui*, the pilot and a second man fought over you in the Square Louvois. The second man was Oliver, *non?*"

I stared stupidly. "How did that get in the newspaper?"

"Everything is in the newspapers in Paris. Except for me." She winked. "Though you can 'elp me change that. I want to meet the Spirit-Hunters."

"You want to meet them?" My brow wrinkled. "I'm afraid none of them are here now—"

"Then introduce me later. Or—*je sais!* Show me their lab."

"Really?" I squeaked. "You want to see it?"

"*Bien sûr!* These Spirit-Hunters are famous! I can imagine

274

my parents' faces when I return to Marseille and tell them who I 'ave seen."

"The lab is probably locked—"

For a moment her face fell. But then she flashed a grin. "Ah well. Then I will merely take a peek at the *door* of their famous lab, and that will be enough."

"Well, all right," I said grudgingly, waving to the stairwell. "I suppose there's no harm."

Less than a minute later, we were standing on the second floor and staring at the Spirit-Hunters' lab door.

Laure marched to it. "Let us try it, *oui?*"

"I'm certain it's lock—" I broke off, for Laure had pushed the handle, and it was most assuredly *not* locked.

She shot me a grin. "Do you think I could 'ave a peek?"

I gulped. I knew Joseph—or Daniel—would disapprove . . . but if we looked inside, I could also quickly search for the note from Jie. "Yes. Hurry." I strode toward Laure. "We'll go in, but only for a moment."

"*Parfait.*" She eased back the door, and we crept inside, closing it softly behind us. "It smells," she whispered.

"Because there is a corpse over there," I murmured, pointing.

She made a gagging sound and instantly pinched her nose. "A *corpse?*"

"Yes." I grinned at her. "The Spirit-Hunters do hunt the Dead, after all." Laure only cringed in response, so, leaving her to stare around the room, I darted toward the windowsill where Jie's note still lay. I snatched it up and held it to the light.

Gone out. Be back later.

—Jie

For several moments the only sound was Laure's feet padding over the carpet as she inspected anything and everything. I read the note again. And again and again, my heart picking up speed each time. This was *not* Jie's handwriting. It was similar; but after exchanging letters with her for months, I knew her wobbly style. This lettering was too smooth. Too assured.

So what did that mean?

I shot a glance at Laure. She was reading the titles of Joseph's books and mouthing them to herself, her eyebrows arched high.

My gaze returned to the note. Had Jie been taken? And by whom? For what purpose? In the end it didn't actually matter—what mattered was that Jie's absence was *bad.*

I needed the Spirit-Hunters to return. I needed to tell Joseph to send out *all* of his new patrol force. I *needed* to find Jie.

I could ask Oliver to look, I thought. Except that I was not ready to. I so desperately wanted to trust the demon . . . but I couldn't. Not after his display yesterday. *If only I could talk to Elijah . . . ask him about Oliver and the letters—*

My thoughts were interrupted by a choke.

I whirled around—only to find Laure standing beside the butler, her face green. "It smells so strongly."

I grimaced. "That's because you're right beside the body. Come stand here. Next to the window."

She clasped a gloved hand to her mouth and rushed to my side. As she worked on opening the window, I turned away and tried to refocus my thoughts.

The words of Joseph's book came to mind. The words about a séance. *A longer-dead ghost will require more power and therefore more people.*

I straightened. I couldn't hold a séance by myself, but I could *mimic* one, could I not? I could pretend to have more people by using a crystal clamp to enhance my power.

Triumph rushed over me—but then a crash sounded. I jerked toward Laure. On the floor was Daniel's ornate cream box—upside down and with the lid popped off.

"*Excusez-moi!*" Laure wrung her hands. "*Je suis désolé,* Eleanor! I am so sorry!"

"It's fine," I muttered, shoving Jie's note into my pocket and kneeling. *Please don't be broken.*

Laure crouched beside me. "When I opened the window, I did not see the hatbox."

"I don't think it is a hatbox." I yanked the lid off the floor.

"Then what is it?" She slid the box over, revealing what had spilled onto the floor . . . and she gasped.

My heart sank like a stone. It was a mechanical hand. Bronze gears shone in the place of knuckles, and polished wood flesh gleamed in the afternoon sun. At the wrist there were a series of tendon-like wires: the muscles to operate this creation.

I gulped, and with shaking fingers, I reached out to stroke it. The detail was immense and meticulous, from the small, carved fingernails to the soft curve of the palm.

Tears burned, welling in my eyes. Daniel *had* told me there were ways to make mechanical hands, and when I had asked if he was offering, he had answered, *I can always try.*

He had not only tried, but he had succeeded. No wonder he had been so upset by my phantom limb.

"Are you . . . are you all right?" Laure's voice was gentle.

"No." I wiped at my eyes. "Daniel made this . . . and it was meant for me." I picked up the hand and laid it gently back in the box. Then I placed the lid on top.

"*Was* meant for you?" Laure pushed herself up and helped me rise. "Why not *is* meant for you?"

"Because I have this," I answered bitterly, lifting my right hand. "I have this cursed, magical abomination."

She shook her head and returned the box to the windowsill. "I cannot pretend to 'ave any idea of what you speak. But"—she gazed at me, sympathy dragging at her eyebrows—"I do know a broken heart when I see it."

All I could do was bite my lip and nod.

"*Il t'aime.*" She offered me her handkerchief. "He loves you."

I took the lacy cloth and dabbed at my eyes. "Perhaps. Or more likely he was experimenting—"

"*Non,*" she interrupted. "He loves you, Eleanor. *Je sais.* I saw 'ow he looked at you on the street, 'ow he listened to you. And now, there is this." She waved to the green box. "He loves you. The question is, Do you love him in return?"

I stayed silent, avoiding her eyes.

"Perhaps," she said at last, "it would be best if I leave you alone for a bit."

"Y-yes." I gulped. "I'm sorry."

"Do not be. I will explore the 'otel for now, and when I am finished, if you are—'ow do you say?—*recovered*, we will go out for lunch. Unless you are attending this ball tonight at the *palais*? The one in all the papers?"

"Ball," I repeated numbly. I had forgotten all about that— and it was quite possibly the last thing I wished to deal with right then.

"If you are too busy preparing for the party," Laure said, "then perhaps we can meet for breakfast tomorrow. Before I return to Marseille."

"Or perhaps we can do both." I gave her a small smile. "Lunch *and* breakfast. Thank you, Laure." I offered her the handkerchief, but she shook her head once.

"You keep it. You 'ave more need of it than I." Then, flashing me her own tiny grin, she waved good-bye and glided from the lab.

I instantly crumpled onto a stool and began to cry. "Why didn't he just tell me?" I mumbled to myself, wiping at my tears. I knew I could not blame Daniel for my own mistakes. *I* had bound myself to Oliver; *I* had chosen a phantom limb; and *I* had covered my tracks with lie after lie.

I would ask the Spirit-Hunters to forgive me—for hiding the truth and for betraying their trust.

But I would *not* be ashamed of the magic inside me. This was who I was now, and I would have to show Joseph and Daniel that there was nothing to be afraid of.

And, by God, I would find Jie.

With a final sniffle, I pushed away all the sadness and locked it up, far out of reach in the back of my mind. As I pushed to my feet, my eyes caught on the crystal clamp. A séance. It was something I could do.

I snatched up the clamp's box, grabbed Joseph's book on spirits, and marched from the room.

Once I was safely stowed in my bedroom, I assembled the crystal in the device and plopped down, cross-legged, onto my bed. Opening the spirit book, I flipped to the proper page.

My pulse thrummed as I scanned the text. It told me I needed to focus all my power, fix my target firmly in my mind, and then find the curtain.

I lowered my eyelids. "Step one: focus my power." With a deep breath, I began to draw in my magic. Immediately it tingled through me, up from my toes and in from my fingers. The same delicious buzz as always, warm and intoxicating. And as always, my worries evaporated one by one. Daniel and demons and corpses—they all felt meaningless compared to this feeling. To this *power*.

But I didn't let Joseph's warnings go completely. I knew this was an addictive warmth, and I made myself cling—if only by a thread—to the reality beyond. Soon, the last drop of soul had poured into my chest, and I could feel the well pulsing in time with my heart.

"Now think of Elijah." I imagined his auburn hair. His glasses—the way they constantly slid down his nose. I thought of his smile. His sea-green eyes. His goofy, braying laugh . . . Then I slowly squeezed the crystal clamp.

Electricity—a sharp zap—slid up my arm and into my chest.

The well grew bigger, and my heart raced faster.

I sent my senses out, groping for the golden, glowing curtain. It was always there, always present . . . and then I found it.

I opened my eyes. The curtain shimmered before me as clearly as my bedroom had only moments before.

I grinned, proud. I *could* use this power without letting it taint me.

All right, now I simply say his name.

"Elijah Fitt," I whispered. "Elijah Henry Fitt, your sister, Eleanor, wants to speak with you. Answer my call."

Nothing happened. I tried again. "Elijah Henry Fitt, your sister, Eleanor, wants to speak with you."

Still nothing happened, and now my chest was starting to ache. "Elijah," I called, a sharpness creeping into my voice. "Answer me!"

Maybe he was busy . . . or . . . or blocked! I could try someone else.

"Clarence Wilcox," I rasped, quickly running out of breath. "Clarence Wilcox, come to my call!"

Still nothing. Was I doing something wrong?

And why was electricity still zapping up my arm?

I looked down in horror at my right hand—it was still squeezing the crystal! I tried to pry the clamp from my fingers, but I couldn't let go. My muscles would not release, and the well continued to grow. Blindingly bright, it pushed every last drop of air from my lungs. As my heart beat faster, I knew with terrifying certainty that this would kill me.

No! A whimper escaped my throat, and with it, the last of my air.

I needed to cast a spell, needed to get this magic out of me . . . but I couldn't remember any spells—not with my pulse careening and the room spinning. All I could think was that I had to stay awake, had to keep my eyelids up. . . .

Just as I toppled forward, I latched on to the only words I could conjure. *Awake, awake, awake . . .*

When I finally came to, I was facedown on my bed. My head was pounding, and the instant I peeled back my eyelids, I wished I hadn't. It hurt. Everything *hurt.*

I pushed myself up. My vision sparkled with painful stars, and yet I felt so relaxed . . . aching, but somehow good.

It's from the magic, I thought. Whether I meant to or not, I had found a way to cast the power from me.

I scooted off the bed. For a moment I swayed unsteadily, but I knew that if I did not move, I would collapse into sleep. I had failed, and now it was time to move on. I needed water, needed to find Laure, and needed to launch a full search for Jie.

I scuffed to the door, but just as I was leaning on the doorknob, a scream erupted from outside.

I wrenched open the door. An old woman barreled toward me, her eyes huge. "Rat!" she shrieked. "Rat!"

My breath whooshed out. A rat—nothing dangerous.

But then another door burst open, with a fat man toppling out. *"Les oiseaux sont enragés!"* He sprinted frantically toward me. *"Aidez-moi!"*

I barely had time to sort through this when three more doors—no four, then five—tore open and panicked guests came screeching toward the stairs. Toward me.

As the first old woman scrambled desperately by, I finally caught sight of the rat.

But this was no rat. The giant, raw hole in its neck crawled with white maggots, and its eyes were milky white. This rat was Dead—a Hungry Dead.

And it wasn't the only one.

I kicked into a run. I needed the Spirit-Hunters. If all the animal corpses in the area had come to life, I could not face them alone. I had wasted all my energy on the failed séance.

I bounded onto the stairs. A flight below was a black-uniformed steward. "Help!" I shrieked. "Get help!"

He didn't react, just continued his quick descent. I clambered after. Someone needed to find Joseph and Daniel. "Help!" I yelled again. *"Á l'aide!"*

He paused on the second floor, and I jumped the remaining steps between us.

But I stopped midstride.

The stairwell reeked of carrion, and this was *not* a steward—

it was the butler from the lab.

No, no, no!

I lurched back around. So did the butler, his jaw gaping and bloody eye sockets close. Stiff arms flew up, grabbing for me.

Somehow I managed to sweep up my skirts and leap two, three steps at a time. "Run!" I screamed as guests came toward the stairs. "*Les Morts*! Run!" Thank God, they listened, and as I raced up floor after floor, the broken beat of footsteps stayed close behind.

It felt as if it took forever to climb those stairs. My legs burned and my chest was on fire. I couldn't maintain this pace—and the hotel had to dead-end eventually . . . because I was almost to the top floor. I would have to face the Hungry here. Now.

I scrambled onto the top landing and surged into the hall.

But I instantly skittered to a stop, my mind erupting in panic. There were rats everywhere! And mice and sparrows and a mangled cat. They were all dead yet somehow brought back to life.

I couldn't stop them all.

A door flew open behind me. "No!" I shrieked, lurching around. "Stay inside!"

A woman in violet stumbled into the hall—Laure! Oh God, where had she come from?

She screamed, and in a flash the Hungry tackled her to the ground.

I flung up my arms and threw out every ounce of power I could muster.

"Stay," I chanted. "Stay, stay, stay!"

The Hungry slowed, its jaw chomping a staccato beat. Laure fought and clawed to wriggle free, shrieks flying from her throat, but the corpse was much heavier, much stronger.

And its teeth inched closer and closer to her neck.

"Don't move!" I screeched. "Stay, stay, *stay*!"

But the corpse was stronger than me too, and its teeth were now clamping down on her neck.

Then pain burst through me, bright and sudden. My concentration broke. The decomposed cat was latched onto my arm.

I screamed and jerked back, but the animal's fangs were deep. And now the other animals had reached me.

I lost sight of the butler as a mangled bat flew into my face, teeth bared. From every direction, I was ripped and scratched and bitten. Each slash stabbed through my mind, blinding and white.

I toppled back, tripping over my skirts, and hit the ground hard.

The corpses kept coming. Everywhere, everywhere. Rat teeth and jagged fangs knifed into me. I flung out my power. I kicked, I shoved, I screamed. . . . My fingers dug into jellied flesh and rotting fur. My feet crunched through bones . . . but there were still so many. So *many*!

"Eleanor!" a voice bellowed. Oliver. "Command me! Say the words!"

But I couldn't speak—I could not even breathe. All I could do was think, *Sum veritas*.

It was enough. The magic oozed from me, and a breath

later, Oliver roared, *"Dormi!"*

But only some of the animals stopped their attacks. So I kept fighting.

"Dormi!" he shouted again. Though I felt the attack lessen, it was not the end. I pumped even more energy into clawing my way free.

"Dormi! Dormi! Sleep, dammit! *Dormi!"*

The final rat stopped. It tumbled over, stiff and dead once more.

And the hall was silent. Too silent.

"Laure!" I hurled bloated corpses off me. "Laure!" Then Oliver was there, trying to help me rise. "The butler's victim," I shrieked. "It's Laure!"

Oliver's eyes bulged. He spun around and darted to the collapsed butler. I crawled over, and we shoved the rotten body aside to show an unmoving woman beneath.

Her neck was destroyed—half of it torn out and still in the butler's teeth. Tattered flesh clung to the edges of a gaping hole.

"Laure!" I wrenched her to me. Blood spurted onto her dress, onto my hands, warm and sticky and red. She was dying.

My eyes flew to Oliver's. "Help her!"

"How?" His voice was frantic.

"Heal her!" A river of blood slid down the side of her neck, blossoming onto her violet gown. Her eyelids fluttered slightly, but her chest barely moved.

"It's a death wound," Oliver said, his voice shaky. "It will take all my magic and yours to heal—"

"Do it!"

"Then lay her down."

I placed her gently back on the carpet. Her head lolled to one side, stretching the hole and oozing more fresh blood. Oliver gripped my hand in his and laid his other over Laure's heart. His yellow eyes held mine. "Command me, El."

"Heal Laure. *Sum veritas.*"

His eyes lit up. First a flash of blue—pulsing, pulsing—and then an azure flame. So bright, so blinding, I had to squint.

My heartbeat synchronized with the pulsing flames, and time seemed to hold its breath. I was aware of everything around me. Of how Oliver's eyes shone brighter. Of the fetid stench of the corpses, heavy and gagging. Of the smell of blood, higher-pitched and piercing. Of the animals—rat after rat, sparrow after pigeon. Of how congealed blood and writhing maggots were ground into the teal carpet.

Oliver latched onto my soul and he *pulled*. Each drop of magic slid from me, draining and draining, shriveling my insides.

I wanted to scream at him, "There is nothing left! Stop, *stop!*" But no words would form.

And still Oliver shone brighter. Blue light pulsed in his skull like a jack-o'-lantern, beautiful and terrifying.

Then his whole body tensed up. His hand crushed mine, and suddenly the light burst into his chest. A well of power, glowing through his ribs.

He cried out, and a spark cracked from his outstretched hand. A beam of power shot into Laure's chest, spreading out like a spiderweb over her body.

Oliver's voice ripped out again, an agonized sound. His head rolled back. His chest burned brighter and seared my eyes.

All at once, Laure's body stiffened like a board. Oliver screamed, and Laure screamed too. Then liquid heat rolled over me, bathing us in a perfect warmth.

The light shrank in on itself, smaller and smaller, until it finally winked out completely.

For a moment all was still. My eyes were too blinded to see, my body too stupefied to move. But I saw a shadowy form teetering back. Oliver. I lunged over and caught him. He sank into my arms, a tiny smile on his face.

I looked at Laure. Her neck was as smooth and unblemished as a baby's, and her chest moved at a normal, steady pace. Her eyes were still closed, but she was alive, and she would be *fine*.

The moment was so strange and calm. The awful smells and blood *everywhere* seemed separate, as if I were viewing it all from afar. My heartbeat in my ears was nothing more than a distant drum, my ragged breaths a far-off breeze.

But the fragile calm was soon shattered. Footsteps hammered up the stairs and into the corpse-laden hall.

"Demon!" Joseph shouted. "Demon!"

CHAPTER SEVENTEEN

"Demon!" Joseph hissed. He stood over Oliver and me, a crystal clamp in his hand. Behind him stood Daniel, with a pistol—a real pistol—aimed at Oliver's head.

"Eleanor," Joseph said, "get away from that creature."

"It's fine," I said tiredly.

"*Non*. He may look like a man, but he is not. He is a demon."

Oliver wound his fingers around my arm. "She knows what I am."

"Let her go!" Daniel barked.

When Oliver did not budge, Joseph lifted both hands. "I will blast you to the spirit realm."

"No, you won't." Oliver's fingers tightened. "I'm bound to Eleanor. Use that *gadget*, and you kill her too."

"Silence!" Joseph roared. "I will not hear your lies." He squeezed the clamp.

"Wait!" I screamed, lurching to my feet. "It's true. Oliver is my demon."

Joseph froze, and his face paled. "*Non, non*—it cannot be."

"It . . . is."

Daniel choked, and when I glanced at him, I saw horror rip over his face. Horror and betrayal.

Joseph stared at Oliver, his eyes as hard as stone. "What lies have you planted in her?" he growled. "Show me your binding piece."

"No lies." A smugness settled on Oliver's face. He stood and slipped out his locket. At that, Joseph's eyes closed, and he finally lowered his hands.

Daniel, however, did not move. His pistol stayed trained on Oliver though his gaze was on me. "Have you been bound to this thing the—" His voice cracked. "The whole time?"

"Yes. I had no choice, Daniel. Please, I—"

"It's a monster." Daniel's voice was barely above a whisper.

"Oliver isn't a monster. He saved my life," I added. "And Laure's."

Joseph and Daniel flinched, as if noticing the bloodied woman on the floor for the first time. Yet neither approached.

"Why?" Joseph demanded. His neck bulged. "*Why* would you bind to a demon?"

"You make it sound as if I set out to do it, but I did not." I tipped up my chin. "As I have said over and over, *I had no choice.*

Marcus sent the Hell Hounds after me." I raised my right hand. "He had a spell on me, and the only way to survive was to bind to Oliver."

"Why did you not tell me?" Joseph straightened to his full height, and his voice bellowed out. "I told you I thought a demon was responsible for *les Morts*! How, Eleanor, *how* could you hide a demon from me after knowing that?"

"Because Oliver is not the one raising *les Morts*."

"How do you know that?" Daniel lowered the pistol, and I noticed that his hands trembled. His voice too. "And how do *we* know this creature isn't the one raising the Dead?"

"Because I'm *telling* you it is not Oliver."

"And you are a liar," Joseph spat. "A liar and a necromancer. I should have seen it—you are no different than he."

It was like a punch in the gut. *He. Marcus.* And for a split second my heart clenched . . . but then all regret vanished in a seething rush. After everything we had done together, after we had stood side by side against the Dead, after Joseph had *seen* what Marcus had done to my family, he thought I was no different? All my past loyalty had bought me *nothing?*

"No!" I spat. "*No.* I am not like Marcus. I am not the corrupt necromancer you so desperately want me to be." My lips curled back. "Do not look at me like that—as if you do not understand what I mean. All you see, Joseph, is black or white, and I am sorry, but I do not fit into those lines."

I drew back my shoulders. "Necromancy has not corrupted me, but Marcus *has* corrupted you and how you view the world.

I am still Eleanor and the same girl I have always been. Only I'm stronger now. Stronger than you, Joseph, and stronger than your machines. I can use my magic—my *necromancy*—without turning into Marcus."

"Is that what you think?" Joseph gave a growling laugh. "That you are somehow immune to the darkness inside you? You are not, Eleanor. You are only blind to it, and eventually it will take control."

"And if it *does* take control?" I threw my arms wide. "So what? I don't care—and you shouldn't either. I am on *your* side! If this magic is the only way to stop Marcus, then so be it!"

"Is this truly what you believe, Eleanor?" Again Joseph laughed, his face twisted with disgust and his scars stretched taut. "You believe you are powerful enough to face Marcus? Do not mistake the feeling of strength for *actual* strength."

"Tell yourself that," Oliver snarled. "Tell yourself she's weaker than you if it makes you feel less afraid. But know that it isn't the truth. Eleanor *is* strong; and once she is trained, she will be as strong as a demon, as strong as Marcus, and certainly stronger than you." He flourished a hand at the corpses littering the hall. "She raised these. All of these, and all by herself. The rats, the birds, the butler—it was all Eleanor's magic."

I spun to Oliver. "Why are you saying that? I didn't do this!"

"Oh yes, you did. It might not have been on purpose, El, but I felt your magic all over it."

"But I couldn't have!"

"Yet you did." He gave me a sad half smile. "It *was* you who raised the Dead."

Bile rose in my throat. "But how? There is no possible way!" Then I remembered the words I'd thought before passing out: *Awake, awake, awake* . . . "Oh God, oh God, *no*." My breathing came faster. I clutched my stomach. "It *was* me. Oh no, no, no . . . it was an accident! I was trying to hold a séance."

"You need multiple people to hold a séance," Joseph declared.

"So I used the crystal clamp. But it overwhelmed me, and I couldn't reach any spirits."

"Of course not!" he yelled. "The séance is not about power. It is about focus. Focus and *discipline*—neither of which you have!"

"Because you have not taught me!" I screamed. "If you want me to learn, then *teach* me! Do not tell me simply to *resist* my magic. I cannot; don't you see?"

Daniel took a step toward me. I jolted. He had been so silent, I'd forgotten he was here.

"How," he said in a rough voice, "can Joseph be expected to teach you? You lied to him—to *me*." His eyes ran desperately over my face. "What . . . what *are* you?"

A fresh wave of fury crashed into me. I scoffed. "That is a stupid question coming from you since, pray tell, what are *you*, Daniel? You prance around the city pretending to be a gentleman in your fancy suits and with your fancy manners. Well, you are not a gentleman. You're a *criminal*, remember?" I rounded on Joseph. "And you—you have the same magic in you. It must be *so* wonderful simply to fight the corruption. But how, Joseph? *How* do you do it? I can't solve this on my own!"

Joseph's mouth opened, but I surged on before he could fling out any more unwarranted accusations. "Both of you are running around chasing your tails and attending parties and *salons* while *les Morts* run free. While an amulet with seventy-three compulsion spells hides somewhere, waiting to be detonated. While Jie is *missing*! And while Marcus could be here any blasted moment. The Spirit-Hunters are an ineffective joke." I pounded my chest. "But I have power, and I intend to use it."

Before Joseph or Daniel could answer, I spun around and knelt beside the still-unconscious Laure. "Ollie, can you lift her? She's small."

"I can manage," he answered, crouching beside me. Together we hefted the woman into his arms.

"We will take her to the lobby and call for a doctor," I said as we trudged past the Spirit-Hunters toward the stairs. But I barely made it two steps before Joseph's voice rang out.

"Stop. I cannot let you go free."

Oliver and I paused, but I nudged the demon to keep going. Then I pivoted around and advanced on Joseph. "And what will you do to me? Blast me to pieces like one of the Dead?" I spun to Daniel. "*Shoot* me?"

"If we have to," Joseph answered quietly, "then yes."

"Well, you do not have to because I am not your threat. You *know* me, Joseph. Daniel." My gaze darted between them. "All I want to do is search for Jie, and after I find her I will leave

Paris—leave *you*—for good." I pushed out my chest, pumping all the assertion and command I could muster into my words. "I am *not* a threat to you—not unless you try to stop me. If you get in my way, then this"—I motioned to the corpses—"will seem like child's play."

Without waiting for a reply, I marched after Oliver, and together we descended.

It was a bluff. I couldn't fight Joseph. Oliver and I could barely carry Laure down the stairs, much less use any more magic. But it didn't mean I *wouldn't* fight Joseph if he got in my way.

The truth was, despite my exhaustion, I felt ablaze with potential. I would finally *do* something. I would find Jie and stop Marcus.

"Are you . . . all right?" Oliver asked between gasps for air, his cheeks bright pink.

We were passing my floor. Tufts of putrid fur and feathers littered the carpet, only broken up by brown bloodstains or by mounds of rotting corpses. And every so often, a dazed hotel guest gawping at the disaster. It was a replica of the top floor—as was every floor in the hotel.

"I am . . . fine," I answered, panting. Laure was a small woman, but Oliver and I had no energy left. We rounded a bend in the stairs, and the dull roar of a distant crowd hit my ears. *It must be all the guests—they must have gone downstairs.*

"That . . . didn't go well." He slowed and shifted his grip beneath Laure. "With . . . the Spirit-Hunters, I mean."

"It went how we thought it would go."

"And you're not . . . sad?" Oliver pressed.

"No," I said stoutly as we trekked past the Spirit-Hunters' lab and the sounds from below grew louder, nearer. I wasn't sad. Not at all.

"That's the magic, you know." Oliver spoke the words carefully, watching me for a reaction. "When the power wears off, you *will* feel this."

I wiped my face on my shoulder, but the movement was sloppy . . . and I realized I was shaking. We were almost to the foyer, and the frantic cries of all the guests were now thunderous; but it wasn't the noise that tremored through me. I was keyed up on magic.

And that meant that Oliver was right. When this passed, I would probably feel a great deal of guilt over Laure, over the Spirit-Hunters, and over all the damage I had caused. But for now I did not. All I cared about was finding Jie.

And, I thought, anticipation warming my blood anew, *if the magic begins to wear off, I can always use more. . . .*

Most of the hotel's patrons had taken refuge in the restaurant. Everyone was a disaster—clothes torn, eyes wide with shock, and skin coated in bits of animal corpses. No one even noticed Laure and me, and while I dealt with her slowly rousing form, Oliver had his eye out for the Spirit-Hunters.

It was all going surprisingly well. We had called for a doctor to tend to Laure—not that she had any injuries to tend—and she seemed to have no memory of what had happened. She

296

thought she had fainted, and she was in a happy buzz from Oliver's magic.

But then Laure noticed the blood on her dress, and the panic set in. "*Qu'est que c'est? Qu'est que c'est?*" she breathed over and over again. "It is blood, *non? Mais comment?* How, Eleanor, how?"

I grabbed her hands and forced her to look at me. "Listen, Laure: it's not your blood. It's mine."

This was perhaps a poor response, because although she stopped her frantic questions, she now looked incredibly suspicious.

"Your blood?" Her lids lowered slightly. "But you are not even hurt."

"I'm not?" I glanced down, and for the first time I realized the state I was in. My sleeves and skirts were ripped to shreds; my hair hung in thick, crusted clumps before my face; and my arms were covered in jellied animal blood. Yet the skin beneath was as smooth and perfect as Laure's.

Oliver had not only healed the young woman.

So I wound up telling her the truth. "It was magic, Laure. We . . . we were both attacked by the Dead, and I healed us."

Her brow furrowed. "Magic. You healed me with magic?"

I nodded wearily. "I am afraid there's much more to it." I glanced at the restaurant's entrance. Oliver was motioning to me—the doctor had arrived. I turned back to Laure. "But I cannot tell you everything now. And your doctor is here."

She pushed to her feet, the picture of vitality. "I do not

need one. I shall call a cab and return to my friend's house. However"—she leaned close, her eyes boring into mine—"I expect to hear the whole story tomorrow, Eleanor. I will call on you. We have plans for breakfast, *non?* So tomorrow morning before I leave for Marseille, I will return."

"Fair enough," I murmured.

After walking with her to get a carriage, I returned to the crowded foyer to search for Oliver. Sometime in the last hour of hell, I had decided I would turn to the demon for help finding Jie. I had been willing to give him my letters—had decided I could rely on him—until he'd ruined my moment with Daniel and my temper had clouded everything. No, perhaps I would never trust the demon completely, but he at least deserved my respect. He had saved my life and Laure's. . . .

Besides, he was all I had left now.

"Mademoiselle Fitt!"

I paused, searching for who had called me. "Mademoiselle Fitt!" The Marquis's dark hair and oily mustache appeared nearby, and he pushed through the throngs to finally pop out directly in front of me. "*Mon Dieu*, are you hurt?" His eyes ran over my destroyed gown.

"I'm not hurt." I tried to smile, but I found I was too distracted by all the panicked people closing in. What if the Spirit-Hunters were here? What if I missed Oliver?

As if sensing my distress, the Marquis took my elbow and guided me through the people to the relative calm of the stairs.

"I heard *les Morts* were here," he said, breathing heavily and leaning on his cane. "I came immediately! *C'est horrible—très, très horrible!*"

I nodded, unsure what he wanted from me, and turned my gaze back to the crowds.

"I cannot find zee Spirit-Hunters," the Marquis went on. "I went to zee lab, but it is empty. Are zey hurt?"

"Uh . . ." I glanced at him just as he set his cane against the wall.

And suddenly I found I could do nothing but stare at it. The handle had changed shape again—I was sure of it. Now all five craggy fingers were curled inward into a fist . . . a fist that would fit perfectly into my hand. . . .

I wet my lips, unable to look away. All I wanted to do was touch the ivory. Feel the grooved carvings, see how the ivory could form such a realistic human hand. And above all, how it could change its shape.

"*Mademoiselle?*"

I started and jerked my gaze to the Marquis's face. "Pardon me? Wh-what did you ask?"

"Are zee Spirit-Hunters hurt?"

"Oh, um, no." I blinked quickly and tried to clear my head. "I-I believe they are fine."

"*Dieu merci, Dieu merci.*" LeJeunes pressed his hands together as if praying. "I was so, eh . . . so *worried* when I could not find zem. Do you know where zey are?"

My eyes flicked to the cane and then back to the Marquis's

worried face. "They must be somewhere in the hotel, sir, for I saw them not too long ago."

"And zey will still be attending zee ball tonight?"

"Ball?" My eyebrows shot up. Yet again I had completely forgotten about the ball—not that it really mattered. It was hardly something I would be attending now. "I do not know, but I would assume they will still go. Although . . ."

"*Oui?*"

"One of the members is missing." I bit my lip. "Jie Chen— the Chinese girl. She has been missing since yesterday."

The Marquis nodded. "It is very bad. Monsieur Boyer asked for extra men on his patrol force. I gave zem to him gladly. Gave him zee best inspectors we have."

"Oh." My brow knit. Perhaps Daniel and Joseph were not as unconcerned for Jie's safety as I had thought. "And have these inspectors found anything?"

"*Non.*" LeJeunes wagged his head, almost sadly. "Zey have not . . . how do you say? Have not found any clues. But zey are looking—and will continue to look until zey find Mademoiselle Chen. But listen." He bowed toward me, peering at me from the tops of his eyes. "It is *impératif* zat Messieurs Boyer and Sheridan come tonight. All of zee other senators will be in attendance— over seventy men and families—and despite zee missing *mademoiselle*, a public appearance such as a ball is *vital* to zee Spirit-Hunters' continued support. And to my own continued support for zee election."

I found myself nodding in an almost emphatic agreement.

Madame Marineaux had said the same thing, had she not?

"*Très bien*—I am glad you understand, Mademoiselle Fitt. You must tell zem zis, *oui*? Tell Messieurs Boyer and Sheridan what I have told you."

"Perhaps you should tell them—"

"*Non, non.* I will let you tell zem. It is better. Zey like you. Zey listen to you."

Not anymore, I thought. But I bobbed a polite curtsy, hoping LeJeunes would interpret it as compliance.

He did; and with a delighted grin, he tapped his nose once and said, "*Merci beaucoup*! Madame Marineaux is right about you. *Une fille intelligente*! Smart girl. Now, I must be off—I have much to do before zee ball! Much to do!" He twisted around and hobbled back toward the crowds.

But he left his cane. I knew he left it without even checking. And I also knew I ought to call out after him . . . but I wanted to see it. Wanted to . . . touch it. . . .

Holding my breath, I gently lifted it by its base and brought the ivory near. Up close, it was even more beautiful. A craftsmanship like nothing I'd ever seen—so real, I thought it might start moving at any moment.

My hand trembling, I gently reached up to stroke one of the long, jagged fingernails. But then the Marquis's voice rang out.

"*Mademoiselle*!"

I tensed, confused. Angry.

And then the Marquis was beside me once more and taking the cane away from me. "Oh, *merci, merci*! I almost forgot it, and, *oh la*, zat would have been bad! Zis is my good luck charm—I need it if I am to win zee election." He winked at me. "Until tonight, *Mademoiselle. Au revoir.*"

"*Au revoir*," I mumbled, my chest aching as I watched him disappear back into the crowds.

"Eleanor."

"Huh?"

"El, snap out of it." Oliver stood before me. I stared stupidly at the demon as the world behind him shifted into focus. I was still at the foot of the stairs, yet the crowds beyond had thinned. "How long have you been standing here?" he asked, concern obvious in the squint of his eyes.

"I . . . I don't know."

"Well, come on. Let's go to your room." He took my arm gently in his, and we began a careful trek up the stairs. "What happened? You seem utterly lost."

"I feel utterly lost too." I chuckled nervously. "I . . . I was talking to the Marquis and then . . ." *Then I saw his cane, and he took it from me.*

"And then?" Oliver prompted.

"Um . . ." I cocked my head. "He was . . . was looking for the Spirit-Hunters and insisting they were not here. Did you see them?"

"No." Oliver's head swung once. "I think they must have slipped out in all the . . . er . . . *excitement.*"

"Maybe to search for Jie." I hoped this was the reason.

302

"Or perhaps *les Morts* have struck again."

"Number seventy-four," I murmured. Then I froze mid-stride. Hadn't the Marquis said something about seventy? "'All of the other senators will be in attendance.' . . ."

"What?" Oliver moved onto the step above me and gazed down. "What about senators?"

"Something the Marquis said about how over seventy men and their families will be at the . . . oh, merciful heavens." My eyes grew huge as something else he'd said played in my mind. "'This is my good luck charm.'"

"El, what are you whispering about?"

" . . . I need it if I am to win the election." I moved onto the step beside Oliver, and my words rushed out. "Oliver, what does an amulet feel like? How would I recognize one?"

He shrugged. "I don't know. I've never seen one."

"Would it be attractive? As in alluring—would someone want to . . . to touch it?"

"I don't know, El." He peered at me slantwise. "A necromancer might be attracted to the power, I suppose, but the average person—"

"The cane!" I almost screamed the word. "The Marquis's cane is the amulet."

"The Marquis? As in the man who is—"

"Hosting the Spirit-Hunters, yes!" I burst into a run up the stairs, shouting, "His cane—it isn't normal, Ollie. Every time I have seen it, the handle has been in a different shape, and all I can think about is how much I want to *have* it. Maybe he is a

303

demon—you said yourself that you wouldn't be able to sense one nearby."

Oliver's feet pounded behind me. "Well, there's one easy way to tell. What color are his eyes?"

I slowed. "Blue. Damn, they're blue." I resumed my racing stride, and we rounded the stairs, flying past the Spirit-Hunters' lab. "But even if he is not a demon, he could still have an amulet."

"But why would he need an amulet?"

"To control the senate, win the presidential election—power. There are seventy-four corpses and I bet seventy-four senators."

"No," Oliver called after me. "There are seventy-*five*."

"But seventy-five minus the Marquis is seventy-four! And . . ." I trailed off, grinding to a halt. I turned horrified eyes on Oliver. "He said they'll all be at the ball tonight. What if he intends to *cast* the amulet then?"

Oliver frowned. "But why would he want the Spirit-Hunters there? Surely he wouldn't want to cast it with people around who could stop him."

Now it was my turn to frown. "I-I don't know, Ollie, but we cannot risk leaving the amulet with the Marquis. We have to stop him."

"Why do we have to stop him?" Oliver demanded, but I did not respond. I had already resumed my desperate race to my room.

And all I could think of was that stopping the Marquis would lead to Jie. Something in my heart told me her disappearance was connected to *les Morts*; and if the Marquis was the man behind *les Morts*, then . . .

My lips quirked into a smile. Then I would destroy him.

Just as I skittered to a stop before my bedroom door, Oliver jogged up behind me.

"What do you"—*gasp*—"intend to do, El?"

"Stop him."

"How?"

"I'll take the amulet." I wanted it—I couldn't deny that. "I will go to his house and take it." I pushed through my doorway.

But Oliver shoved into my room and forced me to stop. "And then he'll cast the amulet and *compel* you to return it. Your plan won't work."

"Then tell me what I can do."

"Your only choice is to stop the necromancer who made the amulet."

"Stop him how?" I shut my door.

"Death." He spoke with an intensity I'd never seen. "*Murder*, El. And despite all your . . . your bloodlust and dark promises, I don't think you can do that. I *know* you cannot."

"Yes, I can," I said softly.

"No. You are not Elijah, and I won't let you become him."

"I thought you wanted this. That you *wanted* death and sacrifice and blood."

"I told you what I meant by that, El. In the lab, I *told* you I didn't mean violence." He grabbed my arms. "Listen to me. One

305

death—even if it seems necessary—will only be the beginning. I know. I *know*."

No, you do not know, I thought. But I pretended to wilt in agreement. "Then what do we do?"

"We leave it to the Spirit-Hunters, and you and I deal with Marcus."

"Marcus . . ." The name rolled off my tongue. I looked into Oliver's face, my back straightening. "Will you try to stop me from killing *him*?"

He shook his head once. "His death is different."

"How?" I demanded.

"Because . . . his time already came. He doesn't belong in this realm." Oliver pulled away, his shoulders tensing. "So leave *les Morts* and Jie to the Spirit-Hunters. Let us go after the Old Man in the Pyramids. Let us fulfill Elijah's final command *and* stop the monster wearing his body."

Find Marcus, my heart nudged. *Find the Old Man and stop Marcus* . . . The Spirit-Hunters could handle the Marquis—it was their job, after all.

"All right," I said at last. "We'll go after Marcus and the Old Man. Though not until I make sure Joseph knows about the Marquis and his cane."

"Fine." Oliver's lips eased into a smile. "Then we should start with Elijah's letters. *That's* where we'll find a clue to this Old Man and his blasted chicken."

"Chicken? What do you mean?"

"Pullet. *Poule*. It means 'chicken.'"

"But the Black Pullet isn't actually a chicken . . ."

"Yes, it bloody well is. But don't make that face. It's also a chicken that lays golden eggs and grants its master immortality."

"Wait." Massaging my forehead, I crossed to my bed. "Are you telling me that everyone is chasing after a chicken that lays golden eggs? It's like something out of a child's fairy tale. . . ." My voice trailed off as something from Elijah's letters came to mind. Something about a fairy-tale joke.

"'Jack and the Beanstalk,'" I whispered, easing onto the edge of my bed.

"Huh?" Oliver strode to the bed and plopped down beside me.

"Didn't the story of Jack and the beanstalk have a chicken that laid golden eggs?"

He shrugged. "Perhaps."

"But didn't you tell Elijah a joke about it? When you were in Marseille—in some crypt?"

Oliver's eyebrows drew together. "We were never in a crypt in Marseille. Not together, at least. And I certainly never told him any Jack and the beanstalk joke."

I lurched off the bed. "So it's a clue!" I began to pace. Four steps forward, four steps back. Exhilaration pulsed through me, laced with magic. I tossed back my head and for two long breaths simply basked in the heady warmth.

"So what do we do?" Oliver asked.

I smiled and skipped back to my bed. "We can look at Elijah's letters and see exactly where in Marseille they lead us.

But again"—I wagged a finger at Oliver—"I won't leave this hotel until the Spirit-Hunters know about the Marquis and the amulet."

Oliver scoffed. "And I said fine, but do you think they'll actually listen to you?"

I crouched down and pushed aside the floor-length bed-cover. "I will make them listen. I peered underneath the bed. "I will not let Jie . . ." My words died.

My carpetbag wasn't there. Nothing was there.

And that meant all my money was gone—and all of Elijah's letters with it.

CHAPTER EIGHTEEN

*I shot upright from the floor. "Did you take my car-*petbag, Ollie?"

"Of course not."

My stomach turned to lead. "Oh no." I scrambled to my feet, lunging for the wardrobe and yanking back the door. Yet other than my undergarments and gray walking gown, there was nothing.

In a panic, I tore through the room, Oliver right beside me. Under tables and chairs, and even in the bathroom, I searched.

But my bag was gone.

I grabbed Oliver's sleeve, on the verge of hysteria. "You are sure you didn't take it?"

"I didn't!" His head shook frantically. "Where was it?"

"Under the bed."

"*What?*" He gripped my upper arms. "Why would you keep the letters in such a damned obvious place?"

"Because I didn't think—"

"No, you didn't think! Are you completely *stupid*, Eleanor?" He was shouting. "Anyone could bloody take them—*including* Marcus!" His fingers dug into me.

"But can't you find them?" My voice was shrill. "Sense them with your magic?"

His grip loosened.

"The way you found the letters on the boat," I pleaded.

Oliver swallowed and then nodded. "Yes. Yes, I-I'll try that." He released me.

"Do I need to command you?"

"No. I . . . I can simply feel for it—the same way I sense you. Now be quiet." He closed his eyes, and the faintest shimmer of blue shone through his eyelids. Then they popped up and he pivoted around, aiming for my balcony.

I scrabbled after, and we both tumbled through the glass door.

And instantly stopped. For there were the letters, reduced to a pile of smoldering ashes. The carpetbag was open beside it.

"Oh no, no, no." Oliver dropped to the embers and shoved his fingers in. "No, no, no—*please* no." But his hands came up with nothing but soot. Tears slid down his cheeks, and he rolled his head back, eyes closed. "This was *all* I had left of him, El. How could you just leave his letters out?"

"They weren't out—"

"And they damned well weren't hidden either." He jumped to his feet, rounding on me. "You are an idiot."

I skittered back into my room. "I-I'm sorry."

"Sorry isn't enough! I *told* you that I was still under Elijah's command. I needed those letters to find the Old Man! Those letters and this locket"—he clasped the chain, his knuckles white—"were the *only* things I had left from Elijah."

"Me too!"

"But he wasn't your—" he broke off, his eyes twitching.

"Wasn't my what?" I demanded.

"Nothing!" he roared. "It's bloody *personal*, and none of your damned affair. I cannot believe you could be so stupid as this." He twisted away from me, and when he spoke again, his voice was low. "I need a drink. I'll be at the bar." He released the locket and stalked to the door.

I ran after him. "You can't just leave! What about the Old Man in the Pyramid? The Black Pullet? Or *Marcus*?"

"What about Marcus?" He stopped at the door. "He's obviously in the city, and now he has burned our only chance of finding the Old Man. You wasted away our time, and now he caught up to us." Oliver spun back to the door.

"Don't go." I grabbed his hand. "Please, Oliver. There's no reason to be so mad."

"No reason?" He flung off my hand. "You call losing our only clue to the Black Pullet no reason? You call losing my only connection to Elijah *no reason*?"

"We do have a clue," I snapped. "We at least know we have to go to Marseille."

"No, Eleanor. We *think* we have to go to Marseille." He resumed his stomp to the door.

"Stop!" I shrieked. "This isn't fair for you to be so angry. I can try to remember what Elijah said! Or I can try to set you free before the command—" I broke off. He was already to the door.

I lurched after him. "Please, *please* do not go. If you do, I'll . . ."

Oliver paused, his whole body tensing. Slowly he looked back. "You'll *what*, El? Command me?"

I gulped and nodded.

His eyes flashed gold. "Oh, I dare you to. I dare you to command me. Because I will fight it. I will fight it until you and I are both on the ground weeping from the pain." He ripped open the door. "Now let me go. I want to be alone." Then he stormed away, slamming the door behind him.

And I was left standing there, watching the empty space where he'd just been. "But *I* don't," I whispered, "I don't want to be alone."

My bedroom door had barely been shut for four shaking breaths when a knock sounded. My heart heaved—was Oliver returning?

The knock came again. "Mademoiselle Fitt?" a man asked—a man I didn't know. "*Est-ce que vous-êtes là? J'ai un télégramme pour vous.*"

Telegram? Maybe there was word from home! I hurtled to the door and swung it wide. A startled, blue-uniformed steward gawked at the state of my gown and hair. In his hands was a silver platter atop which lay a neatly folded telegram.

I snatched it from him—"*Merci, merci!*"—and then I kicked the door shut, already unfolding the telegram.

In Le Havre. Will reach Paris Saturday. Have news.

Allison

My jaw went slack, and for several moments I could do nothing but reread the message again and again.

Allison Wilcox was coming to Paris. On Saturday . . . that was tomorrow!

"Have news," I whispered, my eyes searching the scant message for some sort of sign; but there was nothing to be found.

Why hadn't she telegraphed from Philadelphia? To be arriving so soon could only mean she had left shortly after me—on some indirect voyage, I assumed. Yet . . . what could have possibly prompted such a trip?

Panic began to creep in. Panic and guilt and a growing shroud of black dread. Allison was coming tomorrow with news. I had almost killed Laure. I had threatened the Spirit-Hunters. I had raised a hundred animal corpses by *accident*. I had left Elijah's letters out, and now someone had destroyed them. And my demon—the one person I thought I would have left—had abandoned me.

And Allison Wilcox was coming tomorrow. Oh, why, why, why? What news could she have? *Nothing good, nothing good* . . .

The sound of rustling paper hit my ears. I blinked. My hands shook violently, and my stomach churned. I staggered toward the bathroom, certain I would vomit. Certain I would collapse at any moment.

I paused at the door, clutching at the frame. "What have I done? What have I *done*?" I slid down to the floor. Daniel was right. I *was* disgusting for being so foolish . . . so weak.

And now I was alone too, and very, very lost.

Without thinking I pulled in my power—what few traces had returned since raising the corpses . . . since healing Laure. There wasn't much, but even that little trickle was enough to soothe me. It was like a prayer to a nun, and simply *feeling* the blue energy slide into my heart. . . .

I summoned the only spell I knew. "*Hac nocte non somniabo,*" I whispered. The magic eased out of me, taking my dread and my panic and my problems with it. I exhaled slowly, sinking into the heady feeling and savoring it.

Take a nap. Just a small nap until Oliver returns.

Using the doorframe, I dragged myself up to stumble to the bed. And as I drifted off into a dreamless sleep, a smile played on my lips.

For I was not completely lost. I still had my magic. . . .

I awoke to another knock at my door. Terror rose in my chest, bright and paralyzing. Was it the Spirit-Hunters? I snapped my eyes open, only to find that the sun had barely moved.

"Who——" I tried to call out, but my voice cracked. I swallowed and tried again. "Who is it?"

"Mademoiselle Fitt? It is Madame Marineaux."

I shot upright, my fear receding with each heartbeat. Here was someone who did not hate me. Someone who did not know all the horrors of my life, who sought my company simply *because*.

I bolted toward the door, black briefly clouding my vision . . . but then it receded, and I staggered to a stop. I was still wearing my ruined brown gown—the gown she had given me! And my arms were coated in animal blood, and my hair—

"Mademoiselle Fitt? May I come in?"

"Uh . . ." I crept to the door.

"The Marquis told me you were caught in the hotel's *Morts*."

I reached the door and with great care cracked it barely an inch. "Yes, *Madame*. I fear I am a terrible mess. Perhaps you ought to return later." Through the space, I saw her face tighten with worry.

"Nonsense, *Mademoiselle*. If you are hurt, then I can help. Please, let me in."

I reluctantly spread the door wider, taking in the Madame's impeccable silver-gray gown and feathered hat.

As she examined me, her hands flew to her cheeks. "Oh no! You are injured!"

"No, I'm fine," I rushed to say, but she had already shoved in.

"You are covered in blood!"

"It isn't mine. I assure you, *Madame*, I am not hurt." *Not on the outside, at least.* I gulped and pushed away the thought.

"Then let us clean you up." She grabbed for my arm, then— clearly thinking better of it—withdrew her hand and motioned toward the bathroom. "The dressmaker will be here any moment for your final fitting before the ball."

I flinched. "The ball? Oh no, I cannot possibly attend."

She tutted and bustled toward the bathroom, not even bothering to see if I followed. She seemed to know I would . . . and I did—though slowly.

"You *will* attend the ball," she said lightly. "It will be the best solution to your afternoon of horrors." She paused at the bathroom doorway and finally glanced back at me. "Trust me, Mademoiselle Fitt. I know these things."

"A-all right," I stammered. Even though I was determined to avoid the ball—Jie still needed finding, and Oliver . . . who knew when he would return? But in the meantime, I could at least enjoy a bath.

Her lips curved up, making her bright eyes crinkle. At that smile, my chest loosened. Some of my earlier worries pulled back, almost as if . . . as if I were using my magic.

And it occurred to me that maybe friendship was a better balm for my problems than magic.

CHAPTER NINETEEN

I floated on air. Giddy. Positively brimming with joy and perfection. My gown was beautiful, and *I* was beautiful—more beautiful than I had ever been in my entire life. The bloodred color of the fabric made my skin glow and my cheeks bright. My hair was coiled and curled, and roses were tucked in at the back.

Madame Marineaux had spent the entire afternoon with me, helping curl my hair, pulling my stays until I could hardly breathe—yet, oh how tiny my waist was after!—and pinching my cheeks to add color.

Now we rattled in her carriage on our way to the ball— a *ball*! My very first ball, and in Paris no less. Oh, how proud Mama would be if she were here to see this.

Or—my brow furrowed—would she be proud? Something

was wrong with that thought; but before I could identify precisely *what*, Madame Marineaux gestured to the window.

"We are almost to the Palais Garnier. I think you will like what you see."

I slid across the velvet bench seat and swept aside the matching curtain. "You have *such* a lovely carriage, Mad—ohhh." I stopped speaking, too enthralled by the gleaming and golden palace at the end of the street. As party guests alighted from their carriages and glided toward huge archways that marked the building's entrance, bright streetlights bathed them in an ethereal glow.

And as our own carriage slowly rolled closer, the full splendor of the palace came into view—the giant golden angels flanking its sides, the copper-domed roof, and the elaborate faces and statues that peered out from every spare inch. All I knew of the palace was that it was meant to be a theater—yet we had no theaters even half as magnificent in Philadelphia. Even the lovely Arch Street Theatre I had visited with Clarence seemed a drab, tiny thing in comparison to *this*.

"Come." Madame Marineaux's sweet voice broke into my gawking. "We must make our grand entrance. An old lady and a stunning young *femme*."

"Old lady!" I cried. "Hardly! You look positively *perfect* tonight." And I meant that. Madame Marineaux's gown was a vivid black silk—so unusual yet so striking against her pale skin and dark hair. I was elated to be spending the evening with a hostess as remarkable as she.

A footman opened the carriage door and helped me bustle out. Other guests sailed past, all of them in pairs and chattering happily. Drifting over their conversations was the faint sound of a thrumming waltz. A breeze caressed my bare shoulders, sweeping beneath my curls.

It was a perfect night. I had no cares in the world. Only this delicious buzzing *happiness* in my chest.

Madame Marineaux swished past me toward the columns, her face beaming as she declared, "The ball calls us, *Mademoiselle*! Let us dance and dance until our feet hurt and the sun rises!"

Dancing! I gathered up my skirts and traipsed after her, my heart singing at the thought of real dancing! I had certainly learned the waltz, the mazurka, and all the other popular dances, but I'd never had chance to *do* them! As we approached, the music grew louder, and I could see dancers soaring past on the second-floor balconies.

But staring out from above those balconies were staid, golden statues of composers, and I grinned up at Mozart as he watched me approach. It was with such silly distractions in mind that I finally reached the wide steps leading to the Palais Garnier's entrance. I followed Madame Marineaux up through an archway, and after passing through a wooden entryway, found myself in a high-ceilinged hall, where dim lantern light flickered over life-size statues of more composers.

Madame Marineaux whirled around quite suddenly, her gloved arms outstretched. "Oh, I almost forgot! You must take a dance card."

I blinked and then realized she held a palm-size white booklet with a delicate cord attached to the spine. I gasped excitedly and snatched it up. My first *dance card*! I flipped it open and scanned the list of all the dances—we were currently on the polka redowa.

"I shall introduce you to everyone," Madame Marineaux continued, clearly enjoying my pleasure, "and then I am certain all the men will be vying for a dance with the pretty American girl." She hooked her arm into mine, our enormous skirts pressing inward, and gave a long, contented sigh. "I have been so lonely until you came along, Mademoiselle Fitt. It is . . . *wonderful* to have a companion once more."

"But . . ." I looked away from the card. "What of the Marquis?" At that name something tickled in the back of my mind, yet when I tried to pinpoint why, the feeling flittered away like a hummingbird.

Madame Marineaux tugged me into a walk, leading me toward an archway. Beyond was an enormous staircase, glowing golden and warm. "I adore the Marquis, but a man is no replacement for one's female friends. Nor is he a replacement for my m—" Her lips puckered. "My first *man*."

"I . . . I am sorry."

"Do not be! Did I not tell you only two days ago, *c'est la vie*? And look." Smiling, she pointed to a bronze statue beside the stairwell. Beneath its elaborate candelabras stood two men in deep conversation. "There is a friend of mine, and"—she flashed her eyebrows at me—"he has a very handsome son who

I am certain will wish to escort you to the dance floor."

After our introduction, the young man, a Monsieur Something-or-other, did escort me. Up and up the stairwell we went. The music grew louder with each step, and my fingers traced along the balustrades. At the first landing the stairs split in two, and the *monsieur*—who prattled endlessly in French and did not seem to mind that I neither understood nor listened— veered right.

The moment we reached the second floor, however, we were forced to slow. People were *everywhere*. Women clad in all shades of a pastel rainbow hung on their black-suited partners. As we waited for the crowds to thin, the young man took my dance card, withdrew a pencil from his waistcoat, and scribbled his name beside the galop. I grinned delightedly as I slipped the dance card's cord around my wrist. My first dance! And with such a dashing gentleman on my arm . . . except, I felt there was someone else I would rather have on my arm. But for whatever reason, I could not remember who.

I brushed it off, intoxicated by the atmosphere. My escort said something and motioned to our left. Yet before I could even try to comprehend his French, he was tugging me through a dim doorway and into a round room with a bright sunshine painted on the ceiling. Mirrors adorned the walls, magnifying the light from a gold chandelier and reflecting a flushed, bright-eyed me.

I had just enough time to evaluate if my roses were still in place in my hair (they were) when my escort pulled me through the tiny room and into an alcove crowded with men. They debated in excited French, hands wild and mustaches wiggling, as completely disinterested in the dancing going on beyond as I was in their debates.

Fortunately, my partner was of the same mind, and we finally managed to wedge ourselves into the ornate ballroom just as the first strains of the galop began.

And moments later, with his gloved hand on my back and his other hand clasping mine, we sashayed onto the dark-wood floors. Crystal chandeliers hung overhead, dripping with light and illuminating all the swirling faces. My partner smiled; I smiled.

The dance passed in a blur, and I barely had time to catch my breath before Madame Marineaux had a new young man to meet me—and to sign my dance card. One after another, I waltzed, polkaed, skipped les lanciers, and hopped into another galop. And one after another, my partners' faces blurred together. . . .

Just as the first bouncing beats of a waltz began, my newest partner drew me into his arms. But then another man shoved through the crowd. He snarled something at the Frenchman, and before I could even process it all, this new young man had me in *his* arms.

His suit was like all the other gentlemen's, his patent leather shoes just as gleaming, his white gloves just as crisp, yet something about the way it all came together on Daniel was a thousand times more striking. His hair was slick and combed, but a ruffle at the front meant he'd run his fingers through it anyway.

I observed it all in a flash, and a combination of delight and fear bubbled through me. Though why I would be afraid of Daniel Sheridan, I did not know, so I let the pleasure take over, and I beamed up at him.

The music began. He shot a look to his left, his brow furrowed, then he tugged me into the waltz.

One, two, three. Step, step, step. "Empress, what the hell are you doin' here?" His voice was low as if he did not want us overheard.

"It's a ball, Daniel! I am dancing." My skirts billowed out as we spun. "And I am so *glad* you came—you're a lovely dancer."

"What?" He scowled, staring at my face. "What is *wrong* with you, Empress?"

"Nothing!" I smiled even wider, my face hurting. Everything beyond Daniel had blurred into a myriad of colors and sound. All I cared about was this moment—Daniel's green eyes gazing into mine and his hands guiding me over the floor. "I have never felt better in my entire life, Daniel! And oh, I'm so *glad* I get to dance with you. I had no idea you could waltz."

"Why?" he spat, anger brightening his eyes. "Because I'm not a gentleman?"

"Oh, but you *are* a gentleman. You're the most handsome gentleman here."

Now his scowl eased back, replaced by confusion. Yet on we danced—step, two, three, step, two, three.

"Where's your monocle?" I asked. "I bet it would look very jaunty on you tonight."

"Jaunty?" he repeated.

323

"Yes! You look so *wonderful*, and I think the monocle would look lovely with your suit. So where is it?" One, two, three, step, step, step.

"With . . . with my other clothes." His eyebrows curved down. "Joseph and I've been out all afternoon in search of Jie. We had to change into our suits here. . . . Eleanor, why are you smiling at me like that?"

"Like what?"

"Like . . . like you're drunk. You don't smell of alcohol, so what *is* this . . . this giddiness?" He whirled me past Madame Marineaux, and I gave her my brightest, happiest grin. "And," he said, "I still don't understand why you're here."

"Why wouldn't I be here?" I laughed. "It's the most fun I've ever had!"

"See? That's not *normal*. Not after what happened this afternoon."

"What happened this afternoon?"

His careful step-step-step faltered. "Are you jokin' with me?"

"I would never joke with you, Daniel—not unless you wanted me to."

He stopped waltzing, and I spun directly into him. I grasped at his shoulders, melting into his chest. *Maybe he'll kiss me.*

But he didn't. He twisted me around and yanked me off the dance floor.

"The waltz isn't over!" I cried.

"No, but you are. We're done dancin'." He pulled me roughly

324

toward the archways leading back to the stairwell, yet before we could get to the marble steps, Madame Marineaux strode into our path.

"Monsieur Sheridan, where are you taking Mademoiselle Fitt?" Her eyes darted from my face to Daniel's.

"I'm takin' her to . . . to talk."

"You can talk here." Madame Marineaux bared her teeth in a smile. "First you refuse to follow the rules of the dance card, and now you are stealing her from the ball."

Daniel glared. "I wish to speak to her in private. I told you that before, but you seem to think *you're* in charge of her dance partners."

"And I told *you*, *Monsieur*, that I am her chaperone for the evening."

"I'll speak to her one way or another, *Madame*. We have personal things to discuss."

My heart fluttered. Personal things? Love, perhaps?

"It is not appropriate," Madame Marineaux declared, "for a young woman to wander off with a young man." She raised her chin imperiously. "Monsieur Sheridan, please release Mademoiselle Fitt."

Except I did not want Daniel to release me. I turned pleading eyes on Madame Marineaux. "Please, I will only be a moment. I promise."

Madame Marineaux's nostrils flared, and if it wasn't for her wide grin, I would have thought she was angry with me. "I do not think that wise. I am your chaperone, after all."

"But I *know* Daniel, and it will only be a moment."

She stood taller, suddenly seeming to tower over me despite being several inches shorter. "Mademoiselle Fitt, I absolutely insist you leave this young man and you come with me. Why, simply consider what the gossip mongrels will *say* if you leave with—"

"Gossip be damned," Daniel snarled, pushing past Madame Marineaux. "She's comin' with me, and that's final." He yanked me onward.

As I stumbled past, I opened my mouth to offer Madame Marineaux an apology. But her eyes blazed so brightly that their golden sheen was almost yellow—and I was so startled, I forgot my words.

Daniel towed me down to the first floor with the bronze statues and their glowing candelabras. He guided me around a bend and farther down. At the stairs' lowest landing, we passed a small fountain before hurrying into a round room with a velvet sofa at the center. It was a waiting room beside the theater's back entrance. Daniel hauled me to the sofa and forced me to sit down.

He crouched on the floor before me, his face barely visible in the dim candlelight. "What is going on, Empress?"

"I do not know. You are the one who led me here." I batted my lashes at him, hoping he would find this attractive.

It would seem he didn't, for he gave a low groan and shot back to his feet. "Something's not right. You're actin' like a lunatic, and you have no memory of what happened earlier—"

"What happened earlier?" I puffed out my lips.

"That's exactly what I mean. Something's not right." He stared down at me. "I'm gonna go grab our things and find Joseph. *You*"—he pointed his finger in my face—"are gonna stay right here. I don't care who comes down here or who tries to talk to you. Tell them you're waiting for the Spirit-Hunters. Do you understand?"

"Yes." I flipped at my curls. "I wait here."

His jaw clenched, and his eyes ran anxiously over me. Then he lowered his hand. "I mean it, Empress. *Don't move.*" Then he spun on his heel and marched off.

I watched him go until he passed the small fountain and I could no longer see him, then I smoothed my bodice, adjusted my skirts, and fingered the roses in my hair. I could hear the mazurka overhead, and I wanted to *dance* it. I wanted to glide over the dance floor with Daniel again—to feel the air on my shoulders and the men's eyes on my face. . . .

With a sigh, I slouched back on the sofa—or I slouched as much as I could in my corset—and examined the elaborate floor beneath my slippers' heels. Mosaic tiles spread out in wild designs, leading in all directions. That was when I noticed there were two hallways branching off this room. A wide hall to my right that must lead to the theater's back exit . . . and then . . .

I twisted around to inspect the narrower hallway in the back corner. It slid off into shadows.

But then a shape materialized in the dark. Closer and closer it came into the room until I could finally see it completely.

It was a young man with dark hair and a perfect smile.

My stomach hitched, slamming against my corset. Memories came flooding back. Memories of an opera, of a handsome face, and of a night that ended in death. *No—it's not possible! It can't be!*

But it clearly could be, for I was absolutely certain that the young man smiling at me was none other than my old friend and suitor, Clarence Wilcox.

CHAPTER TWENTY

I forced myself to stand. Forced my lungs to draw in air. Forced myself to *move.* "Clarence!" I shouted, and in half a breath I was tearing full speed after him.

Instantly, he lashed around and fled—away from me. Down the hallway.

I ran after him, speeding into the dim hall. I had tried to speak to Clarence Wilcox, hadn't I? Somewhere in the farthest corner of my mind, I remembered I'd tried to call him recently . . . and that there were so many things I wanted to say to him.

So faster and faster I went, my ribs slamming into my corset with each breath until, moments later, I found myself on a winding stairwell. I bolted forward just in time to see Clarence's dark head vanishing down it.

I dove after him. My feet beat out a racing rhythm, and I

descended as fast as I could. With each step, the strains of the mazurka faded.

It was as if something compelled me to keep chasing—to keep hoping that if I followed long enough, he would stop and let me see him.

He reached the end of the stairwell and slithered into a dark archway. The instant my foot hit the final landing, I darted into the darkness too. Candles flickered every twenty feet or so, illuminating the white bricks in the walls and low, curved ceiling. No mazurka hit my ears now, only the drumming of my feet on the flagstones.

"Clarence!" I shrieked. "Wait!" But he did not wait. I tried to push my legs harder, but the dress weighed a ton and the corset flattened my lungs. If he didn't slow, then I would never catch up.

But I could not stop trying either.

As I hurtled past white bricks and archways, the air grew heavier—damper—until soon I raced through puddles that splashed icy water up my ankles and dragged at my skirts. It slowed me, and in two desperate heartbeats Clarence had faded from my sight completely. I rushed forward but instantly stumbled to a stop as the ceiling opened up. I was in a round room with more tunnels splitting off in each direction and candlelight flickering over each archway. Yet none of the tunnels were lit— none of them held any clue as to which path Clarence had chosen.

I stepped tentatively forward. My harsh breaths echoed in my ears, and my heart slammed against my ribs. "Clarence?" I called. "Where are you?"

A cold wind licked at me from the right. I twisted around. There he was, walking backward, his handsome grin wide and his fingers hooked and beckoning for me to follow.

"Wait!" I shouted. In an instant he was gone from sight.

I lunged forward, straight into the blackness. My eyes took only moments to adjust to the ever-increasing darkness, to the ever-shimmering figure of Clarence Wilcox ahead. I was so focused that I failed to notice the changes around me. The way my footsteps rang out on the flagstones and the room opened up. The way the air smelled like long-standing water.

Or the way Clarence's glowing form reflected beneath him like a mirror.

In a final push, I shoved all my strength into my legs. He was so close!

He stopped abruptly, spinning to face me. "If I cannot have you," he said, his whispers snaking into my brain, "then no one shall."

Before I could comprehend this statement, my foot flew through the air, towing me with it . . . and I plunged into a world of ice.

The air punched from my lungs, roared from my mouth. Water clawed into my throat.

Water! I was *under*water!

I flung out my arms—I had to swim, had to break the surface, had to *breathe*! All of my air had been pushed out; my lungs had *no* reserves. But the dress was like a bag of stones. I strained and kicked and flailed, my chest burning, but no air kissed my skin.

And no matter how hard I fought, the crushing in my lungs didn't lessen.

Then, in a blinding moment of terror, I realized that I didn't know which way was up or down. Everything was black. Everything was empty.

I clapped my hand over my mouth and squeezed out the last of my air, trapping the bubbles in my hand. Yet I couldn't feel which way they rose.

I flapped my arms and swung my legs in what I could only pray was the right direction . . . but my lungs were filled with razors, and my muscles were drained. Frozen. I could barely throw one arm in front of the other, barely keep my fingers flexed. . . .

I was going to drown.

Golden light flashed before my eyes. The curtain—it had to be the curtain to the spirit realm. But I was not ready for it. I fought the water, fought the death I had walked into.

The light flashed more brightly, a yellow stream across my vision.

Then the water shifted and fresh cold swirled over me. It shoved my lips apart, rushing into my mouth, into my chest.

Someone grabbed my wrists . . . someone pulled me up. . . .

But whoever it was was too late. My world had already twisted into nothing.

"Empress, breathe!"

A force slammed into my belly, and I doubled up, coughing. *Dying.* Water sprayed from my mouth.

"Breathe, dammit!"

Hands clamped over my face, a mouth pressed against mine, and breath blasted into my throat.

Like a knife was in my chest, I choked on this air that was not mine. But then it came again, searing my lungs. My body convulsed, and with a desperate wheeze, my chest heaved.

Real air slid in. But it wasn't enough.

"The corset is too tight." The voice sounded like Joseph's.

"Give me your knife, then," Daniel said. "I'll cut her out of it."

"You cannot—"

"She'll *die*, Joseph. Give me the goddamned knife."

Then came the sound of ripping cloth . . . then the snap of breaking stays, until suddenly my ribs could move. My lungs could expand.

I coughed. Hands pressed to my belly, pumping. Water dribbled down the sides of my face. More coughing. More water, and then . . . more *air.*

I gulped it in, desperate and starving. It hurt, but I sucked in more and more. I opened my eyes, blinking as the world shifted into focus. A lantern beside me on wet flagstones . . . Joseph crouched by it with a white sack at his feet . . . and beams of light bouncing off black water.

I twisted my head and stared at Daniel—at his wet hair matted to his head and his bright, shining eyes.

"You," I tried to say, but all that came out was a raw croak.

His arms slid around me and pulled me close. "Don't talk, just breathe, Empress. Breathe."

So I did. I sank into his arms and listened to his heart

hammering against his ribs. For several, rasping breaths, we stayed this way, until a tremor of cold whipped through me. I realized that my dress and corset were gone; all I wore were my chemise and drawers.

I shook again, and Daniel drew back. Joseph shimmied out of his coat. They draped it over me, and then Daniel tugged me into his arms once more.

"What . . . what happened?" I managed to ask through my chattering teeth.

"You almost drowned," Daniel murmured into my hair.

"B-but why? Wh-where are we?"

"Far beneath the Palais Garnier," Joseph answered. "It would seem this theater connects to a series of underground tunnels. We heard your shouts and we followed. You ran into these cellars and to this reservoir. We called and called for you, Eleanor—did you not hear?"

I shook my head. Why would I have come under the theater? Why . . . why was I even *at* the Palais Garnier in the first place?

"You were shoutin' 'Clarence,'" Daniel said. He brushed sopping hair from my face. "Why?"

"I . . . I don't know." I screwed my eyes shut. My head felt so foggy. Why couldn't I remember anything?

Daniel hugged me closer. "You were actin' so strange at the ball. So I brought you downstairs, told you to wait. By the time I found Joseph and got our things, you were already gone."

I opened my eyes and stared at Daniel's wet shirt. At the way it clung to his chest. He had to be just as freezing as I.

"Eleanor," Joseph said, "you truly remember nothing? Not how you came to the ball or what you did there?"

I shook my head.

"Daniel told me Madame Marineaux declared herself your chaperone," Joseph continued. "She was in charge of your dance card—and she would not let Daniel sign it."

I pulled back, frowning up at Daniel. "I was dancing?"

"And acting quite the flirt." His eyes roved over my face. "It . . . it wasn't like you at all. I thought maybe you were under a spell."

"A spell?" I looked to Joseph.

The Creole nodded. "It is possible. A compulsion spell would—"

"A compulsion spell!" Suddenly the discoveries I had made before the ball careened into my mind.

I wrenched away from Daniel's arms. "The Marquis! H-his cane is an amulet, and I think it has seventy-four compulsion spells inside!"

Daniel's face scrunched up. "What the devil are you talking about?"

"There have been seventy-four of *les Morts*, and there are seventy-four senators, and I swear, something about his cane isn't right."

"Empress, you're speaking in gibberish."

I forced myself to take a deep breath and slow down. And step by step, I explained why I thought the cane was an amulet.

When I finished, Joseph's lips pinched tight. "Why do you believe they are compulsion spells?"

"Because *les Morts* have all had their ears and eyes removed, but they also had their tongues drained of blood. Oliver was able to sense what . . ."

At the demon's name, both Daniel and Joseph stiffened. And at their reactions, the rest of my day rushed into my brain. I'd had no intention of attending the ball. No intention of staying in Paris. And no intention of ever seeing Daniel or Joseph again.

"Oh God," I breathed. "You both hate me." I scuttled away from them.

Daniel's eyes widened, and his hand lifted—ever so slightly—as if to reach for me. But then it dropped. He twisted his face away.

"You betrayed us," Joseph said carefully. "Your magic—"

Joseph didn't get to finish, for at that moment the passageway filled with the slap of running feet. I jerked around just as Oliver flew into the lantern light.

"El!" He launched himself at me, completely unconcerned when Daniel leaped up and grabbed him.

"Let go of him!" I tried to stand, but the room spun. All I could manage was a swaying crouch. "Stop, Daniel!"

But Oliver didn't even notice that Daniel held him in a stranglehold. All he saw was me. "Where have you been, El? I couldn't sense you—I couldn't find you! I thought you were dead. I searched and searched and strained, but I couldn't feel our bond—"

"Enough," Daniel snarled. He wrenched upward, closing off Oliver's air.

"Stop!" I shrieked, and this time I got to my feet, only to

find Joseph leaping to his—a crystal clamp in hand. "He won't hurt you! *Please!*"

Daniel looked to Joseph, who nodded once. Daniel released Oliver, and the demon toppled to me, yanking me into an embrace.

"I'm sorry, I'm so sorry," he whispered, his voice shaking. "For yelling and for leaving—I thought I had lost you. I thought you were *dead*. But you aren't—you're alive and you're here. . . ." He pulled back, as if suddenly realizing where "here" was as well as the absence of my clothing. "What the hell happened? When I couldn't sense you, I went to the hotel. They told me you had gone to the ball with Madame Marineaux, so I came here. But when I reached a few blocks away, suddenly I could feel you again. So I came running as fast as I could . . ." His head swiveled as he took in the dark tunnel. "But I still don't understand what happened."

"Joseph thinks I was under a compulsion spell."

Oliver reared back. "The amulet? The Marquis's?"

"The Marquis has not been here tonight," Joseph said, his crystal clamp still held at the ready.

"That doesn't mean his amulet could not be cast." Oliver turned a cool eye on the Spirit-Hunter. "They are meant to be used *long*-distance."

Joseph bristled. "Yet if, as you believe, the Marquis's cane has seventy-three compulsion spells in it—"

"Seventy-three?" I interrupted. "Have there not been seventy-four *Morts*?"

"No," Daniel said, his eyes never leaving Oliver.

"Then where were you all day? After . . . after . . ." I didn't finish the sentence. They knew what I meant.

"We followed a lead on Jie," Joseph answered. "It led us all across the city."

"And?" I asked hopefully.

Daniel's eyes slid to mine, thin and hard. "The trail went cold at the train station, and we were late for this damned ball."

"What if," Oliver said quietly to me, "you were meant to be the seventy-fourth victim?"

Daniel sneered. "Except that she almost drowned. A dead victim ain't any good for a sacrifice."

"Unless she wasn't supposed to drown at all." Oliver pointed into the darkness. "What if she was meant to go down that tunnel?"

"Tunnel?" Joseph whirled around. "I see no tunnel."

"Well, *I* do." Oliver sniffed derisively. "There's a crack in the bricks at the end of this reservoir. Maybe it goes somewhere."

At an almost imperceptible nod from Joseph, Daniel lifted the lantern and crept off along the flagstones. The light swung with his steps, and beams of yellow shot over the water—and illuminated a path running alongside it. Soon enough, Joseph, Oliver, and I were left in blackness and Daniel was nothing more than a beacon in the dark.

And still Joseph's hand stayed around his crystal clamp. "Even if that tunnel goes somewhere, it does not explain how Eleanor was bespelled. Everything about her behavior and lack of memory suggests she was compelled."

"Does it really *matter* how she was compelled?" Oliver

demanded. "The fact is that this Marquis or demon is powerful enough to make an amulet *and* powerful enough to compel his victims. So what actually matters is that you're up against something much bloody stronger than you." He sounded almost pleased by this.

I, however, was not. Yet before I could speak, Daniel shouted, "There's a tunnel here." He jumped into a jog toward us, and with each step closer, the light grew brighter, until he stood right beside me and I had to squint to see.

Daniel set the lantern on the floor. "It looks like it connects to a limestone quarry."

Joseph frowned. "Limestone quarry?"

"Yeah. Most of Paris is riddled with underground quarries—limestone, gypsum . . . there's the catacombs too."

"*Wi*, but what good would such quarries be to a demon?"

"A lot," Oliver muttered. "Seems obvious to me. This cellar here isn't the only entrance into the quarries. All the tunnels connect, and there are entrances all over Paris. This demon simply has to trick his victims into any one of those limestone holes, lure them through the mines to his lair, and *voilà*."

"Limestone," I repeated softly, thinking of the burned-out palace and how the white dust had clung to my skirts. How Oliver had groused, *Do you know how hard it is to get limestone off a suit?*

I had seen that same dust somewhere else. . . . Then it hit: the butler at Madame Marineaux's. "The white dust on the butler!" I turned to Joseph. "You said yourself that it was on several bodies. It's limestone—it's from these mines. This demon *is* taking his victims there."

Joseph's eyes thinned. "You could be right. It *would* be a safe place for the demon to hide, and if there are truly entrances all over the city, then these quarries would give the demon citywide access to victims. If it drew its victims in with a compulsion spell, it would never even have to leave the underground."

"But why use compulsion spells to make *more* compulsion spells?" Daniel asked. "That doesn't make sense."

"*Non*," Joseph murmured. "Yet the rest of it does. The white dust on the victims and . . . the fact that they were all missing a loved one." He looked at me, his head at a thoughtful angle. "You were shouting 'Clarence' when you ran here. What if you were chasing an apparition? Each of *les Morts* of which I can think were missing a loved one."

I gasped. "You're right! The butler's wife had just died. And when I first arrived, the Dead that morning had been a baker who had lost his son."

"Well," Daniel said gruffly, "there's only one way to find out if this theory is right."

I nodded. "We go into the mines and see."

"*We* nothing," Joseph said.

"I have to agree," Oliver chimed in. "*We* nothing, El. You and I—we need to get out of here. Find a new place to stay, get some food . . . and definitely get you some dry clothes before you freeze to death."

I stared, speechless. I had forgotten the cold. Forgotten my lack of clothing. Forgotten *everything* but *les Morts*.

Daniel cleared his throat. "You can have my spare clothes." His head dipped to his sack. "But after that, you and that *thing* need to leave."

"Agreed." Oliver nodded once. "The creature in the quarries is too strong for us, El. Let them die trying to stop it—"

"No." I thrust out my chin. "*No*, Oliver. What if the Marquis or the demon or whatever's behind *les Morts* also has Jie?"

"Then she's probably dead," he answered matter-of-factly.

I clenched my teeth. "No. I refuse to believe that. Not yet." I advanced on Joseph. "You cannot face something this strong by yourself. You need my help."

Joseph turned toward Daniel as if I hadn't spoken at all. "You ought to keep your dry clothes—wear them yourself. Eleanor can have my suit, and then we need to—"

"Do not ignore me!" I shouted. "You have no chance against this necromancy. And you have almost no equipment!"

"Silence, Eleanor." Joseph did not turn to look at me. "How many bullets do you have, Daniel?"

My blood warmed, rage escalating through me. I would *not* be ignored. Not like this, and not now. "Do you even know how to fight a demon, Joseph? Are you willing to risk your lives and *Jie's* all because you're too stubborn to work with a necromancer?"

His body tensed, and he looked right at me. "A necromancer who lied to me. A necromancer with a *demon*, and a necromancer who almost killed people today with her foolishness."

"You cannot stop me from coming with you."

341

Joseph rounded on me. "I most certainly can, Eleanor." He lifted the clamp, and the crystal sparkled yellow in the lantern light. "And I most certainly *will*."

"Do it," I snarled. "But I will—"

Daniel stepped in front of me. "That's enough, Empress. Both of you are wasting time." He glanced at Joseph. "Just let her go. It obviously ain't her demon that's causing *les Morts*, and maybe . . . maybe she's right. Maybe we can't face this thing by ourselves."

"Now wait a minute," Oliver declared. "We are not going in there, El. You are not going to risk your life—and *mine*—for them. They don't care about you!"

"No," I answered, my eyes scoring into Joseph's, "but this isn't about them, Oliver. It's about Jie. About *les Morts*. About making a choice to do the right thing."

For several long moments Joseph matched my stare, his nostrils flaring. But at last he gave a single, curt nod. "You may come, but only if you swear to me that you will obey my every command and cast no spells. *No. Black. Magic.*"

I hesitated. I didn't want to obey him—and I certainly didn't want to deny my power if it would help find Jie . . . but I *did* want to join them, and if that meant cooperating—or at least pretending to cooperate—then so be it.

"I swear."

"Good. Now get dressed. We are going to end this once and for all."

CHAPTER TWENTY-ONE

Joseph's trousers and shirt were too long . . . but they were at least dry. As I sat on the flagstones and stuffed the boots with pieces of petticoat, I stretched my mind to remember the ball—to recall some detail that might help explain how I had fallen so easily into a spell, but I came up with nothing. For now, I could only hope that one day the memories would return.

Somewhere in the dark beside me, I could hear Daniel changing as well. Joseph stood with the lantern at the tunnel's mouth. Oliver skulked along the water, staring into its black depths. He twisted around and approached. "Are you sure this is what you want to do?"

"It isn't a want," I said, tying my final bootlace. "It's a need."

Oliver held out his hand and helped me stand, but he didn't

release my fingers. "And you realize how strong this demon is, right?"

I nodded, even though I had no idea, not even an inkling, of how strong a demon could be. In the end it did not matter, for it would not change what I intended to do. "You don't have to come, Oliver."

"But I will. If I hadn't left you, you wouldn't have almost drowned."

I squeezed his hand. "And if I had not been careless with Elijah's letters, you would not have had to leave."

"Empress?" Daniel called softly.

I turned and in the flickering lantern light saw him padding close. Four pistols hung in a leather bandolier across his chest.

Daniel didn't meet my eyes. "We're going now." Then he strode past me, heading for the lantern. For Joseph. For the tunnel into darkness.

I hurried after, Oliver on my heels. Soon enough, I could see the tunnel: a jagged crack in the white wall with barely enough space through which to squeeze.

"Look." Joseph waved Daniel over. "There is blood. And cloth."

I crept closer, until I too could make out the dark stain on the bricks as well as several tiny tatters of brown fabric. "Signs of the Dead?"

Joseph did not answer. He merely backed away from the crack and said, "Eleanor and the demon go first."

Daniel's gaze flickered uncertainly to me. "Or maybe I should go first."

"Let Eleanor's demon face its kin."

"Unless . . ." Daniel swallowed. "Unless he leads us into a trap. I think you should let me go first." He scratched his neck. "Eleanor and the demon can pick up the rear."

Joseph nodded curtly and handed Daniel the lantern. Then, after checking that his bandolier was well fastened, Daniel hefted the lantern high and slithered through the crack. Joseph squeezed in just behind.

I threw Oliver a glance.

"No chance you'll reconsider?" he asked, his eyebrows high.

"None."

He spread his hands. "Then lead the way, *Master* Eleanor."

I wedged myself in, and after wriggling through several feet of rough rock that scraped and latched onto my clothes, I finally toppled out the other side. Water dripped from the reddish walls like blood, and I couldn't tell if the rust color of the stones was from the lantern's flame or their natural color.

Daniel's face flickered ahead. He was waiting, his head crooked to keep from hitting it on the low ceiling.

"There are clear signs of passage," Joseph murmured, his gaze cast down. "Many footsteps have come this way—dragging, uncoordinated footsteps, I would say. And if it was this easy for us to enter here, then why not *les Morts*?"

I glanced down, trying to see whatever Joseph saw, but I

did not have enough light.

Seconds later Oliver squirmed out behind me, his yellow eyes glowing in the dim light. Without a word, Daniel pivoted around and crept off.

The passage descended steadily, and the air turned thicker— as if I were breathing in the stones themselves. Our feet crunched on the sandy floor, but soon the walls sweated so heavily, the droplets collected on the ground in unseen puddles. Cold water sloshed into my boots, numbing my toes.

Yet on we went, the tunnels twisting and winding like a snake. Always sloping down. Always growing colder, until eventually my breath curled out in smoky tendrils. How many years—or centuries—had Parisians been mining beneath their city? To have opened up a honeycomb of caves so extensive and so deep . . . I felt like an ant descending into the anthill. But instead of a queen, we sought a demon.

I do not know how far we traveled—it felt as if we walked for hours—but by the time the ceiling finally lifted enough for Daniel to unfurl his lanky form, I was bone-cold and shambling like the Dead.

And all I wanted was for this descent to end. I was more than a little tempted to call on my power—not only for warmth, but for courage. Yet if Joseph sensed me casting a spell . . . It was not worth his wrath. Not when we were this close.

Of course, several twisting tunnels later I was already regretting my decision to ignore my power, for now we were not only cold and exhausted, we were forced to stop.

Two branches split off.

I hugged my arms to my chest. How much *longer*? I bounced on my toes, trying to get feeling back into them. Trying to quell my impatience and ignore the now *insistent* craving for magic.

The lantern cast shadows on the wall in phantom-shapes— long figures with even longer arms that seemed to wriggle and writhe in time with Daniel's and Joseph's soft murmuring.

I licked my lips. *Fight the magic a bit longer.* To distract myself, I whispered, "Oliver, how do we stop the demon?"

"If it's bound to the Marquis, it won't be too difficult. Its magic will be limited to the Marquis's commands, and we simply . . . I don't know, rope it up."

"What if it's unbound?"

"*Then* we'll be in trouble." He didn't get to explain further, though, for Daniel suddenly declared, "This one." He stood before the right passage. "It has fresh tracks." And with that he whirled around, spraying us briefly in light, and then strode off, with Joseph behind.

I scampered after, grateful to move. But we almost instantly stopped again, for our way was blocked by an old cave-in.

"No, *no!*" I cried. A mound of dusty rubble stood as high as my chest. By now my body was so numb, I could no longer feel my fingers as I rubbed them on my cheeks.

But I bit back the tears brewing in my chest. I was embarrassed to be reacting this emotionally. No one else was showing frustration, but no one else was having to constantly resist the pull of magic either . . . and I couldn't resist much longer.

Daniel clambered up a few steps, and then, leaning on the mound, he held out the lantern. "It's not a dead end," he said softly. "We can get through the space at the top. The cave-in doesn't go far beyond that, but . . ." He looked up and inspected the ceiling. "That ceiling ain't stable. We've gotta be real careful. If it all collapses, we'll be stuck on the other side." He glanced back at Joseph.

Joseph set his jaw. "I . . . I believe we have no other choice. If we see no signs of *les Morts* on the other side, then we will return."

I screwed my eyes shut and prayed we would find signs. We had not gone this far simply to turn back.

Daniel climbed up the mound, his feet sliding and pebbles flying. At the top, he set the lantern in the dirt. "I'll leave it here so you can see . . ." His eyes slid down to me. Then, almost as if he was coming to some decision, he set his jaw. "Empress, you bring the lantern through."

For a second I thought Joseph would argue. But after a momentary hesitation, he planted his foot in the limestone and started to ascend. Meanwhile, Daniel scrabbled around and crawled into the tiny space above the cave-in.

I moved forward, but Oliver grabbed my hand.

"What?"

He shook his head, clearly waiting for Joseph to disappear through the rubble. Then he bent in close, whispering in my ear, "I will only say this once more, and then I fear it will be too late."

"Say what?"

"We can still turn back. Take that lantern and run."

"And abandon them?" My shoulders locked up. "In the *dark*?"

He gave a small shrug. "I don't care about them. At all. And I still don't know why you do."

I didn't answer him. Instead, I spun on my heel, dug my hands into the powdery rock, and climbed.

At the top, there was just enough space for me to wriggle through on my stomach and then twist around to snag the lantern. A few more feet of squirming and I slid out the other side. Joseph took the lantern, and Daniel gripped my hand and helped me clamber down.

But the moment my heavy boot hit the hard floor, Daniel released it. He even wiped his hands on his pants, as if I'd contaminated him with my touch.

And all my earlier irritation flared bright. I had not *asked* for his help. Not to mention, he'd had no trouble touching me after I had almost drowned. No trouble jamming his lips on mine or pressing me to his chest.

The scrape of dirt told us Oliver was on his way, so Daniel held the lantern high. There were distinct footprints all around, and I breathed a grateful sigh.

At Joseph's nod, Daniel resumed his march into the low tunnels. But it didn't stay low for long—nor did it stay narrow. Soon Daniel could stand upright, while I could spread out both of my arms and not reach the walls, and the ground beneath us became smooth. Well-worn as if *very* well-trod.

We should have realized this was a bad sign. We should have known right then to stop—especially when we reached an abrupt turn in the tunnel.

But we were too desperate to reach the end, so we traipsed right around that blind bend. Or rather, Daniel did. . . .

And then his voice roared out. "Dead!"

Panic flooded my brain, and for a heartbeat all I could do was stand there, frozen.

Then came the crack of a pistol shot, and my body surged to life. I twisted around and shoved Oliver into a run.

Behind me came the scraping sound of bone on bone. *Crack!* The blue glow of electricity flashed through the tunnel.

"Faster!" Daniel cried, his voice right behind me. And the snapping of bones just behind him.

So I hurtled faster, the lantern light listing and rocking and Oliver just ahead. Until Oliver stopped and spun around.

We were at the cave-in.

"Command me!" he shouted, his hands flying up.

"Stop the Dead! *Sum veritas!*"

"*Dormi!*"

Daniel's arms flew around my waist, and he yanked me past Oliver just as the demon's blue magic erupted. We hit the pile of rubble, knocking down fresh bits of ceiling.

But the limestone falling on my face barely registered over the stampeding feet and the empty eye sockets everywhere. There were far too many to fight with our fists. We needed magic—lots of it.

"*Dormi!*" Oliver roared again, and a few corpses on the front line toppled over—only to be replaced by more skeletal claws.

Daniel fired a pulse pistol, knocking back the next wave. But more followed.

And in the distance, somewhere in the middle of the sea of skeletons, electricity thundered over and over again.

I let my instincts take over then. As I sucked in my breath, I drew in all my power with it. Then I hurled the magic out. It was like the time at Madame Marineaux's, but now, instead of one corpse there were three—no, there were four, five . . . *seven*. Somehow I anchored myself to seven Dead.

"Stay," I murmured. They did not stay. Nor did they come as quickly—though the corpses behind them were not slowed. Their bone fingers reached over felled corpses and fought to get by.

"*Dormi!*" Oliver cried again, and three of my seven crumpled. Instantly, I mentally grabbed onto the next corpses.

"Stay, stay, stay." Out of the corner of my eye, I saw Daniel reload his pulse pistols, his eyes never leaving the Dead.

It was then that I noticed that Joseph's electricity had stopped. No more blue flashes, no more thundering blasts.

My grip on the Dead faltered. Two hurtled for us, fingers reaching and jaws wide.

Pop! They collapsed, and pistol smoke wafted into my nose. "We need to get out of here!" Daniel shouted.

No one moved. Oliver continued bellowing, "*Dormi!*" Yet with each of his attacks, fewer and fewer corpses fell.

And though I still chanted "Stay, stay, stay," fewer and fewer corpses listened.

"*Go!*" Joseph screamed, his voice distant and desperate.

Daniel lunged forward, as if to force his way into the Dead. I threw myself at him. "No, you can't—"

"He needs me!"

"And you'll *die.*"

Daniel hesitated, his gaze whipping from the lines of never-ending skeletons to the rapidly draining Oliver. Then he snatched my hand and hauled me to the pile of limestone. "Climb!" He twisted to Oliver. "You too! *Climb!* I'll cover you."

He flipped out two pulse pistols and aimed at the shambling bodies—bodies that crawled over their felled brothers, their heels sinking into ancient flesh.

Pop! Pop! I raced up the rubble, my hands digging into the dirt and my legs propelling me up as fast as I could go. Oliver was right on my heels, and in his hand was the lantern.

We reached the top. I pushed Oliver in front and twisted back to get Daniel. "Come on! Hurry!"

Pop! More Dead toppled over, almost at Daniel's feet. He wouldn't make it.

"*Hurry!*" I shrieked, reaching for him.

"I have one pistol left and no time to reload." He grabbed hold of my hand, and I poured all my strength into towing him up. He reached the top, and the Dead climbed up after.

"Go!" He shoved me violently into the narrow space. "Faster, Empress—*go!* I'll hold 'em off."

I did as he said, dragging myself with my hands and kicking with my heels. Dirt crumbled over me, and I thought the ceiling would fall at any moment. . . .

Then Oliver had his fingers around mine. He was yanking me through and into the calm of the empty tunnel beyond. I was about to tumble down the limestone, to keep running, until I realized that Daniel wasn't behind me.

I twisted around. "Daniel!" I met his eyes, wide and scared.

And still faraway on the other side of the cave-in.

I knew without even seeing it that the Dead had reached him.

"Shoot them!" I screamed. "Shoot!"

But he didn't. He aimed his pistol directly at the ceiling, and in a final roar he screamed, *"Run!"* and pulled the trigger.

Chapter Twenty-two

"*No!*" *I launched myself at the cave-in. The entire* tunnel was blocked, but I had to get through. I kicked rocks aside and flung at the dirt. "Please, please, *please, no!*"

Oliver's arms slung around me. "Stop! You'll bring down more of the ceiling."

"But they're on the other side!" I shrieked. "Daniel's *on* the other side!"

"And we can't do anything about that now!"

"We can go through!"

"No, El, we can't." He spun me around to face him. "Your man shot the ceiling, and he did it on *purpose.*"

"B-but why?" I found I was shaking and . . . and *crying.* "They have no light and th-there's hundreds of Dead."

"I don't think the Dead were hurting them."

"Wh-what?"

"Joseph—he kept blasting them down and was still able to shout. He didn't sound *hurt*. More . . . detained. Think about it, El. Why would the demon want to hurt anyone who walked into its lair?"

"It . . . it wouldn't." I pressed the heels of my hands to my eyes. "It cannot sacrifice a dead victim." My hands dropped. "But that means Joseph and Daniel will both be . . ." I spun back around and lunged for the rubble. "We *have* to get through!"

"But there's no *point*." He was yelling at me. "If we get through, then *we'll* be demon-food."

"But we can stop the Dead!"

"No, we can't." He shoved in front of me and gripped my chin. "There were *hundreds* of bodies back there. This demon must collect them from the catacombs and use them as sentries to patrol the tunnels. I can't take down more than a few Dead at a time, El, and you . . . you don't know how to take down *any*."

"So teach me!"

He lowered his hand. "Even if I did, you wouldn't be able to stop any more bodies than I can."

My stomach curdled, and the tears fell harder. "B-but I can't just leave Daniel . . . or Joseph . . . or that *demon*. Please, Oliver!"

"Please what? We have only one option: go back. We can get the hell out of here and—"

"No. *No*." My tears stopped abruptly, cold trails on my face. "We are not leaving. Though . . . we *can* go back." I swooped up the lantern and strode down the tunnel.

"And do what?" He surged beside me, his hands up. "Oh no.

You mean go into the other passage?"

"Yes."

"What if it leads nowhere?"

"I have to try."

"Well, what if it leads to more Dead?"

I hesitated at that, and Oliver charged on. "See, El? We need to go back to the surface."

"No," I snapped. "Absolutely not. There must be some spell I can cast to protect us, right?"

His shoulders dropped an inch. He looked away. "There *is* an awareness spell. It would allow you to sense anything living—or Dead—nearby."

I nodded curtly. More magic. More spells. It would give me strength, and that was something I needed. I set off back toward the branching tunnels and said, "Tell me what to do."

Oliver followed just on my heels, the lantern swinging in his hand. "First you say *Sentio omnia quae me circumdentur*. It means 'I feel all around me,' and it will form a web. You sort of toss it out." He spread his arms, and the light sprayed out with the movement. "Do you understand?"

"Yes." We were almost to the split. With each step, I drew my magic into my chest. It trickled in slowly, warm and safe. A balm to my fears, an embrace against the cold, and a light in the dark. And with each drop of soul that slid through my veins, my steps grew stronger, and the blue glow grew brighter.

"*Sentio omnia quae me circumdentur.*" The words trilled over my tongue, and as I threw my magic wide, casting it in all directions, I slowed to a stop at the fork in the tunnels. My magic spread and spread until finally sinking into place like a net sinking to the bottom of a pond.

"Well?" Oliver asked. "Do you sense anyone?"

"No." Other than Oliver behind me, I sensed nothing—though I tried to sense more. Tried to push the web just a bit farther, to feel for Daniel and Joseph . . . but they were too far away, or . . .

No, they are alive, and I will find them.

With a final glance at Oliver, I set off down the other passage. How long we went or how far, I could not say. Though the winding limestone tunnel was the same as all the others, this journey wasn't like the earlier one. I had my magic now, so I felt no irritation—only determination. And worry. Always, *always* I had to battle thoughts of Daniel and Joseph getting closer to death with every second that passed—if they weren't already . . . dead. . . .

And always I had to focus my web of awareness. More than once I found my thoughts wandering, for I could not help but wonder where we were beneath Paris. We had walked so far. What part of the city was above us now?

Eventually Oliver pulled me to a stop. "The path ends ahead."

"What?" I choked. "What do you mean 'ends'?"

"There's a wall." He motioned ahead, beyond the range of the lantern's light. "A dead end."

I scurried ahead, frustration exploding in my chest—only to grind quickly to a halt. There *was* a wall. But it was cracked, like the wall by the reservoir had been.

"I can squeeze through that." I darted forward, but Oliver latched on to my arm.

"Don't be ridiculous! It probably leads *nowhere*."

I yanked free and surged toward the wall again. "Just let me check. Please." Yet I only made it two steps when a black, putrid wave slammed into my senses.

I cried out, dropping to my knees. The stench of grave dirt invaded my nose.

"El, what is it?"

But I couldn't answer. My stomach heaved, and bile boiled up my throat. I vomited into the black. Acid splattered my hands.

"El, what's wrong?"

"D-death," I stuttered before gagging again. *"Wrong."*

"Draw in the web." His voice was barely a whisper, yet the urgency was clear. "Hurry, you'll feel better."

I did as he said, frantically reeling my awareness back to myself. Instantly the nausea and the smell vanished.

Clutching my arms to my stomach, I sank back until I hit the tunnel wall.

"Are you all right?" Oliver murmured, his hand patting my arm until his fingers found mine. He squeezed. "El?"

"No, I am not all right." My voice trembled, burning my acid-raw throat. "It was . . . it was so, so rotten. Death every-where."

"It's the demon." Oliver's voice was barely a whisper.

"Can you sense it?"

"Not yet," he admitted, squeezing my hand again. "But I'm sure I will soon. Your web of magic extends your range of awareness

359

much farther than my own. Tell me: which way was it?"

I pointed behind me, toward the crack in the wall. "Just beyond there."

Oliver's eyebrows shot down. "Did you sense Joseph? Or Daniel?"

"I-I did not try."

"What about the Dead?" he pressed. "Did you feel any corpses?"

"I did not *try*, Ollie. The black and the grave dirt, they over-powered everything."

He took my other hand in his. "You have to try, El. If this demon is just through that hole, we need to be prepared. We need to know if it's alone."

I gulped and nodded. Tentatively, I sucked in my magic, but rather than fling out my awareness, I let it creep through the crack . . . then onward and up . . . until the rotten sense of wrong rolled over me. I screwed my eyes shut, forcing myself to keep fumbling, keep feeling. . . . Then I sensed two flames amid the black: Daniel and Joseph.

I yanked in the web, popping my eyes wide. "They're there," I breathed. "Daniel, Joseph. And I couldn't feel any Dead." My breath shot out, thick with relief. "Oh thank God, they're there. Alive . . . *alive*."

"And how far ahead is the demon?"

"No . . . no more than a hundred yards."

"And you are sure you want to keep going?"

"Yes."

"Then let's go. Quietly." His hand gripped my elbow, and without another word, he helped me cram myself into the slanted crack. I had to shove and wiggle until the rock tore my clothes and slashed my skin, but I was numb from the cold and the magic. I felt no pain. After several feet of this clambering, I finally wedged through—and into a pitch-black, yet open, tunnel.

Oliver eased out behind me—but without the lantern. "I couldn't carry it and still fit through. I'm sorry."

"Can you see?" I whispered.

"Well enough. I will go first." Then he clasped my hand in his and pulled me into a careful tiptoe. Our pace was barely above a crawl, and everything seemed loud. Each of our steps, our breaths, our fingertips brushing on the cave walls. And everywhere that my straining eyes landed seemed to move. Every spot in my vision sent my pulse racing.

Suddenly Oliver's hand clenched mine in warning. I froze, holding my breath trapped. Ever so slowly, Oliver pulled me to him, and then I felt his lips at my ear. "It's ahead. Joseph—he's shouting. Can you hear?"

I shook my head once.

"We'll keep going, but be prepared to fight. Have . . . have your commands for me ready."

"What will I command you to do?"

He gave an almost inaudible laugh. "Just tell me to destroy it." He drew away from me, and together we crept forward, the tunnel curving right . . . then left. After twenty measured steps, the faintest sounds finally began to slide into my ears. Forty steps and we rounded another bend—and now Joseph's bellows sounded clear. Seconds later we veered sharply left . . . and halted. Light, painful even in its orange dimness, shone ahead. I squinted, trying to see what was *in* the light, but we were still too far away.

Then a scream—a sickening shriek of pain—tore through the tunnel. But I couldn't tell if it was Daniel's or Joseph's. All I knew was that we were out of time.

I pushed Oliver to go faster. The screams masked our footsteps until the shrieking ceased. We instantly stopped . . . waiting, not breathing. A new sound broke out: a tinkling, happy sound. Someone laughing.

I glanced at Oliver, and at his nod I slunk forward. He slid along behind me, both of us hugging the walls and craning our necks.

But once I *could* see, I instantly wished for the darkness again. Because knowing what was in there—seeing the horror—was so, *so* much worse.

It was a cavern, tall, round, and as large as the ballroom, yet lit by torches that cast the scene in an orange, shadowy light.

And there, hunched over a stone table in the center of the cavern with long, jagged claws extended and her dainty mouth lapping up blood, was none other than Madame Marineaux.

And the blood was Joseph's. It poured from the side of his head, from a gushing, jagged hole where his ear had once been.

CHAPTER TWENTY-THREE

Madame Marineaux still wore her black ball gown, her coiled hair as perfect as ever. . . . Even her face—her smile— seemed as sweet as it always did. But her fingernails—they were as sharp and long as knives. And her mouth . . . fresh blood dribbled down her chin.

It took all of my self-control not to run straight to Joseph or completely the other way. She was a friend. I had trusted her, and yet . . . something twisted in my gut. Something that said, *You knew this all along. You simply did not want to see it.*

But I would deal with that guilt, that hurt, later. For now I had a demon to face.

I dragged my eyes away from the Madame, searching for some sign of Daniel. It wasn't hard—he was loud despite being bound and gagged against the left-most wall. He rolled and writhed beside a narrow tunnel descending into darkness. Yet his struggles did no good; he was too tightly fettered. Tossed on the dirt nearby was his bandolier, the crystal clamp shimmering beside it.

I flicked my gaze the other way, forcing myself not to look at Joseph's shuddering chest or Madame Marineaux's bloody face. Forcing myself to evaluate the enormous cavern.

There was a third tunnel on the far right. Torchlight flickered into it, showing a rising floor—a well-worn, rising floor.

"Y-you," Joseph rasped, his voice weak yet penetrating every crevice in the room, "c-can kill me, but you will not go unpunished."

Madame Marineaux laughed, almost gleefully, and rose to her full—albeit tiny—height. "You have no idea what you say, Joseph Boyer. Your blood is very strong. Very strong, indeed. And when my master learns whom I have *killed*. Oh, how pleased he will be."

At the word "killed," Daniel's struggles grew more frenzied, and muffled shouts seeped through his gag.

Madame Marineaux clucked at him. "Monsieur Sheridan, I do wish you would stay quiet. Your turn will come soon enough."

"Stop," Joseph commanded hoarsely. "W-we know what you"—a shiver wracked him—"plan. You and the Marquis . . . cannot succeed."

"The Marquis?" She chuckled and dragged a claw almost lovingly along Joseph's jaw. "Is that who you think is behind this? Oh, you naive little Spirit-Hunter. The Marquis was merely a tool. A source of income . . . and *power* for my master. He had no idea what was happening around him—or to him."

A hand landed on my shoulder, and I flinched. But it was only Oliver. His eyes told me plain enough what he could not say: *We need a plan.*

And as much as I did not want to go—as much as my body screamed at me to run into the chamber and *do* something—I had to think this through.

Madame Marineaux was a demon, and she was strong.

So I forced myself to look away, to turn around and leave. We did not stop until there was no more light and Madame Marineaux's wicked crowing had faded to a distant whisper.

Oliver pulled me to him, breathing in my ear, "Joseph's hurt badly, and that *demon* is . . ." He trailed off.

"It's Madame Marineaux," I whispered.

"No, El." I heard him gulp. "Her claws . . . I think she's a Rakshasi."

"Rakshasi?" That name sounded familiar, though I couldn't place why.

Oliver moved closer, pulling my body to his. "They're the most deadly a-and," he tripped over his words, "and *powerful* demons of all time. And they're the only ones I know of with claws like that. She has venom that works like a compulsion spell . . . venom that makes you see things that aren't real."

I sucked in a breath as all the pieces clicked together. So *that* was why I'd gone to the ball. Why I'd forgotten every moment spent with her. And with this realization, some of my memories came *back*. The sound of her voice as she plied me with questions about the Spirit-Hunters. The sound of *my voice*—flat and monotone—as I answered. And all it had taken was a drop of venom in my champagne; I had been hers to control. Except, I'd had nothing to drink tonight. . . .

"With power like this," Oliver went on, "she must be thousands of years old. I'm a bloody *baby* next to her, El." His whispers sliced into my ear, and with them came icy fear.

"So . . . so what can we do?" I asked.

"We can get the hell out of here—"

At that moment, Joseph's ragged screams ripped through the tunnel once more. Oliver cowered into me, his yellow eyes flashing in the black.

"Please, El," he breathed. "Please, let's just *go*."

"No. We can't. We are out of time." I pivoted around, pulling away from Oliver. Joseph's screams continued.

"We need a plan!" he hissed.

"I have one. I saw Daniel's pistols on the left wall. If I can distract Madame Marineaux long enough, then you can get the Spirit-Hunters' equipment and free them. The pistols will need reloading, so I will keep Madame Marineaux's attention until I see that you're ready to fight." Then, before Oliver could protest or point out the ten thousand holes in my plan, I ran toward Joseph, toward Daniel. . . .

Toward Rakshasi.

I did not bother to stay quiet. Did not even pause to check my surroundings. Joseph and Daniel needed me—*now*—and as soon as I had enough light to see the ground beneath my feet, I burst into a sprint.

When I finally skittered into the cavern, it was to find Joseph still bound to the stone table. But now Daniel was sprawled out on the floor beside him. His mouth was still gagged and his limbs still tied. Madame Marineaux, her back to me, hovered over him.

"Stop!" I said, my voice a low growl. "Let them go."

With unnatural speed, Madame Marineaux twirled toward me, her dress billowing around her. A genuine smile spread over her lips. "You came!" She clapped with delight. "I am so glad."

I looked past her, terrified that I'd find Daniel's body mutilated. But he was fine, and at the sight of me, his eyes bulged and he burst into a fresh struggle. Joseph also saw me, and despite the blood oozing from his head, he also strained against his bonds. For whatever reason, it looked as if Madame Marineaux had made no more wounds on his body.

"But," Madame Marineaux continued, "how did you get in here from *that* passage?"

I turned my attention back to Madame Marineaux; she bustled to me as if we were merely meeting on the dance floor. Her little steps covered surprising ground, and she stood before me in only seconds. "And," she said, "where is your dress? Who removed it?"

"We did," Joseph croaked. "And with that amulet off her, your spell ceased."

So the dress was how she had compelled me tonight. She had turned it into an amulet.

Madame Marineaux rolled her eyes. "You are bothering me, Monsieur Boyer. First Monsieur Sheridan will not be quiet while I am sacrificing you, and now *you* will not stay silent." A single fingernail clicked out, growing as long as a dagger. "I wish to speak to Mademoiselle Fitt in *peace*." She whirled around, flying for the stone table.

"Wait!" I screamed. "Madame Mari—Rakshasi!"

She paused, her skirts swishing forward. "You know my true essence?" She looked back at me, her eyes glowing yellow. "How?"

"I . . . I made a good guess."

Her lips curved up. "You *are* like Claire. So feisty. So clever." She twisted back to me, forgetting Joseph completely. "Are you here to join me, then? To help free me from my master? He is a false master. A *liar*."

She was close now. Close enough for me to see the streaks of blood around her mouth, the bits of flesh stuck in her claws.

I needed to draw her away so Oliver could sneak in. I retreated, strolling for the wall and aiming for the tunnel in the far right corner. *Twenty steps to the wall, then twenty steps to the tunnel.*

"A false master?" I asked, still moving as casually as I could.

"He *tricked* me." Madame Marineaux's lips puffed out in a pout—but almost immediately curled back, baring her fangs. "He killed her. His own mother. My Claire—he *killed* her! Then he broke Claire's bond and trapped me in an agreement."

My mind raced to understand what she had just shared. She was an unbound demon, yet she still had some sort of master. So how?

"What sort of agreement?" I asked, continuing to walk.

"I must do as he wishes for as long as he wishes, and perhaps one day he will let me go home. . . . Where are you going, *Mademoiselle*?" She frowned. "Stop walking. *Now*."

I froze. The altar was forty paces away. That would have to be enough space. . . .

Oliver must have thought the same thing, for barely a breath passed before he crept into the cavern and darted for the stone table.

Madame Marineaux tensed as if hearing Oliver, but before she could turn around, I blurted, "Will he free you? Will your false master keep his promise?"

Her posture drooped. "I do not know. He is *cruel*. Nothing like his mother, my Claire. And he is strong—too strong for me. But you . . ." She reached out and stroked my cheek with her claw. "You and I, Mademoiselle Fitt—he could not beat the two of us. Not together." She leaned in, inhaling deeply. "So much power. It radiates off you."

I gulped, trying not to breathe. She *stank* of blood. Her breath, her claws—a metallic, keening stench.

She did not seem to notice my reaction. "Think," she purred, "what we could do with your strength and my experience. Just *imagine*." Then her fingernail pierced my jaw. Only the slightest poke, but it broke the skin . . .

And the venom overwhelmed me.

It is Christmas, and I am in my family's drawing room. There is snow falling outside the window, and a fire billows in the hearth.

369

Father sits beside the fireplace, the Evening Bulletin *in his hand, and Elijah sits on the floor at his feet, a book upon his lap.*

Elijah glances up at me and smiles. He looks not so different from when he died—older, stronger, and wider jawed. Yet his spectacles still slide down his nose, and his goofy grin is as I've always known it. He looks happy.

Father says something in his bass voice; it makes Elijah laugh. Then Father laughs too, and my heart swells.

A new laugh chimes in—Mama's twitter—and I spin around just as she walks into the drawing room.

"Would you like mulled wine, Eleanor? Your friend was kind enough to bring us mulling spices."

"My . . . my friend?" I step, confused, toward her. My dress rustles, and for the first time, I notice I'm wearing a stunning blue taffeta with black trim. I smooth the bodice, gaping. But then Mama speaks, dragging me back to the moment.

"Yes, your friend Mr. Sheridan." She glides to me and takes my hands in hers. "He said he has an old Irish recipe for mulling, and—"

"Did you say Mr. Sheridan?" I interrupt, my chest cinching. "Is he here?"

"Yes, dear. He only just arrived. Do not look so worried." She winks at me and pulls away—Father is calling her. "You look as beautiful as ever," she trills.

I try to swallow but find that my throat aches. My mother has never called me beautiful before . . . and yet I feel beautiful. Feel safe and certain—

"Empress."

I gasp and twirl back to the door. And there he is, wearing a handsome gray wool suit and with his cheeks bright pink from traipsing through the winter snow.

He grins, making his whole face relax and his grassy-colored eyes twinkle. Then he strolls to me. "I appreciate you invitin' me to Christmas supper." He only stops his easy amble once he's directly in front of me. I have to tip back my head to meet his eyes.

But then a frown knits onto his brow. He reaches out to clasp my chin. "Why are you cryin', Empress?"

"I am?" I reach up, and my gloves slide over wet cheeks. "I . . . I am. It's just . . . I'm so happy, Daniel."

"Then you shouldn't cry, Empress. You should laugh."

I laughed—a shrill, desperate sound—as the vision faded away . . . as Madame Marineaux's face swam back into my vision.

My laugh broke off, replaced by a sob. I toppled to the hard earth. "Where is it?" I screamed, clutching at her skirts. "The vision, bring it back! Please, I want it back."

The edges of her lips twisted up. "And you can have it, Mademoiselle Fitt. You can *have* it if you join me."

"Do not believe her!" Joseph rasped, still bound to the table. "It is only a fantasy."

"Ah, but it is *not* only a fantasy," Madame Marineaux whispered. "Together we can make it real. With your power and mine, we can do anything. They"—her voice lifted, as if she wanted the Spirit-Hunters to hear—"do not appreciate you.

These Spirit-Hunters think you are dark, but they simply do not understand that this is who you are. But I understand, for you have told me all your troubles.

"You are not dark," she went on. "You are *selfless*, Mademoiselle Fitt. These Spirit-Hunters have no idea how hard it was for you to get here. They do not realize all you had to do to survive. All that you gave up for them. For those you love."

I shook my head, my eyes burning with tears.

"They do not understand that your mother hates you. That your friends have all rejected you. Or that your fortune is gone. What do *they*"—she flicked her wrist dismissively in Joseph's direction—"know of the dresses you had to sell to pay for your mother's bills? Your ungrateful, *cruel* mother? What do they know of the friends who avoid you on the street or laugh behind your back?"

A sob shuddered through my chest. Everything she said was true. What *did* the Spirit-Hunters know about me? About what I had *lost*?

"Nor," she continued, "can they see the fine line you walk between life and death. The Hell Hounds await you—still these guardians hunger for your blood. You *must* use your necromancy to stay alive, but these Spirit-Hunters cannot see that." Her voice grew louder with each word—and my conviction, my *hurt*, grew too. "So tell me what the Spirit-Hunters actually know about you at all?

"I will tell you," Madame Marineaux declared. "The Spirit-Hunters know nothing. Their lives have gotten better, while *yours* has spiraled into pain and hate and memories best forgotten."

Madame Marineaux bent to me and whispered in my ear, "I feel your pain as strongly as my own, *Mademoiselle*. I know what it is to be denied what you deserve. To have everything you love taken from you." She dipped her pointed chin and watched me from the tops of her eyes. "I am unbound yet unfree. How is that any different from you, who are far from home yet never able to escape it?"

"What—" My voice cracked, but I tried again. "What do you want from me?"

"Oh, it is easy." She brushed my hair lovingly from my face. "My master—my *overseer*—expects me to meet him in Marseille, but you can free me before then. We can get your friend, the Chinese girl, back from him, and together we can *crush* him. You, Mademoiselle Fitt, could become my true master. A woman worthy of my magic and my devotion."

"What do I have to do?"

"Don't!" Daniel roared. "Empress, don't!"

Madame Marineaux twirled around, and I realized with a start that Daniel and Joseph were both free now . . . that Daniel was running toward me.

But then a bolt of light flew from Madame Marineaux's hand and blasted Daniel in the chest. He toppled backward, flipping over like a rag doll to crash into the stone altar.

And for several heartbeats I only watched. Completely indifferent . . . until a noxious wave pummeled into me—a shock wave from Madame Marineaux's spell that was filled with complete *wrong*. And like a hypnotist's snap, it jerked my mind back to reality.

"Daniel!" I pushed off the wall, trying to skitter around Madame Marineaux. But she was faster—so much faster.

She lifted me up and slammed me against the wall. Pain cracked into my skull, and sparks raced through my vision. I reached for her, tried to scratch at her face, but she merely straightened her arms—and somehow her arms were suddenly longer than mine. Much longer, and my fingers reached nothing but air.

So I punched her elbow.

Her arm shuddered, and a wail broke from her lips. "After all I have offered and given, *this* is how you repay me?"

"Offered?" I croaked. "By sacrificing *les Morts*? By building an amulet of compulsion for your precious Claire's brother—"

"An amulet for the Marquis?" She gave a giggle. "Whatever are you talking about?"

"His cane. I know what it is."

Now her giggle became a howl of laughter. "How quaint! You think his cane is an amulet. But it is not; it is a far more powerful artifact than any amulet. I told you I found it in India, did I not? I have no need for silly compulsion spells. My venom compels anyone I want. Why, a drop of venom in your wine, a drop of venom on your dress—*Mademoiselle*, you were my *puppet*." She stepped in close, and her claws poked into my skin. I held my breath—if I moved, if I breathed too heavily . . . those razors would slice me. "Perhaps you are not as clever as I once thought. As I told your friend, the Marquis had no idea what I was up to—no idea what I really am."

Her claws dug deeper. She wanted to poison me. Wanted to overwhelm me with her visions . . .

"Then why did you need sacrifices?" It took all my strength to stay still. To fight the shudders racking inside me. "If you can compel and you had wealth, why sacrifice all those people?"

"Those were not for me. Though the blood was *nice*." She ran her tongue over her lips. "My master was the one to sacrifice. There is someone who requires compelling, and a single spell will not suffice."

Over her shoulder, I saw Oliver hauling Daniel to his feet. Satisfaction—triumph, even—washed over me. At least Oliver and the Spirit-Hunters could get out alive. Now, I was the only one who had to walk the fine line between life and death. . . .

And with that thought I recalled Madame Marineaux's comment: *Nor can they see the fine line you walk between life and death. The Hell Hounds await you.*

The Hell Hounds. If there was one thing a demon—even one as powerful as a Rakshasi—could not face, it was the guardians of the spirit realm. And thanks to Marcus's spell, I knew just how to call them here.

I creased my face into a sneer—a victorious smile I could not contain. "Why would your master," I crowed, "want compulsion spells? I thought, Madame Marineaux, that he could simply make you—make his *slave*—cast a compulsion spell for him."

She gritted her teeth, her nostrils fluttering. "He wants a spell that lasts days. Weeks, even. Mine only maintain for hours at a time."

"Because your magic isn't good enough? Is that it? He does not think your magic is strong—"

"Stop!" she screeched. "I see what you try to do, *Mademoiselle*. You wish to rile me, and that, I fear, will not do. If I cannot have you, then *no one* shall, and so it is time for you to die."

"Oh?" I lifted my eyebrows as if this piece of information were utterly uninteresting. "Perhaps you ought to wait a moment, *Madame*. I have something you might like to see."

Her lips pursed into a smug smile. She waited.

"Oliver, remove my hand. Take it back."

"Oliver?" Her eyes thinned. "To whom do you speak?"

With my own wicked grin, I screamed in her face, "*Sum veritas!*"

Instantly she released me, rearing back. "Another demon?" She twirled around, her nostrils sniffing the air wildly.

Then she spotted the Spirit-Hunters, standing on the opposite side of the cavern with the crystal clamp and pulse pistols trained on her. I saw no sign of Oliver.

A scream ripped from Madame Marineaux's mouth, inhuman and ear shattering. "*Veni! Veni!*" She bolted for the Spirit-Hunters, her skirts and feet barely skimming the ground.

Daniel fired his reloaded pistols. Madame Marineaux slowed but didn't stop. Two more shots cracked out, and this time Madame Marineaux did halt.

But it was not because she was hurt. It was because, crawling out of the dark tunnel behind the Spirit-Hunters, was an army of corpses. The skeletons from before.

"Behind you," I shrieked just as Daniel twisted around, his next pistols firing.

I dove forward, desperate to help, but all at once pain sliced up my arm. Phantom pain. I glanced down. My hand was gone. It was just a stump once more. Instantly, Marcus's spell took effect.

First came the wind—so fierce and so cold. It blasted through the cavern, winking out half the torches. Then the stench of grave dirt assaulted me.

Madame Marineaux whirled toward me, disbelief—and betrayal—in her eyes. She knew what was coming. Knew there was no escape from the Hell Hounds.

Crack! Electricity lashed through the air as Joseph blasted skeletons away. He and Daniel were holding off the Dead, but only barely.

A howl tore through the cavern, and the pain in my missing hand screamed. Stars blurred across my vision. The Hell Hounds were close—so close—and all I had to do was keep Madame Marineaux here.

I staggered toward her, reaching frantically for any piece of her I could grab. But my right hand flared blue, blinding in its agony. Madame Marineaux's eyes locked on it.

A grin swept over her face, and I knew she understood that the Hell Hounds were here for *me*, not her. Her grin shifted into a frown. "I am sad," she said. "This is no way for a girl with your talent to die. Yet, you made your choice—and it was not me. Too bad, too bad. If you had only seen things my way, then they could have lived too." She waved disinterestedly toward the Spirit-Hunters. Their backs were to the wall, and an ocean of skulls and groping fingers surrounded them. But they weren't defeated—not yet.

"But *c'est la vie, Mademoiselle.* The bad choices—*c'est la vie.* And now I must wish you *adieu.*" She surged for the gaping black tunnel in the right corner. It was the only way out now that the left tunnel was swarming with Dead. Before I could even try to lunge into her path, she swept around me, soaring for the exit.

"Ollie!" I screamed. "Hold her! *Sum veritas!*" Then I launched after Madame Marineaux, sucking in all my power. Every ounce of soul in my body I drew into my chest, and in a wave of heat that scorched through me, I let all my magic loose.

"*Stay!*"

Madame Marineaux froze only feet away from the exit. I could feel her pulling, pumping her own magic into a counter-spell.

"Stay, stay, stay!" I shouted, and from the other side of the room, Oliver bellowed, "*Mane, stay!*"

A thunderous roar filled the cavern. All the torches whipped out, leaving only the electric blue of my magic and Joseph's crackling attacks to see by. Not that I could see—not now. The agony in my hand was too much. I toppled forward, my arms windmilling and all focus on my spell lost.

The Hell Hounds had arrived.

Time seemed to slow. I heard the Hounds' monstrous jaws snapping behind me, coming closer each fraction of a heartbeat. I felt each throb in my hand and each tiny gust of unnatural wind.

"Bring back my hand, Oliver," I whispered, still falling forward, still trying to regain my balance. "*Sum veritas.*"

A body hurled into me, screaming in Latin. I crashed down, and the squalling Hounds boomed over us. In that instant the pain in my hand ceased. It was its usual phantom limb—flesh and blood—once more.

Yet the Hounds did not stop their frenzied chase. They blasted straight into Madame Marineaux. Her body rose up and up, and the Hounds swirled around her in a tornado of blue flames. Her shrieks pierced the cavern, shaking my soul.

I am not ready. Not ready. The thoughts cleaved into my brain. Her thoughts—her fears. *Claire!* she yelled into my mind. *Claire! Help me—save me! I am not ready. . . .*

And then finally, a thought that nestled so deeply into my heart, I knew it was meant only for me: *I was wrong about you. You* will *topple him.* An image flashed next—the cane . . . no, only the ivory fist. Then the vision shifted to a gray Oriental fan on a low shelf in Madame Marineaux's sitting room.

The image vanished.

Her agonized screams crescendoed, dominating every thought. I watched as she spun . . . as the Hell Hounds' roars shook through everything.

Then her body bent backward, snapping in half like a stick, and in a final rage of howling, the Hell Hounds swirled Madame Marineaux from this world and into thin air.

Into oblivion.

CHAPTER TWENTY-FOUR

Vibrations from the Hell Hounds shimmered in the air, and I waited for the sounds to vanish. My stomach pressed to the cold ground. Oliver's heartbeat stuttered against my back.

One breath, two breaths—the sounds of struggle were not lessening. If anything, they were growing worse. Bones clattered and lightning blasted from the back corner. A pistol cracked and Daniel bellowed, "Empress—*help!*"

Oliver rolled off me. I scrambled to my feet and surged for the flashes of blue. Toward the horrors of the Dead.

No, not Dead. *Hungry.* For these corpses were no longer under Madame Marineaux's control. They were free now, and rabid.

Skeletons crawled over their brethren, tatters of clothes loose on their bodies and chunks of brittle hair on their gleaming skulls. Hundreds poured from the mouth of the tunnel, crawling and climbing and scuttling for the nearest life: the Spirit-Hunters—their backs still to the wall and surrounded on all sides.

A corpse, its ragged shirt falling off its bone shoulders, twisted around and lurched at me. Without thinking, I latched onto my spiritual energy and flung. Magic flared from my fingertips and raced out, blasting into a skeletal rib cage.

And for half a moment I was bound to the ball of soul that animated the body. I did the only thing I could think to do. "Sleep," I said. "Sleep." The soul flared once and winked out like a match.

The corpse fell—one single corpse out of hundreds. Panic and frustration boiled through me . . . yet this was the best I could do, so I had no choice but to keep going.

"Oliver!" My vocal cords snapped as I screamed for the demon. "Stop as many Dead as you can! *Sum veritas*!"

His eyes flashed beside me, and then his voice took up with my own. "*Dormi*!"

"Sleep!" Blue light shot from my hand, and more Hungry toppled over. If I could only make a path and get the Spirit-Hunters out, then we could run.

Over and over, Oliver and I took aim one after the other and chanted, "*Dormi*, sleep, *dormi*!" And all the while, Joseph's electricity never stopped blazing and Daniel's pistols never stopped cracking.

But my magic was getting weaker—Oliver's too. The light whipping from our hands was paler and our chanting fainter. Would he keep going until he was so drained he collapsed? "Stop," I ordered him.

He didn't stop. "They're almost free! *Dormi*!" His eyes shone blue, and a final flicker of power pierced the nearest corpse.

And he was right: the Spirit-Hunters could get out.

"Come on!" I bellowed at them. *"Come!"* Then, grabbing Oliver's arm, I wrenched him toward the tunnel in the right corner. If Madame Marineaux wanted to take it, it *had* to be the best way out. It was also our only choice.

I spared one glance back to check that the Spirit-Hunters followed. They did.

And so did the Hungry.

I could barely see—only the flash of Joseph's electricity gave me any light—but Oliver held fast to my hand, and he seemed to know where to go.

And behind us, the corpses' jaws did not stop chomping. The sound—that clattering and snapping of long-dead teeth—covered *everything*. Louder than my rasping breaths, than my thrashing pulse, than Daniel's screams for me to run faster . . .

Then we reached the tunnel and were barreling through. Ahead was the faintest flicker of orange—torchlight. But I could not spare a moment for relief. For the grating sound of the Hungry Dead had reached the tunnel too. The sound echoed, and at every bend in the passage, I expected to see a fresh army of corpses. But forward was the only way to go—one foot in front of the other—so forward we went.

Abruptly, the tunnel veered into a white archway, and before I could even process, we had run onto a tightly winding staircase with steep steps and no space. We were rising back up to the city. Though where we might come out, I had no idea.

Oliver rocketed up and out of sight. But I was tired. I could not seem to draw in enough breath, and my legs—they were as weak as pudding. I pumped all I could into each step, but . . . the stairs, and so much spinning . . .

"Don't stop!" Daniel roared. He shoved me against the rounded wall, skittering in front, and then his hand was crushing mine. He wrenched me up the stairs. "Come *on*, Empress!"

Electricity flared behind me, thundering over the skeletal feet. How was Joseph still going? How could he battle so many Hungry and for so long?

I should help, I thought vaguely, instinctively pulling in the dregs of my magic.

And with the magic came a fresh spurt of energy. I straightened, pulled free from Daniel, and let Joseph catch up. His bloodied head rounded the stairs. "Go!"

"Duck!" I threw out my hands and screamed, "Sleep!" The power lashed out like a whip . . . but I only connected with a single corpse—not even the closest.

Joseph heaved into me, forcing me up the stairs. "Run!"

"But I can help."

"They are too close. Just *run*!"

So I did, because Joseph was right. The Hungry were *so* close, I could hear individual toes clattering on the stairs. Hear their fingers scraping the walls. They were just around the spiral, almost on us . . . almost on us. . . .

Then Oliver's voice burst through the stairwell: *"You're at the top! Run!"*

And that was all Joseph and I needed. With a final burst of power, we flew up the steps—two, three at a time—around and around . . . and then we tumbled through a doorway and into a dark cellar.

A heavy door slammed shut behind us. I fell to my knees, breath scalding my lungs and my bladder burning. I needed to vomit. Needed to catch my breath . . . but there was no time. Blinking, I lifted my head and tried to gauge where we were. . . . The tunnels had led us to a random entrance in someone's wine cellar—Oliver had been right about the honeycomb of quarries.

Nearby, the demon held on to a wooden shelf, his head hanging and chest heaving. Beside him stood Daniel, a pulse pistol aimed at—

Bang!

I jerked around. The door shook dangerously, while the rasp of bone on bone vibrated through the stone floor. Joseph, who was somehow still on his feet, had his crystal clamp in hand and his eyes locked on the door. The hole where his ear had been still oozed blood, but most of it had crusted and scabbed down the side of his head.

Another dangerous slam against the door, and this time the wood groaned.

Oliver stalked to me. "Let's go!" He yanked me to my feet. "That door's going to break."

"He's right." Daniel said. "We're out of time."

"I cannot leave." Joseph's voice was weak, but his words were fierce. "If we go, this door will break, and these Hungry will overrun the city. I cannot let that happen." He turned to us. "You all must leave while there's still time."

"Hell if I'm leavin'." Daniel spat on the floor and, fingers flying, began to reload each of his pistols. "I can fire four shots, then you attack."

Hinges squealed, filling the room with their high-pitched keening. The door was coming free.

"I'm staying too," I said hoarsely. "But I cannot stop more than one corpse at a time—"

"And you're exhausted," Oliver cut in, glaring at Joseph. "There's no way the four of us can stop all those Hungry."

"*I* can." Joseph fixed his gaze on me. "I can magnify your power. Remember the library in Philadelphia? I stopped Marcus because I used *your* magic. We can do that again."

I nodded slowly. "Will it be enough?"

"I do not know, but I must try." His jaw clenched, and a fresh trail of blood slid down his neck. If Joseph could still fight, then so could I.

"I'll squeeze the crystal clamp, then." I hurried to him and took the gleaming device from his hand. Wrapping my fingers around the clamp, I shot a glance at Oliver. "You could also magnify—"

"No."

"Please." I had to yell to be heard over the pummeling corpses.

"No." Oliver's eyes thinned to slits. "I can fight the Dead on my own."

"*Please*." I grabbed his hands. "We can stop these Hungry—"

"Yes, we *can*. You use your magic, and I use mine. I will not let that electricity touch me. We can fight these Dead without it. Or, better yet, we can leave before that damned door breaks!"

"I will not leave! Joseph can lay all the Dead to rest—at *once*—so if you—"

"*No!*"

A hinge broke free and pinged across the cellar.

"You *will* help me," I shrieked. "Squeeze the clamp, Oliver. *Sum veritas*."

Betrayal and fury flashed in his yellow eyes, quickly replaced by blinding blue. He snatched the clamp from me, his face contorted with rage, and his fingers gripped mine with bone-breaking strength.

For a brief flash I connected to Oliver—his anger seethed through my veins; his pain lanced into my chest. He *hated* me. Elijah would never have done this to him. I would pay for my cruelty.

Abruptly the connection ended, and if not for the roaring groan of the wood, I would have clawed at Oliver and begged his forgiveness.

But I did not. I threw out my free hand and screamed, "Joseph!"

Joseph hesitated—only a breath, but it was a breath too long.

In a deafening explosion of splinters, the door smashed inward. The Hungry toppled in.

Pop! Pop! Daniel's pistols fired, and the first wave of Dead fell to the floor.

Joseph lunged for me, and the instant he had hold, Oliver squeezed the clamp. Electricity pierced through Oliver's hand into mine. Up my arm, rippling beneath my skin until I *boiled* with power.

The pistols rang out again. Again. Yet for each corpse felled, ten scuttled in to replace it. Yellow skulls, shattered teeth, empty eyes.

My muscles twitched uncontrollably, and my heart raced. Why wasn't Joseph using the power? I wanted to shout for him to attack, but my body was locked in place. I could do nothing but twitch. And watch as the Hungry clambered in. Daniel had to reload, and with each agonizing second, the chomping jaws closed in.

Why didn't Joseph attack?

My heart galloped faster, pumping the hot oil through me and ballooning into my head. Black closed in on the edges of my vision. I was going to die, going to explode—

Blue light snaked from Joseph's fingers. Thunder boomed.

Like a wind through grass, the Dead gusted backward. Flattened and lifeless for as far as I could see—all the way into the black tunnel and beyond.

But again the blue lightning struck out. This time it sizzled into the tunnel, a thousand veins of electricity flowing down, down.

Blue power laced through the air and boiled through my body. Then screams filled the air—*my* screams! Oliver's screams, Joseph's screams! Our heads rolled back, our throats burned raw with the inhuman shrieks. . . .

Until, all at once, it stopped. The hot crawling beneath my skin, our screams, the electricity . . . and the Dead. Everything *stopped*.

And as one, Joseph, Oliver, and I tumbled to the ground.

We stayed in the cellar a long time—too exhausted to do anything else. But eventually Daniel hauled us up and forced us to leave the devastation behind. Rising from the cellar, we came into an empty hallway. I instantly recognized it: Madame Marineaux's house. Somehow, all that winding through the mines had taken us beneath the river Seine and directly into her basement. Obviously she had chosen this house for precisely that reason.

Joseph hung on to Daniel, his dark face drained white and his ear losing blood in bright red spurts, while Oliver stalked ahead of me, refusing to meet my eyes. Refusing even to acknowledge my existence.

"There's a sitting room," I rasped, turning to Daniel. "It has a fireplace. Joseph can rest there until we find a cab."

Daniel's eyes flickered over the hallway. "Shouldn't there be servants?"

"The house is empty," Oliver growled.

I did not ask how he knew—he *did* have exceptional hearing. Instead, I simply nodded and beckoned for Daniel and Joseph to follow. We shuffled to the back of the house until I found a familiar door. It was open, and embers burned in the hearth.

But the instant I stepped in, I drew up short. For there was an old man sprawled on the floor between the armchairs and the fireplace.

A squeak broke through my lips. I recognized the man's elegant clothes—and I recognized the cane lying inches from his open hand. But his chest did not move, so though I *knew* it was the Marquis, nothing about him looked as it ought. His skin sagged with age, and his formerly black hair was brittle and white.

Daniel spotted the Marquis next. He shot me a wide-eyed glance before easing Joseph into my arms and darting forward. He crouched beside the body, but it only took him a moment to check for a pulse. He shook his head once.

"Is it LeJeunes?" Joseph asked tiredly. I helped him shuffle toward the closest armchair, and as Daniel eased the Creole to a seat, I bent down to examine the cane.

The handle was missing, the ivory fist gone, and though something tickled at the back of my mind—something that said it *should* have been around here somewhere—I could not find the full memory.

Daniel's voice interrupted my thoughts. "Do you think Madame Marineaux killed the Marquis?"

"I don't know." I rose, my gaze flicking back to the man's ancient face. "He looks as if he aged a hundred years since yesterday."

"Because he has," Oliver said from the doorway. He stalked toward me, still avoiding my eyes. "The man's body was drained of soul. Look at how desiccated the skin is. How fragile the bones."

Joseph cleared his throat. "How is that possible? I have never heard of such a thing."

"I've only heard of it once," Oliver admitted, leaning over the Marquis's corpse. "Your brother"—he pointed at me without actually looking my way—"mentioned it in passing. He said it was one of the darkest magics there is. Darker even than necromancy."

I grimaced, my stomach suddenly churning. "Can you sense who did it? Like with the butler's body?"

He straightened. "No. There is no soul left. Not a drop of spiritual energy, and without that, I cannot tell you anything."

"What magic is darker than necromancy?" Joseph asked— or tried to ask, but his voice was barely audible. He wilted back in the armchair.

"We can worry about it later." Daniel knelt beside Joseph's chair. "You're losin' blood too fast."

"We should clean the wound," I added. "Before it festers. There must be alcohol in the—" I broke off as Oliver thrust

391

his flask into Daniel's hand.

"Vodka. It'll sting like hell, but it'll clean." Then he strode to the window, ripped down one of the scarlet curtains in a single move, and threw it over the Marquis's body.

I gaped at him, surprised.

Oliver scowled. "It's disgusting. Scares me—not that you care."

"What do you mean I do not care?"

But he didn't respond. He had already pivoted toward the door and marched off.

"Where are you going?" I called, hurrying after.

"To find a cab."

"Are you upset with me?" I knew the answer. I had felt his fury in the wine cellar, yet I had hoped it might have dulled some. "Please, Ollie. Wait. I *do* care. I'm sorry for what happened in the basement."

He skittered to a halt, his body tensing. "Not sorry enough, El. Do you have *any* idea what you did to me? Blasting me with that electricity?"

"It was the only way!" I reached his side, clasping at his sleeve. "We needed all of our magic—"

"That wasn't *magic*," he spat. "It was filthy. Unnatural—"

"And strong!" I clutched my hands to my chest. "You saw how many Dead Joseph stopped. We can't do that with our spells."

"No, perhaps not, but at least my spells won't *kill* me."

I flinched. "Kill you? What do you mean?"

"I *told* you electricity would kill me slowly—"

"I thought you were being dramatic."

He gave a scathing laugh. "Being dramatic? Thank you, El. Thank you *very* much for seeing me as nothing more than a jester." He pushed up his chin. "Electricity kills demons. It blasts away their soul like the Hell Hounds, but instead of all at once, it's bit by bit. I hope you got a good look at what happened to that Marquis, because that is *exactly* what you did to me. You"—he jabbed his finger into my shoulder, pushing me back a step— "just withered away part of my soul. Part of my very *being*. And for *what*?"

"T-to stop the Dead—"

"I didn't want to stop those Dead in the first place. We had time to get away—to *leave*."

"But then the Dead would have overrun Paris!"

"So?" he snapped. "That was not my problem, Eleanor. It was *your* problem, and then you *made* it mine." He leaned into me, his face scored with rage and pain. "You gave me no choice. You betrayed my trust."

"I-I'm sorry." I cowered back. "I truly am, Ollie. Please . . . what can I do to make it up to you?"

"Free me. Free me and get the hell away from me."

"I-I do not know how—"

"Because you're not training!" His roar blasted over me, and I shrank back farther. "You're running around Paris with everyone *but* me! You seem more upset about that damned Marquis's death than you do about hurting me. I really am

393

nothing more than your tool!"

"I'll start studying—I promise."

"You're bloody right you will, but don't think it will be enough for me to forgive you."

"Empress?" Daniel stepped into the hall, his hands in fists. "What's goin' on here?"

"Nothing," Oliver snapped. And without another word, he went through the front doorway and stormed into the night.

Daniel looked at me, clearly expecting an explanation.

But I couldn't speak. Guilt and shame coiled inside me. Only the blackest magic in the world could drain a person's soul, yet I had done exactly the same thing with electricity. I had *killed* a part of Oliver.

For several minutes, all I could do was stare silently at Daniel—and somehow he understood that staring was all I was capable of, for he did not speak. He simply waited for me to return to the moment.

And as time ticked past and the world slowly cleared before me, I began to *see* Daniel. To see how his lanky body slouched with his weight on one foot. How his face was streaked with dirt and sweat. How his hair was dusted white and poking up in all directions. How his chest moved beneath his shirt—a shirt that used to be white but was now mottled gray. . . .

And above all, how beautiful he was—not just on the outside but on the inside as well. He knew me; he understood.

My mouth went dry. I took a step toward him. "Thank you."

His brow creased. "For what?"

"For . . ." Two more steps, and I was in front of him. "For still caring, despite everything."

"Caring? I didn't do anything. I heard shouting from the other room and—"

"I mean, thank you for caring enough to save my life tonight. Twice."

His eyes ran over my face. "You saved my life, Empress. And Joseph's. I reckon that makes us even."

"Even," I murmured, not particularly aware of what I was saying. My eyes were stuck on Daniel's throat. On the faint flutter of his pulse. It was . . . fascinating. It meant he was alive. We were both *alive*.

Without thinking, I rolled onto my tiptoes and brushed my lips over that patch of skin, over his heartbeat.

He stiffened. I lurched back.

Heat flushed through me. "I-I am so sorry," I tried to say, but my voice barely squeezed through my pinched throat.

And Daniel simply gaped at me, slack-jawed and frozen.

"I sh-shouldn't have done that." I skittered back several more steps, humiliation boiling inside me. "Please—forgive me."

Still he did not move, did not speak.

I retreated farther, wishing the front door were open so I could flee as far and as fast as my legs would go. Oh, why wasn't Daniel saying something—*anything*? And why was he staring at me like that?

I turned to go, my hand outstretched for the doorknob.

"Wait," he breathed.

I paused, glancing back.

And in three long steps he reached me. Then, his hands trembling, he cupped the sides of my face, and I swear his chest was so still, he could not have been breathing.

I know I wasn't.

He ran his thumbs along my cheeks, down my jaw, over my lips. And his eyes seemed to scour every inch of me. Then, ever so slowly, Daniel Sheridan lowered his head and grazed his lips over mine.

And I felt as if my heart might explode.

Yet despite that—despite the fragile perfection of his touch—it wasn't enough for me. It could *never* be enough. He smelled of sweat and blood and gunpowder. Of caves and torchlight and everything we had been through.

I loved him, and I would not let him walk away—not this time. So before he could draw back or change his mind, I pushed forward and kissed him again. Hard.

A low groan broke from his mouth, and now I *knew* my heart exploded. My brain, my skin, my lips—everything burned with feverish need.

His hands dropped to my waist, pulling my whole body to his. And now he kissed me, determined at first and then almost desperate. No matter how many times we pressed our lips together, it was not enough.

Then came the nip of teeth, a flick of tongue, and my knees turned to jelly. I almost fell backward.

But he would never let me fall. He crushed me to him, his body hot through his clothes—hot through *my* clothes. Then he guided me backward and pressed me to the door.

And all I could think—all I could *feel*—was that I needed more. More of him, more of Daniel.

His stubble scratched my face raw. I did not care. I was too lost in the feel of his lips, of his tongue . . . of any feeling that proved we were *alive*.

His lips left mine, but before I could beg him to stay, his mouth was tracing along my neck, biting and possessive, and now it was my turn to groan. I could barely breathe, my heart hammered too hard against my lungs, and I certainly could not see straight.

But the moment couldn't last forever. Always, the real world had to interfere.

A weak voice called out. "Daniel? Eleanor?"

Daniel and I paused. Our hearts drummed and our breathing rasped—so loudly, I almost thought I had imagined that voice.

But the voice called again. "Daniel?" It was Joseph, and at that realization, Daniel and I staggered apart.

"Is all well?" Joseph called.

"Yes," Daniel croaked, scrubbing a hand over his face. He blinked quickly, as if trying to grab a hold of who he was, where we were, and what had just happened. . . . He looked as completely lost as I felt.

"We're . . . we're coming," he said, his head swinging toward the sitting room.

"Just a moment," I chimed, forcing my legs to walk, to step away from Daniel. I *knew* that now was not the time for love, but that did not change how much my body *wanted* it to be the time. Did not change how much my pulse pounded in my stomach, painful and confused . . . and unfulfilled.

"Wait." Daniel reached for me.

"No." I slipped away from him, and a bitter laugh broke through my lips. It never seemed to be the time for Daniel and me.

I glanced back at him. "Joseph needs us, remember? He's hurt. *Badly.*" Without another look, I marched away from the door, away from Daniel, and away from everything we had just shared.

CHAPTER TWENTY-FIVE

While Daniel tended Joseph's wound, I wandered through Madame Marineaux's sitting room, skirting the Marquis's curtain-covered body. The memory from before tickled at my brain. It had to do with the cane. With something I was supposed to do . . .

Then my eyes landed on it. The low shelf from Madame Marineaux's vision—and the Oriental fan on it. There was something glowing behind the flowered folds.

My breath hitched, and I dropped to the floor, sliding the fan aside to reveal the ivory fist. Now uncovered, the clenched fingers glowed as brightly as a magical well in my chest—and the artifact was mine. I could finally *have* it. Clearly Madame Marineaux wanted me to take it, for she had shown me where it was.

Ever so gently, I grasped it with both of my hands and held it up.

"What have you found?" Joseph rasped.

I flinched, my fingers closing around the ivory as fast as possible. "N-nothing," I stammered, stuffing it into my pocket. I stood. "It's just . . ." My gaze lit on a different shelf—a shelf with hair clasps—and something Madame Marineaux had said flittered through my mind.

We can get your friend, the Chinese girl, back from him.

"Daniel," I said slowly, "when you followed that lead on Jie—to the train station—why did you think the trail had gone cold?"

"Because people saw a Chinese boy there with a young man. They both boarded a train." He walked to me—though I couldn't help but notice he stopped three feet away. The air between us practically shimmered.

I gulped, and he rammed his hands into his pockets. "I don't think," he said gruffly, "that Jie would willingly get on the train if she'd been kidnapped."

"No, but she would if she was compelled." I held the hair clasp out to him. "Madame Marineaux said she could put her venom on anything—compel anyone to do as she wished."

Daniel pulled back from the clasp—or perhaps he was pulling back from my hand. He nodded. "Yeah, I reckon it's possible she was under a spell, but then where was Jie going? And who was she with?"

"Marcus." Joseph's voice was barely above a whisper, yet

the name seemed to roar through the room. "Jie was . . . with Marcus."

The clasp fell from my fingers. I whipped my gaze to Joseph. "Wh-why would you say that?"

His finger lifted wearily, and he pointed at the portraits above the fireplace. "That is Marcus's mother."

"Claire?" I gaped at him, horror rising in my chest. "Claire LeJeunes——"

"Claire *Duval*," Joseph corrected. "And, trust me: I know what she looks like."

I gripped the sides of my face. "I should have realized! Madame Marineaux *showed* me this portrait—she told me over and over how much I *reminded* her of Claire."

"You could not have known," Joseph murmured. He took a quick swig from Oliver's flask and, wincing, said, "If anyone should have realized, it is I. The Marquis told me his sister lived in New Orleans, yet the connection eluded me. I had no idea she was French aristocracy."

"But . . ." Daniel wet his lips. "Didn't Madame Marineaux say that Marcus killed his mother?"

"Yes." My hand eased into my pocket, my fingers sliding around the ivory. Just touching it made me feel better. Stronger. I stood taller. "The Madame also said that Marcus tricked her into a binding agreement. And she *also* said Marcus was going to Marseille."

"And if Jie was with Marcus at the train station," Joseph said, "then she is also bound for Marseille."

"But what's there?" Daniel asked.

"The answer to the Black Pullet." I closed my eyes, my fingers clenching the ivory even more tightly. "Marcus found my letters from Elijah, and he must have solved the riddles within. He must have seen something in them that *I* did not." In a flat voice, I told them what happened with the burned letters and the Jack-and-the-beanstalk riddle. "There's a crypt in Notre-Dame de la Garde, and something important must be in there. *That's* why Marcus is going to Marseille, and it means . . ."

Joseph sat taller. "It means we must also go to Marseille."

"Unless it's a trap." Daniel tugged at his hair, a grimace on his face. "Why keep Jie alive unless it's to lure us down there?"

"Perhaps you are right." Joseph's fingers went absentmindedly to his wound.

Daniel snatched Joseph's wrist. "Don't."

Joseph blinked. His hand lowered, and he quickly tossed back another swig from the flask. Then he drew back his shoulders. "But, trap or not, I will not leave Jie in that monster's hands. We go to Marseille."

"I . . ." I bit my lip. "I want to save Jie too, but if Marcus left yesterday, then he's a whole day ahead of us. He also knows what was in Elijah's letters. He knows where to go. He'll be ready and waiting long before we can even get train tickets."

"No," Daniel said. He stepped to Joseph's side. "You forget: I have an airship. It's faster than any train. We can be in Marseille in a few hours. Then *we* could trap *him*."

Desire blossomed in my chest. Desire and something darker—something violent. I was ready to go after Marcus. No more waiting, no more looking for clues or answers. I was ready to face him *now* and to make him pay.

Make him pay for wearing Elijah's corpse. For hurting Joseph. For taking Jie and killing, killing, killing so many innocent people. For killing his own mother and entrapping Madame Marineaux . . .

And for all the hell I had had to endure over the last three months. It was time for Marcus to pay.

As Daniel placed a hand behind Joseph and helped the Creole stand, I asked, "How long does your balloon take to prepare?" My words lashed out, overeager and hungry. I swallowed and forced myself to add, "To prepare it for flying, I mean."

Daniel's eyes flicked to mine, but he instantly looked away. "It can be ready to go in an hour."

"Then let us go." Joseph motioned to the door. "Hopefully your de—" He broke off. "Hopefully *Oliver* has found a cab by now, for there is no time to waste." He and Daniel shuffled past me toward the door.

I took two steps after them. "Joseph?"

He glanced back at me, his eyes dark and inscrutable. "*Wi?*"

"When you said 'Let us go,' did you mean . . . all of us?"

His lips twitched up ever so slightly, and he nodded once. "Yes, Eleanor. I meant all of us."

I could not help it. I grinned.

Several hours later, with the sun almost risen and the sky a stunning blue, I found myself at the gates of the Tuileries Gardens. Daniel's balloon drifted overhead, packed and waiting. Oliver was already on board, sulking . . . furious. Daniel was still in the lab, grabbing his final things, and the last I had seen of Joseph, he had been beneath the hotel doctor's none-too-gentle hands. I'd had just enough time to get cleaned up and don a fresh suit (awkwardly borrowed from Daniel) before the airship had arrived, ready to be loaded with the Spirit-Hunters' equipment. I left letters for Allison and Laure, explaining everything and begging for their forgiveness. Whatever news Allison had would simply have to wait. If she had made it this far from Philadelphia, she could make it a bit longer.

The same went for Laure. I felt rotten for abandoning her. After the horrors of yesterday, she deserved better, but I could not—*would* not—risk Jie's life waiting for both girls to arrive. Perhaps I would see them in Marseille.

And now it was time for me to go.

My feet padded lightly on the steps into the garden. A breeze licked through the chestnuts and sent the balloon floating toward me. It strained against its leashes, a creaking melody to the rustling leaves and curious voices of passers-by. Even at this early an hour, a crowd had gathered to watch the airship.

To think that none of these people knew what had happened in the night while they slept. What had happened beneath their homes. What we had saved them from or how much it had cost us.

To think that, for them, it was just other day.

It annoyed me. Angered me, even. Philadelphia had been the same as Paris—so much work and so many tears, and all for

404

what? So people could simply get on with their lives.

"And so," I whispered to myself, pausing on the final step, "the wheel is come full circle." But Shakespeare quotes held no comfort for me today, no matter how true they were. I had too many unanswered questions.

For one, where was the compulsion spell—the one built from *les Morts*? It had sounded as if Marcus was using the seventy-three sacrifices to build a long-lasting spell, so did he take it with him when he left Paris? Madame Marineaux had said nothing about the amulet's final destination or final purpose.

For two, what had happened to the Marquis? Had Marcus been the one to kill him? I would have to press Oliver for more information on this black magic that was even darker than necromancy—as soon as the demon was willing to speak to me again.

And the ivory fist—what was it? My fingers slid into my pocket, where it rested. It was not an amulet, yet Madame Marineaux had claimed it was special, powerful. And for whatever reason, she had *wanted* me to have it. Oddly enough, its fingers had started to loosen—only slightly, but enough for me to notice that the fist was unfurling. . . .

With a yawn, I withdrew my hand and rubbed at my stinging eyes. I would find answers to my questions soon enough.

Then, my hair whipping in my face, I sent my gaze flying out over the small crowd of airship-viewers. Over their top hats and feathered bonnets. Over the flowers and maple trees. Over the burned-out palace and the Rue de Rivoli, with its neat, beige buildings and endless gray rooftops.

I sent my gaze out over Paris.

And I let the faintest smile pull at my lips. Seeing this perfect, *perfect* morning was exactly what I needed. The reminder to dig deeper until . . . until . . .

Until I found it, hiding within my heart and wrapped beneath layers of anger and grief. It was wound up so tightly in hollow regret that I would never have found it if I had not searched.

But there it was: a tiny flame—only the faintest glimmer, really, yet a flame nonetheless. A hope in the darkness.

"Eleanor?"

I turned and met Daniel's face, peering at me from the top of the steps. He was clean-shaven, freshly dressed. The wind pulled at his damp hair, and he looked as sharp as ever . . . yet sad. Worried.

But he did not need to be. I knew what I was doing.

"Are you ready?" he asked.

I reached into my pocket and slid my fingers around the ivory fist. Then I grinned. "Yes, Daniel. I am ready."

Acknowledgments

$\mathcal{T}$his book almost killed me, and the only reason I survived it is because of my best friend, soul sister, frequent sounding board, and fellow author: Sarah J. Maas. You held the megaphone to my ear and shouted at me to keep going. I kept going, and the book *wasn't* the death of me.

Huge thanks to Biljana Likic for all her help with the book's Latin phrasing. If not for you, my characters would be speaking in gibberish, and I am so grateful for all you've done.

To my Hero Squad, Erin Bowman and Amie Kaufman— thank you, thank *you* for listening when I needed it and for reading the book when I needed that.

To my critique partner, Katharine Brauer: your honey badger feedback turned this manuscript from pure drivel into an actual *story*. I love you for that.

A giant thanks to Meredith Primeau, Erica O'Rourke, and Amity Thompson for being beta readers when I needed criticism and cheerleaders when I needed support.

Endless love and thanks to Sara Kendall and Joanna Volpe for going above and beyond the call of duty over and over again. There is literally not enough space in these acknowledgments to convey just how much I appreciate *everything* you do.

Karen Chaplin, you (and the wonderful Alyssa Miele) helped me transform this book from a giant tome of "talking heads" into a story that made sense. Circumstance might have brought my book to your desk, but I truly believe it's where Eleanor and the gang were meant to be.

To the entire Harper team working tirelessly (or I assume tirelessly, but in all likelihood you're terribly exhausted at this point) behind the scenes to design my dazzling covers, set up events, and keep things running smoothly: a million thanks and a million cookies too.

Finally, to my dear husband, Sébastien, and my family—Mom, Dad, David, and Jennifer—you all believed in me long before I believed in myself. I love you.